OH, TITLE!

Other books by Daniel Donatelli

JIBBA AND JIBBA

MUSIC MADE BY BEARS

Oh, Title!

25 Short Stories, 7 Essays, 3 Pastel Parades, 2 Teleplays, And 1 Poem

Daniel Donatelli

H.H.B. Publishing, LLC

Paperback ISBN: 978-1-937648-08-4
EPUB ISBN: 978-1-937648-09-1
Kindle ISBN: 978-1-937648-10-7
PDF ISBN: 978-1-937648-11-4

With the exception of "The Poops," "'Dan, It's Jenna...': A Tragedy," "Now Here's This," "Riding The Rail," "Some Open-Ended Thoughts On The Importance Of Our Circuses," "The White Dog Of Light," and "My Ideal Man/Woman: A Case Study," this collection is a work of fiction, and all characters and events contained herein—even those based on real people and real events—are entirely fictional.

Published by H.H.B. Publishing, LLC
Henderson, Nevada

Cover Design by Zach Kuzmic
www.zachkuzmic.com

Layout by M. Wang

Manufactured in the United States of America

www.hhbpublishing.com

Contents

"While dictating a rather long report to the district Chief of Police, towards the end, where a climax was intended, I got stuck and could do nothing but look at K., the typist, who, in her usual way, became especially lively, moved her chair about, coughed, tapped on the table and so called the attention of the whole room to my misfortune. The sought-for idea now has the additional value that it will make her be quiet, and the more valuable it becomes the more difficult it becomes to find it. Finally I have the word 'stigmatize' and the appropriate sentence, but still hold it all in my mouth with disgust and a sense of shame as though it were raw meat, cut out of me (such effort has it cost me). Finally I say it, but retain the great fear that everything within me is ready for a poetic work and such a work would be a heavenly enlightenment and a real coming-alive for me, while here, in the office, because of so wretched an official document, I must rob a body capable of such happiness of a piece of its flesh."

—the diaries of Franz Kafka

"Creation seems to come out of imperfection. It seems to come out of a striving and a frustration. This is where, I think, language came from. I mean, it came from our desire to transcend our isolation and have some sort of connection with one another. It had to be easy when it was just simple survival. 'Water.' We came up with a sound for that. 'Saber-tooth tiger behind you!' We came up with a sound for that. But when it gets really interesting, I think, is when we use that same system of symbols to communicate all the abstract and intangible things that we're experiencing. What is 'frustration'? Or what is 'anger' or 'love'? When I say 'love,' the sound comes out of my mouth, and it hits the other person's ear, travels through this Byzantine conduit in their brain, through their memories of love or lack of love, and they register what I'm saying, and they say yes they understand, but how do I know? Because words are inert. They're just symbols. They're dead. You know? And so much of our experience is intangible. So much of what we perceive cannot be expressed. It's unspeakable. And yet, you know, when we communicate with one another, and we feel that we have connected, and we think we're understood, I think we have a feeling of almost spiritual communion. And that feeling may be transient, but I think it's what we live for."

—Kim Krizan,
from the 2001 film *Waking Life*

The Inventor

Part One

HE'D BEEN inventing for as long as he could remember, and he could remember nearly everything from his eternal lifetime.

In fact, where he was from, everyone lived forever.

So glorious was his immortal homeland that for all citizens but he—The Inventor—further creation was discouraged, even prohibited. With an immortal population, there resulted an eventual limit on what could exist before the accumulation amounted to a garish, cumbersome, endless hoard. And because any superfluous creations would only add clutter to and subtract beauty from the timeless harmony of the world they had all exhaustively refined, most of the immortals were able to distract themselves with other infinite tasks.

But, and this should serve to show just how masterfully talented he was, The Inventor was one of the very few immortals ever given permission by the ancient governing councils to continue creating. Whenever the creation of something new became necessary, The Inventor was called upon.

In fact, he was so talented that he had done something nobody else had ever even risked attempting. He had a home, and he had a lab, and that was all he was permitted to have, which was one more lab than any other immortal was ever given. But he also had another lab—an unauthorized, additional, *hidden* lab, deep underground: a personal sanctuary—that he had built himself, slowly and carefully, over the course of centuries.

When completed, the lab was a fountainhead of joy for The Inventor. He'd tunneled beneath the foundation of his home and then slowly emptied out a large chamber to house his equipment—a place where he could really let himself off of the proverbial leash. He loved inventing so much that he couldn't stop himself, couldn't ask for permission, either.

He knew about the delicate balance and about the councils that oversaw everything, and he respected it all, to a point, in public.

But his was an afflatus that resisted any containment—by councils or otherwise. Consequently, instead of making a petulant, emotional show of what he considered an injustice—the injustice being the bittersweet inventive permissions/restrictions given to him by the councils, cold as handcuffs—he quietly took matters into his own, free hands, and created a sanctuary governed by one.

Nobody else knew about it—it was too valuable a secret to share with anyone, even his closest friends. Despite the fact that a small part of him wanted to burst with the news of the awesome things he was creating down there, he knew he could not risk the additional indulgence. He hadn't felt this good in what felt like forever—getting to invent things for the pleasure of inventing them, not just because they had been deemed necessary by a calculating council.

The Inventor's basement lab was lit from the floor, ceiling, and walls. Each surface was a light fixture as well as a surface. In the middle of the basement was a large, smooth, box-looking piece of equipment that was his own brilliant invention: it was an invention that made inventing easier for him.

He invented using a coding system he'd created for the box. He could string the code together in his mind, transmit it into the box, and the box would translate the code into tangible reality. The machine worked silently, or almost silently—as the invented code was being made into a reality, the box issued a soft, mechanical hum.

Eventually he built hallways branching away from the laboratory, and he filled the hallways like a museum, or a trophy room, with displays of the things he had created over the millennia.

And this is how he lived for ages and ages more. He invented things, observed them, and decided if they were worth keeping or if they needed to be reworked. It filled the endless eons with dynamic beauty. He loved his new life, to every extent possible.

But then one day, as he was coding together what he considered the first step in his career's masterwork, he *coughed*.

Never once in his life had he coughed before. He and the rest of those like him had never known even a moment of illness—had only known eternities of health and vitality.

He coughed again, worse than the first time.

Part Two

UNDERSTANDABLY WORRIED and confused, he sought the head of the council that governed all councils that governed the immortals. He requested and was granted an emergency meeting immediately.

He entered The Leader's office, which was open to the day. The office was a small, circular grove in the forest at the foot of a mountain. The head of the councils had a great smile for The Inventor and welcomed him warmly.

"Please sit wherever you like, and tell me what is on your mind, my old friend."

The Inventor sat on the thick hump of a root that had curled out of the ground. As he labored from standing to sitting, he could feel a wheeze in his chest.

"I come with troubling news, sir. This morning, while working, I . . . coughed. I am sick. Please tell me it is one of The Jokester's pranks."

The Leader's smile collapsed and was replaced by a frown—a suddenly grave, ruminative aspect.

"The Jokester is away."

The Inventor's face, if possible, became even graver than The Leader's.

"Then I am . . . dying. But how? We are all immortal. I have done so much good."

"You have not broken any of our rules?"

"I have broken some, yes. I was never told that my immortality would be revoked if I broke them. I was told they were simply for the betterment of all of us."

The Inventor coughed. The Leader was disturbed by the alien sound of it, but he recovered his thoughts and made a slight correction to The Inventor.

"They are for the betterment of all things. This is unprecedented. Who knows about this?"

"Only you . . . and I."

"Things here have changed before, but not like this. We do not always know all of the reasons for the changes, and there are enough theories around here to confound The Philosopher."

The Inventor waited as The Leader gave the matter the full weight of his aged, specialized wisdom.

The Leader shrugged weakly and then appeared to reach a mild certainty. "There *must* be a reason for it, Inventor. You *must* find the reason. There is *always* a reason."

The Inventor left with no more comfort than when he arrived. As he walked, he attempted to summon the unknown reason in his thoughts.

His coughing only grew worse. Between coughs, he could taste the mild fragrance of his world's vibrant environment—a bittersweet kiss goodbye. He grew weaker with each step.

He had killed so many things in his ages of inventing; it had been necessary for the betterment of his creations. There were times when he had considered the idea of death, and he had picked at it to see if there were anything useful in its core. But, so far in his existence, he had not spent much time wondering about the full ramifications of his people's deathlessness. Now, the end of his life was all he could think about, and even though he as yet couldn't conceive of a way in which death had any value, the layers between himself and the problem were decaying rapidly. He was already feeling the intense heat of emotion—and the intense cold of reality—around the question of mortality. Now, he had the same disease within himself. What was the value? What was the reason? Why should he die?

He could barely make it to the basement below his house. He was sluggish and weak. He coughed in violent rasps that fell away in wet gargles, which he choked on, triggering more painful fits.

He knew sadness. He had not known sadness before. It was born within him now, and from out of the rotten pain of his new misery and confusion, the code popped into his head.

He'd been building the code for as long as he'd been inventing, which seemed to stretch back as far as he could remember—a powerfully long time. It was the interwoven code of everything he'd ever invented, and he'd been patching it together in his mind through all the many millennia.

He fell to the floor in the basement of his hidden laboratory.

To want to live, he thought. *To live is not enough, but to* want *to live. To live and to* want *to live.*

The code, complete, in his head—woven together so intricately and beautifully that he began crying over how much he loved and would miss all of this—would be his magnum opus, and it would exist here forever. It would be his immortality—it would be the only immortality left to him.

His chest rattled, and he coughed a mouthful of black fluid out of his lungs and into his hands. The rising stench was the stench of death. He knew.

Gasping for breath, he took his sputum-covered hands and held onto the sides of the box. Still on his knees, crying, he faced the input device. The code was there. He had checked and double-checked his memory. It was all there, but the box would not register it.

There was no soft hum.

He tried it again, painfully and painstakingly, but still nothing.

His world started swimming away from him. He felt death rising through his shuddering body.

He pulled his head back and, with the tattered, desperate remains of his dying, immortal energy, he smashed his head into the input device. Nothing. He smashed it again and again. Nothing.

With the last of what he was or would ever be as he existed from that moment on, he filled his head with the code and put everything that was within himself into the input device.

Then there was a big bang.

Fractal Traveling

ALL ROADS have brought me here, he thought to himself.

It's not that all roads lead to Rome; it's that all roads lead to all places where those roads go. Yes, they go to Rome, and they go home, and they go to me when I am on the road. He liked that idea, and he saw all those little cars and trucks and wagons within himself, going here and there as needed—each passenger listening to the tinny sounds coming from his radio, her phone, his murmuring inner monologue. The morning commute, the afternoon commute, the evening commute, the graveyard commute—the roads of his circulatory system thronging with pushy drivers, moving at great speeds and under pressure from all sides. *It's like that everywhere, on all scales*, he thought, and he placed, in his mind, a marble on each side of each scale. High above his head, the first marble rolled off the top scale, and on each scale down the marbles rolled off, until they all thunked heavily on his throat.

He felt at his throat and felt beard, and beneath the beard was his voice—sensitive with illness, raspy with sound, but his.

There was more room on the bench where he sat—a long, thickly lacquered, wooden plane along the outside edge of a busy airport terminal—and a traveling family of four was looking to sit down to his left, each stepping over the bearded man's bag while the bag's owner pensively stared at his own thoughts, considering the precious transportation system within and outside of himself, counting scales and marbles and diving into the fractals of metaphysics. The family father was too distracted with leading his beloved brood to the waiting area to give much notice to the bearded man. The family mother noticed him with concern and wariness, and as she stepped over his luggage, she turned to look back at her two children, to (ludicrously) make sure that in the moment between when she last saw her children a moment ago, and this moment, where she was seeing the man, he had not somehow raped and murdered one or both of them.

They were there, safe, following her, and she scanned seemingly the rest of not only the airport but the whole city for any other spots that might accommodate the family. Unfortunately, there weren't any.

"Is anyone sitting here?" the mother asked the man, attempting to gauge the stability of the stranger's mind by reading into his eyes as he collected and gave his answer.

He gazed over at the rest of the empty bench, looked at the woman, and shrugged.

"It's a pretty simple question, beardo," said the elder sibling—a young girl just entering her "tweenage" phase, who looked like what her mother used to look like, but with her father's wide-set brown eyes. She had a sneer of vast impatience on her face, as if shouldering her travel bags were a labor of Dickensian cruelty.

"Anyone sittin' here run to the bathroom or somethin'?"

"Forgive me," he said to the entire family, "but I haven't been paying attention. I don't travel well."

"Well, I can understand that," the father said. "I've never known anyone who travels well—even people who *like* traveling."

With that, and with the way that the father confidently sat his butt onto the bench and propped his ankle up on top of his ol' knee, the ladies set their bags down and joined the two gentlemen already sitting.

Looking straight into the faces of the people seated on the bench, a traveler would see, from right to left: the family father, checking his watch, checking the board of flights, and checking his watch again; the family mother, angled so as to be able to see, at all times, both of her dear children and the unusual, bearded man; the elder daughter, seated so low on the bench that her head was held upright by the backrest/wall, listening to music on her headphones, eyes closed, seemingly to shut out the mortifying horror of her family; the younger daughter, not much more than three years old, mimicking her older sister's lying-seated posture, her feet dangling in the air; then a large stack of the family's travel bags, effectively working like a border fence; and then the bearded man, leaning on his right arm, which was leaning on the right armrest while he stared straight into the floor, pensive.

One of these things is not like the other.

Individuals, families, lovers, and teams clattered by with their big bags. Male and female voices sounded informational soundings to the hustling travelers— *"Cleveland to Minneapolis, Flight Three Eighty Four, is now leaving from Gate Sixty One, repeat Gate Six One"*; *"Marcia Brendowicz, please pick up the white courtesy telephone"*; *"We at Hopkins International Airport hope you are having a great day today"*—and the bearded man barely heard any of it. He was back in his head.

Two philosophers sat under an ailanthus, near a gurgling brook, with the late-afternoon sun golden on their faces as they watched two children toss pebbles into the water.

"One of those children will die within the year," the philosopher Cheng said. "And what purpose will he have served?"

Cheng's friend, Qei, a notoriously negative man, did not answer but instead himself picked up a pebble and tossed it into the brook. The pebble disappeared beneath the running surface.

Then Cheng understood, and neither said anything else for the remainder of their visit.

The bearded man could feel that sun on his face. It worked its way within him. He heard jostling sounds, soft—rhythmic and arrhythmic.

His eyes focused again on the floor; then he turned and saw the three-year-old's face looking at him—her little cheeks buoyant as hot-air balloons—just over the stack of bags. She was breathing a *heeshy* laugh at the change in the man's face from thought to perception to his recognition of herself.

"Tessa, baby, leave the man alone," the mother said, trying to sound like she was trying not to inconvenience the stranger, rather than what the father heard, which was his wife helicoptering again. *Really worked for Kelly*, he thought, and he looked over at Kelly, still lying back, still eyes-closed, still embarrassed as hell.

Three-year-old Tessa ignored her mother and kept looking at the funny man. He looked at her, began scratching his face, and with a sleight-of-hand motion, he appeared to pull a tiny metal toy airplane out of his beard. Tessa again heeshy laughed—this time at the barest look of faux-surprise on his face when he saw the airplane in his hand.

He held it out to her, but she didn't move to take it. She was still feeling shy, but she was emboldened by the bags between them, which she kept bumping her chest and belly into lightly with an uncoordinated consistency that was somewhere between rhythm and nonrhythm.

"I understand," he said to her, but so low that only she could have heard him, and he winked at her. She liked the wink and responded by trying to wink back, but she just closed both eyes—elaborately blinked—when she did it. The bearded man almost floated into the air from his amusement at that. The amusement filled him, but the only evidence on the outside was a little upturned corner of his mouth.

He held out the toy, but she still didn't take it, so he slipped it back into his beard.

"C'mon, Tessa," the mother said, picking up the little one. "Let's go find the potty."

Tessa watched the bearded man as she was being carried away. He sat forward and put his elbows on his knees, face in his hands, and stared at the carpet.

Two philosophers sat on a craggy precipice high up a mountain. Below them was a great grassland valley dotted with trees and shrubs, with animals all around. The animals had gathered near a small watering hole—the hole too small for the great numbers of dehydrated animals there—and the animals waited patiently their turn, even as the two philosophers watched the level of the water go down inch by inch.

They continued watching then as a large, predatory cat chased down a sturdy-legged grazing animal on the periphery. The field of dehydrated grazers fled in all directions but the direction of the attacking cat.

Qei said to Cheng, "Can you believe the price of gas these days?"

The bearded man began to see the floor again, his bag, his feet. His cheeks, above the beard-line, were red from the pressure of his hands.

"I said can you believe the price of gas these days?" the father said. "It's actually cheaper for me to *fly* the family out to Lauderdale this year."

The bearded man looked at the father. He saw in the father's face, and heard in the father's voice, that this man had something else on his mind that he wished to talk about, but couldn't. The elder daughter opened her eyes briefly, looked at her father, looked at the bearded man, and shook her head in embarrassment and disapproval before closing her eyes again.

"The price—the moral price?" the bearded man asked.

For some reason, this really charmed the father. "Ha! Well, I guess you're right." He said to himself, "The moral price—" Then he continued, "No, I was just talking about how frickin' expensive it is—money expensive—these days. Can't trust any of these markets, I guess."

"I think," the bearded man said, "that it would have been better if you and I had met under different circumstances, if you don't mind my saying it."

The father's affable smile disappeared. "Why's that? What are you some kind of flit?"

The bearded man enjoyed the question, even smiled introspectively, and responded. "It seems as though you have something you wish to talk about, but you can't, because your daughter's headphones might be on mute right now, and you don't want her to hear whatever's really on your mind."

"What? Kelly—" the father said. She did not respond. "Kelly, you can take the headphones off; I know you're not listening to them; I can hear it when you are."

Busted, the tweenager pulled off her headphones.

"Well what's on your *mind* then, *Dad?*"

"The man was wrong, Kelly; there's nothing on my mind."

The bearded man said, "There's always something on our minds—"

"There's nothing *unusual* on my mind, okay?"

"What's your name, fella?" Kelly asked the bearded man.

"My name . . . that's a good question," said the bearded man, giving the question more weight than the girl anticipated.

"No, it's not! It's just a stupid name. What's your stupid name?"

"It's really none of our business, honey," the father said.

"*He's* the one who's telling *you* what's on *your* mind, *Dad*. I just want to know who he thinks he is, is all."

"I think . . . I am here," the bearded man said, "and I am also in my thoughts sometimes."

"What the *heck* does that mean? You're *weird*."

With that observation, Kelly closed herself off from the conversation. She put on her headphones, and soon both the father and the bearded man could hear the muffled noise of loud pop music.

"It's something about your wife," the bearded man said. "Anxiety—"

"Okay, we're back!" the Tessa-carrying wife announced happily, relieved to see her husband and eldest daughter still alive and safe. She settled back down onto the bench, and her eyebrows briefly furrowed in curiosity as it finally registered in her mind that it appeared as though her husband had been talking to the bearded weirdo while she was walking back just now.

Tessa was beaming and drooling with a big yellow sucker in her mouth. She reached with both hands towards Kelly, to be held by her.

"Mom, this guy is *weird*," Kelly said taking off her headphones again and accepting Tessa from the mother.

"Kelly, honey—don't say that about people. It's un-lady-like."

In the bearded man's head, the philosopher Cheng said, in a particularly effeminate voice, "I can't help it if he's *weird!*"

The bearded man saw the floor again, felt the family's eyes on him. He said, "Don't worry about it, ma'am; I already knew."

A woman's voice, pleasant, over the intercom, announced, *"Flight Two Twenty One, Cleveland to Anchorage, is now boarding."*

The bearded man stood and picked up his bag.

"What's in *Alaska?*" Kelly asked, one last attempt at a barb against the creep before he left, and also showing off she knew where Anchorage was—nobody's fool.

Tessa scrambled across Kelly's lap and stood and bumped her belly against the bags again, heeshy laughing at the now-standing bearded man.

"Another good question, miss," the bearded man said to Kelly. "That's something else I'm trying to figure out."

As distracted by his thoughts as ever, he picked up his bag and entered a gap in the river of gate-bound travelers, and he worked his way perpendicularly across the river until he melded into it and was gone from the family's view.

After the unusual man disappeared into the crowd, three-year-old Tessa continued bumping her chest and belly into the family's stacked bags, but she wasn't heeshy laughing anymore. Instead, her eyes were fixed on something where the bearded man had been sitting.

A small toy airplane.

The Poops

THE WEEKEND before I left for college was the first time I ever smoked weed. Because of how seriously I took baseball in my youth, and because of the then-depths of my profound Catholic-moral guilt, I just never had any interest in puffing the magic dragon.

But then high school ended, and I had one last summer of baseball—one last summer of trying to get a scholarship, to continue my athletic successes in college. But I didn't get shit.

Baseball used to be my life. Everyone knew exactly where they could find me nine months out of the year: practicing, running, hitting with friends . . . whatever. It was the heartbeat of my adolescence.

Now picture this: I played for the best summer-league team in Cleveland. The best of the best northeast Ohio had to offer. We were cocky, talented, locally successful, and better than you or anyone else (at least from Ohio). Every season ended with a State Tournament in Youngstown OH—the most depressing place in America this side of anywhere else I've ever been—and the tournament after my senior year was particularly special, not only because we'd made it further than any other team I'd ever played for, but also because I knew it was the final season of my baseball career. And after a childhood of playing tournament baseball, it was particularly special for me to be pitching in the state-championship semifinal game.

The thing about tournament ball is that usually both teams' aces face off in the semifinals because there's no point in saving your best starter for a championship game you might not even make it to. And in fact I wrote about a similar situation in my novel *Jibba And Jibba*, but I needed to enhance the drama of the situation, so I had young Jibba, who was his team's ace, pitch in the finals. My defense is that JAJ is a sloppily written work of fiction, and this particular story is not (fictional, that is).

In front of dozens of scouts, my friends, my family, and a smattering of players from teams left behind who'd come to the game to give me a hard time (I'd been responsible for the defeat of a number of top teams in that, the greatest tournament I ever played in), I took the mound, and the game began.

Two hours later, the game ended. We won 3–0. I pitched a complete-game shutout, had a home run, two doubles (one of which short-hopped the left fielder like he was playing shortstop) and after my last swing of the game, as I came to a standing stop at second base, my longtime coach shouted over to me, "What are you gonna do next, drive the bus back to Cleveland?"

(Like I said I've written most of this story in JAJ, but it's worth repeating for what follows, as a juxtaposition—to show where I started compared to where I find myself at the end of this story.)

That was the game I finally hit one of the main goals of my life: I threw a ball ninety miles per hour.

I know that doesn't seem like much when you consider the speeds tossed around in the professional leagues, but 90 mph for a 5'8" white dude is pretty fucking sweet.

After the game ended, all four of the semifinal teams, their friends, families, and the scouts were treated to a fireworks display given by the organizers of the tournament. The whole show was underscored by a crackling-speakers song that seemed to be directed directly at me—"My Way," as performed by Frank Sinatra.

I've always taken a certain pride in being my own person and in doing things my own way. Everything from my awkward sartorial choices to my unusual, grunting pitching delivery was a personal signature, was done my way—with an oxymoron-busting volitional intransigence that goes back as far as I can remember, the individualist to a fault.

It's not often you're actually aware of the fact that you're experiencing one of the truly memorable and important moments of your life—usually you're too busy living within the moment to think about it. A lot of the time you're ignorant of the moment's importance until six months later (or five years , or . . .) when it hits you just how *special* and important and profound that moment in time was. How much it mattered. How much it represented to the person you were at that period, during that part of your life.

After the game, I was sitting on a picnic table with teammates I'd been playing baseball with since I was six years old, and as I looked up and down the line of faces gazing up at those radiant, colorful explosions, which cast shadow-splashes of light across their dirt-streaked aspects and within their lacrimal, reflective eyes, I realized, in that rarest of moments, that I had achieved everything I'd ever wanted to achieve with baseball. There was nothing baseball had left to offer me, because a few weeks earlier I had been named to Ohio's all-state baseball team (2nd team), which meant I had achieved my other main goal, of getting my picture put up on my high school's athletic wall of fame, which had been my dream for the previous decade. I had reached the pinnacle of my youth, and I knew it was time to move on and become a goddam adult.

Which was especially true when you consider that this was at the height of the steroid era (A.D. 2000), and there was no way a professional team was ever going to draft some short, right-handed, balding white dude who couldn't even get a better offer than a half-scholarship to a miserable D-III school.

The following afternoon we lost the state-championship game to a team of Mexican immigrants—all of whom were the size of NFL tight ends, who were flown in by some rich asshole—and the following week our team bowed out of the Midwest Regional Championship Series in Cincinnati.

I cried long and hard after that final loss in the regionals. Thundering shudders. In front of everyone. A massively pathetic display.

But I knew it was the last game I'd ever play.

"My Way" had been my swan song.

Because I was so good at baseball all my life, I was friends with the "popular" kids. Well, at least until my late junior/early senior year, when I realized that I never had any fun when I was hanging out with them besides on the baseball field, and none of them appeared to want to be my friend outside the field anyway. Getting drunk and into fights had never been my thing, and it was seemingly the only thing they ever did.

Eventually I befriended a kid from one of my classes with whom I'd always shared a similar sense of humor—named Wes. He wasn't "popular," but he was funny, weird, and way more like I was than my other "friends."

So throughout my senior year I hung out with Wes and his good friend Jordan. It quickly dawned on me that I'd almost never actually had any real friends before. After all, here were two relatively dateless pussies like myself—excellent!

We became good friends quickly.

Two weekends after my final tearful game was also the weekend before my new/real friends and I were scheduled to leave for college. During the last night we were ever to hang out together as piece-of-shit high-schoolers, we drove down to Lake Erie, and Wes pulled out a joint. My friends—Wes, Jordan, and our friend TJ—had smoked up before, but my lungs practically still had a blushing, voice-cracking hymen.

But now that baseball was over, and seeing as how I was headed to college *sans* sports and would probably experiment with drugs there anyway now that literature would be my heartbeat and nearly all of my new heroes were dead drug addicts, I figured I'd take a rip with these fine friends of mine and see what happened.

What happened was we all got fucking baked like astronauts in an explosion of blissful alien wondercolor.

Way, way, *way* baked.

Wes then incompetently drove to a nightclub in downtown Cleveland (the entire time I was in the backseat PAR-ANOID out of my mind, wholly convinced that EVERY-THING was the COPS), and when we finally and terrifyingly arrived, we spent the next hour standing in the middle of a dance floor, totally unable to cope with the situation we were open-mouthed gazing at.

Namely that we were way fucking baked.

All around us coked-out girls were grinding against each other as they danced on the tables. Tough-guy dudes looking for a fuck or a fight were milling between us, and the bass from the speakers was making my eyes and vision vibrate awesomely.

In a way, being stoned resulted in my doing the same thing I'd be doing anyway (staring at writhing, beautiful women), but every perception was amplified and highlighted by a million percent.

And from thence was born the stoner you have typing these words today.

So I first started smoking a week before I left for college, and when I got to college it turned out my roommate was a bona-fide stoner. Great kid. Former baseball player, turned hip-hopper, turned stoner, turned Daniel Donatelli's freshman-year roommate. His name? Josh. His nickname? Jibba! (For the record, my Jibba[s] are nothing like the real Jibba, though—I just loved the linguistic fun and the necessary mask of my great roommate's great nickname.)

Unfortunately, because I was so new to the game, I was still morally working my way into the new pot-smoking paradigm, so for my first year in college, I didn't smoke nearly as much as I do today. My roommate and our friends would smoke nearly every day, whereas I would smoke only sometimes. Maybe twice a week.

I don't know what I was thinking.

But anyway, that's important to remember—I was a very late bloomer, and at the beginning even when I bloomed it wasn't very frequently.

So two academic quarters later and it was time for Spring

Break. Now, it just so happened that Ohio State's spring break (where Jordan went to college) and mine fell on the same week that year, so what other choice had we than to spend the week partying . . . .

In Salt Lake City.

In a dorm.

Yeah.

But a dorm in Salt Lake City was where our good friend Wes could be found, so a dorm in SLC was where we were bound. My first ever trip farther west than Indianapolis.

So the plane slams (seriously, a jarring slam) onto the tarmac, and we get into SLC and for the first night just chill out after whatever the hell that landing was. The second day, a day which will live in infamy, our friend Wes goes out and picks up a bag of some weed he refers to as "The Poops."

"You know," he says, when we ask for clarification, "like, 'The Poops' is The Shit!"

And indeed it is. Whenever Wes merely opens the bag to examine its contents, the room STINKS like a blunt had just been smoked in there. I'd never come across such an absolute potency before (and still haven't)—particularly coming from Ohio, where there were no different names for different hybrids like the cannabis culture the West takes for granted. In Ohio A.D. 2001 there are only two types of weed: thirty-dollar weed and fifty-dollar weed.

With thirty-dollar weed, you basically get the roots of the plant, some stems, a few leaves, trace clumps of soil, and maybe a toy G.I. Joe arm or something. And the fifty-dollar weed in Ohio would be given away to the homeless out West.

So bear that all in mind. There are three important factors to consider when trying to understand what happens next:

1. My then-neophyte stoner status. My body was still relatively pure after a particularly active and ascetic youth filled with constant athletics and Catholic privations;

2. The vast difference between Ohio "weed" (plants of

some variety that somehow got the job done) and Rockies 'n' West Weed (Ghostface Freight Train, Snozberry Three-Alarm Whoopsidoodle, Cannibusiness Pleasure Farm Hallucinogen Bubbleclouds, or whatever the hell the names are for the wonderful weed out there);

3. SLC is in the Rocky Mountains, nearly a mile up, and therefore the air there is much thinner, so any intoxicants will tend to intoxicate-the-hell-out-of.

So the evening of day two in SLC comes around, and we (Jordan, me, and our U. of Utah–matriculating friend Wes) decide to walk over to Wes's friend's dorm to take something called President Hits.

President Hits Tutorial

(I'd never heard them called that before, and I've never heard them called that since, but that's what Wes called them that night, and that's what they'll be to me forever now.)

1. Obtain a midsized bottle of Gatorade or some similarly packaged beverage;

2. Consume or empty the contents;

3. With a lighter, burn a hole through the very bottom of the bottle, small enough to be able to be blocked with one finger;

4. Again with a lighter, burn a hole through the cap of the bottle, large enough to be able to fit a makeshift aluminum-foil bowl into the top;

5. Fashion the aluminum-foil bowl;

6. Pack the bowl and set it into to hole in the cap of the bottle;

7. Fill the bottle with water (making sure to cork the bottom hole with your finger);

8. Fit the enbowled-and-weed-packed cap back on;

9. Light the bowl using a lighter, and with your finger, uncork the bottom of the bottle (this allows gravity to drain

the water out and in the process create a natural pull on the bowl up top, which fills the bottle with more and more smoke as more and more water falls out and weed is burned);

10. Once the water's completely run out, quickly unscrew the cap, fit your mouth over the bottle, and . . . .

And that's a President Hit.

It's a lot like a gravity bong, only a little more *MacGyvery*.

So anyway we get to Wes's friend's place—Wes's friend is a dude nicknamed "Yoda"—and there are a couple other kids there as well. Together it was me, Jordan, Wes, Yoda, some other kid, and a dude named Colt.

Before too much fore-twenty-play has gone on, Wes suggests we adjourn to the bathroom and smoke (precautions still being necessary as we are in a freshman dorm in godforsaken Utah).

When it is my time to take a President Hit, I inhale and cough for five minutes like everyone else. I watch a thick, milky, almost liquid smoke roiling inside the Gatorade bottle; I briefly look down into the swirling madness below the cap just before I fit my mouth over the portable gravity bong, and I watch an eruption of smoke explode from my mouth shortly after my lungs, and indeed my entire being, reach critical mass-weed-inhalation.

I cough for no less than five full minutes—thick saliva flooding my mouth not unlike in pornos when a girl's taking The Dick a bit farther than normal into her mouth/throat/stomach. My eyes are immediately three-quarters shut. I don't know if I'll make it. I keep fucking coughing and spitting.

I seriously can't stop.

While I am in my personal misery, spitting thick saliva and coughing myself silly, Jordan, Wes, Yoda, that other dude, and Colt all take their President Hits.

We stumble out of the bathroom and into whatever flat surfaces we feel would be comfortable enough to sit around on. At first I'm a little disappointed. I just smoked a bigger hit than any I'd ever taken, at a much higher altitude than I'd ever smoked in before, but I wasn't really any higher than I would be after smoking a bunch of thirty-dollar weed at my sea-level school.

But I can't smoke anymore. My lungs are . . . well, pardon the pun, but my lungs are smoked.

Fortunately/unfortunately, soon things start to get super-stoney, and after five minutes of grooving on my exponentially expanding, interstellar buzz, Colt suggests (adamantly) that they go back to the bathroom to smoke a bowl.

(Wow!)

Every moment I sit there I notice I am getting more and more baked.

"No, thanks," I say to them, hoping they can hear me from five-thousand light years away.

So Jordan, Wes, and the gang head back into the bathroom to smoke another bowl (which to this day stills seems surreal, if not suicidal, to me, and Jordan later told me that that "Colt" dude was in rare form, taking huge hit after huge hit—his thirst for baked goodness apparently incapable of being quenched).

So eventually they come back out, and by then I'm trashed. Fucked. The protective layers of my being having been stripped away, I sit there like an exposed nerve—twittering and twitching in reaction to even the lightest stirrings of the air, jerking my head violently towards any sounds I perceive, real or not.

At some point—I have no idea how or when—Wes and Jordan decide to head back to Wes's dorm. (Perhaps they see how I'm entering another dimension.)

So we stumble back to Wes's dorm, which is probably about two-hundred-yards away, and just as we're about fifty yards from the front door of the building, this VERY AUTHORITATIVE VOICE calls out, "HEY!"

"HEY, STOP!"

And all of a sudden, Wes is running.

And then all of a sudden so are Jordan and I.

We book into Wes's dorm, shoot up the stairs, sprint down the hall, and crash into his dark room. We all agree that we're just way too baked to do anything else, and seeing as how we had plans to go snowboarding the next morning, we decide to call it a night (though I can hardly remember any of that line of thinking or discussion).

So we're just about settled into our bed/couch/floor/etc., really swirling into our profound pre-sleep buzz, when . . .

WHOOP! WHOOP! WHOOP! WHOOP! WHOOP! WHOOP! WHOOP! WHOOP! WHOOP! WHOOP!

(It's not stopping.)

WHOOP! WHOOP! WHOOP! WHOOP! WHOOP!

(The light under the door leading to the outside hallway is flashing.)

WHOOP! WHOOP! WHOOP! WHOOP! WHOOP!

"That's the fire alarm," Wes says. "Fuck."

I think to myself, *Can that VERY AUTHORITATIVE VOICE have wanted to talk to us so bad that he decided to (devilishly coincidentally) smoke us out? Am I really about to go to federal prison for smoking weed?*

No matter the situation, we have to get out of there.

So we stumble downstairs, keeping our eyes locked on the ground, avoiding eye contact with everyone (our eyes are exactly red—almost alarmingly red).

Once we're outside, someone calls out, "Holy shit, dude! Look at that!"

I look up from the rock I'm voidishly staring at and try to see what he's talking about. As I look at Wes's dorm I begin to notice that the windows exposed to the face we are looking at show a Dark Cloud slowly blotting out all the light. It is headed from the side opposite of Wes's room towards his room.

It looks like the place is filling up with smoke from a fire.

All our belongings, our plane tickets, identification, money . . . everything is in Wes's room—in a building that looks like it is burning down.

And I am STILL getting progressively higher. It starts to feel like a fucking *nightmare*.

Now my understanding of the way the U. of U. campus is set up is like so: all of the dorms surround one main central student-relations building. This building houses the dining hall, a lobby, a small grocery store, and a bunch of other stuff I'm sure. We are told to head to this building while the fire department comes.

So keeping our eyes to the ground we shuffle into the center building and head for a group of two couches off to the right, somewhat away from the masses.

Now imagine this: the building we're in is predominantly made of marble and currently houses about one-hundred-fifty irritated, concerned, very talkative college students. Now imagine what the sum of all of their conversations sounds like bouncing off of four marble walls and a bunch of other odd, hard acoustical architecture.

It sounds a little something like this:

"ANGIEINENGIONAKDMALDISLAMGMEK-POAINBSAIEOPAHGAMKLSDMMBAOIEGTNVR-WRBXLWOPGHAGHAHAHAHAGHWORINVAEHA-HAHAGNAJHSFOANHGOAIWHASEMWNAMPEWUE-BZVRWJSMJFOPEJWBDCWERWEMGKWOMWAP-MAGNAWINDLIUTPLJMURSXZKFDOPELFMJYWHD-KLDNAGTYWRAMG . . . ."

Now imagine that horrid chorus of tongues lapping at the ears of a young man spiraling certainly into insanity. A TRILLION voices at once, none of them any more distinguishable than the others. Wes and Jordan are pretty much asleep on the couches. I'm lying there on the floor, unable to put any coherent thoughts together. Baked absolutely out of my shelter. Impossible to think, or for the world to have any semblance of order. It's like I've returned to when I was a baby: the world is nothing but a washing machine of colors and sounds, all whooshing and swooshing around, and I am in the center, unable to tell a painting on the wall from my own mother. The voices bouncing from wall to wall to wall to my eardrums making no sense whatsoever. Nobody is talking to me, yet I can hear absolutely everything everyone is saying.

Certain that we have been "smoked out" of the dorm by an AUTHORITY, I search for ways to hold onto the tattered cordage of my rapidly unraveling sanity, in case it's needed when I'm being raped to death by gleeful, shrieking Mormons in a Utah gulag.

So what do I do?

The only thing that makes any sense to me.

I start repeating a sort of sanity-mantra in my head.

Your name is Daniel Donatelli, your social security number is . . . . Your name is Daniel Donatelli, your social security number is . . . .

Over and over again I repeat this to myself. It is the only way for me to hang on. (Wes later tells me that I was actually saying this OUT LOUD.)

I am totally fucked. Fucked and fucked and fucked. I try to hang on.

Your name is Daniel Donatelli . . . .

What feels like THREE HOURS of that later, we receive word that it is safe to go back to the dorm—that it had been some pranksters playing with the fire extinguishers that caused the "smoke" to fill the halls.

So we head back to Wes's dorm and lay down for the night. Wes and Jordan go back to sleep, but not I.

I lay there praying to God in my head.

Dear Lord, please, if you have any mercy at all, please, I beg of you, let me be sane again when I wake up.

Dear Lord, please, if you have any mercy at all, please, I beg of you, let me be sane again when I wake up.

Over and over again until I fall asleep.

When I wake up, the sun is shining and things are gloriously comprehensible. And then a little while later, at The Canyons, on the chairlift, Wes, Jordan, and I get baked on The Poops again.

'Dan, It's Jenna...': A Tragedy

Prologue (aka The Big Buildup)

I ONCE told this story at a rooftop barbecue party in Hermosa Beach CA, and the whole thing went so well that I've decided to put it here on the permanent record, in this fine mothafucka in your hands, despite the fact that the story casts a terribly poor reflection on virtually every aspect of my personality.

The whole big telling, back on the rooftop deck, took two hours—with the late-afternoon, late-summer sun inching towards the diamond-blue horizon, seemingly itself with an ear for my humorous, shameful story. And the reason the story's scope kept growing was because of a tremendous number of corollary, got-'em-on-the-line, biographical asides, as well as the legitimately curious questions the partygoers (SoCal's ubiquitous perfectly ripped men and hot-bodied women) had for me, the clearly insane, truthful narrator of this physio-chemically corrupted story.

The long-limbed, beautiful woman who hosted the barbecue told me she had never seen anyone tell such a compelling story over the course of so long a time. Thus, the following—all of which is unfortunately true.

In many ways, this is the story of my life. But not really. But also, pretty much.

I started losing my hair when I was fifteen. Yes, fif-fucking-goddam-teen. It was a cruel fate—a kick-in-the-dick defeat in the genetic lottery.

And yet despite that early and piteous setback, I still had some minor success with girls in high school. I had a nice smile (via orthodontics? You betcha!); I was sometimes funny; I was sensitive and generally handsome—I've often said I'm a seven out of ten on the attractiveness scale for bald white men, but like a high-five, low-six on the broadest male spectrum. So although I mentioned some successes, I don't mean to imply that girls were throwing themselves at me; it's just that every now and then, either because of my baseball successes (I was awesome) and general "popularity" (via baseball successes) or because she had no self-esteem, a nice girl would sometimes let me prematurely ejaculate in her vicinity.

But that pretty much ended in college. Well, it didn't end, but the quality of girls shot way, way down (or, more accurately, "blew up"). Wider hips, thicker waists, more facial hair—on the girls, not me. And being a loner in just about every sense of the word since as far back as I can remember, I spent most of my days in college in a pot haze, not really worried about all those girls out there who preferred those damnable "attractive" guys rather than we the funny-looking majority. Again, I still heard about rare crushes but primarily from the sorts of girls who put the "crush" in crush—as in heaviness and stomping ability.

In high school I didn't drink much. I was too concerned with being the best baseball player possible—and being short, white, and right-handed, I needed every competitive advantage I could get. Not to mention the fact that I didn't really enjoy drinking (I couldn't stand the hangovers, nor could I stand enjoying myself, because of my widely known profound capacity for Catholic guilt). Plus, I had great friends who drank heavily and who became just okay friends, and then not friends at all. Embarrassments. The kinds of teenagers who reveled in the fuck-everyone-I'm-young danger of drinking and driving.

They wanted to kill others, and I wanted to kill myself.

High school can be a brutal time for anyone.

But then, when college came, I started to enjoy drinking more—got my beer-legs. My university was a walking campus—

everything was within walking distance of everything else. No need to worry about drinking and driving; we needed only worry about getting busted by the cops for being so drunk we stood out amongst a campus of twenty-thousand other drunk buffoons. So no worries, really.

Now here's the way I drink when I'm a twenty-one-year-old college junior: most of the time, I have about six to eight beers, which is enough to get me drunk to the point my friend refers to as "Sailor's Choice," which is that perfect level of drunkenness between sobriety and sloppiness, and then I would head home and smoke weed and get Absolutely Kablooey—rock-starring the fine line between The Kablooey and spewing my insides into the crotch of a toilet. But sometimes . . . sometimes I drink to the point of scientific impossibility. I never really know when it's going to happen—I rarely plan on it. But sometimes it just happens. Way, way, way too drunk. Obnoxiously drunk. Homer Simpson and Hunter S. Thompson—live and rowdy and in your face.

So, with all of that out of the way, I can begin the telling of this truly pathetic tragedy.

SOPHOMORE YEAR in college, a girl lived on my floor who was un-fucking-believably hot. Seriously. Unreal. One of the sexiest girls on the entire campus. I shit you nuns. (In fact, I recently stumbled upon a high-class porno of a girl who looks A LOT like my beloved pretty woman, but fortunately/unfortunately it wasn't her.)

I only talked to this supergirl once during that whole year—on September 11, 2001.

I was in the same elevator as she, on my way back from a speech class, when nervously she cleared her throat and said to me, "Did you hear? America's under attack." I, in all my witty glory, open-mouthed and still blown away by her smoldering sexiness, countered with this gem: "Nuh-uh. What do you mean?"

She briefly explained the uncertain things she'd heard, and then the elevator doors opened, and I shot over to my room to turn on the news. That was our only encounter all year besides all the times I stripped her naked with my eyes whenever I saw her.

Anyway, our junior year rolls around, and it turns out this sexy girl shows up at one of our house parties. I lived with seven other dudes in the rattiest piece-of-shit house on campus, but honestly we were seven of the coolest people I've ever been associated with, so we threw incredible parties. (Unfortunately, two of our roommates were on the baseball team, so we always had a little too much baseball sausage for my tastes, but with baseball sausage comes some hot drunken girl groupie peppers, so it rather balanced out.)

So 9/11-girl—I shouldn't call her that, because even though we'd never met formally I already knew that her name was Jenna, because I'm a real creep—surprisingly showed up with another girl I knew well, and we three started talking, and for whatever reason I decided to be like George Costanza in that *Seinfeld* episode where he does everything that's the opposite of his instincts. I was a total dick to this unusually attractive girl. I figured, *Fuck, what the hell do I have to lose?*

And she ate it up!

At the end of the night she ended back up at our place briefly, and she gave me her phone number. Huzzah! The hottest fucking girl on campus gave ME her number! The ugliest dude in our house! Some bald douchebag! It was too good to be true.

So the next weekend rolled around, and I was supposed to meet up with Jenna at a party at a mutual female friend's house. Big party. My roommates were all stoked for me and decided to get me pretty drunk. So my roommate Aaron *("Dan, I don't read books; I do shit people write books about!")* Smigelski started pouring me copious shots of vodka and wicked screwdrivers (Phillips-head screwdrivers, four points of vodkontact). I'm downing them like I've got a pair because metaphorically I don't have a pair and was literally worried that Jenna would discover what a loser and tool I was. So I figured if I allowed myself to go well beyond the realm of Sailor's Choice, I could blame it on that.

I was five oceans past Sailor's Choice when I stood up to leave for the party.

Between the time we walked out of our house and the time we arrived at the party, I had become an absolute WRECK. And this party was seriously like eighty-percent female. A true gem.

And then there was I.

I remembered hearing that Jenna hadn't shown up yet, so I was going around the party interrupting people's nice conversations with my drunken insanity and generally ruining everyone's good time like I like to do when I'm poisoned. I think it's funny.

I ended up running into a girl who after meeting me said, "Wait, YOU'RE Dan The Columnist!" (background: I had a weekly humor/politics/philosophy/shitty column for three academic quarters for the main student paper during my time at school). Absolutely fucking thrilled to have met a fan (there were a tragi-terrible number of people on campus who thought I and my column were useless pieces of monkey shit), I hugged her, uh, creepily, quite a few times. I'm pretty sure I ruined my standing in her eyes after that.

So later now, and drunker—far, far drunker—the sexy girl still hadn't arrived yet, and I was in a conversation with my roommate Jonathan and two girls, a brunette and a blonde who both claimed to know us (but I couldn't remember either of them—or who I was). The conversation wasn't really going anywhere (or anywhere my totally fucked-up, drunken self cared about, mostly because I couldn't hear a goddam thing they were saying from all the music and the packed party), so I spent the majority of the time staring at the blonde's massive breasts.

And the more I stared at them, the more they began to annoy me. They represented everything I hated about what I was going through. This girl was wearing a "shirt" that just screamed, "Hey, everybody! Look at these fuckers! Adore them! They are all that I have, and all that I am, and I'm still too good for this bald dickhole who's staring at them!" So in my twisted, drunken logic, I thought to myself, *Okay, sweet-tits, you want titty attention? I'll GIVE you titty attention!*, and I crossed my arms and casually brushed one of them (the left one) with my left hand.

"Dan, did you just touch her boob?" the brunette said, busting me.

"Um . . . ."

I'm caught. I go in for the full grab.

The conversation all of a sudden makes an awkward shift in direction. The people around me are abuzz with . . . well, I'm not sure. Anger. Disappointment. Creeped-out-ness. Lots of bad vibes.

"What the hell is wrong with you? She's not an object! Blah, blah, blah, blah," the brunette was shouting. At me. *(What's with her?)* So once again in my twisted drunken logic, I thought to myself, *This'll shut her up*, and I grabbed (double-fisted) BOTH of HER tits.

"We gotta get Dan outta here," one of my roommates says to another. And all of a sudden we're leaving. What, a man can't molest two girls in the middle of a party anymore?

I'm sorry, I thought this was college.

(Brief parenthetical aside that nobody ever seems to believe: it was not rapey lust that drove me to unleash such unwanted boob-grabbing, and I know this not only because I've never done anything like that before or since, but also because I'm certain that that sort of thing goes against every part of my personal moral/ethical philosophy. My never-believed-by-anyone-besides-myself explanation is that my gropings were not gropings but were rather misguided, intoxicated—yet I argue still somewhat meritorious—*statements* about the convoluted social standards that combine inhibition-shedding alcohol with carnal-attraction clothing in environments not conducive to conversation.)

Anyway, we end up going to a bar after I'm physically escorted from the party, but at this point my memory starts to go spotty. All I can recall of my time at the bar is repeatedly trying to check my voice mail on my cell phone—quite unsuccessfully, just mashing my drunken fingers on the keypad—looking to see if the unbelievably sexy Jenna had called/left a message.

At some point, after spending an unknown amount of time drooling into my phone, begging for it to work, I decided that I was just too drunk to stay out anymore.

I knew my limits.

So I walked back to my place, dragged the garbage can over next to my futon, and spent the next hour vomiting like a Bobcat.

And I swear the last thoughts I remember that night were, *Well, this is it. I'm not waking up tomorrow. I'm about to die. It's been a decent run, I guess. I pretty much enjoyed myself. So long, everything.*

When I woke up the next morning, my first thought was, *Oh, my God . . . I am IMMORTAL!*

Epilogue (aka The Big Payoff)

I HAD three voice mails waiting for me the following morning. The first, received at 1:03 a.m.:

"Dan, it's Mom. It's one in the morning. You keep calling here. I hope you're okay."

The second, received at 1:15 a.m.:

"Hey, Dan! It's Jenna! Sorry I didn't catch you at the party, but I'll be at [a bar we'd frequent] 'til it closes. Hope I see you there!"

*The third, received at **2:58 a.m.**:*

"Dan, it's Jenna. It's like three in the morning, and I'm really scared. I really don't want to be alone right now. Is there

any chance I could come over there? Please call me back."

I slept through it.

Jenna got back together with her ex-boyfriend the next day.

GODFUCKINGDAMMIT!!!

A Helicopter That Didn't Crash (Or, A Modern Short Story)

THE AIRPORT bar—Uncle John's Bar—was closed. Daphne walked past its darkened, hollow face and watched a chubby-but-cute Mexican woman pull the security gates closed. A small machine vibrated in Daphne's pocket. She fished it out and flicked it to her ear. It was Harry—calling from Gallimont.

"I don't see how it's possible you're calling me," Daphne said as she walked through a corridor tinted vitamin-urine yellow by bad lighting and old paint. She looked at her watch. "You're supposed to be at the Coldwater plant right now, and they're not allowing outside calls yet."

"That's it—That's just it, Daph!" Harry said. "We're not there! It's gone!"

A little boy, tugging a small suitcase on wheels, worked his way through the human stream, towards his family. His face was a sleepy little moon. His mother and sister—a skin-harried, blonde-curled copy in scale—thumbed through a magazine and pinched and pulled long ropes of wadded chewing gum, respectively. No father in sight. Probably not coming. The boy rolled his little suitcase into his sister's shin. It was just a moment.

"What?" Daphne asked, inured to Harry's hysterics. She caught a glimpse of herself in a dark window, and as always she sadly remembered how fat she looked in profile. An unflattering angle, certainly.

"It's gone, Daphne! It burned to the ground! It's just ash an—"

"Burned?" she asked, a bit unsettled by Harry's phrasing of it. "You mean financially or something? Jack said the Coldwater CFO was a crook, but—"

"*Burned*, Daphne!"

"Harry, brand-new munitions plants don't burn to the ground," she said, stepping out of the human river flow and leaning against the floor-to-ceiling window overlooking the tarmac. A plane safely taxied across a soft-glowing-orange band of asphalt. "They explode."

"You haven't seen the news today?" Harry asked. "Daphne, it's national news! We're still at the hotel. This town is going nuts!"

A man in an orange vest, with those runway earmuffs around his neck, leaned against a rail just below Daphne's feet and puffed a cigarette. Daphne, a little surprised to see this, thought the man looked like her brother's friend Lawrence Darrow. It turned out it wasn't the friend, but you can't forget a name like that.

"I've been on a plane for the last fourteen hours, Harry," she said. The man with the earmuffs couldn't see it, but another man—vest, earmuffs, but also a sense of *overseeing the ground operation*—was striding towards him. "What happened?"

"Oh holy jeez, Daphne, I forgot. How'd everything go?" Harry said.

She replied automatically. "It went fine, thank you," she said. "What in the world is going on out there?"

"It's all sorts of crazy!" Harry said. "James and I got here last night—"

"Is Jim okay?"

"Yeah, he's here in the room," Harry said, sounding a little relieved. "He's showering now. Told me to call."

Mr. Overseer, in the earmuffs, long-striding away from the sunset, towards a plane being unloaded by only one baggage handler, didn't look happy from what Daphne could make of it. And the cigarette-smoking Looks Like But Isn't Lawrence Darrow still couldn't see Mr. Overseer on the way.

"Good," she said. "So you got there last night—"

"Yeah, and everything was fine," Harry said. "We get up this morning at about six ay em, because you know how those Coldwater engineers are—the *weirdos*—and we're on this *noth-*

ing road when there's these two cop cars blocking the way. James pulls up to them, and they flashlight him! They point behind us, you know. Tall Cop says, 'This area is off-limits. Go back.' Well, you know how James can be, especially that early in the morning, *especially* on the road, so I try to calm him down some, and—"

With the hard toe of her stiletto, she soundly tapped the window just above Not Lawrence Darrow's head. Immediately he turned around with an upset look. He mouthed, *(What the fuck?)*, and with a gesture of her head in the direction of Mr. Overseer, she let him know exactly what the fuck. Not-Darrow turned, saw his boss, and, quick as a hiccup, the cigarette was covered and smothered by his boot. He re-eared his earmuffs and set off towards the unloaded plane. A few steps later, he turned and gave Daphne the uplifted thank-you thumb. A little corner of Daphne's mouth joined it, and she heard Harry in her ear again.

"And you should have seen the Short Cop's face, Daphne! He was so pissed I thought he was going to *shoot* us!"

"Harry—" Daphne interjected impatiently.

"So anyway the cops tell us that there's been an accident up at the Coldwater plant and that the authorities are on top of it and that we just need to go back to our rooms until they get everything back to normal. They said, get this, you'll love it so much you'll just hate it. The Tall Cop said, 'Everything is fine—we just need to make sure that everything is okay.' You tell *me* where you can find sense in *that!*"

"Did you tell them you were there specifically to visit that plant?"

"Of course! Yes, we did. *Several times,*" Harry moaned. "They said the charcoal team was there already. God knows when *their* investigation will end or when their report will come out. We'll probably *never* find out what happened. Oh, it's just the strangest thing, Daphne, just the—"

A disgustingly fat man in gray sweatpants. A dusty old couple, waddling like dying windup toys, with the wife asking,

"Is this Los Angeles?" and the husband answering, "No, honey," and the wife asking again, "Is this Los Angeles?" A large black janitor wrist-flicking a large black garbage bag to inflation. "No, honey." A self-conscious teenage boy hiding behind his long hair. "Is this Los Angeles?" Daphne looked at them and felt, briefly, that heavy curtain of sadness, like the lead bib for an X-ray. "No, honey."

"Does anyone have any clue of what happened?"

Daphne couldn't look at that teenage boy's awkward face anymore. She turned her visual attention to a billboard on the far wall. It was half-completed. The first half said, "The Best Things in Life." The billboard bore a picture of a man shouldering an ax. Daphne didn't like the smug look on his face at all.

"The pictures on the news—aren't there any TVs in the airport?—anyway, the pictures on the news show this circle of black ash where the Coldwater plant was. There are some pictures of the blaze itself, but the helicopter that was circling and filming the burning plant had some sort of mechanical breakdown. It crashed right into the fire! No survivors! I'll tell you, I'll never step foot onto a helicopter—I've *never* seen a helicopter that didn't crash!"

Daphne reached a pair of sliding glass doors. Above them, a sign read **Ground Transportation**, and a line of cabs waited with their sundry immigrant drivers standing beside the long row. Her eyes and eyebrows began a commission with the man at the front of the line, who turned on his heels and opened the rear door for her.

He was round in every way. His spheroid face bore a round mountain of a nose that whistled lightly as he breathed. His fists were little ham rounds and the rest of him a composition of spheres stretched in the various ways that always end up looking like a cab driver.

She gave him the address, and as he circled his way around to the driver's seat, she gazed down the long row of cars and pedestrians in the airport breezeway. A city bus raced past the outermost lane, past people standing alone together waiting for parking trolleys or the ride from a friend's favor. Everywhere somewhere else, but close. One girl, a quietly radiant teenager in intentionally sliced jeans, sat on her suitcase reading a thick book. The binocular effect of Daphne's eyes revealed the book's title: *The Facts of Astrology*.

That book should be very helpful to you, dear, she thought and dipped her head into the dark cab.

She entered a new atmosphere. After the multitude of crisscrossing currents in the airport/breezeway, it was like stepping into a vacuum. It smelled like the remains of a battlefield on which war was waged between the foul stench of careless sickness and the medicinal sterility of flavored cleaning compounds. Like the way her roommate once described a dormitory bathroom as smelling like "Peaches and Ass." She realized Harry was still talking.

"—ght, Daphne? Daph?"

"For chrissakes, Harry . . . Is Jim out of the shower yet? Put him on. I need to ask him something."

Daphne heard a garbled voice as the phone changed hands (it was Harry muttering *"Bitch . . ."*), and then Jim was on the line.

"Daphne," Jim began with a smile in his mellifluous voice, "Welcome back. You were in my prayers the whole time, despite your protests."

The taxi cut through traffic, and the air through the slightly open window felt good. She opened it more. She felt better. The fabric of land that spread out across her field of view looked like a black blanket showered with white-hot sparks. There was either the cold of nothing or the fire of light. Little dots and bigger dots, and always that vegetal cool air. It was a wonderful summer night now. And Jim.

"Yes, Jim; I'd rather you hadn't, but I know the . . . *gesture* means a lot to you, so thank you. It all went as expected, really. It was a general thing."

"There's that funny way of describing it," Jim said. "What do you think about this Coldwater business? Weird, huh?"

The cab driver's hat was pulled pretty far down on his face, she noticed. And the car was moving pretty fast.

"I think it's just all so strange," Daphne said snuggling her head into the back corner of the cab, where it was soft and sleepy. The yellow sled sped down the freeway, and the air stuck its fingers through the open window to play with her face and her hair. "It's like it doesn't all add up."

"Hold on a sec, Daphne," Jim said. She heard a garbled discussion between Jim and Harry. Then Jim was back. "Sorry 'bout that. Anyway, you had a question for me?"

"Yeah, Jim," she said, trying to remember what her question was.

"Hey, shut up, Harry, all right?" Jim said with his hand cupped over the phone.

"What did he say?" Daphne asked.

"D—Daphne, um . . . Let me call you back."

"Why? What's wrong?"

Jim had to whisper. "It's Harry. I don't know what happened, but he's starting to freak out."

Jim said, *"Relax*, Harry. Everything's okay."

"What's he saying? Jim? Are you there?"

She heard a loud clattering. The sounds of struggle. "What's going on? What's he keep saying, Jim?"

The line went dead.

The hum of the road.

Peaches and ass and a cool breezy hand playing with her face.

Daphne felt the cab begin to slow before she recognized that they had arrived. She tossed a pair of twenties to the driver and let herself out. "Thank you," she said, distracted. "Very good," she added, not sure why. Just some nice words.

Outside now. The lighting was all wrong. It flickered, and she felt a momentary sense of vertigo. She looked up at her apartment building.

Flames licked at the black sky through blown-out windows. The building burned, and she felt the small machine in her pocket vibrate again.

Enjoy The Matrimony

Part One

THE BRIDE had only chosen one color for the floral arrangements.

When she had seen that both the church and the reception hall consisted of rooms that were decorated almost entirely with the dark brown hues of rich, lacquered wood, she decided that, as a gift to her husband, and because it was always one of her favorites, she would simply choose the color orange for her wedding. Consequently, orange, brown, and white, the colors of the bridegroom's favorite team—the Cleveland Browns—filled the church (and the reception hall) with an essentially classic Cleveland feeling, which felt, for better or worse, like family.

As a result, the church, as the groom's younger brother entered it that morning, looked, to the groom's brother, like a mix between the setting of a wedding and a spiritual football rally. He loved it.

He stood at the back of the empty room, the lights half-lit, and looked at the decorations while listening to the hum of the building's ventilation and the mumbled voices of the people in the vestibule behind him. He hated churches when they were filled with people and preachers. He had long ago dropped this pernicious religion from his life—as much as he could, at least—but he'd never quite gotten to the point where he loathed even the buildings themselves. In fact, he liked the buildings, when they were empty. There was a wonderful calm to this big quiet room that was built for finding peace with and answers to the biggest questions. (*Just get rid of the people and all the statues of Jesus's dead body*, he thought.)

At the side of each pew—just below the bench's elbow rest—hung a small burst of orange nasturtiums set against the dark brown of the wood. The flowers were affixed to the ends of each pew all the way from the back of the church to the front row. At the front of the church, on both sides of the altar, were more explosions of orange—crowds of zinnias in large glass vases—and these were set against the rich paneling of the back wall and the brilliant, gilded gleam of the large tabernacle.

Above the altar, flowers, and tabernacle was a statue of a man whose hands and feet had been nailed to a cross. His side was cut open. The man was dead, but there was kindness and forgiveness in his open eyes. Here was this religion's most important person, and they chose to commemorate his loving memory with an image of the man as he was put to his grisly death.

The groom's brother shuddered and looked away. He'd entered the church because it was obvious he wasn't needed in the vestibule yet. He'd decided he would try to see if he could rekindle the candle of his spirit—a flame that had gone out seemingly for forever—and also because he liked empty churches and the big questions they lubricated.

There was another reason, but he felt foolish admitting it to himself.

Nevertheless, his waxy internal candle remained unlighted, and he turned and while adjusting his uncomfortable bow tie went back into the room off to the side of the church, where the bridegroom and the best man were getting ready.

"But I don't think you'll be needing that anytime soon," the best man said, and then he and the groom laughed. The two of them turned and saw the groom's brother, who was the only other person in the groom's side of the wedding party.

"How is it out there?" the best man asked.

"It's quiet," the groom's brother said. "Looks really nice, though." After a moment, he added, "Go Browns."

The groom and best man laughed again.

"She's a great girl," the best man said. It wasn't the first time he had said that.

The groom, Paul Duke Karrington, was born thirty-one years and seven months earlier. Five years after Duke's birth, his younger brother, Walter Maynard Karrington, was born. That same year, Duke started attending a Catholic preschool, where he met and befriended Anthony Michael Sclarisimmo. Consequently, Duke Karrington had known Anthony Sclarisimmo for literally the entire duration of younger-brother-Walt's life.

Duke Karrington, the bridegroom, was about fifteen pounds underweight. He was bald, and his pale bald pate gave way to a horseshoe of short curly red hair. His dazzling blue eyes—really, the only part about him that could be considered traditionally attractive, and in this case extremely attractive—were bespectacled, with a pair of glasses that framed his face and brought out the surreally colorful quality in his eyes. Like the other two members of the groom's wedding party, he was wearing a black tuxedo with an orange vest/bow tie. His cheeks were pockmarked with the scars of horrid teenage acne. The acne disappeared in his early twenties; the scars remained. He was an accountant.

Anthony Sclarisimmo also looked underweight, but he was actually about ten pounds heavier than he appeared. He hid tight, compacted muscles beneath his too-big clothes. In a tux, he looked like a child. But he was no child. Earlier in his life, he'd been a highly decorated up-and-coming boxer. He'd been forced to retire from fighting, however, after he spent two days and nights puking from the effects of his third concussion in as many months. The two of them—Duke and Anthony—when they were in high school, had been nicknamed Anorexia Nervous (Duke) and Anorexia Balboa (Anthony). Anthony was a blackjack dealer at a local casino.

Walt Karrington had brown eyes—eyes far inferior, aesthetically, to his brother's, though they had a certain intensity some people found alluring and some unseemly—and a wavy shock of brown-red hair that he had let grow past his ears. For the formal event, he'd combed his hair behind his ears and spritzed it into place with hairspray. Duke and Anthony agreed he looked better than they expected from him. Universally otherwise, Walt could be found in an ironic T-shirt and seemingly the same pair of jeans he'd worn since his freshman year of high school, with his hair going god knows anywhere. Today, Walt's feet felt like prisoners in those hard shoes. He felt the formal suffocation of the bow tie around his neck. He was just out of college, unemployed, and his tux fit him terribly (sleeves a little too short, the chest of the shirt much too tight, threads everywhere), but it was too late to be adjusted.

"I'm very lucky," Duke said. He meant it. He felt it. All three agreed that the fair bride was an unenumerated wonder of the world.

The gray-haired, square-headed priest, Fr. Michael Anthony Ferlinghetti, entered the room—the sacristy, which was also where the priest got ready for mass—already fully dressed in the day's ceremonial vestments, seemingly floating over the densely carpeted floor in his silent black shoes. He was taller than the three of them by a few inches. He had a permanent grin that creeped out Walt but which most people seemed to find charming. Fr. Michael, too, had blue eyes, and it looked like the surface of the blue quivered when you looked at them closely enough. (*Probably from all the lies pressing against the sides of his skull*, Walt thought to himself half-humorously and -bitterly.)

"I just saw the first car of guests arrive," the priest said. "Do you gentlemen have any questions before we begin?"

"I never question anything, Father," Anthony said, which made Walt laugh.

"No, sir," Duke said, giving his younger brother a disappointed-older-brother look.

"Which side is the groom's side? You know, for seating people," Walt asked, partly out of curiosity and partly as a peace offering to his brother on his brother's big day.

"Traditionally, I believe the bride's family and friends are on the left, and the groom's are on the right. Friends of both can have their choice," Best Man Anthony said before the priest could answer. (Evidently Anthony too felt the sudden need to be helpful.)

They all looked at the priest for confirmation.

The priest nodded, but it looked to Walt like the priest simply didn't want to contradict what was said. This made Walt think it didn't matter which side was which, and that seemed to take some of the pressure off, for some reason. Walt didn't even realize he felt any pressure until some of it was relieved.

If Duke and Walt had not been brothers, they would have been enemies. In fact, they were enemies, but their familial link—and more accurately their mother—did not allow the nemeses to actually do battle.

Perhaps they would not have been enemies had they not been brothers. Duke was the kind of guy Walt could ignore just as easily as he could ignore anyone else; nevertheless, he wasn't allowed to ignore his brother. They lived in the same city, and their aforementioned mother loved nothing more than to have them over for lunch every Sunday. They honored their mother, and fortunately, through the years, as they grew into adulthood, they found ways of getting along with each other. Had it been three years ago, Walt would not have been one of Duke's groomsmen. Maybe both men were maturing. And then maybe it was just, to quote their late father, "the goddam way it goes sometimes."

Whatever the reason, Walt pulled Duke aside. The priest had gone out to the altar to make the final preparations, and the best man had gone out to greet the first guests.

"Duke," Walt said, "I feel like someone needs to say this. Anthony is too nice to say it, but I think our relationship makes me perfect for this. I know we all love June, but I need to ask: are you absolutely certain about this? You know I don't hold shit as sacred, so matrimony probably won't mean much to me if I ever do it, but I just feel like I need to offer you one last out before you're all the way in—no pun intended. Are you sure this is the girl and that you're ready to commit to this marriage for the rest of your life? This whole arrangement is loaded in her favor, so you gotta be pretty goddam—you gotta be certain."

"You couldn't ask me this at the bachelor party or something?" Duke asked. "It's a bit late now, Dubs."

"But not too late, man."

"Walt . . . Yes. I was certain when I met her, certain when I asked, and I'm damn certain now."

"Okay—good," Walt said. He was glad that was over. "You look great, you skinny piece of shit."

Duke clapped his hand on Walt's shoulder, "You too, you crybaby faggot. Don't ever talk about my wife again."

Walt looked in his brother's eyes to search for the truth and indeed found certainty. Consequently, he sarcastically did the *Top Gun* locker-room jaw-snap at his brother, and they both laughed. Then Walt shook his brother's hand in confirmation of their mutual good faith and turned and walked through the door to the church.

Alone in the sacristy, Bridegroom Duke sat down and breathed a deep breath. He was unhappy with his brother for asking him that. But as he sat there, he started to get it. He really would be making that same commitment, only for superreal this time, in a half-hour, and he needed to be goddam—he needed to be sure.

Fortunately, he was.

In another odd room of the church, across the way, built for the brides-to-be, June Hypenette, the bride-to-be, wasn't so certain.

Part Two

THE BEAUTIFUL June Kathleen Hypenette looked at herself

in the mirror and didn't see anything but what was happening behind her, where her two bridesmaids were shuffling flesh around within their dresses—smoothing out fabric and otherwise preparing themselves to look their lady best. They were so focused on their pursuits that they temporarily forgot the bride was even in the room.

June could almost literally feel this relief from their attention, and she used it now to look at herself with full honesty. Was she ready for this? Was she happy? She looked in the mirror and saw a woman who was unready and unhappy. An unmistakable frown bent her mouth. Through the mirror and her periphery, she saw the porcelain shoulder blades of her younger sister as they started to turn, away from her, and the frown disappeared and was replaced with June's finest forced smile when she was mirror-face-to-face with Millie.

Millicent Vera Hypenette wasn't fooled. She could sense that her sister was bothered by something, unhappy and uncertain. The problem was that she, Millicent, didn't know what to do about it. She was nearly a decade younger than her older sister, and what the *heck* did she know about getting married? She'd never had a relationship that lasted longer than three dates. Hell, she was still technically a virgin! But she wanted to help, so she gave her sister a little shoulder massage.

"You ready for the fight, champ?" she asked. "Big purse for this one, so get mean."

"Leave her alone, Millie," the maid of honor said.

The maid of honor—Tiffany Ilene Taylor—had been June Hypenette's best friend since college. They were paired together as roommates during freshman year, and they maintained that arrangement all the way through college. People used to joke that they'd lived together so long it was technically a common-law marriage. Sometimes, they did feel like an old married couple—in that they were comfortable in silences together and never had sex with each other.

June Hypenette could be described as physically perfect, at least according to the majority of heterosexual men who ever met or saw her. She had a golden fountain of platinum-blonde hair and eyes so blue they appeared to be radiating light, like if one were to turn out the lights, those two gleaming blue gems would be visible to everyone else in the room. A graceful face gave way to a thin, sultry neck, which gave way to two delicate-looking yet appropriately bearing shoulders. Her arms were slim and elegant. Her breasts fit her torso perfectly, at least according to Da Vinci. And they were a symmetrical wonder of softness and firmness. She had a slim, flat waist, perfectly rounded hips, and long legs. There were times in her life when men would try to talk to her and would be so overwhelmed and nervous they would literally mumble in complete incoherence. June would giggle and say to them, "Aw, you're very sweet." It was a diplomatic and kind rejection. She was a kindergarten teacher.

Tiffany Taylor didn't exactly have the same tact, but she, too, was incredibly beautiful. She had tight spirals of brown hair leading to an obsessively worked body and augmented breasts. She ran five miles every morning and always watched what she ate. She was almost powered by men's attention, and in that case it was a symbiotic relationship: men fell all over her for her attentions because they thought she was beautiful, and she kept in attention-falling shape because of it. Nevertheless, although she liked the unspoken attention of men's eyes watching her every move when she, say, went to the DMV, etc., she was almost instantly creeped out by any man who spoke to her—any man who wasn't an Adonis, that is. Consequently, her rejections were much less diplomatic than June's. In fact, most people would describe her as a bitch. She and June seemed to get along because of how different they were. June needed Tiffany's unbridled (and often humorous) bitchiness to offset June's almost pitifully abundant kindness, and Tiffany needed June's wonderful kindness to offset the bitterness that seemed to spill into every aspect of her life. Tiffany was also an elementary-school teacher.

Millicent Hypenette was a mistake—a gorgeous mistake.

Her parents only wanted one child, but ten years after June was born, first came their father, then came Millie. The child was saved by Catholicism. (Millie was saved by her mother's fear of Catholic retribution.) Either way, here arrived the bounciest baby in the world—in fact, a child model. Millie was so kindhearted that she once cried for hours when she accidentally ran over a worm on the sidewalk. The worm was already dead, which June tried to explain to her, but that didn't matter to Millie, who felt so awful it almost made her parents laugh when they heard about it. That kindness receded a bit, however, when she matured. It was still there, but it was further under the surface than it had been. Too many people had taken advantage of her heart, and there is no level of kindness so deep that the person can forgive repeatedly being taken advantage of and used. So, she grew quiet and reticent. Her heart still filled with feelings of empathy, compassion, and kindness, but those feelings often only found their way into the world through a deep, hollowing pain in her innermost soul. Otherwise, she almost always appeared aloof, unattached. She found it kept people from figuring her out too quickly. Millie was still in college, but this being the summer, she was on break and working as a volunteer at a hospital in New York.

"Stop it, Tiffany," June said. "She's just trying to help—it's something Dad used to say to us."

"Well what's wrong? Besides these hideous dresses," Tiffany said. It was true. It's hard to look good in an orange dress, and although these two women were able to pull it off, it didn't change the objective fact that it's hard to look good in an orange dress.

"Yeah, they make my skin look like I'm in a Terry Gilliam movie," Millie said. Neither of the other two women got the joke. They both gave Millie that *Oh, it's just Millie* look.

"Can one of you tell me I'm doing the right thing?"

"What—Of course you are!" Millie said. "Duke is a *great guy*."

"Yeah, so what if he's not a hottie; he loves you," Tiffany

said. June gave her the *Oh, grow up Tiffany* look. "I mean, that's the problem, right? You're not sure if you can commit to someone who isn't—"

"Shut up, Tiffany," June said, and she started to apply the last layers of her makeup, with Millie supervising.

"You're just nervous because of Mom and Dad," Millie said. "I get it."

"What about them?" Tiffany asked.

"Well, they fell in love, and they've stayed together for the past forty years. That's such a long time. I'm sure it kind of feels—"

"Like I'm about to lose who I am," June said. "I'm June Fucking Hypenette, you know? I'm *me*. Pretty soon, I'm going to be June Wifey Karrington. I'm going to be one of two. But I like being me. But I love Duke. God, I feel *sick*. I shouldn't be thinking these things. This is supposed to be the best day of my life! Right?"

There was a knocking at the door.

"Just a second!" Millie said to the door and turned to June. "You're going to be June Fucking Hypenette Karrington, and that name is *fucking awesome*."

There was another knock.

"June, sweetie? It's your mother. I'm coming in."

All three women looked at each other with the same sigh.

"Come on in, Mom," June called to the door.

June's mom, Willa Louise Hypenette, who looked like an old, time-engorged, humorless version of Millie, waddled in and saw the three women looking at her uncomfortably. "Is something wrong?" she asked.

"June's got cold feet," Tiffany said.

June and Millie stared icy daggers at Tiffany.

"Oh, honey! You were so excited! What's wrong?"

"It's nothing," June said.

"I don't think—" June's mom said, but she was interrupted by Millie.

Millie faced what she called "a real shituation." She had

to get her awful mother out of there, but if she left June there alone with Tiffany, Tiffany might further poison her against Duke and make things worse. She had to do *something*, though, so she decided to take her mother (a big negative) out of the equation. While her mother was talking, she slipped her bracelet into her bra.

"Mom, I can't find my new bracelet *anywhere*. I know I had it in the car. Can you come look for it with me? I think June and Tiffany can work this out. We're not going to help."

"But of course I can help—I'm her mother."

"Go help Millie, Mom. I'm okay; I promise," June said.

In a rare act of interpersonal perception, Willa Hypenette recognized that her daughter truly didn't want her there, even if she was trying to look like she did. "Okay, honey. You know I love you."

"I love you, too."

"Let's *go*, Mom," Millie said, leading her through the door.

"I love Millie," June said when they were gone.

"Where'd that come from?" Tiffany asked. "What's to love?"

June gave Tiffany a cross-brow look. "Why are you being so shitty today?"

Tiffany didn't want to admit that she was internally roiling with jealousy. June wasn't even sure she wanted to be married, and Tiffany had wanted to be married since she was twelve, and yet here they were: June getting married, with cold feet, and Tiffany alone like an unmatched shoe that's running out of baby-making magic, or something.

"I'm sorry, J-F-H," Tiffany said. "I'm just stressed out. You know you love Duke, and you know you'll always be yourself, no matter where you are or who you're with, so what's the problem? I mean, after all, look at those breasts!"

June laughed.

"Do you think he really loves me? I just love that goofy bastard so much it hurts sometimes."

"If you've ever trusted me in your life, June, trust me now.

Get married, and tonight at the reception I'm going to tell a story that will prove to you just how much he loves you."

"Can't you tell me now?"

"Nope. I'm only going to tell you if you go out there and make an honest man out of him. Otherwise, you'll be like that mythical guy who went to Hell to get his bride back, but he wasn't allowed to look at her as they made their way out of Hell. But that guy looked, and he never got to bring his wife back. Is that what you want? Huh?"

"What are you talking about?" June asked, even though she knew what Tiffany was talking about.

"I'm talking about love, baby," Tiffany said, and then got serious. "Your love. You deserve Duke's love, you lovable bitch!"

June looked in the mirror again, and this time she actually saw herself.

There she was, as always, and she stood and turned and looked at her maid of honor for a pre-ceremony appraisal.

Tiffany looked the bride up and down.

"Prettier than life itself," she said.

Part Three

When Walt Karrington reached the vestibule of the church, the first thing he noticed was that almost instantly the room had become crowded with friends and family. Ten minutes ago, a handful of these people were here; now, there were waltzing pockets of well-dressed people all around, chattering loudly.

He saw his cousins Kevin and John talking to his other cousins Jamie and Sean—each looking sharp, healthy, and contented. He saw his Aunt Goldie and Uncle Glenn, who were wearing the same dress and suit they wore to every formal occasion. They were standing together, looking over a bulletin board tacked with photographs from the attached school's end-of-the-year outdoors day. Walt had looked at those pictures earlier. They were nice, and Walt asked himself what happens to adults that they can't look so nice in pictures. He knew the answer, but he didn't dwell on it.

He saw his friends Dwight and Herb. Dwight, who came from a very wealthy family, was wearing an impeccably cut suit. Contrastingly, Herb was wearing black running pants and one of those T-shirts that looks like a tuxedo. Walt waved to them, and Dwight nodded back while Herb did the finger-shoot thing. They both looked like they (probably definitely) were high. Neither of them looked comfortable in the church—that made the three of them, at least. He saw June's friends Alicia and Sarah with their dates, though he'd forgotten their names. Alicia and Sarah weren't as attractive as June, Tiffany, and Millie, and their dates matched them in ordinariness.

He also saw June's grandparents on her father's side. They were two unintentionally hilarious old people—age-short, hobbled, shouting at each other conversationally.

Then Walt saw his mom, Dorothy Judith Karrington (née Thompson). She was talking with Fr. Michael. Walt looked at her and frowned. She was wearing a new dress, and she looked so classically pretty, like an old-time movie star.

God, he thought, *I wish he were still here.*

James Paul Karrington—Duke and Walt's late father, Dorothy's late husband—had passed away a little more than a year ago. It had come as a surprise to all. James had seemingly been in good health right until the moment of the massive and fatal heart attack. The death brought the family closer together. The husband/father had always been the biggest presence in the family, and with him gone, a large void resulted, and the pulling force of the void brought the remaining members together to where each filled a part of the hole left by James' death. Dorothy had been forced to become more independent, Duke had been forced to become more of a family cornerstone, and Walt had been forced back into the lives of the family he had been slowly abandoning since he left for college. The night after the funeral, Walt and his mother cried together. Duke was there, too, but the reality of their father's death didn't hit him for a few more weeks. Sure, he cried a bit, but only because it killed him to see his mother crying like that. He had been otherwise numb, perhaps even incredulous about the whole thing.

One of the thoughts that flashed in the storm of Walt's mind that night was that his mother's faith must not be as strong as it would otherwise appear. How could she cry like that if she truly believed her infinitely kindhearted husband was in the perfect and eternal state of Heaven? It makes sense to miss someone, but the way his mother was crying that night was more than just sadness. There was something scary about it. All his life, Walt had seen within his mother the closest thing to unwavering religious conviction he could believe possible, and then at the first truly horrible tragedy of her life Walt saw that her protective layers of faith had split like dry-rotted wood, and the pain hit her core like it hit the core of a nonbeliever—like a dentist's drill hitting the tooth's nerve. Time, of course, had anaesthetized the pain, but Walt could not forget the image of watching his mother almost lose her soul.

Now, she looked good—good, but not great. Incomplete might be it. In a way, however, he liked her like this. She'd always been so dependent and timid. Now, because of what Millie would describe as her "real shituation," she appeared to have become more independent and bold. She'd had to take on these traits, and they fit her surprisingly well.

"Hi, Mom!" Walt said and leaned in for a hug. Dorothy diplomatically ended her talk with the priest and smiled at her youngest son and hugged him back. "Walter, you look so handsome," she said.

"Thanks, Ma," he said. "You look great, too. Where's Uncle Homer?"

Ever since her husband's death, Dorothy Karrington had been spending a lot of time with her single-for-life brother Homer.

"He's outside talking to Mrs. Featherly."

"He knows she's married, right?"

"I don't ask him about anything he does anymore," she said, and they both laughed. "He's a nut."

"Have you seen Duke yet?" Walt asked.

"I saw him this morning—he came by for breakfast—but not here," she said. "Is he around?"

They both looked around but did not see Duke. "He was back in the church earlier. Might still be there. You want me to get him?"

"No, no, honey," she said. "I'll see him eventually. So, have you talked to Millicent?"

Walter's face flushed red with embarrassment, and he looked around for any nearby Hypenettes, and he smiled. "No, Mom," he said. "I don't think she's into me like that."

"Don't be silly, Walter; what's not to like about you?"

"Ask *her*," he said.

"Please—I'm sorry, Wally—please don't let this get you down," she said. "I was just asking. You seemed to like her, and I was curious."

"I'll be fine, Mom," Walt said rather unconvincingly. "Anyway, I think they want us to start seating people. I know you've got people to catch up with here, so let me know when you're ready."

"Sounds good, sweetie," Dorothy said and hugged Walt again.

Walt went to the door between the vestibule and the church itself. There waiting for him was a very professional-looking couple.

"Hello," Walt said with a tiny bow. "I'm Walter—the groom's brother."

"Hello, Walter," the man said. "I'm Cliff—the groom's boss."

"Hey, awesome," Walt said. "Duke says you're the man."

"How can I be the man when *he's* the man?" Cliff said and chortled to himself. "Heard that one on the radio. And this is my wife—Maria."

Walt greeted the older-but-still-relatively-attractive Maria with a handshake.

"Well, may I show you to your seats?"

"Certainly," Cliff said and backed away from his wife, in good form. Walt held out his elbow for Maria, and she took it. They walked down the main aisle—Maria smelling like a bouquet of old flowers—and Walt let them pick their favorite row on the groom's side. "Enjoy the matrimony," Walt said, and they both seemed to like this because they smiled as he walked back to the vestibule.

Coincidentally, next he escorted the principal of June's school, alone, to her seat on the bride's side, near another member of the faculty. The principal, as seems to always be the case, was a cunty, rat-faced woman, and she was obviously only invited because she was June's boss.

Next he escorted his cousin Noelle to her seat. She walked like such a little lady. She felt light as a bird next to him, and he found it hard to believe she was twelve already.

"Oh, you look so handsome, Wally!" Aunt Goldie said.

"Thanks, Aunt Goldie."

"Lookin' strong, too," Uncle Glenn said. "Been working out?"

Walt's answer came in the form of a faux-left-jab. Glenn put up his fists to block the blow and laughed with Walt.

Aunt Goldie leaned against him rather heavily. He hadn't realized how old she and Glenn were getting. He loved this couple. They were just classic. One time at a previous wedding he'd seen Glenn pluck and hand Goldie a rose, and while Goldie was looking at the rose, Glenn stared down Goldie's cleavage with an *"Ooooo, that is sweet!"* look on his face. Duke walked them to a row near the back of the groom's side, where they struck up a conversation with one of Duke's coworkers, which started when Uncle Glenn asked the man, "How much beer do you think I've already had today?"

When he returned to the vestibule again, laughing, there

was only his mother there, who was looking at the pictures of the kids on the board.

"Do you remember when you were at this school?" she asked.

"Of course," Walt said.

"You kids were so adorable," she said.

"Yeah—what the hell happened to us?"

They both laughed.

"Come on, Mom," Walt said.

Dorothy Karrington took one last look at the field of pictures and faced her son, who looked more like James every day. Walt saw her frown and realized what it meant, recognized the recognition and sadness. "I wish he were here, too," he said.

He escorted her to her seat in the front row, next to Uncle Homer, and he returned to the groom's room off to the side of the church—the sacristy—for the beginning of the ceremony.

Part Four

THE CEREMONY was taking place in a church in downtown Cleveland OH, and the grand majority of guests were Clevelanders themselves, so the church colors and decorations were a huge hit with the attendees. The men loved the football/Browns tribute, and the women were surprised by how lovely everything looked, after they'd been warned about the bride's unusual coloration decision.

Additionally, most of them had never expected Duke to get married, especially to a woman like June! All his life, he'd been a loner. He'd never brought a date to a family wedding or event, and nobody ever really heard about him having any trysts at all. Everyone was sure he got laid now and then, but nobody had ever heard of any actual incidents. Truly, these unexpected nuptials were something worth celebrating. Duke may not have been generally seductive, but he was obviously much-loved.

Which is a way of explaining just how ubiquitous and buoyant were the smiles that morning, when the first piped chords of the Mendelssohn's "Wedding March" filled the shuffling air of the church.

Everyone stood, with a youthful strength in their knees, and turned to face the back of the church, where Walt Karrington and Millicent Hypenette had begun walking down the aisle together.

Just before they started, Millicent had turned to Walt and asked, "Oh my god, are you nervous? I'm so nervous."

He thought and said, "Not really." He was nervous to be around her, but not nervous about what they were doing.

"Really? How could you not be nervous with all these people watching us?"

"Because they're not going to be watching me," he said.

Millie blushed.

"That didn't help."

"Sorry."

The song started, and they walked. Walt asked himself how he could be so shallow as to already be in love with a girl he met three days ago. And he was right about what he said to her. Everyone was looking at Millie, and rightly so. She was the prettiest Terry Gilliam character anyone had ever seen. The orange in her dress also brought out vivid aspects of the green in her eyes. (What a collection of eyes at this wedding!)

At the base of the altar, Duke the bridegroom stood waiting. To Walt, he looked great. This was not Duke's scene at all, but he filled his position perfectly. There was a look of honest intensity and earnestness in his face, an unconscious revelation of how much this day actually meant to him.

Both Millie and Walt beamed big smiles at him as they passed. Then the two turned and walked to their respective sides of the altar. A yearning voice within Walt wished they could have just stayed in the middle and made the event into a double wedding. He thought about it as he stood looking over the gathering, all turned away from him now, watching Anthony and Tiffany walk down the aisle together—people whispering to each other, flashbulbs flashing, pipe organ piping. He thought it would be fitting for Millie to wear an orange wedding dress; she seemed like the kind of girl who would do something just like that.

Anthony and Tiffany marched. Anthony looked his classic, underfed, handsome self. Tiffany reveled in the same crowd's attention that had so obviously bothered Millie. In the moment, she looked quite good to Walt, even though he didn't consider her particularly attractive.

There are some girls who are very pretty, but their personalities take it all away. It's not often, but it happens, and it happened to Walt with Tiffany. She must have been able to sense that, too, because she'd been a dismissive bitch to him all week.

When Anthony stood next to Walt on the groom's side of the altar, the two did a fist bump, which sent a low murmur of laughter through the crowd. Walt and Anthony were also close friends and would have been even if Duke were to disappear.

After the best man and maid of honor were settled in their standing positions next to Walt and Millie, the music faded. For a moment, the church was filled with an almost awkward, anticipatory silence. Then the first bars of Wagner's "Bridal Chorus" whistled from the organ's pipes—the irony of a song written by an atheist being played in churches every weekend not being lost on Walt—and there, at the back of the church, stood the bride. Her dress a simple, white, sleeveless affair sewn perfectly to glide over the grace of her statuesque form, she took the breath away from a few of the women in attendance. Escorted by her father, Robert Wallace Hypenette, who was a tall, thin, gaunt man with an affable face, the literally blushing bride appeared to be walking on nothing at all, not even air. She—like her dress—just seemed to *flow*. For that minute, Walt was not obsessed with sweet Millie in his periphery; he was enraptured by the beaming bride. It was so nice for him to see something so nice, especially in a church full of people and statues of a dead savior.

The father symbolically handed the bride to the groom—both bride and groom almost glowing with happiness to be together here for this momentous event—and Bob Hypenette walked over and sat next to his blubbering wife.

The priest addressed the attendees from the altar.

"We are gathered here today to witness the union of Paul Duke Karrington and June Kathleen Hypenette . . . ."

It was a fine ceremony. Walt mouthed all the praises and responses that were called for in the mass, having memorized them long ago. He could not forget them, no matter how much he wanted to, and he mouthed them for the same reason this ceremony was being held in a church: to appease the parents of the bride and groom. The only other remarkable thing Walt noticed (again and again) was the bride's sister, Millicent. God (no pun intended), he couldn't keep his eyes from her. He felt indelibly pulled to her—not only his eyes but the full scope of his attention and self. She was the only thing, besides the momentary trance of seeing the bride, that made being in that church palatable.

The exchange of rings went off smoothly, and the first kiss as man and wife was a beautiful moment and was met with a few catcalls from Dwight and Herb. Then things wrapped up.

"Go in peace, to love and serve the Lord," the priest said.

"Thanks be to God," the crowd said in unison.

"Ladies and gentlemen, it is my honor to be the first to introduce you to Mr. and Mrs. Duke and June Karrington."

A cheerful applause—and more Dwight-and-Herb cat-calls—pealed through the air. As the applause died down, the first thrilling notes of a symmetric-yet-more-enthusiastic replay of Mendelssohn's "Wedding March" were sounded, and Millie and Walt were reunited at the front of the altar. They walked together down the aisle, with Walt cocking his head in her direction ever so subtly, to try to catch wisps of her wonderful scent. They were followed by Anthony and Tiffany. Finally, the bride and groom walked back down the aisle, together. Soon, the vestibule was totally packed.

Everyone was in a celebratory mood. "Good job, Walt," Millie said and quickly shuffled over to be with her sister and parents, and Walt listened to the sound of dozens of conversations crashing against each other and swaddled himself in the trance of hearing Millie say his name.

Duke and June greeted people with smiles and hugs. Walt soon found himself alone in a corner and was quickly located by Dwight and Herb.

"Holy fuck that chick you were paired with is hot," Herb said.

"Told you, man," Walt said. "I seriously think I'm in love with her."

Dwight and Herb laughed. "I don't blame you, man," Dwight said. *"Shit."*

"Hey, Walt—it's time for the pictures," Anthony said over the din of the crowd.

"Okay," Walt said.

"What are you guys going to do until the reception?" Walt asked his friends.

"Probably going to The Dome," Herb said.

"You'll be there for a while?"

"Yeah. Definitely."

"I might meet you guys there, then," Walt said.

"Sweet."

"Later, fellas."

"Later."

The wedding crew, and their parents, had worked their way back into the church. When all were gathered, everyone was led outside by the photographer, who brought them to an immaculately landscaped and picturesque alcove outside of the church, and for the next half-hour the photographer snapped hundreds of pictures of various combinations of the bride, groom, their parties, and their parents/families.

Walt still had not worked up the nerve to say anything else to Millie, but as they all were leaving, he felt the air and life being sucked out of him, and he bucked against the feeling, resulting in a too-loud call to "Millie!"

She turned and smiled at Walt. "Hey, what's up? I was wondering when you were going to talk to me."

"What are you doing now?" Walt asked.

"Probably just going back to the hotel with my parents," she said. "Why?"

"My friends and I are going to hang out at this cool place. I'd like you to come, if you want to."

Millie looked at her parents and looked back.

"Sure!"

Part Five

"HOLD ON a second," Millie said to Walt.

She hustled over to her parents, spoke to them, pointed to Walt, and her parents nodded. She came back.

"Okay, my parents said we can meet them at the reception," she said. "Can I grab a change of clothes from the car, though?"

He changed in the bathroom and she changed in the bridal room in the church, and he picked her up out front. She came out wearing a pair of jeans and a plain blue T-shirt.

The sight of her in her normal clothes, away from the Gilliam-inducing orange dress, was such a beautiful-and-thus-intimidating sight that Walt felt his bowels loosen a bit from anxiety. "Shit," he said to himself, looking at her. "Oh, shit. Okay, man, you can do this. Be cool. Be cool, man."

Happily she pulled the door open and popped in and said, "Okay, where are we going?"

"It's this cool place my friends and I heard about a few

years ago, and we go there all the time now," he said. "I'm not sure how to describe it, though. We just call it 'The Dome.' It's not that far from the reception hall."

"That works for me," she said. "Going back to that hotel with my parents was my only other option. *No, thank you.*"

"So, what do you think of Cleveland so far?"

"It's nice," she said. "It's not so bad. Back in New York they made it sound like I was going to have to milk the mayor."

Walt laughed.

"So you grew up out here?" she asked, looking around.

"Yeah," he said. "Spent eighteen years here, went away to college, and then moved back a couple months ago. Not sure what I'm doing next. Taking a few months off before I finally have to grow up."

"Where did you go to college?"

"Boston."

"Is 'Boston' an unpretentious word for Harvard?"

"Yes."

"No way! That's where I'm going, and I say the same thing! I always hated when I heard people say they went to *Harvard*, like that's some big deal. It doesn't make you superior to other people—which is what it always sounded like to me, and I hated that—it just means you—"

"Did well in high school," they both said.

Millie looked at Walt now. Really, almost like for the first time. Like now that he had passed some sort of test, she could really look at him. She liked him, but she didn't quite *like*-him-like-him. He was cool, though.

"Yeah, but now I'm one of them," Millie said. "I'm one of those people I hated."

"So why are you going there, then?"

"I got in, and my parents are paying for it, I guess."

"Where do you want to be going?"

"I don't think I do—anywhere," she said. "I don't think I need it. I've always been an autodidact. I don't see why my parents should pay so much money for me to learn things I would have learned anyway."

They were making great time, like the Fates were divining the traffic for them, and soon they were pulling off the freeway and onto a rural-looking road.

"The place isn't far from here," he said.

"What do you want to do, like if you could do anything, what would it be?" Millie asked.

"I would write this story," he said.

"What?" she asked. "What story?"

"Never mind," he said. "Weird answer. I get weird sometimes."

"I can *tell,*" she said, but faux-mockingly.

"Okay, so we're almost there."

Millie looked around and saw, on both sides of the car, stretching columns of trees marching by. "There's a building around h—?"

She went silent when Walt took a left into what didn't even look like a place where you'd be allowed to turn left, and before them opened a vast field within the otherwise surrounding forest. In the middle of the field was a small building, and seemingly bursting from the ground, like a reverse comet collision—an asteroid flying *out* of the earth—was a massive geodesic dome, around a hundred feet in diameter. (A geodesic dome is like the skeleton of a dome, without the covering. It is open to the elements and the air.)

"Wow!" Millie said. "'The Dome!'"

"Yeah," Walt said, smiling. He drove along the long lawn and parked his Jeep next to Dwight's BMW. Millie and Walt walked down a path to the building itself and then into the middle of The Dome, where Dwight and Herb were seated, talking.

"Hey, guys," Walt said. "This is Millie. Millie, these are my friends Dwight and Herb."

She shook each's surprised hand.

Is anyone still with me? I wish I could tell you, reader, what the hell is happening here, or why I'm writing this story, or where it's going. I don't know. I'm just pulling this out of myself like it's a tapeworm, like it was in there, doing its thing, and I'm realizing as I place it into a sterilized surgical bowl, that its purpose is singular to itself. J. D. Salinger could pull off shit like this, but I don't have his depth. I need to entertain, or provoke thought, and I can't rightly say I'm doing that with this plot-free piece of dumb waste. I was in a wedding this summer, so that's part of the inspiration, and Millie is obviously this girl I thought I fell in love with recently. It's obvious to me, at least. I guess I'm not yet ready to let go of her. She lives far away and hasn't replied to any of my messages in more than a month, so I guess my mind is just stupidly trying to tug at the tail of a tiger as it runs away from me.

I was really hoping this story would sort of create itself in the writing, and I suppose it's done that, sort of, but I'm not excited to write it. It's amateurish.

Certainly Mr. Salinger knew where he was going with his stories; even if they were going nowhere, they were going nowhere with a certain class and timeless aesthetic. I feel like a ventriloquist's dummy without a ventriloquist. In a literary sense, I'm moving my mouth up and down and telling myself that it's interesting and worth hearing.

But, oh well. I've gotten this far into it, so I might as well just finish it out. There's not much left anyway—just more bullshit.

The four of them sat on the grass in the middle of The Dome.

"This place is so cool!" Millie said, looking around.

"You should see it at night," Dwight said.

"Yeah, the lighting is crazy," Herb said.

"I'll *bet*," she said. "So how do you guys all know each other?"

"We met in middle school," Walt said. "During recess.

Dwight and I were on opposing football teams. We were both super competitive, and we were jawing at each other, about to fight, when Herb here stumbled over to us, holding out a bottle of rubber cement he had in his pocket. He said to us, 'Why you guys wanna fight, man? Wouldn't you rather just huff some glue instead?'"

"Somehow, it worked," Dwight said. "We both started cracking up."

"Everyone loves rubber cement," Herb said.

"Isn't that terrible for you?" Millie asked.

"Oh, yeah, totally," Herb said. "I wasn't actually huffing it or anything. I just had it in my pocket, and I remembered it made me feel peaceful in art class, and I thought I could spread some peace . . . or something."

"Yeah, none of us was actually into the huffing, you know besides the normal amount; it's just that what Herb said was so crazy that we forgot what we were fighting about."

"I always tell Herb he should be the Ambassador to Druggistan."

"Druggistan's too commercial these days," Herb said. "It used to be about the *drugs*."

"So what do you guys do now?" Millie asked.

"I work for my dad's steel company," Dwight said.

"Just got a job for this fall as an English teacher here in Cleveland," Herb said.

"My sister's a teacher!" Millie said.

"Oh, cool," Herb said, but it didn't sound like he really thought it was cool. He was high and distracted and probably nervous to be talking to a girl as pretty as Millicent.

"I can see why you guys come here," she said, looking around, her eyes tracing the angled lines of the dome all the way to the top. "I really like it!"

"I love it here," Walt said. "So many great memories."

"You want a drink, Millie?" Dwight asked, handing her a bottle he pulled from his backpack. "Figured it's a celebration."

"*Sure,*" she said and took a swig of vodka straight from the bottle.

"Nice!" Walt said.

"Whooo!" Millie sighed from drink.

Walt himself took a slug, to calm his nerves.

"Hey, so, Walt, I think I left something in your car," she said. "Can you help me find it?"

Evidently Millie left all her excuses in the car.

When they got back to the car, Walt could sense that she wanted him to kiss her, and he did. He stepped in, pulled her close, and kissed her with all the passion he contained, which was volcanic. They slipped into the backseat of the car, and she pulled down his pants and started to wrap her mouth around him, fully—

"Walt!"

Walt snapped out of his daydream and saw Anthony laughing at him. They were still by the alcove near the church. Millie was walking away with her parents. He'd blown it again—had chickened out of asking her to join him, or even talking to her.

He drove to The Dome and drank and smoked with his friends, distracted by the lost opportunity, kicking himself for his cowardice. After a few hours, the three friends drove to the reception hall.

It was party time.

Part Six

FROM THE outside, the reception hall looked like a dramatically lit, big brown box.

Cleveland does the best it can.

Two stoned, red-vested, teenaged valets waited near the front door, which consisted of two large panes of blacked-out glass bearing a cardboard sign—"Hypenette/Karrington Wedding"—across the front.

Through the door, stepping into the room, one would notice that there was no main source of light. There were white Christmas lights along the walls, and there were candles aglow on the tables, and there were lights in the glass shelves along and behind the large bar. The result was a sort of permanent twilight, and the effect was soothing and very adult-feeling.

It was a large room, with a U of tables surrounding a softly glowing dance floor. The tables were covered with a white tablecloth, and then a smaller orange tablecloth. Each place at each table was set with the standard two-fork, two-knife, two-spoon, dinner plate, bread plate, two-glasses setting, but in addition to that, there were also beer mugs filled with Cleveland's finest. (The children were given root beer and good examples of why not to drink.)

Even the Cleveland-dreading Willa Hypenette admitted to her husband, "Well, this is very nice. Good fun."

As things were getting started, the bride, groom, and their bridal parties greeted the attendees. Walt met and forgot a tremendous number of people in a relatively short amount of time. Everyone just wanted to get to the bar anyway, and who could blame them?

Millie looked unspeakably great. It was like there were little magnets within the center of each of Walt's cells, and they were as naturally pulled to her as any measurable magnetism. But he still knew nothing about her, goddammit. That had to change.

It wouldn't be too weird to marry your brother's wife's sister, would it? Two brothers and sisters getting—yeah, that's weird. Shit. But fuck!*, look at her. Sense* her.

There was another cute girl in the line of people he met, so he made sure to try to remember to swing by at some point in the night and talk to her—thereby getting Millie curious and/or jealous. And if not, maybe he could do the other chick.

Party!

Walt had had a few drinks.

Everyone else joined him in that pursuit. The Karrington family contained a large number of people who could just pack away shit-tons of beer and keep on going. The Hypenettes could not match this, of course, but they were drinkers; make no mistake about it. The bartender was tipped well that night.

People again settled into pockets of conversation, and goddammit Millie was *still* talking with her parents and whoever they were goddam talking to. He didn't want to talk to *them*. He must have been eying the situation for longer than he thought because before he knew it people were heading towards their tables for dinner, and before dinner he had to give his speech, which the night's emcee was just pointing out to the hungry crowd.

"Okay, before we eat, we have some people who would like to say a few words on behalf of the bride and groom. First, let's start with the groom's brother . . ." the emcee looked at the card in his hand, "Walt Korvington!"

There was a responsive applause—and some laughter at the emcee's mistake—until the emcee handed Walt the microphone.

Walt cleared his throat and began.

"When Duke asked me to speak at his wedding, I immediately agreed. It's an honor, because I love him. But later that night, after he asked me to do it, I began thinking about what I would say. I asked myself what I could possibly have to offer to you all on this occasion that would be of be any value, seeing as how my love life is like a whale flopping around and dying, confabulated and miserable, in a lifeless desert—you know, getting sand in its eyes and blow hole and between its teeth and on its tongue, looking for water that isn't there . . . . Anyway, what I realized is that this isn't about me at all; this is about what's happening right here.

"Right here we have something truly real and wonderful in this plastic world. Right here we have friends and family coming together because of *love*. We have food and drinks and togetherness. We have music and dramatic lighting and adored women in celebratory dresses. We have slobs like myself and Anthony dressed in formal tuxedos. We have my fine brother Duke and his beautiful bride, and, fuck it, I'll say it, we have the bride's un*believ*ably sexy sister, whom I celebrate like a God-struck pagan. And we have all of this tonight—the family, the friends, the drinks and lighting, beautiful Millie—because of two people we love and cherish, Duke Karrington and June Hypenette, being united . . . and that, to me, is something well worth celebrating.

"Duke, if our father is watching us now, I know he is proud of the man you are, and he is happy. Duke and June, we drink to you. May your first child . . . be an *intentional* child. Cheers."

"Cheers," the crowd laughed and piped back; drinks were downed, and the Hypenette parents shared a bemused grin.

Next, it was the best man's turn.

"Thanks, Walt," said the emcee. "Now here's the best man, Anthony Sclari . . . smo."

"Thank you," Anthony said. "Um, I think Walter pretty much covered it—wiseass. What I can add to that is that I've known the Karrington family for nearly my whole life, and I wanted to tell any Hypenettes out there that you are lucky. I consider myself very fortunate to be their friend, because they are truly talented and great and kind people. And you all seem great, too. But let me just end by saying June, they call my position in the wedding the best man, but in all honesty Duke is the best man I've ever known, and he is going to make you very happy. I wish you a long life together, filled with laughs and happiness. Cheers."

"Cheers," repeated and drank.

When the emcee offered the mic to Millie, she blushed and repeatedly turned down the requests to make a speech, say-ing, "Trust me—I'd just cry the whole time." (The bride had never asked her sister to give a speech at the wedding, because she knew how much Millie loved her, and Millie was a *crier*.) So, the emcee shrugged and introduced the maid of honor, who began her speech.

"Hi, everyone. I'm June's friend Tiffany. I've known June for—how many years is it, June? Wait, you know what, forget it, too many years!—let's just say I've known June for a long time.

"One of my ex-boyfriends used to say that his way of measuring if someone was his friend or not was he would ask himself if he were living on the other side of the country, would he fly back for their funeral. You can see why we broke up, right?"—crowd laughter—"But even though it's pretty dark, I hated to agree that it made sense, sort of. And the only reason I bring it up is because my ex-boyfriend was wrong in this way: there are some friends for whom you'd rather be the dead one yourself, if you could spare their life. June is the only friend I have like that, and I love her. Never once in her life has she ever been anything less than the sweetest, most genuine person I know, and I know enough to know how much of a gift that is.

"Earlier today, I promised June I would tell her a story about Duke that proved to me just how much he loves her, and I'd like to tell that story now:

"As many of you know, and some of you may not, Duke's father, James Karrington, died last year. He was a great man, and his family and friends continue to miss him. A couple weeks after Mr. Karrington passed away, I got a call from Duke, which, if you know Duke, is *rare*. The guy refers to his cell phone as an electronic pocket watch. Anyway, he called me, and even though I could hear that he was really sad, he sounded better than I expected. Anyway, I asked him, you know, why he was calling, and he said to me, 'These have been the worst two weeks of my life.' And then he started crying"—at this point, Tiffany, too, began crying—"And I started crying. And then he said at first it didn't hit him, you know? How could he be dead? He said they'd just gone to an Indians game together a few nights earlier. And then it hit the night before, so hard. Duke said to me, "He's dead. He's dead, Tiffany, and I can't cry hard enough. I've tried. There's no bottom to it.'

"I said to Duke that he needed to tell this to June, not me—that she needed to hear all this. And he just kept repeating that he couldn't tell her this stuff, that the only thing that was keeping him upright was that she wasn't worried about him. He could think about her going about her day, and it was the only thing . . . normal. He said if June were as worried about him as he knew she would be if she knew all this, it would make things so much worse. It would be too much.

"Then he apologized and said that he would've called Walt but nobody could find him. He said that he just needed to tell someone. He said something that I immediately wrote down after we talked, because I knew it would be worth repeating today. He said, 'I love her, and it's killing me that I can't share this with her, but I can't. I need her to think I'm strong. At the same moment the thing about my Dad hit me, I realized she's the one. I thought about myself dying suddenly like that, and I realized the only regret I would have would be that I died before the world knew that I loved June Fucking Hypenette more than life itself. I don't feel like I deserve her, Tiffany, but I need her more than anything.'

"At the end of our talk, Duke said to me, 'Please don't tell anyone about this.'"

The crowd laughed.

"June . . ." Tiffany said, but she couldn't go on—the whole thing had become too emotional for her.

There was a long, sniffle-filled silence before Tiffany could say, "A toast: to Duke and June."

"Cheers!" the crowd piped up and drank down.

The emcee announced that the food was served, and the party returned to its more informal swagger.

Dinner was eaten, more and more drinks were imbibed, and the people there were forced to agree with Mother Hypenette: "This is very nice. Good fun."

People started dancing—Dwight, Herb, John, Sean, Noelle, Aunt Goldie, Uncle Glenn, Dorothy Karrington, even Uncle Homer with feet like landed fish, the bride's friends and their dates, the groom's boss and his wife, and others, and others. They danced in celebration of love and life.

This story closes with a short scene amidst the drinking and dancing, with a nervous Walt Karrington sliding into a chair next to the finally-alone Millicent Hypenette. After an anxious moment, each looks into the eyes of the other and smiles in the warm mood produced by the wistful, dulcet notes of Louis Armstrong's "What a Wonderful World."

Walt breathes a deep breath, takes Millie's hand in his, and guides her onto the softly glowing dance floor.

They lean into each other and dance.

"Walt," Millie says.

"Yes, Millie," Walt says.

"I'm like—I'm sorry to say it, but it won't work. I'm too like you."

"What?" Walt pulls away a bit and asks her perfect face. "What d—"

"I'm a chick-chick, Walt. I eat puss'—never been much of a cock girl."

Walt stops dancing. "Oh. Okay. Uh, cool, for you, then . . . ."

Oh well, he thinks. *I never had a chance—fuck it.*

He starts looking around the reception hall for the other hot chick, from earlier, before it's too late.

"Her name is Kelsey, and she's my girlfriend," Millie says, reading Walt.

Millie can feel all of Walt's muscles tense up, and he's now a black hole on the dance floor. She can actually hear his jaw grinding in frustration—she smiles. Eventually, Walt speaks up.

"Millie?"

"Yes, Walt?" Millie says.

"Are you fucking with me?"

The First Pastel Parade:
Lines Alive Rising From Dead Novels

-Men who because of their illness and weakness were allowed to board the life rafts with the women and children, and also men who because of their strength and numbers were left to the icy waters' bottom alone, frozen and blue, their ghastly white ankle bones embedded into the gray silt, their bloated pale flesh flaking bit by bit into the mouths of unseen, hideous fish.

-The air in the room was thick and dry, like breathing through a rug. The tenants didn't seem to notice, or didn't seem to mind, nor the flies, nor the thin shaft of light that cut through the golden air and glowed on the groaning, dusty floorboards.

-The little boy looked up and saw the big yellow sun hidden by a large, fast-moving cloud, and suddenly the entire neighborhood was shrouded in shade, and icicles raced up the boy's spine.

-She was the type of girl who, when socially uncomfortable, turned nasty, with her teeth showing, and her fingers curled to predatory hooks. She was uncomfortable often, but people still loved her because of how pretty she looked when she glowered.

-"Polar bears," the cashier said, "are all left-handed. I read that somewhere. If I had to have a bear paint me a pretty picture, before any other bears, I think I'd try to find me a right-handed polar bear. You know?"

-Her father died two weeks ago, out of nowhere, and with a weird mix of emotions, the horny young man realized that he might have a shot with her now.

-She laughed softly, dipping her head forward self-consciously to muffle the laugh into her own chest, but the downward movement of her head, towards mine, sent a waft of her hair's conditioned scent into my face, and in that moment I was connected to everything I've ever loved.

-I thought we got along, but we only got along because he was doing an impression of someone like me. It turned out later that we didn't get along at all. He wasn't my friend. It turned out I didn't even know him. And I try not to think about it anymore, but I sometimes wonder if there was even anyone in there to know.

-She clasped her arms around his beloved big fat leg and squeezed. *Uncle Jim is always so soft*, she thought, and this made her happy, because all her favorite things were soft, like her blanket and teddy bear. Uncle Jim always felt self-conscious about his weight; maybe he wouldn't if he knew just how much joy it brought his little pint-sized niece.

-The longer he looked at her, the worse he felt about himself, and he tented his fingers as he ruminated.

-Embarrassed by the first one, the little boy ran upstairs, and with each successive step, he accidentally let out another loud, wet flatulence (twelve steps, thirteen barks in all), which only compounded his mortification, and the boys and girls at the birthday party laughed and laughed and never forgot it for the rest of their lives.

-"It's hard to think of any good reasons," he said. "It's hard to think of any good," he said. "It's hard to think of any," he said. "It's hard to think of," he said. "It's hard to think," he said. "It's hard to," he said. "It's hard," he said. "It is."

-Pvt. Hernandez knelt on one knee, put the German paratrooper in his sights, blinked away the salty sweat from his eyes, and pulled the trigger. Click.

-Is it any wonder you're alone right now? Apparently it is.

-The dog nosed the handle of the door, sniffed it, and padded back to the warm spot on the carpet, circled around, sat down, curled into a dog-ball, and slept.

Now Here's This

7 January 2007, Malibu CA

WE EMERGE at the top of a long path that curves through a valley my friend and I had been warned earlier might be overrun with packs of coyotes. The twisted path forms a mild downhill hike followed by a mild uphill hike to a horizon-line that, when reached, will undoubtedly reveal the chilling expanse of the Pacific Ocean. On either side of us, Southern California dried-out desert winterized vegetation stretches up and down—a long field of differently sized shrubs, waist-high, brown starbursts of sharp twigs, with the yellows and browns of the desert broken intermittently by the odd lively green push of somehow-living, somehow-breathing plants, probably with very deep roots. This—the moment I turn the corner by a sun-blasted boulder and see the path wriggle through the tinderlike vegetation—is when the psilocybin mushrooms take hold, digging their neon claws into the soft underbelly of my consciousness, and I begin to feel giggly and absurd as I become a part of where I am.

I begin to think about where I've been, what I'm doing here, and where I'm going to be tomorrow.

Seven-million years ago I was probably already dead by this point in my life. If I weren't, I was walking with my family in this same valley that is overrun with coyotes and god knows what else. If I had somehow managed to avoid a major calamity, a common disease, and the inherent threat of starvation in a prehistoric culture, I would be a seasoned veteran of the wild, my hands cut and calloused, my wisdom of survival a deep and yet narrow pool which I passed on to my offspring more through the gleaned wisdom of my behavior than by direct tutelage, for which there would simply be no time, nor words. My mind—a surging force desperate to innovate various methods of protection for my family, from wild animal attacks or the threat of gang violence at the hands of my fellow new humans, who were still grumpy from having awakened from the ignorant bliss of the beast—would have to worry about finding food to feed my family and places to keep them safe at night, and on top of that, probably a concern over some sudden illness that was harvesting death in my youngest child, again. In this capacity, I would at nearly every moment need to make rapid, perfect decisions. Dark clouds in a mighty distance over the ocean would signal something I'd have to figure out before it was too late and we were bogged down in a potentially fatal deluge—or lightning storm, or flash flood, etc.

Today I am on a trippy Sunday hike through Malibu Canyon, and I am abubble and agiggle as the world's friendliest poison flips my brain upside down and lets the pale underside sizzle in the sun. I am at once nauseous and ecstatic—something I describe to my friend as "neaseousty." We're both carrying fist-sized rocks in case the weird foreigner who earlier warned us about the coyotes in this valley was right. Not that the rocks would really be of any particular use to two stoned-out funny monkeys, but I still cling to my rock and hope just the same.

Tomorrow afternoon I'll be seated in a cubicle that I call my office because I'm in denial. I am employed in one of the world's most unromantic and unnecessary jobs. Tomorrow, instead of challenging myself with productive effort, I will be looking up various health maladies on the Internet, wholly convinced I have some terrible disease. I am a borderline hypochondriac and have already been diagnosed as having a Generalized Anxiety Disorder.

My life consists of waking up in a warm apartment, going to work in one of the most laid-back atmospheres in the work world (a laid back attitude befitting toil at the far periphery of human usefulness), coming home to a refrigerator full of food, and doing some reading and writing before going to sleep and starting it all over again the next day. A cakewalk life. And yet I have a goddam Generalized Anxiety Disorder.

How can this be?

It dawns on me, or at least the me that I am when I am both rejecting and being seduced by a poison, that my near-constant state of anxiety is based largely on the juggernaut brute I had to be when I descended from the trees and began to manipulate the environment to suit my many needs seven-million years ago (the date of the true dawn is always changing, but let's call it seven-million, to be simultaneously objective and winkingly biblical-sounding).

Seven-million years ago I had real reason to have Generalized Anxiety. Every day was a mortal battle on a particularly unforgiving terrain within a painfully indifferent universe—every day was a fight for my life and the lives of the only people in the world with whom I shared a vital bond and the earliest vestiges of love that went beyond that of beast for fellow beast. A poetic love. They and I were in constant danger.

Those were legitimate worries. But while things got easier over time, the crashing wave of evolution has, until only recent centuries, always been a white-knuckle ride. The brains of the lowest beasts to the great mortal monkeys of humankind have always been operating at the maximum. Survival of the fittest goes far beyond a bench-pressing competition. The engine of our minds has nearly always been in overdrive.

It's an adventure.

Or at least it was.

Now it's a day job, a warm apartment, and, for me, the constant worry that it will all come crashing down due to neurodegeneration, malignancy, or some unseen menace—a stray bullet, a rogue wave, a foreign aggression.

When I compare my two lives—my life seven-million years ago and my life now—the only constant I can see is the still-surly stupor of man, again, having molted the protective layer that kept our minds from meta-thought and asking the bittersweet question, "Why are we really here?" My children have doctors. My stockpiled food contains long-lasting preservatives. My hands are soft and pudgy and well oiled from near-constant masturbation. I don't have a family. At my age, I am yet young enough that I need not concern myself with the ticking clock counting down my chances at producing progeny.

My brain, having developed over the course of millions of years of white-knuckled grasping for a hold on the surfboard of life during the tidal wave of evolution, is not sure what to do in such a controlled and calm environment. While it's true that we'll never truly descend from the trees entirely—that we'll always be animals—we are very strange animals at this point. Without life-and-death concerns occupying our amazingly capable minds, many of us make trivial matters into life-and-death problems.

Take what you find on reality television shows, where fifteen people with no jobs and nothing to do start throwing their own shit at each other over little nothings. These are not things they should be concerned about, yet they are, with revolting passion. Take what you find coming from groups like the Christian Coalition, who regard exposed nipples with the same fervor we used to hold against a pack of stampeding wooly mammoths crushing our slower ancestors' spines.

Perhaps this is why Ayn Rand advocated man striving to be the best at whatever he was undertaking—be it architecture, proofreading, or what have you. Perhaps she knew that our minds have been in a certain high-octane gear for millions of years, and when those minds aren't being put to a useful or productive purpose, they don't simply slow down and relax but instead turn into runaway trainwrecks.

It's all a matter of the things we choose to care about. We're going to care either way, but what matters most is that we choose a useful direction in which to point our tremendous mental capabilities.

For now, as I mount the distant hill and overlook the chilling oceanic expanse, the direction of my mind is every direction—thanks to chemical manipulation. But I will come down, and the soft light of my mind today will refocus tomorrow and will most likely turn inwards again, searching within for certain malignancies. For now, I just want to throw up, because although it is certainly the best and most smile-inducing kind, there is a poison in my stomach.

"Don't forget not to puke," my friend cryptically says to me with sarcasm. If I puke, it only makes sense the toxins will spill, and my light will refocus, and this runaway dynamo will find its awful track again, and I will agonize over the misdirections I have followed. But if I don't forget not to puke right now, I'll have found temporary relief from the bittersweet reality that what I (and we) do best is also what I (and we) do worst.

So I sit atop what my friend has named "Simba Rock"— a hillcrest boulder that overlooks this whole valley—and I do what I do while I'm doing it. I am abuzz with a buzz, and it feels like each and all of my cells is a giggling ghost. It is a joyous vacation from the responsibilities and worries of the inescapable heaviness of my real life—a rare opportunity to let my thoughts be anything but the steady worry they almost always are.

The sun is slowly and quietly dipping into the dazzling water, and we must return soon to the lovely-awful buzz of civilization. My buzz is wearing off. The day is ending.

Now here's this.

Maggie The Moment

It was the only magazine within reach—a thick, glossy, square-shaped, distinctly European fashion rag. He didn't have the strength to walk to the corner of the room and rifle through the stack there on the mahogany end table. It didn't matter anyway. The guided arrow of his perception was rounded to the point of uselessness. It was rounded by a combination of his uncertain condition and his jittery anxiety. He flipped through the pages of the magazine, and nothing registered; it was like sun rays bouncing off of snow. The heat of his perceptions didn't melt the cold facts into knowledge in his brain. There actually was no heat to his perceptions. They had no penetrative ability—no spark, no pressure.

Here was an interview with a fashion designer. Here was an article about handbags. Here was a picture of a handbag. Here was a model-looking model with her mouth open and smeared red-glitter eyeliner splayed across her rather mannish-looking, square-jawed face.

He looked up at the clock and thought about what he was waiting for and quickly ducked his head back into the glossy magazine. He turned pages idly while anxiety sent the mildest twitches through his hands. The air in the room was warm. It made him sleepy. He was much too anxious to sleep.

His head felt funnier than fuck.

His thoughts were as monotonous as a marathon: *test results test results test results test results test results test results test results*.

One foot after another for miles and miles.

He flipped through the pages, with the funny feeling creeping into him again.

He flipped pages until the sunlight returned.

Maybe it was the cloud that finally moved and let the sun

back in through the tall window behind him. Something changed. Maybe it wasn't even the cloud or the sun; maybe it was the image itself. He stopped flipping through the pages, and his gaze settled on and began to melt into a picture in the magazine.

The pretty, young woman—she wasn't a model-looking model; she was normal-looking, though distinctly attractive—had her eyes closed and her head leaned back. She was standing in a field. Long, lazy leaves of overgrown grass bent over each other at her feet. Sailing atop these waves of grass were the sharp-edged joints and leaves of berry shrubs. Behind the girl, to her left, was an unmistakably summer-looking tree, fully grown and green, its hands and fingers catching the sun's rays and letting a few filter through to the brown-golden grass. The young woman must have also been standing under a similar tree, because the sunlight warming her deeply contented, almost childlike, upturned face was broken intermittently by leaf-shaped shadows. The image—the woman, the field, the grass, the shrubs, sky, trees, and shadows—reminded him of, looked just like, his favorite place on earth, the place where he and his family had vacationed during the summers of his youth. The girl was any idealized young love, made him feel at peace.

He was falling into the picture.

He was not scared as he fell. He did not even look around to see if anyone else saw it happening. He just wanted to be there, with that pretty girl, standing in that natural field, breathing that fresh air, and he was getting his wish.

All the unnatural sounds of the waiting room disappeared—the hum of the heater, the inscrutable conversations between the receptionist and whomever she was on the phone with, the tapping of the blinds' plastic rods against the windows, the automobile traffic outside, below. The sound was replaced by a new sound. The distant wind. Then the wind in his ears. The shush of the leaves, the trees. The birds and insects scuttling and calling to each other.

She was still there, with her head leaned back, letting the sun-puddles warm her face. She was wearing a sleeveless white blouse, buttons all buttoned, with her slim arms at her sides, and she was wearing a brown skirt, knee length, that bloomed outward from her thin waist. The blooming was a result of the fabric, he could tell, because two skinny legs emerged from the bloomed fabric, almost porcelain, crafted, so pretty, and not just sexually pretty. Structurally pretty. She was still there and he was still watching her. Then he could see that something within her had registered his presence, and he saw her eyes move behind her closed eyelids, and then she opened them and looked at him. She did not look surprised at all. She just took him in, and she spoke.

"I know you're there."

"I wasn't sure. I wanted to be here."

"Where did you come from?"

"I'm not sure you'd believe me if I told you."

"Oh, you're one of them, huh?"

"One of—?"

"You needed this."

"I did. I do."

"It's wonderful, isn't it?"

He looked around, and there were miles of golden grass, more trees, more shrubs, and within himself nothing but that comfort of being safe and warm and *home*.

"I don't want to go back. I've never wanted to go back."

"But you have to. You've had to."

"Who are you?"

"My name is Maggie."

"Maggie . . . That's my favorite name. I'm glad your name is Maggie."

She smiled sheepishly into the grassy ground.

"Am I dying, Maggie?"

"Follow me," she said, turned, and walked away from him.

He followed close behind. The smell that lifted off of her

and was carried to his nose by the breeze was the smell of his first girlfriend, from high school, small, fragile, and beautiful— the first girl he ever kissed. He hadn't smelled that smell in decades. It filled his head with memories that danced as they swam and sang and burst in his mind.

I'm dying, he thought.

He followed her anyway, across the field, for her loveliness. The fresh air invigorated him, but the thought that he might never breathe this air again made him want to cry. The pretty way the sun hit her skin, the perfect way the sun felt on his own, the way the wind sounded as it swooped through the leaves of trees and grass, the way his muscles carried him forward through this perfect wilderness . . . His heart swelled.

"I don't want to die, Maggie," he said when she looked back. Her childlike mouth frowned down at the corners. *She could feel my pain*, he thought. *She is not real*, he thought.

He followed her, but he knew they were together, and he could breathe for what felt like the first time ever.

After a while, he had worked up a good sweat, felt great, and she stopped. He saw nothing but more endless wild and the back of her perfect form, until she stepped out of the way so he could see where she had brought him.

It was a chair. A waiting-room chair. In the middle of the endless field.

"Who are you, Maggie?" he said.

"I'm just a moment," she said. "I'm impossible. I'm already gone. They're ready for you."

She took him, by his shoulders, and guided him slowly— almost like dancing—towards the chair.

In the same way he fell into the image, he fell into the chair. As soon as he sat, the world swirled away from him and reappeared, and there was an overweight woman standing in the doorway, looking at him.

She repeated herself. "Excuse me, sir—they're ready for you."

He placed the magazine back on the table, stood on his

unsturdy legs, and followed the overweight woman into the catacombs of the office, his mind at peace as it orbited his memories of the pretty blonde impossible Maggie and the fields that were her frame.

I'm just a moment, he thought.

I'm impossible.

I'm already gone.

Objective

A SCUFFED-UP leather football spirals through the autumn air and into the pale-Irish hands of 19-year-old Kevin Caise, who is sloshingly intoxicated. The polyhedral, crumbling, concrete pebbles of the Peden Stadium parking lot make clattering noises beneath his feet as he drunkenly pivots and throws the ball through a westward breeze and into the arms of 20-year-old Marty Yoder, who is also staggeringly drunk and having a great time this gray-skied early afternoon.

A male Eastern Bluebird, 1 year old, flaps and darts through the ever-swirling stacks of invisible pillows of oxygen and carbon dioxide that comprise the breathable environment, and the bird curiously watches the two humans throw the football to each other through those same pillows, but then its eyes are drawn to a scattering of seeds near one of the empty benches on the grassy green field inside the stadium, and it rides an eastward pillow-breeze down to the spot and begins pecking at the lucky abundance.

A worm, beneath the field, churns soil through itself, and there are thousands of more worms down there. They can feel the vibrations produced by the roving villages of synchronized drums booming above them.

Two blonde freshmen—Jessie Reed, 18, and Kelly Thompson, 18—have a desperate (drunken) need to urinate, but all the bathroom lines are too long, so they take turns watching out as the other squats and sets urine free between a suitably secluded red Ford Mustang and black Chevy Suburban.

"Oh my God, Kelly—I just peed on my shoe again," Jessie slurs.

Derek Penton, 23, a senior linebacker for the Ohio University Bobcats football team, clenches a rosary to his forehead with his right hand and rocks back and forth. He is anxious and preparing for war. Meanwhile, his younger brother, Dustin, 19, an undeclared freshman, throws up in a toilet in the stadium bathroom. He is hung over and preparing for more partying to come.

There is a homogeneous pane of gray wallpapering every visible horizon. The overall cloud system, in fact, covers nearly half of the state of Ohio itself, and it (the cloud system) spits drizzle in unpredictably natural places, but not here in the middle, over the stadium, where it is just one fungible gray.

In the stands, having just found the right spot, Dale Goodwhistle, 42, is treating his two sons, Froggie (Francis, but a mother's term of endearment that stuck), 12, on his (Dale's) left, and Cyrus, 14, on Froggie's left, to their first football game at Dale's beloved alma mater. So far, the boys don't seem to give very much of a shit.

Our Eastern Bluebird friend, stuffed with seeds from a spilled "NatureStorm!" health-food mix, is spooked into flight by an approaching Eastern Michigan University medical trainer, who watches the bird flap up into the invisible pillows of the atmosphere and out of the stadium. Then the trainer, Elizabeth Mondrian, 22, checks to make sure all of the towels are dry enough after the light drizzle from a half-hour before. They're fine—only barely damp at all.

The elder Goodwhistle brother, Cyrus, has not been able to stop following every movement made by Ohio University cheerleader Dawn Grace, 21, since he first saw her as she gyrated her hips in an unintentionally sexy warm-up with the other cheerleaders down on the field. In fact, Cyrus has what American storytellers might call an ongoing, earnest, teenaged boner.

There are many hundreds more fans in the bleachers than the Goodwhistle men. There are, for example, seven members of the Alpha Sigma Phi fraternity drinking liquor out of flasks while baring their green-painted chests to the late-autumn cold. There is also a cluster of nine male floormates from the all-male dorm Read Hall, and they are much more warmly dressed, but they too are drinking liquor out of concealed means. They, too, like the bare-chested frat guys, are sharing jokes and observations. And they, too, or at least most of them, like Cyrus Goodwhistle, are worshipping every taut-skinned, voluptuous movement made by Dawn Grace as she mingles with her fellow cheerleaders down on the field before the game.

"My buddy in S-A-E fucked her once," Kevin Caise says, "and said he came in like *a second*, dude."

Two small armies of padded humans run onto the field from opposite directions. The Ohio University Bobcats are wearing white helmets, dark green jerseys, and white pants. They have all different kinds of football cleats. And that goes for the Eastern Michigan University Eagles, whose school colors are the same as OU's, and whose jerseys are the inverted version of the Bobcats': green helmets, white jerseys, green pants.

Both teams form into tribes, jumping up and down and letting their adrenaline take over. Their heart rates rise from anticipation of the violent presentiments being mentally conjured by the brutal physicality of the coming competition, and their blood pumps with the electricity of determination and fear, and soon they are all howling in a frenzy, except for those of them who have to go deeply inside themselves instead.

An eastern gray squirrel, 4, leaps from a bending Blue Ash branch onto the sturdy brick wall on the outside of the stadium and scurries along the top before leaping from the wall to a steel girder beneath the bleachers, where the concession vendors and bathrooms are.

Froggie Goodwhistle is hungry. He tells his dad, and his dad asks his son Cyrus if he wants anything while they're up. Cyrus, distracted, shakes his head no. His father follows the boy's gaze down to Dawn Grace, and inwardly Dale Goodwhistle smiles. He's kind of surprised at how relieved he feels to see that his son is a heterosexual, and he doesn't know how to feel about that. He'd never considered himself homophobic before, and he decides he's not. *Men have hormones, too—it's probably more chemical than ideological*, he thinks. *Or something. What the fuck.*

The quarterback of the Ohio University Bobcats, Colin Wilson, 20, didn't think he'd be this hung over. He can't think right, and his eyes are dry and blurry. *We are in trouble*, he thinks. *I really didn't think I'd be this hung over.*

"Oh, my God, Kelly," Jessie says, looking at herself in the mirror in the bathroom and frowning at the pockmarks on her cheeks before turning to the closed stall door. "You BLEW him in front of the whole party!"

"No, I *didn't*," Kelly says with insistence after urinating, before wiping.

"I was THERE, Kelly!"

"I don't remember that," Kelly says, emerging from the stall off-balance, steadying herself on the rim of the sink where Jessie had already placed two cans of beer she'd smuggled in.

"Oh, my God, Kelly—I wish I had your ability to forget things."

"Well," Jessie says, "it all starts here, bitch!" and they toast cans of beer and begin chugging.

The eastern gray squirrel scurries along the beam and catches the attention of young Froggie Goodwhistle standing in line with his father.

"Dad, there's a squirrel up there," Froggie says.

Dale Goodwhisltle, however, is distracted, looking at his phone and reading an email from his lawyer.

"What?" he asks.

"There's a squirrel up there," Froggie says.

Behind them, Kevin Caise says to his friend Marty Yoder, "Do you remember that fuckpig I took home from the bar?"

"No," Marty says honestly.

"Me neither!" Kevin says, and they both laugh.

"There's a squirrel up there, on the beam," Froggie says to

his father.

Dale Goodwhistle pulls his eyes from the phone and looks where his son is indicating, but by that point the squirrel had scuttled to a different location, so Dale sees nothing unusual, no squirrels.

"Wow," Dale says artificially.

Froggie quietly resents his father, and he doesn't like the feeling, not only because it is a bad feeling but because he thinks he isn't honoring his father like he should. By the time they get to the front of the concession stand, Froggie doesn't want anything anymore, and Dale just gets a coffee.

"GO BOBCATS, YEAAAHH!" Jessie Reed shouts as she emerges from the bathroom, and everyone under the bleachers lets out a drunken din of agreement.

Theater major Sherri Bliss sings the National Anthem—the birds all listen and watch cautiously.

The worms churn.

The squirrel leaps from the beam and scurries up a vertical hallway between a wall and the back fence of the bleachers. She climbs to the light at the top, where she emerges on the rim of the stadium, and is tempted to dart down the stairs and onto the field when she sees the football kicked high into the air—for a moment she thinks it's a winter's worth of acorns in one. But there are too many people down there, and they have already claimed it.

"Sanchez! Sanchez! Get out there!" Ohio University Offensive Coordinator Joe Patta, 35, screams down the bench, as Freddie Sanchez, 19, bounds onto the field with his long, quick strides.

In a luxurious booth near the press box, Ohio University President McGeorge Gerard, 56, says to his wife, "No; the other one—with the pink label. The blue one would *kill us all.*"

"What?—Why can't I ever get a straight answer out of you?" asks his wife, Sheila Gerard (née Beauregard), 48, in reply.

"It is wise, sometimes, to be intentionally inscrutable, my

dear," he says.

"Certainly, George, but with me?"

"Marriage is something I plan to *win*, Sheila, my love."

Elizabeth Mondrian's hands are shaking—EMU's half-back, Kevin Taylor, 22, is having cramps in his calves again, and he's asked her to rub them out for him!

Kevin lies back on a table and lifts his left leg for her to work on. She takes the cleat in her left hand, cradles the leg under her right arm, and begins working the calf with her right hand. At this point, to her, there are only two people in the stadium, and as she loses herself in the moment, she presses her pelvis against the trainer's table and smirks into the wonderful frottage it creates down below.

I deserve this, she thinks to herself.

(Kevin Taylor had chosen the nearest trainer to help him with his cramps; he did not know anything of Elizabeth's ongoing carnal lust.)

Colin Wilson hits the last step of his three-step drop, and immediately his porous protection breaks down, and there are two massive Eastern Michigan defenders running after him and grasping at his jersey. Wilson ducks out of their pursuit and heads towards an open spot on the field to reorient himself, but by then the linebackers have broken through, too, and he has to continue on his trajectory towards out-of-bounds territory while looking down the field to see if he has any open receivers.

Freddie Sanchez recognizes the busted play almost immediately and breaks from his route and looks for an open spot on the field along Wilson's line of sight. He finds it and sprints in that direction.

Wilson sees him, and while still running, he throws the football ten feet ahead of Sanchez, who strides into the path of the pass, catches the ball, lowers his shoulders, and blasts through the off-balance cornerback, Marvin Walker, 21, but is then hit hard to the ground by the EMU defensive back JeVarreous Stanley, 22.

The majority of the people in the stadium cheer loudly in favor of the outcome of these actions.

The sudden eruption of noise startles the squirrel, which had been consuming discarded "P-NUT!" peanuts from the ground in an unoccupied part of the bleachers, near the top. The startled squirrel decides the number of humans here makes her nervous, and she runs up the steps and up a fence, along the top of the stadium, and leaps confidently to a naked branch offered by a 40-year-old Blue Ash tree.

Dawn Grace proves to one of her teammates (and, as a corollary, to every male watching her from the stands) that she can do the splits effortlessly.

Kevin Caise and Marty Yoder clap hands and dap-tap with their friends Sean Wenn, 19, and their friend everyone calls "Penthouse," (Donald Torgedson, "long story"), 19.

"Wenn and Pent," as Marty calls them, are seemingly inseparable. Where there is one, there is inevitably the other. Rather than "Wenn and Pent," Kevin Caise calls them "Johnson and Johnson."

"You guys try any of that shit yet?" Sean Wenn asks as they sit down in a secluded area of the bleachers.

"I think I did last night," Kevin says.

"You *think*?" Wenn says.

"Bro, you'd *know*, bro," Penthouse says.

"Probably, but I don't remember shit except some horse I took home from the bar saying she wanted to get high and fuck," Kevin says. "And I'm pretty sure we fucked, so I guess we got high, too."

"Great story, Kevin," Penthouse says, and Marty and Sean laugh.

At halftime, a team of musicians and dancers ruin a melody of pop songs by squeezing hit music through a great many lungs of brass.

The dancers are mostly chubby, and their faces are made into caricatures by forced smiles and piles of makeup.

The drunks in the stands—students and alumni—love

it all because it's loud and they recognize the songs. They're drunk during the day, and now they got some tunes and tiny dancers and that permanent yawp of being fuckin' OU shithoused.

When the teams return to the field, so do the cheerleaders. Cyrus Goodwhistle thought he would never breathe again, having to endure that interminable, damned halftime! Where could she have disappeared while he was forced to talk to his stupid dad about a stupid science project?

"*She* is my project, father!" he wanted to shout, but he knew it wasn't true, but sometimes our emotions can build an entire lifetime for us in a moment.

"Dad, how long do two quarters usually take?" Cyrus asks his father.

"You got about an hour an' fifteen minutes," Dale Goodwhistle says. "You know, that's kind of what your mother used to look like."

"Jesus, Dad—that's gross," Cyrus says with a shudder.

"I'm just sayin'," Dale says. "Your old man was cool once."

"No, you weren't," Cyrus says.

He gets that from his mother, Dale thinks to himself and grinds his teeth.

It's not just birds and invisible pillows in the atmosphere. The mild westward breeze now carries with it the floating seedling of a wicked but survivable airborne influenza that has existed for two-hundred-million years, and the virus catches on the lid of an open flask, and when Derek Shepard, 21, of the Alpha Tau Delta fraternity raises the flask to his lips, the viral lid rides gravity to Derek's cheek and kisses the virus onto the corner of the young man's mouth, away from the virus-killing alcohol, and within minutes the virus has done its DNA thing, and Derek can feel that he's starting to come down with something.

"Shit," he says and horks up some mucus from the back of his throat and spits it onto the ground at his feet.

One of the people in the stands is not drunk at all, but

rather high. His name is Jamo Smang, 19, and he's thinking about how there's a comfort in the idea of an infinite universe. With infinite space and time come infinite possibilities—and within those possibilities sits a world or planet or life where there's a version of Jamo Smang who didn't make so many wrong decisions, whose life was a "vast feast where all hearts opened and all wines flowed."

That morning he had woken up looking at a poster of a test nuclear explosion. His first conscious thought was, *Jesus Fucking Christ, I'm still here.* Without knowing exactly why, and almost buffeted by that fact, he no longer wished to be alive. He did not wish to kill himself, but he simply wished, in his heart, for his life to just simply and mercifully pop out of existence.

He came to the game because he couldn't sit in his room anymore, like he always did, so he chose to go to the football game because he'd never had any luck at the library.

He got high in a plastic bathroom outside the stadium, paid the four-dollar-with-student-ID admission, and ogled his way up the stairs of the bleachers, eventually settling in a spot behind a row of girls from the Chi Omega Mu sorority, near the top.

"Dad?" Froggie Goodwhistle says to his father.

"What's up, Froggie?"

"Do you think things at home will ever get back to normal?"

Dale Goodwhistle sighs. He'd brought the kids to the game in order to avoid this conversation. But here it was anyway.

"I think so, Froggie," Dale says. "It'll just take time."

"Yeah?" Froggie asks.

"Yeah. And even if they don't return to the old normal, there'll be a new normal eventually, buddy," Dale says. "Your mother is a good person, and I don't blame her for the way she reacted to what I did. Maybe, if anything, you boys can see how our personal decisions can end up affecting other people without our intending them to. But even if that's the best we can pull out of this, I'm really sorry you had to learn it this way, Froggie."

Behind them, Dante Riddle, 19, who bet two-hundred bucks on the game, shouts, "That's cheating, ref! Fuck your ass with broken glass, you *racist fuck!*"

"Dad, can I check out the view over the top of the wall back there?" Froggie asks his father, who turns and looks up the stairs that lead to the top of the stadium.

"Sure," Dale says. He looks over at Cyrus, who is still fixated on Dawn Grace, and stands. "We'll be right back, Cyrus."

Cyrus does not respond.

Inside Ohio University's "Rufus the Bobcat" mascot costume, there is a brief moment when, between dance moves, for half of a second, Kent Wallaby, 21, thinks to himself, *This is fuckin' stupid.*

"Remember how whenever you saw me, my dear—?" President McGeorge Gerard says and turns in his seat, to better address his wife. "Remember when we were younger how you said every time I was nearby it was all you could do from bending over and putting your bottom up way high in the air?"

"I never said any such thing," Sheila says with mirthful certainty, "you old *loon.*"

"You said it to me once, Sheila," McGeorge says and returns his attention to the game. "You went into great detail, if I remember."

Sheila chortles and dismisses her husband's silliness with the indifference it deserves.

EMU quarterback David Hanes, 22, hands the ball off to Kevin Taylor, who fakes right and cuts left. Two of the ligaments in his knee are shredded by physics when he cuts left, and he falls to the ground immediately, and the pain is so great that he momentarily loses consciousness.

There are trainers standing over him when he comes to. Kevin, having forgotten the injury that caused him to pass out, tries to stand up, but the pain kicks him back to the ground, and Elizabeth Mondrian can see Kevin Taylor's eyes fill with tears.

In that moment, the love she feels for Kevin flares wildly, and she, to her later horror, finds herself shouting at her boss, EMU Head Trainer Alexander Yurima, 45, "FUCKING *DO SOMETHING*, ALEX!"

"Hey, dude, looks like EMU's tailback just got hurt," Kevin Caise says to Marty Yoder.

"Good—fuck him, whoever he is," Marty says. "That'll teach him an important lesson about *trying*!"

"Don't do it, dude!" Kevin Caise says, pretending to give Billy Taylor some advice.

"Nothing is worth it, man!" Marty yells. "Just drink!"

When they get to the top of the bleachers, Froggie Goodwhistle jumps and pulls himself up the brick wall and looks over the Ohio University campus, which is a rumpled blanket of dark browns and greens, with tall old trees and red-brick buildings growing out of it. He can see for miles, and it's as peaceful and serene as anything he's ever seen.

"I wanna try to sit up here, but I need you to hold on so I don't fall over," Froggie says.

Froggie is somewhat of a mumbler, and Dale, to clarify, asks his son, "What?"

What Dale, a mumbler himself, said as "What?" Froggie hears as, "Ya!"

There is an unanticipated *"Oooh!"* that runs through the crowd when Kevin Taylor's knee gives out, and Dale Goodwhistle turns to see what happened on the field at the same moment his son begins boosting himself farther up the ledge.

Froggie's arms clutch desperately for a hold, but no hold is found, and the boy's little body falls thirty-five feet to the ground, where the child dies instantaneously as his brainstem is punctured by a lip of concrete.

Dale Goodwhistle finds the source of the *"Oooh!"* on the field and returns his attention to his son.

Froggie isn't there.

Dale looks around in panic and does not see his son anywhere, and then he hears a woman's horrified scream down on the ground outside of the stadium.

He looks over the ledge.

The Ohio University Bobcats defeat the Eastern Michigan University Eagles 28–17. The teams finish the season ranked fourth and fifth, respectively, in their conference.

After the game, an unknowing Jamo Smang disinterestedly walks past the ambulance, towards his dorm (*probably some old dude with a heart attack*, he thinks to himself). On the way back, in the parking lot, he runs into one of his only friends on campus—Jack Keaton, 20, who is a fellow member of the esteemed E.W. Scripps School of Journalism.

"Any luck in there?" Jack asks, on his way back from the library.

"I am, I believe, metaphysically incapable of starting a conversation with someone I don't know," Jamo says. "Which is troubling for an aspiring journalist."

Jack laughs and asks, "Anything else to report?"

The pale polyhedral pebbles of the concrete make clattering sounds as they roll beneath their feet.

"I'm beginning to think that having a bias is important," Jamo says. "Can you imagine how much ink and paper we'd waste if we really tried to remain completely objective with the stories we wrote?"

The Final Inning

THE DATE was 4 August 2008—the day Office Supply began its back-to-school sale, the day Jimmy Ventinanno finally killed that goddam rat in the garage, and most importantly for the purposes of this story, the day of the completion of the tie-breaking world-series game for the nine-and-ten-year-olds of the Winston Boys' Baseball League.

Three nights ago, the red team won. Two nights ago, the gray team won. Last night, just before the start of the final inning of the game, the score was tied when a thunderstorm caused a delay.

The game—the series—was scheduled to be completed tonight.

Mike Detzweiler sat in the back of his van, where the windows were tinted, and shotgunned another beer while he listened to the Cleveland Indians lose a game on the radio. The blue conversion van sat in the Caretti Fields parking lot, under a late-afternoon sun, nestled between two large SUVs.

He pulled out another beer and popped the tab and leaned back. He could see the child-proportioned baseball field through his windshield, and already a few of the players had arrived with their uniforms on. Behind him, in the park proper, he could hear the rusty hinges of swingsets' squeaking, and he could hear the low voices of parents' parenting and the high voices of toddlers' toddling, all like fuckin' jerks.

The beer—ice cold, amazing—fell into his mouth and seemed to just melt into his bloodstream without his even needing to swallow. After a long day of landscaping, his body gratefully soaked it up and was given more.

More and more cars arrived, and with them parents and more ballplayers. Detz swilled the last of his sixth beer and started packing a pipe with marijuana and hash, safe in the blacked-out confines of his plush backseat—"Amsterdam in the back of a van, man!"

He rummaged behind the seat looking for a lighter and pulled out a small pair of women's underwear (a dark-blue thong). He looked at the thong for a moment, and sniffed it (of course), and then he remembered Denise, and he smiled a big beery smile.

Denise done gone to college, but she took a few memories with her, didn't she? Heh heh.

Detz found the lighter—an irono-Catholic thing for which the flame, when lit, produced a spitting image of the Holy Spirit flickering atop Smiling Jesus' glorious head—and took himself a big, big, *big* hit. The hash-heavy armor came to support the battle-weary beer soldiers, and together they continued their ongoing war against all the things that kept Mike Detzweiler down in life's fucked asshole.

He took another rip-roarin' hit and turned on some music. "Fuckin' Tribe," he muttered and changed the radio over to CD, and turned the music way the hell up. Heavy guitar, spine-igniting bass, confounding pounding drums all took over his brain for a bit. During a particular rush in this particular Rush song, Detz hit a heavy swig from a loose bottle of vodka, and after the air had cleared a bit—you know, when most of the weed and hash smell had floated up and out of the slightly ajar top opening of the van—he stumbled out the side door, with a couple of empty beer cans rattling to the ground by his feet, dressed fully in his umpire blues, and walked towards the baseball field, because the game was about to start.

"Okay, coaches, can I see you over here?"

The coach of the gray team, Ernie Hollingseed, sported a tremendous mustache and those socks with the three horizontal bars of color—classic. In his day job, he too was a landscaper. The coach of the red team, Mikey Buonavetti, was about two feet shorter than most grown men, and two feet wider in every way. In his day job, he was a supervisor at the DMV.

"We know the rules, right? Nothing new here, so if ya got any questions, let's have 'em now so we can get these kids playing."

Detz had umped so many games that summer these words didn't even register in his head. It was automatic. Muscle memory.

"You okay, Detz?" Coach Buonavetti asked, which was followed by a concerned "Yeah," by Coach Hollingseed. Both coaches had concerns.

"Never been fuckin' better, boys," Detz said and then walked away and announced, "All right, let's do it!"

"Balls in! Coming down!" the catcher called. The pitcher pitch-tossed the ball in, and the catcher threw it to second base. The infielders tossed the ball around the diamond and got it to the pitcher while Detz cleaned off home plate. He almost fell right on his face in the process, but he was able to throw his left leg forward to catch himself, but in doing so he re-lost his balance and ended up hip-checking the catcher.

"Holy shit, I'm sorry, Davie," Detz said and helped the shocked boy back to his feet.

"It's okay, Detz."

"PLAY BALL, ALL RIGHT?!" Detz called out.

It was the fat pitcher for the red team on the mound. Fuckin' sweet. Defnitely the best pitcher in the league. Nothing but good hard strikes.

Coincidentally, the first batter for the gray team turned out to be ol' Denise's youngest brother—Hugh. He kind of looked like her, but he had what Detz had to assume was his father's nose. "Glad Denise didn't get that honker," Detz said to himself as the batter settled into his stance and the pitcher got his signal from the catcher. *Big ol' thing, ain't it?* he thought to himself and leaned over behind the catcher.

Fsssssss, snap!

"Streee!" Detz shouted.

Detz could barely follow the ball he felt so good and fucking ripped. That fat little bastard was one hell of a pitcher, and that was one hell of a pitch, from what Detz could make of it.

Another strike. 0–2. Ball outside. 1–2. Then the hardest throw yet, with the loudest snap yet, and . . .

"STREE THREE AHHH!" Detz hollered as he made wild gesticulations with his boozy arms.

Half the fans were jubilant as Hugh walked away from the plate crying, and Detz could see that Hugh and his sister made the same crying face, and he knew because Denise'd cried when he'd informed her that there was no relationship coming—that they were "just having fun, baby." Evidently, she wasn't having as much fun as he was, and Hugh was having the least fun of all as he sat down and collected tears in his batting gloves.

The next batter, who looked like he should be weighed in ounces, not pounds, took a big hack at the ball. He made slight contact, and the ball dribbled to the pitcher, who snapped the first-baseman's glove with the throw. "OUT!" Detz roared.

"Fatty's on fire!" Detz announced.

"What did you say?" Coach Buonavetti and half the kids in the infield's faces asked. Detz realized in this moment that he'd spoken, not thought, the thing about Fatty being on fire. His mind delivered his old standby excuse when things like that happened.

"Got a rap song stuck in my head, sorry," he said as he stumbled. They looked at him quizzically still. He continued, though with certain rap-like inflections: "Fatty's on fire, and so is the roof; the roof is on fire, so I go to the phone booth, and put on my cape, uh . . . 'm not a date-rape victim . . . hm . . . nigga . . . ."

He trailed off badly into a forest of awkwardness.

"Oh," Coach Buonavetti said, confused but willing to move on.

There was no such song, and Detz smirked to himself for being such a clever asshole. And then he mouth-belched his cheeks to inflation.

Up next, up now, was Graham Peters—one of the best hitters in the league. A lefty. On more than many occasions growing up, Detz had gotten way more than his share of black eyes and bloody noses from Graham's older brother—Harry. Graham looked just like Harry, only even more like a son of a bitch. Detz looked around to see if Harry were here tonight. No sign, thank fuck.

The fat pitcher for the red team was being cautious with Graham; Detz could tell because the first pitch was about two inches outside.

"Stree!" Detz called out, and the call was met with the groans of half the parents and cheers from the other half. Graham looked back at Detz with a touch of hate in his eyes, and it would be hard to describe the intensity that was to be found in the eyes of the counter-look Detz was already staring back with, but needless to say young Graham turned away nervously.

The next pitch was a foot outside.

"Stree!" Detz announced, and the fans' groaning only doubled. "Oh 'n' two!" he announced over their complaints.

"Way outside!" someone in the stands commented.

"Is he drunk?" someone else asked.

The next pitch went right down the middle, and Graham put a holy helluva smack on the ball. Immediately it shot high into the sky and deep, right down the right-field line, and over the fence. The fans went nuts. *Oh no you don't, you little bastard*, Detz thought as he saw Graham beam into a big smile and hop into his home-run trot.

"Foul ball!" Detz called out.

"WHAT!??!" virtually everyone in the park, except the most avid red-team fans, said in unison.

"Whadda ya mean, what?!" Detz said to them all. "It hooked foul, and you fuckin' know it!"

A thunderous rain of boos, so early in the going, caught Detz off guard. Didn't they realize what a prick this little fucker's older brother had been? Detz stood there and didn't move.

"It's okay, it's okay," said Coach Hollingseed. "He's the ump, everyone."

At the mention of his title, and as the fans' ire was alleviated by the batter's coach's diplomacy, Detz's mind re-joined the action, and he stumbled back behind the plate. Graham Peters picked up his bat and eyed Detz again with his little-boy anger. Detz doubled down on his own fully grown-up, already-vicious hatred, and Graham tapped back into the batter's box while Detz sneered at him with contempt and remembered being punched in the face over and over again.

The next pitch was inside. Too inside. It smacked heavily against Graham's right forearm. Immediately the young boy fell to the ground, clutching his arm, wincing, on the verge of crying.

The crowd let out one of those unintentional gasps of empathy for the boy. The coach came rushing over.

"Foul ball!" Detz called, looking right down at the boy crying on the ground.

That's when the place went crazy.

Instantly the fans on both sides started those complaining noises that Detz had grown inured to over the last few fucked weeks.

"WHAT?!?" the formerly cool Coach Hollingseed shouted. "Kid got drilled in the forearm, and you call it a foul ball?!?"

"What the hell is wrong with you, Detz?!" Coach Buonavetti wanted to know.

Similar cries, from both sides in the stands, continued and only grew louder.

"HEY! HEY! HEY!" Detz said, trying to alleviate the situation. "I heard a ping, okay?! Foul ball!"

"Get off the field, loser!" a dad shouted.

"He's gay!" someone else said.

"Ump, the boy's got a bad red welt halfway up his forearm. I didn't hear no ping. Explain that."

"Riiiii-cochet!" Detz said/sang like that old Ricola commercial. This made him giggle, but it didn't make anyone else giggle. Instead, more irksome voices joined the chorus.

"He's a bum!"

"Ruining the game!"

"Doesn't know the rules!"

"Looks fat in those pants!"

The commissioner of the league—Otis Hanson—had arrived by this point. He had his face pressed against the fence, to better see the action on the field. What he saw right now was a boy still lying on the ground clutching his forearm in pain, with several concerned parents watching over. He saw two coaches right in the umpire's face, and he saw the familiar shape of Mike Detzweiler in an umpire uniform gesticulating defensively. In right field, that weirdo kid Alvin Grimes was twirling in circles while staring at the sky.

Detzweiler turned his head and saw Otis Hanson looking at him, and immediately his stomach flooded with bile.

"Oh, shit," he said.

Coach Hollingseed followed Detzweiler's eyes to Otis and called out: "Otis! Come on out here!"

Otis weaved between the complaining parents and through the red team's bench and entered the field.

"It's okay, Mr. Hanson," Detz said, talking into the fat part of his ump's mask, to better hide the alcohol-and-drugs smell. "A ball hit the batter, but I thought I heard it ping first, so I called foul ball, and then all these people went nuts."

"Otis, it didn't hit anything but Graham's forearm," Coach Hollingseed said.

"Mikey?" Otis asked of the other coach.

"I didn't hear anything either," Coach Buonavetti said.

"Mike, you okay with just calling it a hit batsman and letting the game proceed?"

Mike Detzweiler wasn't so drunk that he forgot how much he needed this job. "That's fine by me, Mr. Hanson, but I swear I heard a ping."

"Might just be all the booze you been drinkin', Detzweiler," Coach Buonavetti said.

"Or maybe your ears are shot from all those painkillers you took last summer," Detz said defensively.

"I had surgery!"

Otis grunted and waved his hands, to calm everyone down, and said, "Jesus Christ, you assholes: these kids just want to play some baseball. Stop being such a bunch of faggots and get the game going, or you're all out of here."

"Works for me," Detz said and picked up his big foam chest shield. The coaches walked to their respective dugouts, and Otis found his way off the field.

Detz nudged the still-crying-on-the-ground Graham with the toe of his shoe. "Runner, take your base."

The runner stood, wiping tears from his stupid face, and waddled to first base. His waddling trip was met with a smattering of applause from the fans, which gave way to still more complaints about the so-called "stupid umpire" who "sucks!"

The next batter stepped into the box, tapped his bat on the plate, and pulled his hands back as the pitcher delivered the ball.

As the ball passed the batter, that little prick Graham took off for second base, so the catcher tossed the ball to the shortstop, at the bag, but it was plainly obvious that Graham was well under the tag, safe.

"OUT!" roared Detz, and he did the "out" hand gesture like he was finishing an epic guitar solo, windmilling the hell out of it.

From the stands, an infuriated and drunken Hank Peters—Graham and Harry's father—finally pulled the trigger.

That was Mike Detzweiler's final inning.

The Second Pastel Parade:
I'm Mighty Sorry,
But I Won't Apologize

The Now-Wordless Old Man

And that's it. I'm out of things to say. I'm all talked out, you could say. I won't say it 'cause I've already said it. You've given me your ear and I've taken it with both hands. Well, here's it back—never ended up doing me much good anyway. And for that I'm mighty sorry, but I won't apologize.

The Sisters P & H

P: Have you seen my black sweater?

H: Which one, the one with the silver—

P: The one you borrowed for the game last week.

H: I didn't give it back to you?

P: No, you didn't.

H: Well, it must be around.

P: I've been looking for ten minutes. It's not—

H: It's not in that pile? I thought I threw it in that pile of clothes.

P: That's the first place I looked, and the fifth. No—both times.

H: Hmmmm.

P: Listen, I already know where it is. Just tell me the truth.

H: What do you—

P: Quit stalling and tell me. I know where it is.

H: Well if you know where it is, then go get it. I don't know what you're—

P: I *can't* get it, *okay*, because you *know* where it is and *why* I can't get it.

H: Honestly, I really don't know what you're trying to sa—

P: Josie Pomeranski told me that she overheard Greg Blevin tell Henry Yates that you used your hand on him and ended up getting some of his "stuff" on "your" black sweater.

H: Whose stuff?

P: Greg's! I saw you go downstairs with him after the game last—

H: That liar—I didn't use my *hand* on him!

P: Puh-leaze! I know you—

H: I used my mouth.

P: Eww, gross. And my swe—

H: Sorry about that.

The Elevator Guest

Man: What floor?

Woman: Thirty-two, please. Thank you.

(No response.)

Woman: (clears throat) Thirty-two, please.

(No response.)

Woman: You can hit the button for thirty-two, if you want.

Man: Oh, no, that's okay. I was just wondering where you were headed.

Woman: Oh, that's weird. But aren't you headed somewhere? There's no other buttons pressed.

Man: Nah.

Father Of The Year

Father: Son?

Son: Yes, Father?

Father: I'm sorry.

Son: Huh?

Father: I'm sorry, son. I've ruined your life, and I'm sorry.

Son: What do you mean, Dad? You and Mom are the best. I've learned so much from you.

Father: Thank you, son. But that's not what I meant. What I meant is that I'm not a tall man.

Son: So what?

Father: So it might not matter to you now, but the world loves tall people and hates short people. Your life is going to be substandard, and it's all my fault. I could have tried to find a taller wife, but your mother makes that chicken dish—

Son: I don't care about that, Dad. You and Mom love me, and that's enough.

Father: For now.

Son: Forever, Dad!

Father: You'll see.

Riding The Rail

"With far-flung steps I crumple miles of streets."
—Vladimir Mayakovsky

I'LL START with this because this is where it started for me: the first time I saw the kind I ended up falling in love with, I thought it looked stupid as hell. (Which is a weirdly consistent theme in my life.)

I grew up in a suburb of Cleveland OH (Mayfield Heights, "A Vibrant Community"), which is in the heartland of Midwestern Sports Country (Baseball, Basketball, Football, Fighting, Church), and although when I was younger I'd spent some time with small skateboards in my driveway (mainly I would stomp on their tails and watch them flip through the air), it quickly became apparent that all my friends were going to be getting around on something else, so I had to ride one of those things, too.

Of course, their choice made more sense considering the long distances we had to travel.

So I put my little skateboard away, in the back of our attached garage, and asked my parents to buy me a freestyle bike.

The next time skateboards came into my life was when I was nineteen, in A.D. 2000, visiting my friend Wes at the University of Utah, in Salt Lake City, where long skateboards (longboards, let's call them) were all the rage amongst the campus-in-the-mountains-bound students (snowboarders all), who had to be in class and thus could not be on the mountain—gliding along on the gravity of whatever way was pragmatically available. When I saw them, they were bombing down one of the many big hills on campus, and because I'd never seen long-boards before—because I was from the heartland of Midwestern Sports Country—I thought all those Utes looked like stupid tools.

I didn't think about longboards again until my friend Jordan and I drove out to live in California after college, in January 2005, where it turned out my really cool friend/new roommate had brought with him one of the very kind of long skateboards that I thought were specifically manufactured to help normal people identify toolbags (the loathsome word "hipster" having not yet been brought into such gushing general parlance as it is today); nevertheless, it turned out that yes indeed the highly-intelligent-and-super-awesome Jordan had brought one of those funny-lookin' things with him to SoCal, and upon further observation, it dawned on me that perhaps he and the girlfriend who'd bought the board for him were actually having a sly wink at the "popular" world: across the bottom of the longboard was a painting of the Alex Grey–created, mystical, fiery eye that can be found in much of the apparel for the rock band Tool—one of my artistic/musical favorites.

(As for the hypocrisy of looking down on "tools" while loving a band called Tool, I once again defer to my dear uncle Walt Whitman and his line about containing multitudes: *"Do I contradict myself? / Very well then . . . . I contradict myself; / I am large . . . . I contain multitudes."*)

Over the course of my first month in California, I realized a few important things. One, almost everything in Los Angeles is a lot closer than it is in Midwestern Sports Country, where a lack of population density lets every province stretch its suburbucolic legs. And two, because of its profound population density, as well as the largely persuasive oil companies centered there, Southern California is almost literally a paved desert—a gently rolling, concrete ocean.

Having flung myself out of the wretched Ohio weather patterns and into endlessly sunny days, I started off riding my bike everywhere, but it quickly became a hassle. Los Angeles is rife with thieves and assholes, so whenever I arrived at my destination I had to do that kind of locking of the bike where the lock is snaked through the frame, around a tall-skinny-strong something, and through the front tire, and most of the time this had to be done with my arms wrapped awkwardly around a my-bike-supporting palm tree or street sign. As I would imagine The Big Lebowski might say, "It was, like, a real bummer, man."

One day, in our first apartment, I was going out to pick up some lunch at Ronnie's Deli, and I looked at my bike and just despised the thing, so, having had some enjoyable success with snowboarding on the aforementioned trips to Utah, I decided to teach myself to ride my roommate's longboard instead. It would be much more convenient to huck that fucker around rather than pedal my bike through the automotive streets and then attempt to seduce the lock around a parking-lot light pole.

So I got high as a cloud in trousers, put on some head-phones, and carried the still-goofy-looking-to-me board down to the street, where the third decade of my life instantaneously changed for the better.

IT ALL MADE SENSE.

The closeness of all these destinations, the ever-expanding field of pavement, the thick wheels and wide body and general tank-like dimensions of the longboard rolling along the smooth concrete and grinding over the viscera of Los Angeles' natural decay. The hot sun, the warm air, the feeling of a well-earned float over the little things—

I was floating over these streets and sidewalks!

By the time my birthday rolled around, my roommate was so tired of me borrowing his board that he and my brothers chipped in together to buy one for me.

The Arbor Rail

(I've been told the company doesn't even make them any-more, which makes mine like totally sweeter, dude. Dope as hell, and extinct as a mothafucka.)

My roommate and I had two friends who worked at The Arbor Collective, a Venice CA–based snowboarding/skateboarding/apparel company, and I'm guessing everyone conspired together for the much-appreciated gift. (Arbor later became somewhat of a Venice staple, with extreme sartorial devotees, and consequently my roommate Jordan, who later ended up writing Conan O'Brien's Twitter bio, began referring to the place as "Arborcrombie.")

The Rail really wasn't much to look at, even then, six years ago. The graphics were pretty lame—Arbor was in its puberty as a business at that time, making good boards but without stylized grace—and one could argue that the board's relatively blank canvas has now been filled in by time and usage, which have drawn their own clever and telltale designs upon it, and it is now its own unique thing.

In my mind, to this day, the board still has a surreal-looking quality to it, like a David Lynchian aspect—an arboreal-mechanical dachshund, with even more parodic dimensions, perhaps something designed by a surrealist artist or a prop comic.

But it rode like a motherfucker! Right from go I found the boundless tennis ball for my inner Labrador. (An "inner Labrador" is a trait I've used to describe people like myself, because when I was a toddler, I would toddle constantly, like a Labrador that will find a way to run around, wherever it is. When I had nothing else to do, I would go outside with Wiffle equipment and hit balls out of my hand and chase them down and hit them back, over and over again until it was too dark to see, and then I'd go inside and try to challenge one of my brothers to a game of table tennis. I was kind of like a permanently Cornholio'd Beavis, if he were really into sports.)

In college, after I no longer had baseball to engage my inner Labrador, I got into weightlifting, and by my senior year I was so "ripped" I was starting to have joint problems because the growing muscles were grinding against the tendons in my pathetically small wrists. After college, I wasn't sure what I was going to do. Baseball and weightlifting were pretty much gone.

And then like I said I found it in Los Angeles.

I found it and I took it as far as I've taken anything besides a couple things.

Over the course of the second half of my twenties, from my twenty-fourth birthday until the day I'm writing this as a thirty-year-old who recently moved back to Ohio, I skated approximately SIX THOUSAND MILES on that board.

I even took to calling it my "therapy." I could just go out and grind along the street and lose myself in the needs of the ride—the ever-jumping hunks of concrete in LA forcing me to hold my attention on the moment, keeping busy the parts of my brain that generally, when not actively engaged, turn against myself. The reasons for that go as deep as it gets, but let's stay on the surface here, because that's what I was doing— carving miles and miles on the concrete surface of one of North America's largest cities.

I spent the majority of those miles on something amazing I discovered, which I later (boringly, simply) nicknamed "The Loop."

You see, I knew enough about the topography of the area to know that if there are mountains to the east (in my case, the San Gabriel Mountains) and there are mountains to the north (in my case, the Santa Monica Mountains), then by and large according to what I know of foothills and such, on the west side of Los Angeles if you're going north and east, you're going uphill.

(I should also mention the fact that I also figured that out by using my ability to know what it feels like to walk uphill, haha.)

Anyway, that's the logic I used to deduce the skating route that I started calling The Loop. I wanted to go as uphill as possible, in order to go as fast and far as possible in one downhill skate.

The Loop is the reason I'm writing this.

In Los Angeles' house there are many mansions, and the mansion in the house of Los Angeles that I lived in was called Santa Monica, which is my favorite city I've ever been to (though, admittedly, I haven't been to that many places).

In case you've never been there—to my beloved Santa Monica—a walkthrough/skatethrough description of The Loop will allow me to paint for you a picture of that oceanic, breezy wonder I called home for five years after Jordan and I moved out of our first apartment in LA proper and into one in SM proper.

The Loop begins and ends in our old apartment on 12th Street (twelve streets away from the beach, kind of), between Broadway Street and Santa Monica Boulevard, and it starts with me taking a long, languid rip from a water pipe while the living-room speakers are blasting wild music through the walls and up to the sky. The pipe is filled with some of the best, greenest, stankiest marijuana on Earth, and I only mention that as an introductory stroke of description of The Loop and the city, for Santa Monica was a place where the city council had recently passed a piece of legislation making marijuana-related crimes the police's lowest priority. (Oddly, even though the city was so supposedly 420-friendly, there were no pot dispensaries in Santa Monica itself—but rather right on the other side of the city border.) And anyway the recent low-priority piece of legislation meant I could take hit after hit of that wonderful shit (which I had to buy in an adjacent LA mansion) and not have to worry about the cops' thunderous knocks upon my chamber door.

So I put the water pipe to my mouth and the lighter to the drugs I packed in there, and I pull in all the goodness, and I hold it in, and at the right moment in the wall-throbbing violence of the wild music coming from the speakers in the living room I blow it all out and watch the smoke crash against the living-room window and spread in every direction but forward.

Little swirls kick off the glass and spin in tight spirals and then uncoil and spread all around the room. The music, to my burgeoning intoxicated delight, gets better. Whatever heretofore unnameable forces that are truly responsible for making something good, or better than something else . . . these additional waterpipe forces make those good things even better at awesome-making.

Then, I detach my iPod from the stereo system and impregnate it with headphones, which I pop in my ears and then pick up my longboard, lock up the apartment, go to the bottom of the steps, have a stoned moment of total paranoia that I left the oven on and forgot to lock the door, then go back up the steps, unlock the door, check the oven, lock the door behind me again, double-check that the door is locked, and *then* I set out on The Loop.

Once outside, the first part starts with a mighty uphill huck.

As I said before, north and east are uphill in Santa Monica, and northeast is the direction I'm heading, so instead of the frustrating and ankle-aching shittiness of skating uphill, I'm enjoying the full-throttle launch of my pot-roasted mind with a pleasant walk up 12th Street, heading north, carrying my board and occasionally riding it on flatter portions of the street.

I usually try to head out a little bit later into the afternoon so the hot SoCal sun is never directly overhead—that way, I could choose to walk in the light when I want, and I could choose to head to the other side of the street to walk in the house-and-tree-based shade when my pale Irish/Italian-but-more-Irish-than-Italian skin couldn't take it anymore.

I entramulate the walk—the whole time carrying my longboard—by listening to whatever is my favorite podcast at the time. Probably Dan Carlin's "Hardcore History." I celebrate that show's entire catalog.

So that's already three layers of goodness: a sunny day, an interesting piece of pedagogy in my ready-to-be-amazed mind, and the best weed in the world stoking everything to bliss. But there is yet a fourth layer! (And more!)

I have an appreciation for the beauty that is capable of being created through architecture—that beautiful and utilitarian combination of art and science—and the farther north you walk in Santa Monica, the more exotic the architecture gets. Every house in my hometown looks the same, and not a single house north of Wilshire in Santa Monica looks the same. I mean, they do, but they don't.

I'm walking up these sunny streets and looking at houses that never fail to impress me. The large, glassy, modern-but-comfortable structures rub the aesthetic clitoris in my brain, and the sensation inspires and reminds me to work harder on whatever project I'm working on when I get back, at the exhausted end of The Loop.

It's quiet up here. Most of Los Angeles is a lot of shitty noise, but northern Santa Monica is quiet in a way that kind of fully brings to my attention how much agitating static I'm now heading away from. The breeze plays with the leaves, and a few Mexicans are running leaf blowers in the distance, but other than that there is only the sound of the constant breeze, sunlight, shade, and the occasional leafy crunch underfoot.

Eventually, I get to a street called Alta Avenue, and I make a right—east. More uphill. Starting to get tired already, uphill the whole time, and more to come, but I've always enjoyed what I call a Catholic workout—where you not only work out but push yourself to an almost punishment level of exhaustion. In fact, more than a few times on this part of The Loop I've thought to myself how I was kind of like a lowercase antichrist: Jesus of Nazareth carried a huge piece of wood uphill to be killed upon it for all of humanity's sake, and I was carrying a wooden longboard uphill to ride it down and have fun because I felt like it. Anyway, temporarily reminded of what a piece of shit I am, I huck my board up Alta to 19th Street and make a left—north again.

The houses here are so beautiful, and it's so quiet, and these people must be so talented and smart if they can afford these properties. Who are they? I never meet any of them in six years of Looping.

19th eventually intersects with San Vicente, which plays a starring role in The Loop, and which deserves a bit of description itself. It's a six-lane street, two functional lanes each way (eastish and westish), with both directions also having a third, outermost lane for parking and a bike path. Between these long chunks of street, along the middle of San Vicente Blvd., is a rather large, grassy, and tree-lined median. Every five or so streets, the median stops, and the pavement continues, and cars can make left-hand turns if necessary. It's at one of those paved intersections that 19th meets San Vicente Boulevard, and across the way, past the six lanes and the median, is the shady opening of what looks like a continuation of 19th Street (but which, technically, is called La Mesa Drive), which is where I'm headed.

After waiting out the traffic, I run to the median, where I usually have to wait out more traffic, but that's not bad because it affords me a few moments to ogle the numerous women who can be found jogging along the grassy San Vicente median. These women aren't actresses and models but rather probably neurosurgeons or banking executives. They're not unbelievably sexy, but they're all at least semi-attractive, and it's just a nice break from the many layers of my thoughts and uphill labors.

After I finally run and wait and possibly skate my way across San Vicente, I enter the umbra of La Mesa and continue walking uphill. This street quickly doglegs and starts heading northeast.

If the houses on the other side of San Vicente were nice, the houses in this neighborhood are architectural poetry. The street is lined with trees that throw shade across both sidewalks and the concrete itself, which is truly rare almost anywhere in Los Angeles. The trees themselves are massive, almost like characters from Tolkien, frozen in time—large, with striated trunks and enormous splintering arms thrusting hundreds of branches in every direction, creating a multilayered canopy, to the point where I can even take off my sunglasses and look around comfortably.

And I do just that.

I sometimes wonder if people notice that I'm always on this path. I also sometimes wonder how it's possible that I've never seen any other boarders here—it's such a beautiful thing; how can nobody else see it?

I truly love these houses and the lives to me they represent, and I keep hucking my board uphill, feeling a physical exhaustion to match my many mental efforts, until La Mesa is intersected by 26th Street (we're twenty-six blocks from the beach now, kind of), and I have to cross 26th, which is pretty intense and requires ample concentration.

Once across 26th . . . .

THESE HOUSES ARE EVEN BETTER!

More wealth, larger grounds, bigger structures. Uphill, Daniel! You're almost there.

It's still a good walk up. A good while. Really tired. Sweating wonderfully. (I love a good sweat from a good workout.)

Eventually, there is a Y intersection, and I go left, onto what is called South Rockingham Avenue, and after the biggest uphill hike yet, the street just ends. It rams into a hilly wriggle of Sunset Boulevard and doesn't go any farther, so that's where it's time to turn around and head back downhill, but first a slight break, because it's about to get intense.

I reach the top of the street and watch the cars whip down Sunset, looking for any that might be turning, which could potentially wipe me out in an instant. Even though I've never surfed (on the grounds that in the ocean I am nothing but a meat bag), I imagine the way that I'm checking the traffic coming up and turning onto the street is kind of like waiting for the right wave in the ocean. Once the noodles of traffic have moved on, I turn around, facing downhill, set my board down, position my feet, turn on the loud music I was queuing up while I waited out the traffic, and start pumping my way down the hill, as hard and fast as I can.

Over the intense years I put into skateboarding and my previous baseball life as a right-handed pitcher, I developed a rather perfect balance on my right leg. I can balance over it with ease, which on this longboard allows me to put nearly all of the rest of my body into the downhill Velociraptor strides of my left leg, which as I ride down the street is churning up chunks of concrete as the suicidal-fuck-it-all demon in my brain sends gallons of adrenaline into my muscles, and the good angels hold their tongues because experience has shown them that on this hill and on this board I can handle it as fast as you please.

Eventually I can't pump any faster, so I settle my left foot onto the front of the board and lean into a better, wider balancing position, at which point I sling over a speed bump, essing back and forth down the street as the air flying by my ears howls in the microscopic gap between my earbuds and the ears themselves, and I can barely hear the faint static of my previously loud music deep below the yowl, but that's fine because I need all of the concentration I can get here. I have to keep on the lookout for people throwing car doors open, parked on the street and visiting friends, unaware of suicide-fast skateboarding stoners leaning into the speed and zigzagging along the sun-pounded pavement, spine alive and reveling in the adventure of velocity, chance, and skill—baked boarders who are good but unfortunately not immortal, so they have to keep their heads a little bit even though a big part of it wants to be dead, doesn't it?

"Bullshit!" the demon roars back. "You're finally alive!"

I'm probably going only twenty-five or thirty miles per hour, but it feels so great under the naked power of gliding gravity. It feels just right, if you ask me.

And here's perhaps a bit more depth to give you an appreciation of these first maniacal steps: they are the beginning of a downhill run of concrete that covers the next *seven miles* of my life—the world-famous California coast.

I'm gliding down the downhill concrete, and I don't need

to worry about manually slowing down, because as if by design, the street starts to gradually level off, hitting a coasting flatness as I approach the ever-hectic 26th, where I stride off my board, pick it up, navigate through the traffic, set it down, and continue downhill, down the sun-shaded La Mesa, starting to run parallel to San Vicente.

I once totally bit it on this street. I was lost in reverie, looking at the canopy of leaves, and the front two wheels of my longboard suddenly stopped, lockjaw-bitten into the teeth of a huge pothole I had neglected to notice, and I went flying off my board headfirst like Superman. I landed like Chubby Man, with a double-bounce, and knew immediately that a huge chunk of skin had just been ripped from my left knee. And because I'm genetically a huge pussy, I started to feel like I was going to pass out like I always do when I get injured in any way, so I walked over and sat on the curb, leaving my board in the middle of the street out of medically based indifference.

Huge chunk of skin gone, good amount of blood on the leg, feeling nauseous (not from the blood but more just because of what a doctor once, when I asked him about it, called my autonomic response), I put my head between my legs, and a moment later I felt a tap at my shoulder, and I saw a Mexican woman carefully poking me for my attention.

"Doctor?" she said, with a phone in her hand.

"No-no-no," I said quickly, after at first being touched by her concern, "I'm okay. Just fell. I'm fine." I gave her a thumbs-up, and she said, "You wait."

I still felt nauseous, so I waited. Eventually I felt another tap on my shoulder, and the woman was handing me a bandage for my knee and a bottle of Perrier that was about as big as my arm. "You take."

I was so moved I wanted to hug her, but I was worried that if I stood up I would feel even more nauseous and vomit on her as I tried to hug her, so I tried to thank her as well as I could with my most thank-you-for-your-exceedingly-generous-help smiles and nods and arm motions.

Every time I ride past that house now I think about how those people were so talented and smart and GOOD that they even hired kindhearted, generous Mexican nannies who, when necessary, would go all the way to the street to help wounded pale chubby skateboarders about to throw up.

It's nice to be reminded of kindness, especially in Los Angeles, but I can't hold on to that feeling for too long because even more of my attention is required in what comes next, which is the most dangerous part of the seven miles of the downhill wonder.

Eventually, just like it had an opening, the sun-shaded street ends at San Vicente, and the pavement around the board will soon again be dazzled with sunshine, but for now I have to keep my head on a swivel because this street is a choke point for automobiles, and I have no idea what's coming down San Vicente going god-knows-how-fast.

This is one version of blind faith. I have to have faith that I'm not about to slam into someone on a bike or hit a car and die.

It's a right turn, west-southwest, downhill as hell, and I take it as close to the curb as I can, and I make it safely onto the bike path, where I am still flying along at probably fifteen or twenty miles per hour. There are cars to my left that are racing by at twice my speed or more, and as always, I have to keep my eye on the cars on the right, parked, with their ever-swinging doors.

My old boss (the amazing Del Necessary) used to joke, "Safety is no accident," and that's as damn fine a bit of logic as I've ever heard, and considering the fact that I was riding on a little piece of wood while gas-breathing monsters were screaming past me on my left, I decided to take a few safety precautions. Wear a helmet? Of course not. (The suicidal-fuck-it-all demon would have none of that, but it would let me defend myself with my wits.) Instead of wearing a helmet, I would always wear at least one item of clothing that was obnoxiously colorful; I'd read of scientific research that suggested that human eyes are naturally drawn to color, light, and motion. I already had motion via the board, but considering my small size—and the considerable ramifications of not being noticed by a motorist and being leg-clipped to my death—I would also take the reflective face of my iPod, angle it towards the sun, and then basically try to light-signal my presence to the drivers flying up behind and past me.

So, wearing my metallic-red shorts and signaling like a motherfucker, I'm now just flowing down the road, in the bike lane, and the best part about it is that this is one of the only streets in all of west LA that isn't constantly broken up by lights and stop signs, so it flows and goes, and so do I.

It levels off for a little bit, almost as a warning, because soon after the leveling it drops fast and furious. This is the Defcon 2–dangerous part of the ride because as I start descending I have to keep making velocity-checking esses in the bike lane/ parking lane, which means I have to trust that no cars are veering into my lane because my turns take me wide, to the curb, and to the very edge of the bike lane, where the traffic speeds past inches away.

I have to keep checking my speed until 7th Street, where there's a stoplight and where I make a quick right and a quick left and take a path that was pointed out to me by my roommate, which is a street that travels along the rim of a large canyon, and as I skate down the street, I can see down into a residential bowl of houses facing the sparkling ocean, and there are stairs on the edge of this canyon that people use to keep in shape, which means that I'll be skating past some of the most beautiful women in the world. These aren't the neurosurgeons on San Vicente; these are women you can only describe to your friends with primal grunts and a vigorous thrusting of your hips.

Right here might be a good time to describe the kind of downhill action I'm talking about, because when I'm fully 'round the rim of the canyon and down and make a left, south, on the appropriately named Ocean Avenue, I reach the point, after a brief uphill walk, where the downhill gradient starts to steady. So far, it's been FAST, then Steep, then flat-but-down, then Steep, then FAST, then the rim of the canyon is flat-but-down, then Steep, then FAST, but Ocean Ave., from San Vicente to the Venice Pier (approximately four or five miles away), is nicely flat-but-down the whole way. If I just stand on the board, gravity will eventually bring me up to around eight miles per hour. If I pump like a champion, I can reach fifteen miles per hour, and I know this because there's one of those speed-reminding flashing signs on Ocean that typically reads something like this 42–38–38–41–40–35–14–39 . . . .

Heading south in the bike lane on Ocean Ave., the large blue cupped hand of the Santa Monica Bay is to my right. It's later in the day now, and as I look over the scene, I can see the giant glowing reflection of the sun on the Pacific waters (it reminds me, strangely, of a light bulb glowing over a bathtub, but on the largest possible scale). In the middle of the right-center of the bay, there is a massive glob of glowing yellow water, and then it's blue and bluer the farther you get from the glob, but the glob is still throwing yellow sparks on all the blue as far as the water reaches.

Here is the full spectrum, from west to east, as I skate, which is along a cliff about fifty feet above the ocean: sun and glowing orb of yellow water, then blue water with yellow tips, then a hundred yards of yellow-white sand, then a snaking concrete bike/walking trail that parallels the coast and is well populated (pedestrians, bicyclists, and skateboarders), then the Pacific Coast Highway, which is also well populated (cars, trucks, motorcycles, and bicycles), and then a fifty-foot, vertical cliff (which I can't see from up here on top of it), at the top of the cliff is a lawn/park to my right, which is dotted with sunbathers, the homeless, yoga classes, families, etc., then a parking lane, then the bike lane, which I'm in, and then five lanes of traffic on Ocean Ave., and then a long row of large buildings: hotels, restaurants, corporate offices, all pushing as many windows towards the ocean as they can.

It's all alive and constantly flowing with motion except the sand and the sky and the buildings.

There is one small cloud over the bay, and it is white and ambling slowly east. The palm trees that line Ocean Ave. are throwing shadows across my face as I roll down the street. There are cars that are passing me no less than three feet away, but I hardly pay them any mind other than to wonder if they think I look cool flying down the street like this.

The thing is that I know I don't look cool. I once read some smarmy, shitty magazine (sorry, I know that describes every magazine) where they were talking about what was In and what was Out culturally, and one of the things that was Out was longboarding. The caption said something like, "You don't look cool, bro."

By that point I was a longboarder, and my immediate reaction was, "We don't do it to look cool; we do it because it's fun as fuck."

So although I, like everyone, wish to look cool, I enjoy these skates so much that I honestly don't care if everyone else thinks I look like the tooliest tool to ever tool himself with a big embarrassing dildo. I've derived too much benefit from it for me to ever be embarrassed about the way I looked while doing it.

Anyway, clearly by this point I've got wild tunes in my ears and I'm a fast-flying skateboarding cowboy space punk who dresses like it's still A.D. 1997 in the heartland of Midwestern Sports Country.

There are stoplights on Ocean, but I ignore them. I fly through reds, with cops waiting there. They don't hassle me as long as I stay close to the curb and am willing to leap from my board if a car or bus were to make too wide of a greenlit turn (and I've had to do that before).

I sling through these lights and keep churning and rolling, ever downhill, towards Venice.

Although it's always been in view, to some extent or another, since I first got onto Ocean, now the pier at Santa Monica Beach starts to really gather my attention, with its Ferris wheel and roller coaster and the boardwalk's ever-moving carpet of people.

I've never been able to understand the people who could ride that roller coaster. If there's ever an earthquake and tidal wave in Los Angeles, the last place on Earth anyone should want to be is locked into a heavy chunk of metal riding on Olive Oyl's groaning legs in the rapidly growing lap of the world's largest ocean.

Seemingly everyone is headed for the pier—as I get closer, the traffic gets denser. Now I'm flying past the cars that were just flying past me. Usually there are now bikers on the bike path, too, and we have our own fractal traffic in our lane, as well as ever yet more parked cars with their doors swinging open.

It's a musical people-watching adventure now. My music is banging in my ears, and my eyes are full of traffic, of the automotive as well as the pedestrian sort.

Briefly about the automotive: in Los Angeles, you spend a lot of time in traffic, and it almost never rains, and there is a lot of money, all of which combines to create a culture where I can skate down the street and within a ten-minute span see a handful of different cars that are each worth more than twenty times my annual salary.

It feels great to so simply glide past these beautiful machines on my time-weathered board—I like to think that we are jealous of each other.

Where Ocean meets the Santa Monica Pier on Colorado Street is always a people-clustered mess. I usually have to pick up my board and huck it through. I cut a path between them quickly, and although by now I'm used to them, they are worthy of a quick description.

These people are from everywhere on Earth. Families and groups and couples and individuals from every corner of the civilized world, all navigating themselves to or from the pier, to take their picture here, at this corner of the world, where I live at the time.

Sometimes I turn off my music around here and immerse myself in the many layered languages at once. It's surreal, yet as an amateur linguist I find an undefinable value in the experience.

Things remain a people-and-car clusterfuck until my beloved Seaside Boulevard, which, because I'm more of a soul skater than a trickster, I huck my board down, west—it takes two blocks to descend the fifty feet to sea level, so it's a rather steep hill.

This one time when I was walking my board down this street, I watched as a dude bombed the same street on his board, straight down, doing a frontside manual (in his natural riding position but balancing only on the back two wheels of the board) and reaching at least thirty-five miles per hour before gracefully hopping off the board and into the sand at the bottom. Whether he intended it or not, I ended up feeling like a real shithead when I saw what he was capable of whereas I was witlessly hucking my board like an untalented gremmie.

Anyway, once I reach the bottom of the street, I go through another one of those times where I have to wait out traffic, but this time of the foot variety. At the bottom of Seaside is an intersection with the running/walking path that I saw from up on Ocean.

Once I find an ample opening I can ride into, I do just that, and I enter the part of The Loop that I always compared to returning a kick in football. The path is pretty wide here, and there are lots of people walking, but I can still skate between them. I've done this so much that I've developed like a sixth sense: I know when the people in front of me are going to stop or change direction before they even know it themselves. As I ride I have to keep in mind everyone's mannerisms and trajectory and infer where they might be headed, all in an instant and constantly changing.

It's great fun for me because it's so complicated and challenging-yet-possible.

There were several times in my history of riding this part of The Loop, however, when I had to throw myself off the board in any variety of directions in order to avert what would've been truly traumatic collisions, usually with other skaters or bicyclists heading in the opposite direction. But that's all part of the fun, isn't it?

The walking path goes the length of Santa Monica Beach, and the beach and path are mainly populated by families of tourists (with their awkward sons and occasionally nymphetic but usually blockish-looking daughters) and ratty homeless people pushing or pulling smelly, trashbag-lined, overstuffed shopping carts or baby carriages, and between all these people are the immobile sand and sky, which are so bright I once described sunglasses in Los Angeles as being as necessary as scuba gear underwater.

This part of the skate is like returning a kick in football because there are lanes of people and I have to cut between and past them, always going forward and faster if I can. And not only that but I have to do this all while keeping enough distance from everyone to avoid violating my own moral sense of trying not to annoy other people through my actions. I already know I look like a tool; I should try not to enhance the perception by showing a lack of grace and/or empathy.

As I cross over into Venice (Venice is a Los Angeles mansion located directly south of Santa Monica), once again these people I'm gliding between are from every corner of my continent and planet. Every age and creed and credo, every spectrum of every gender, in little like pockets taking in the big blue sea and all the other pockets of people as well as the wares that are being hocked on either side of the path.

All these people, the old young ugly and beautiful, and I swear I've seen them all so many times before but I know I haven't. I guess we all just look like each other when crammed together like this and flying by at approximately seven miles per hour.

The Venice boardwalk is also a real clusterfuck of these

galaxies of people, and because by this point I know a few of the local tricks, I cut east briefly and turn south again and take what's known as the Speedway, which runs parallel to the coast/touristy boardwalk but which is more properly paved and for automobiles. Here the oceanic breeze is held in check by the window-throwing oceanfront houses and businesses, and it's still downhill, and I can skate faster here than out with the pedestrians.

Sometimes, though, I'm beat by the time I get to this part of The Loop, and my ankles are aching, and I have to pick up my board and walk for a while, to get my blood and circulation flowing properly again, coming down from the rush of the downhill miles. Things are flatter here. Cars slowly drive by, looking for rarely found parking.

And it's along this long stretch of the Speedway that the truly fun parts of The Loop come to an end. The street eventually pretty much levels off after one more fun plummet—at the bottom of which I see a parking attendant who once said to me, *"There he goes!"*—and when I reach Washington Boulevard, the seven miles of downhill boarding are over, and I turn left, east, go up a few blocks, and turn left again, north, and start heading back to my apartment, perhaps briefly stopping by the business where my roommate bought me the board, where my friend Billy sometimes worked behind the counter on weekends.

Anyway, I carry my board sometimes, and I skate over Venice's man-made canals, and I work my way back northeast, my apartment being slightly east of the famous Santa Monica 3rd Street Promenade, where I once escorted a lost pair of Asian college students to a store they were looking for, and I swear one of them, the much cuter friend, was flirting with me, but I myself was lost in the random thoughts that would happen on The Loop, and I missed it at the time, and to this day it bothers me that I could be so stupid when it mattered, because I was really attracted to that fuckin' girl.

Anyway, I carry my board sometimes, and I skate sometimes, and it's uphill a whole lot, and I really have to Catholic myself the rest of the way. And then I make it back to my apartment, where I walk up the stairs and through the door, where it is almost inevitably two hours and forty minutes after I began. In that time, I've crossed fourteen miles of the sunny, golden coast, and the kind of exhaustion I'm feeling as I enter the apartment can almost be described as self-indulgent.

Afterwards, I take another one of the great showers of my life, and after that I get high again and consume everything that the Taco Bell on Santa Monica/17th has in stock.

I do this pretty much every Saturday and Sunday that I live in Santa Monica, as well as on some days I would take off from work because if I had gone in it would have ended in a violent orgy of bullets and bodies.

Epilogue

ONE TIME *during the first walk uphill on The Loop, probably six months before I would quit my job and move back to Cleveland, a dude on a black beach cruiser boldly said to me, "I'll trade this bike for that board, straight up."*

His bike was pretty cool, and I needed a new one (I still rode my bike sometimes), but I looked at my board, and I remembered the six-thousand glorious miles we shared together, and it was one of the easiest questions I've ever answered.

I'm in Ohio now, and I'm in no great hurry to go back to California, because aside from a very small group of friends I made there, The Loop is the only good thing I have to say about my experiences in Los Angeles, and although now I satisfy my aging inner Labrador with incredibly long walks through quiet Ohio forests, my time-painted, tank-like Rail with six-thousand miles on the odometer is silently resting, waiting, in the trunk of my car, just in case I ever find myself on another gently rolling, concrete ocean by the sea.

Addendum
"The Loop" Soundtrack Hall Of Fame
(Songs For Stoned Skating)

"What Would I Want? Sky" by Animal Collective; "Sleepwalk Capsules" by At The Drive-In; "Pay to Cum" by Bad Brains; "Atlas" by Battles; "Futterman's Rule" by The Beastie Boys; "Off the Grid" by The Beastie Boys; "Lemonade" by Blind Melon; "G's & LOC's" by Bloods & Crips; "Vision Creation Newsun" by Boredoms; "So Much Better" by Childish Gambino; "Get Like Me" by Childish Gambino; "Figure in Your Dreams" by Comus; "Sound and Vision" by David Bowie; "Korea" by Deftones; "Back Again" by Dilated Peoples; "Your Time Is Gonna Come" by Dread Zeppelin; "The Gash" by The Flaming Lips; "Son of Mr. Green Genes" by Frank Zappa; "Inca Roads" by Frank Zappa; "Waiting Room" by Fugazi; "Huddle Formation" by The Go! Team; "When Will They Shoot?" by Ice Cube; "Lust for Life" by Iggy Pop; "Where'd You Go" by J Mascis and the Fog; "Summertime Rolls" by Jane's Addiction; "El Sinaloenese (The Man from Sinaloa; 1943)" by Kronos Quartet; "All Caps" by MF Doom; "Lactose And Lecithin" by MF Doom; "Meeting of the Spirits" by Mahavishnu Orchestra; "No Voices in the Sky" by Motörhead; "The Decline" by NOFX; "Myintrotoletuknow" by Outkast; "Ain't No Thang" by Outkast; "Acid Raindrops" by People Under the Stairs; "Time to Rock Our Shit" by People Under the Stairs; "Thembi" by Pharoah Sanders; "Run and Fall" by Snapcase; "Eric's Trip" by Sonic Youth; "School Days" by Stanley Clarke; "Crosseyed and Painless (live)" by Talking Heads; "Tear Da Club Up '97" by Three 6 Mafia; "Stinkfist" by Tool; "Lateralus" by Tool; "Vicarious" by Tool; "News" by Tune-Yards; "Rock and Roll" by The Velvet Underground; "Roses Are Free" by Ween

What A Picture Is Worth

"WHAT DO you think about pictures of yourself? When you see them. What do you think? Wait!—Let me guess. *Yooooouuu* . . . I think, probably . . . sometimes, I bet you think you look good, and sometimes you think you look bad, you know like *fat*—no offense 'cause you're not, but I could see you looking a little heavy in pictures. I only ask 'cause, when I see pictures of me, I wonder how anyone could stand such a person, such a plain ol' bore. Honestly, I always look the same. I just put on my smiling mask and pose like a cutout—and it's like I don't even really need to be there."

This is what she said to me as I looked at her and as she looked at the book of photographs on her lap.

"I mean, look: same girl with the same dumb smile in every one of them. Seriously. I mean, do they really reflect who we are? I mean, they must, right? It looks like me. But it's just I've seen pictures of *fantastically* attractive people before, and in some pictures they looked so ordinary, even *un*attractive, and I wonder about that: are they actually ordinary, you know, and the picture shows the truth, or was it just a moment—just a half a zenosecond—where they were ordinary or unattractive? Or are they still beautiful, but the picture—the zenomoment, let's call it, because that's what it is, for all I know—robs them of their total self? Like if you were to say that T.S. Eliot's 'The Waste Land' weren't a beautiful work of poetry because you only got to read a single line of it and didn't find it particularly good? Is that right?"

She held two fingertips—thumb and index—to the corner of one photo in particular, a photo of her and another girl. The other girl in the picture, away from the fingers, wore a blue satin dress, a tiara, and a sash that said "Birthday Girl!"

"I hate pictures. I really do. I mean, I have all these, but I'd be just as happy without them, except I need them so much.

It's just that when I see them, I think about all these things that aren't even *in* the picture. I don't even *see* the pictures; I just see the things that *bother* me about them. I don't know. I wish I did. I hate pictures, but I look at them all the time. Funny, huh?"

She started turning the page, but she turned it back, with her fingertips still lingering on the photograph of herself and the birthday girl.

"Like, sometimes I'll see old friends or relatives or something in pictures, and immediately I'm thinking about the worst things I've ever seen them do. I don't remember when the photograph was taken, or the occasion, or anything like that. I hear the people, like, farting in church, or making out with someone else's boyfriend at a party, or, you know, even something like a slight—something that I may not have even understood right. But it slams into my head like a truck and blares on its horn and shines its bright lights right in my eyes, and that's all there is in the world when I see that person smiling back at me, just that thing. God! It's so *annoying*. And I can't stop!"

She angled her body towards me, to emphasize her point.

"Take this girl, for instance"—finally, she consciously pointed to the Birthday Girl picture. "Cindy Simpson. She was my best friend in college—my roommate in the sorority house for two years—and we never had *any* problems. She was always super sweet to me, even when I went through that awful thing I told you about at Carrie's. You know, just a super girl. Not snaky at all. I loved Cindy, really."

She turned her head to look at the picture again.

"But now when I see this picture, all I can see is—well, let me explain this. See, Cindy's the cleanest girl I've ever known, and you know I'm pretty clean myself. I mean *look* at this place. Cindy's way worse, though; I mean she cleaned *everything*. Some of the fraternity boys used to make jokes about it, and they never notice stuff like that! So what I'm getting at is that this one time I was at a party with Cindy, and we were waiting in line for the bathroom—ugh! I *hated* going to the bathroom at a boy's place, dis*gust*ing—and anyway we were talking. Actually I was looking at this crazy painting, and when Cindy turned to see what I was looking at, I noticed that there was a small red dot on her sleeve, by her shoulder. She had this really pretty white blouse on, but it had this little red dot . . . ."

She seemed to be looking at her friend's blouse, in her mind's eye. Then she returned.

"Now, whenever I see her picture, I don't see all the great things Cindy did for me or anything. I don't even see the picture! I just see that stupid *dot*."

After a moment, she closed the book.

"Oh, I must be boring you to *tears*. Jeez, why do I get like this sometimes? Tonight I just feel so . . . *loquacious*. Isn't that a lovely word? I learned it from Cindy, actually. It means talkative."

Just then, the doorway was darkened by a smiling, camera-wielding partygoer, who popped a bulb and took our picture and left. It was a picture of a slender blonde woman, the host of the party, slightly drunk, clutching a book of photographs to her chest, wearing her usual photographic pose and mask, sitting next to me, as I sweated, drunk, looking a little tubby. It was a picture worth about as many words as I've given it just now.

One Thin Slice Of The History Of Life

FOR A BILLION years it was a roiling, red-orange lava field, with roaring comets diving daily into the glowing tide. Over time, the comets' prolific contributions fell to reticence and then to an only occasionally interrupted silence, and on the horizon over that time a spherical planet hardened into shape, and the still-roiling creases of the planet sighed and breathed and conjured and built a sustaining, gaseous atmosphere. The lava hardened to a dark gray crust, and over billions of years the rocky gray plate was rained upon by the primitive atmosphere and washed and filled with water and then amazingly became covered over with colorful forests that grew more and more dense with time—forests that sometimes burned completely or froze and died, but which always returned and overdeveloped once they first started that first time. And then two hundred years ago the thick forest was cleared out, and gigantic skyscrapers replaced the towering trees, and a one-foot layer of concrete was embedded in the brown dirt, and three outdoor basketball courts were erected in the middle of a park, in the middle of a thriving urban center.

Four billion years ago there was a ghost standing in the middle of a lava field, with a ball in his hand, and the ghost shot the ball into the air, and four billion years passed as the ball arced through the air, until it reached the present day, 5 November 2010, became a reality, and swished through the snapping net, as the ghost solidified into a thirty-five-year-old man in basketball shoes, running pants, a hooded sweatshirt, and a knit hat.

The ball hit the concrete and bounced up and down noisily as the shooter jogged over to it, grabbed it, and held it firmly in his hands.

He was in a world of walls. In every direction he was closed in by massive buildings that filled the width and the breadth of his sight, and the autumn wind swirled chillingly in the air between the open-eyed monoliths. The windows of the buildings were clear or black or mirrors, and the buildings were gray, or darker gray, or glass. The stitched-together pattern of architectural styles created, for the shooter, the idea of "urban plaid."

Tossing that odd thought aside, he spun on the ball of his left foot, jumped away from the hoop, found the rim with his eyes, and tossed the basketball into the air with an arc so high that anyone watching would have called it showboating. He landed on his feet and continued away from the basket as he listened for, and smirked at, the always-satisfying sound of the swishing net's brief grasp at the ball.

As he jogged back towards the hoop—an mp3 player in his sweatpants pocket slapping against his hip—he heard, over the sound of the music in his ears, the laughing and basketball-bouncing approach of four male teenagers. When they came into sight, he nodded at them, but they did not nod back. It was not the non-nod of disrespectful youngsters but—it appeared to the shooter—the hesitation of certain teenagers who aren't aggressively self-confident or cranky enough to intimidate outnumbered strangers on a perfectly blue-skied Sunday afternoon at the courts.

The kids walked to the far, opposite hoop, two-and-a-half courts away, and broke up into teams for a game of two-on-two.

The shooter returned his attention to lofting the deep brown basketball through the orange rim and the white net in his favorite green-grass-skirted gray-urban-plaid basketball park.

The music thrummed in his ears, and beneath his sweatshirt and long-sleeved shirt—on his undermost, white undershirt—he was finally starting to feel the presence of sweat. He had been shooting for an hour already, but the air had a November bite to it, rather than the toothless slobber of July, and it had taken an invigorating hustle, replete with the most challenging and acrobatic shots he could reinvent for himself, to feel the warmth he was creating to give the cold air a bite back.

From below the rim, he tossed the ball into the sky, aiming for a bounce on a spot between the foul line and the three-point line, and as the ball fell to the ground at that spot and bounced back up, he ran from where he started, leapt into the air, plucked the ball from its up-bounce, spun to face the hoop, found a swish trajectory with his eyes, translated it to his arms, landed on the ground, and, this time uncertain, turned to watch the ball's path as the ball smacked off the backboard and went through the hoop.

"Uh . . . glass!" the shooter said and laughed to himself.

He thought about a story he heard once, of a man who'd banked in a shot at halftime, from half court, to win ten grand, and who'd refused to accept the prize, he'd said, "Because I didn't call glass."

The shooter continued laughing and smiling as he gathered the ball.

As LeDerrick Swedt was checking the ball to Michael Pollack during their game, Scootie Floyd's attention momentarily shifted over to the shooter on the far court, who was laughing to himself across the way. Scootie thought, *What could that old dude be laughing at?*

"Scootie! D up!" Scootie's teammate, Michael, shouted, and Scootie returned his attention to the game.

Scootie was the best.

They were all good, but they all deferred to Scootie, despite the fact that he was the smallest and youngest of them.

There are some kids who are short, and there are some kids who are thin, and there are some kids who are an almost piteous combination of shortness and thinness. Little, birdlike children.

His birth name was Fawntleroy—Fawntleroy LeVarr Floyd—but everyone had called him Scootie since it started at school one day, in the way that those things just start—embarrassingly. A story he'd rather not be retold.

In a classroom, Scootie's desk looked like the equivalent of a circus clown's big floppy shoes. But when taken out of the classroom and put onto a basketball court, with a basketball abounce, Scootie was no longer a person but a beguiling, inhuman blur. You would swear there had just been a small, birdlike boy standing there, and the next thing you heard was the ball bouncing off the backboard and swishing through the net. Or you would be dribbling the ball, look up to reorient yourself with the hoop, and by the time your eyes were back down looking to reorient yourself with the defense—specifically Scootie—you wouldn't have the ball anymore, and his teammate would be waiting at the three-point line.

Swish.

Scootie was the best of them, certainly.

LeDerrick and Dante Swedt were twins, and they were the poorest people Scootie or Michael knew (who were not exactly wealthy themselves). The twins' father had been a good man who'd gotten an unmarried woman pregnant with twins and who'd stuck around, until he was killed in an industrial accident when the boys were six years old. From that point on, their mother struggled to keep the family warm and fed, and now that the boys were old enough to more or less take care of themselves—twelve—she had more and more returned to her unfortunate, alcoholic indulgences. Consequently, LeDerrick and Dante were almost never home, were almost always looking for something to do.

To most people, LeDerrick and Dante looked exactly the same, but as happens with the close friends of lookalike twins, the more you knew them the more you could tell them apart. In fact, there was one "big" difference between them: Dante was around five pounds heavier than LeDerrick, and consequently Scootie, Michael, and LeDerrick had cruelly given Dante the nickname "Chubs."

LeDerrick was into cars and would always be into cars. Oftentimes, their games would come to a standstill because LeDerrick saw a nice car coming up the street and went into full voyeur mode. Sometimes he would get so excited about a car—perhaps a rare Italian sports car—that he would start clapping at and catcalling the thing as it drove by. His friends kind of thought his fascination was corny, but they all had their obsessions. Already LeDerrick had the idea that he wanted to work with cars when he grew up, and he found himself paying particularly close attention anytime he was in a class in school that he felt might help lead him in that direction, which wasn't often. Otherwise, he could be found at George's Auto Works, where George himself had been tutoring the eager youngster.

Dante ("Chubs") was equally obsessed—not with cars but girls. If the four boys' libidos were set up like the Kentucky Derby, and the gates were opened: Scootie's horse wasn't quite born yet; LeDerrick's horse was jogging distractedly along the outside of the track; Michael's was just starting to get saddled, and Chubs's was already out at full sprint, on the inside track, slobbering at the mouth, champing at the bit. If a game of pickup ever stopped on his account, it was because a pride of lionesses had found their way to the courts and Dante kept veering towards the source of all the pheromones in the air.

In class, Chubs almost never said a word—not because he didn't know the answer but because he so wanted to pounce on his young teacher, whose breasts he watched rise and fall with her every lusty breath. He was afraid of blurting out something, such as, in answer to a math question, while still gazing in awe, "Have you ever heard of sexting?"

It was just one of those wonderful coincidences that his nickname turned out to also be so relevant in the realm of horny bonerdom. Chubs, indeed.

Michael was going into the military. Even his friends

could see it. He loved sports because they were like war. Of the four of them, Michael was the only one who'd ever been in a fight. In fact, he'd been in four. He won three and severely lost one. Although he was obsessed with guns and munitions, he never considered using a gun on the boy who'd won the fight against him. According to the tactics that made sense to Michael, you don't drop a nuke just because you lost a battle. What you do, or at least what Michael chose to do, is enroll in as many free self-defense classes as you can find. And have fun with your friends when you can.

The teams almost always ended up being the same: Michael, the tallest, and Scootie, the shortest, versus the twins, who were much closer to Michael's height than Scootie's.

Just because Scootie was the best does not mean LeDerrick, Dante, and Michael weren't also good; they were all good, very athletic and competitive, but the fact remains that, of the four, Scootie was the best.

The man on the other court was a Throwist, and he could see that Scootie was a Throwist, too.

He'd once read a story by an interesting author—in the interest of full disclosure, whatever that is, and pleasant bragging, which is more like it, I, Daniel Donatelli, was that interesting author—where a word was coined that the ghost of more than four billion years, from that day forward, had used to describe himself:

"Throwist"—noun, a human expert at physically throwing objects.

The old shooter immediately recognized himself as a Throwist—humanity's best when it comes to Throwing.

He had been a wildly successful quarterback in high school, a record-holding pitcher in college, an ace in any act involving a man using his limbs to project something through the air with grace, velocity, and accuracy. Firing—from any angle, mind you—a baseball or football or Wiffleball or Frisbee with authority, precision, and jazz; flicking playing cards more than eighty miles per hour; rolling bowling or bocce balls to the perfect spot; expertly placing darts over uncommon distances; tossing a phone or controller or keys across a room confidently into inexpert hands; and also, let's not forget . . .

Shooting a basketball.

To the shooter, to a Throwist, they were all part of the same family of knowledge, which the shooter's favorite author considered a language—created from the study of the practical physics of the universe in which the body lived, and which is then translated into motion by the mind and body together, to create a desired outcome. Hitting that far street sign with the rock in your hand. Getting the ball to the first baseman in time. Shooting a basketball high into the air and through a hoop, for three points. Understanding yourself and the physical laws of your universe.

He had been doing it so much for so long he had achieved a sort of Throwist's Nirvana—a peaceful combination of precision, coordination, concentration, and sometimes violent velocity.

The shooter was a Throwist, but now all his friends were dead—old married men with young hungry children on their hips—and he didn't have anyone to throw with anymore. His multitalented younger brother was gone, too. Another ghost. Sometimes he'd meet someone, maybe at work, who offered to have a catch sometime, but after the other person's first throw, the shooter would frown. The other person could never handle what the shooter was capable of unleashing—which so much wanted to be unleashed, if only for the sheer exhilaration, like letting a fitful dog bound across a wide open field, rather than tethering it to the truck. He could wind his body up and seriously hurt the person standing across the way, and because of that he had to hold back. He had to keep a leash on the Labrador.

He could still shoot baskets while his dead friends built

their lives, while his dead brother disappeared into the busy mists.

He had never been very social, anyway. He could shoot baskets alone just fine.

So he did.

A Throwist is kept company by the enjoyment of what he is.

He'd never found love, either, or had found it without it finding him, but never both at once, not once, sadly—sometimes a person just doesn't have a match, and there isn't a goddam thing to be done. Hell is hopelessness, and maybe that's why he was always shooting around like that—last place in the universe where he had any control over anything at all.

LeDerrick checked the ball to Scootie, who held the ball, made sure Michael was set on Dante, and checked the ball back.

LeDerrick started dribbling the ball, did a half-step fake to the right, which Scootie bit on, then cut left, free of Scootie, who started hustling back to the basket, and LeDerrick powered up against Michael, who had left Dante by the hoop. Seeing that Dante was open, LeDerrick overhand-passed the ball to him, and just as Chubs was about to bank in the easy two-foot shot, Scootie came flying up and smacked the ball back into his face. The ball hit Dante in the forehead, and the impact befuddled him so much that he ended up spinning around and falling to the ground.

At which point the game came to a stop because LeDerrick and Michael were laughing so hard.

Scootie ran to get the ball and returned.

LeDerrick was especially loving it. "Haaa! Little Scootie-Boo knocked you the fuck out, Chubs! Ain't that right, Scootie?"

Scootie tossed the ball to LeDerrick and said, "Your ball. I think I might have fouled him."

"Ah, shut the hell up, Scootie," LeDerrick said. "You didn't foul shit. Don't take no pity on Chubs."

"Yeah, Scootie," Dante said, standing up. "You know you blocked that shit, little teacup faggot."

"Chubs ain't been rejected that hard since he tried to get Kelly Cavelli to touch his *dick!*" Michael said, and they all laughed.

"Okay," Scootie said in his quiet way. "Our ball."

Scootie had worked out a play with Michael the last time it was just the two of them shooting around. First, Michael would come up and set a pick for Scootie, bunching up all the players near each other. Scootie would dribble awkwardly into the mess of people and then intentionally/"accidentally" have the ball dribble off his foot, away from the basket. Both defenders and Scootie would hustle after the ball while Michael slipped under the basket. Scootie, the fastest, would reach the ball first and immediately fling it back behind himself, over the defenders, in the direction of the hoop. Michael would catch the ball and put it in for an easy point.

It worked perfectly. One to zero.

The shooter returned his attention to the poetry in motion of his own long shots as they rode the winds of the afternoon and swooned into the arms of the withering net. The ball bounced noisily off the ground but softly behind the music that filled his body from his ears.

One day it was just Scootie.

This was later, the following early spring. The worst of the winter had passed, and although there were still large piles of black snow here and there on the big parking lots, both the shooter and Scootie had deemed the weather finally fit for basketball.

Scootie had spent the winter playing table tennis (another Throwist exercise!) with his friends at the Rec Center. There was a basketball court there, too, but there were always adults on the court. The kids never saw the shooter playing up there.

The shooter had spent the winter in a large stack of books. On the first functional day of spring, Scootie emerged

from the Rec, and the shooter emerged from a galaxy of literature, and they both bounced their basketballs up to the courts
downtown, where they started to shoot around on different
hoops.

Of course they noticed each other; how could they not?
The shooter was on the westernmost court, on the hoop near
Hughes Avenue, and Scootie was shooting on the middle
court, on the far hoop, near Fifth Street. When the shooter first
noticed Scootie on the courts, after the long winter, he found
himself building a big smile on his face, but Scootie didn't respond or reciprocate with an appreciative grin. In truth, Scootie was slightly embarrassed to see the shooter up there, because
Scootie had stolen the old man's idea—wearing headphones
and shooting alone, if your friends are too busy, or if you don't
have any friends left.

The shooter had a state-of-the-art music player in his
pocket; Scootie had an old AM/FM Walkman. The shooter was
listening to a carousel of music as he lofted his bombs through
the air; Scootie was listening to national news reports at the
top of the hour—the only channel the old Walkman could still
pick up—as he dashed across the court in pursuit of a rebound.
They both inwardly celebrated the feeling of the spring air on
their skin. What a day!

It was later, around two hours into their personal shoot-
arounds, that they both almost simultaneously bricked deep
threes, with the unforgiving rims punting each shooter's ball
towards the other shooter. They were both in a dead sprint to
their balls when they saw that the trajectories made it simple
enough for the shooter to wait for Scootie's ball and for Scootie
to wait for the shooter's.

When Scootie got the shooter's ball, he lobbed it over to
the shooter with a bounce pass. The ball bounced softly off the
concrete and into the shooter's left hand.

"Thanks," the shooter said.

The shooter also returned Scootie's ball by bounce-pass-
ing it, but instead of with a soft loft, the shooter gave the ball

such an unusual spin that it looked like he'd thrown the ball incredibly poorly, and Scootie started heading over in the direction he thought it was headed, but he had to stop in his tracks when the ball had bounced off the ground and shot into the direction where Scootie'd just been standing.

After he gathered the ball, Scootie looked up and saw the shooter walking contentedly back to the hoop near Hughes.

You can't be a Throwist and not be intelligent. Graceful coordination is physical intelligence, and a Throwist is a physical genius. Unfortunately, there are very few occasions in life where that genius has any practical value at all.

The shooter could do more than two things at once, and one of things he was always doing was thinking. He was thinking while he was doing anything. Sometimes—disturbingly often, actually—he was thinking about his death.

He thought about the last jump shot he would ever take. There would be one; it was a fact of things. He thought a lot about that last shot. It would be a gray day in the late fall, with a drizzle of cold spit in the air. His knees would be a creaky mess, and he'd certainly be "taking it easy out there," and he probably wouldn't even know it would be the last jump shot he'd ever take. Winter would come, and a flurry of Events and Celebrations and Birthday Parties would follow, and he'd fall ill with a bad lung infection, and he'd be bedridden, and he'd die looking out a dark hospital window at thin wisps of snow, thinking about how he should have appreciated it more—that last jump shot.

Sometimes he thought about what happens before and after you die, like maybe in the afterlife all the history of everything that ever existed is over, and you're in some sort of After-Reality, and everything that ever happened is documented, and an After-Person could watch a collection of the greatest feats in the history of the universe—everything from gamma ray bursts to the most vicious pre-civilization hunts. Or a person could pull up the record of another person's life and be able to sit in his or her consciousness and experience life as that person, to be able to mount Everest as Sir Edmund Hillary (or Tenzing Norgay), or hit baseballs as Ted Williams, or conjure relativity as Einstein, or perform any of the unbelievable and exciting secret acts of national espionage that actually took place.

Or shoot baskets as a master Throwist, young or old.

It would just be a waste, the shooter thought, *to be the only person to ever experience how great it feels to be me doing this*.

We all have our ways of dealing with the prospect of that last jump shot.

Michael had gotten in another fight, this time with two bullies, so he was grounded.

Dante and LeDerrick were both sick; they both always got sick in early spring and late fall—bad allergies and no medicine.

Scootie had been touched that Michael had been willing to try to sneak out of the house to go play hoops with him, but one look at Michael's hands told Scootie that he couldn't play anyway. They were caked with blood and cuts, and Michael's face was still lumpy and blue. He winced whenever he did anything.

It was just Scootie again.

Before heading to the downtown courts, Scootie stopped by the nearby convenience store run by "Anoosh Punhajanahab" (as his nametag stated), to purchase a big thing of lemonade with the money his mother had given him for the day.

On his way to the counter, with the heavy and bigger-than-his-head thing of lemonade in one hand turning the line of his shoulders into an inclined plane, Scootie's bad luck continued—he stumbled across the boys Michael had lost to in his most recent fight. The fight had been two-on-one, and had started because Michael knew he could get in at least one good shot at AK, and that was worth it.

The two bullies—whom Scootie knew from school: Aaron "AK" Kellon and James "Juice" Ginn, both older, fourteen, and bigger, with not nearly the telltale signs of a fight fought that Michael had—stood in the aisle, blocking Scootie's path.

"Hey, AK, ain't this little lemonade bird here one of that cheap-shottin' white bitch's little Uncle Toms?"

"Is it?" the other one looked closer. He flipped Scootie's hat off his head.

"Well how 'bout that, Juice."

"I just came from Michael's," Scootie said, stooping over to pick up his hat. "Looks like you guys won."

"Yeah, we did," AK said. "And we're gonna win again."

"And again," Juice said.

"All we do is win, bitch," AK said.

They kept getting closer.

"For now," Scootie said, quietly.

"Whatchu say?" Juice asked.

Scootie didn't clarify; instead, becoming a blur, he shot through the tiny gap between the two colossi, and before they could react, he was slapping a dollar on the counter and speeding through the door, which clanged a bell by its hinges.

A common customer at Anoosh's, Scootie's sudden wordless dollar-slap-and-exit surprised Anoosh, who then turned his attention to the two bullies and addressed them.

"You do not give the other customers a hard time or I will blow your fucking heads off," Anoosh said.

"Fuck you, immigrant dick," Juice said as both young men advanced towards Anoosh.

Anoosh pulled out the shotgun from behind the counter and pointed it at them.

"No, it is you who is fucking! Get out!"

There were three people on the courts other than Scootie. Two of them were teenagers sitting under a netless rim, smoking. The other was the shooter.

Still shaken from his encounter with AK and Juice, Scootie chose to shoot at the basket on the other end of the court from the shooter, who barely noticed Scootie until Scootie boldly walked onto the shooter's half of the court. At which point the shooter stopped shooting and turned to Scootie.

"I always see you up here," Scootie said.

"Me, too," the shooter replied.

"Why don't you play anymore?" Scootie asked.

"I do," the shooter said.

"When?"

"I was just playing."

"I meant against other people."

"Oh."

Scootie waited for the answer.

"Who are you?" the shooter asked instead of addressing Scootie's question directly, but the shooter's question was asked with legitimate curiosity.

"Name's Fawntleroy, but everyone calls me Scootie. Who you?"

"I used to play against people all the time, Scootie. I was very good—hyper-competitive, like, ridiculously successful—but it got to the point where winning felt like nothing, and losing . . . really brought me to an ugly place inside myself."

"How could winning feel like nothing?"

The shooter thought about it.

"I think you're old enough for this: you know about how when adults are in love they like to . . . enjoy each other . . . physically?"

Scootie looked embarrassed; he was young, but he'd heard enough from Chubs to know more than enough. "Sure, I guess."

"My old friend once told me something that stuck with me ever since. He said, 'For every beautiful woman you see, there's a guy who's tired of banging her.'"

Scootie furrowed his brows in deeper confusion. "That don't make sense, either."

The shooter laughed and bounced his ball contemplatively a couple times and tried again.

"Well how 'bout this, then: a poet—another friend of mine, you might say—once wrote: *'Success is counted sweetest, By those who ne'er succeed.'*"

The line was carried over the breeze of the courts, and over the sound of the traffic, and Scootie thought about it.

"What's 'ne'er'?" he asked.

"It's a contraction of the word never—a stuffy little girdle old poets used to like to squeeze their dainty lines into."

Kind of understanding now, sort of, Scootie continued considering the shooter's old friend's declaration. Success is counted sweetest by those who never succeed . . . .

The shooter could tell that the idea was taking Scootie to a weird place inside, and the shooter derailed the train that was building too much momentum too soon by bouncing the ball again and saying, "Anyway, you ever play HORSE? It's the only game I'll play anymore."

For a moment, the shooter internally debated over the better course of action: actually trying, or letting the kid win.

The kid wins all the time, the shooter finally decided. *A loss might give him some context as to how far he still has to go.*

But well son of a goddam fucking bitch, that little Scootie bastard was better than the shooter thought, and the shooter, who incrementally was brought into trying his very best by the increasingly impressive shooting of that never-misses-a-shot-little-prepubescent-jerk, lost to a thirteen year old bird-boy nicknamed Scootie, HORSE to HOR.

"Can I finally get your name now?" Scootie asked after a game that was otherwise wordless besides necessary shot descriptions.

"Today, Scootie, my name is The Defeated," the shooter said. "And look how graceful I'm being."

"Yeah, what's up? I thought you said losing made you upset—most adults yell a lot when I beat 'em."

The shooter enjoyed that.

"Over time I've discovered that if you win enough it becomes less about winning than something else, which is harder to get at and consequently much more rewarding when you find it."

The shooter had enjoyed the difficulty of the competition and the singular concentration it required and manifested within himself. But Scootie still looked confused by the shooter's old-man ramblings. Anyway, the old man really only had one more thing to add, and he'd let Scootie's surely capable mind make whatever sense there was to be made of it.

"Scootie, you've got some great talents—no doubt. But I can't stop thinking of something: another old friend of mine got pretty close, I think, to what I was just trying to get at just now, when he suggested—and this is a fine piece of advice from an exceptionally accomplished man, so listen for your own sake—he said, *'Even those who know the way, study the way.'*"

The warm weather always brought more people to the park.

A few months later, in the dog slobber of June downtown, in the early evening, the courts were packed. Every hoop was the host of at least a game of two-on-two, if not three-on-three or more.

Scootie and the boys had already been beaten off the court by bigger teams, and with nothing else to do, they watched the courts evolve.

"Why ain't that old white dude playin' up here?" Chubs asked. "He's always here."

Scootie spoke up on the shooter's behalf.

"Says he don't play anything but HORSE anymore," he said.

None of the boys could understand what that meant.

"Why not?" Michael asked.

"Said that for every beautiful woman there's a dude who's tired of banging her."

"What—The hell's that mean?" Chubs asked.

Scootie shrugged.

"He's crazy," Chubs said.

They all agreed.

"More than that," Scootie said.

They all agreed with that, too.

In a way, an old Throwist is a rather curious and piteous character, indeed.

It's not like he made every shot he took; in fact, basketball was the sport at which he'd had the least success. But it was not the sport as much as the exertion. All his life he'd been filled with a listlessness, and he'd shaped that listlessness into his cherished Throwitics. But there were plenty of shots that clanged horribly, just as there were plenty of shots that rose and fell perfectly.

But what about away from the court? What is a shooter, a Throwist, when there is nothing to throw? How does a non-professional athlete make money?

He makes money however it takes, with any of his many other talents, and he escapes to the bounding fields, to the downtown courts, to distract himself from the rot that exists everywhere except in the cradle of his tremendous (and ultimately useless) talent.

Everywhere but the court he was a mess. Sometimes he had to find dark corners in populated places because he would suddenly burst into tears. Sometimes he would lie on his couch and watch raindrops race down the window and hope those raindrops would be the last things he'd ever see, because in his mind he would be begging to die, trying to will death into himself.

The only thing that ever came in those moments was not the relieving hand of death but a funny line from a movie that would pop into his head and distract him out of his despair momentarily, or the sound of a toaster popping in an apartment next door, and then the sound of someone swearing really loudly. Otherwise, he just kept going for what felt like a pathetic reason: he coasted on the momentum he had generated when the motors of his life were still working, before he shut them down. And Walt Whitman keeps telling everyone who reads his words that every man who fills his time and place is the equal of any great man if he does.

Unfortunately, it was a perfect storm. It could have been avoided if any of them had been different, or not there, when it happened. But, they were, when it did.

It started just outside Anoosh's convenience store, where the four boys were squatting on the pavement of the parking lot as they drank their big things of lemonade and tried to avoid the worst heat of the day by relaxing in the shade.

Juice and AK hung out with an older boy named Carter Little, seventeen, who was a car-theft maven. Old cars or new, the kid had a knack for boosting the finest rides in the downtown area.

Just like adults, some kids are just real pieces of shit, and Carter Little, who'd just put a damn-fine Cadillac Escalade into gear, was a real piece of shit, so of course he had a beautiful girlfriend who was a sophomore at Lincoln High—a sixteen-year-old model named Younique, who'd been featured on the cover of a bestselling hip-hop album.

Inside the Escalade, Carter drove, Younique rode shotgun, and Juice and AK were in the backseat.

It was Juice who caught a quick glimpse of Michael outside Anoosh's, and seemingly instantly the truck was roaring into the almost-empty parking lot, and they were all stepping out of the SUV.

Before any of the boys could fully register what was going on, they were all lost in their individual ecstasies. LeDerrick couldn't take his eyes off the gleaming behemoth Escalade; Chubs couldn't take his eyes off Younique's already-full-bloom salacity; Michael eyed Juice, AK, and Carter with contempt; and Scootie couldn't help but watch everything as the scene developed.

Michael, who lived for stuff like this, told his friends, "Don't worry, guys—I got these fuckholes."

"What the fuck you doin' 'round here, bitch?" Juice asked Michael, who said nothing.

"You ain't learned shit, huh?" AK asked.

"I was about to ask you the same things," Michael said.

"What, you think you King Shit 'cause your little faggot friends're here? All these bitches are gonna do is pick up your teeth."

"Hey, ain't you the girl from the Greedy Gee album?" Chubs asked Younique, who was flatteringly embarrassed at the way he looked at her as he asked.

"Who the fuck you talking to?" a jealous Carter asked Chubs before Younique could respond.

"That's next year's Escalade!" LeDerrick said. He started ambling towards the car like a revenant son might numbly and slowly unfold the last distances between himself and the home from which he had once departed.

The boys' split attention was unusual for the bullies, but the boys were just being who they were, especially with each of them knowing that the only one who could really handle himself in a fight was Mike.

"I'm talkin' to the decadent piece of chocolate before my eyes," Chubs said, and Younique smiled and twirled a few strands of her hair, as she had no idea the history between the rival parties.

"Who're *you*?" she asked Chubs. She liked this little horn-dog kid.

"Does it have a system in it?" LeDerrick asked as he continued towards the Escalade.

"This little cracker faggot's about to see the doctor," AK said as he began advancing towards Michael.

"We're gonna make you shit your diapers and—"

Younique finally put it all together.

"Geez, *relax*, guys," Younique said to all of them. "They're just *kids*, for crying out loud."

"More than man enough for you, sweetie," Chubs said and winked.

That's when the fight started.

Carter Little absolutely crushed Chubs across the side of his face.

This seemed to break LeDerrick's reverie, because he flew up from behind Carter and tackled him to the ground.

At the same time, Michael quickly cracked Juice across the jaw and ducked to miss AK's wild haymaker.

While Carter wrestled with LeDerrick, Younique ran over to Chubs, who was returning to consciousness, and threw herself on top of him to shelter him from Carter, who'd just freed himself from LeDerrick and was about to kick Chubs in the face. In the process, Younique smothered Chubs's face with her breasts, and Chubs saw God.

Juice and AK had reoriented themselves and were ready to go on the offensive with a more coordinated attack when Michael registered their intentions and surprised them by rushing into the attack, taking away a lot of its momentum, but they still had the upper hand. As Michael struggled in a losing effort against two larger opponents, and as LeDerrick remounted his charge against Carter, who was trying to pry Younqiue away from Chubs, Scootie had an idea for how to break up the ruckus.

He picked up a rock from the cracked concrete, built up a tremendous momentum, and chucked the rock through the two front windows of the Escalade, which both shattered loudly. The crack of the glass was startling enough to cause everyone to stop fighting and figure out what just happened. They saw the broken windows, and then they turned to Scootie, who addressed them.

"Carter, you might as well let Chubs have your girlfriend," he said. "I mean, you're obviously gay, right?"

"I'm gonna kill you, little nigger," Carter said.

As Scootie shot away from the fights and down the street on his fleet feet, Carter ran to the Escalade, got in, and took off after Scootie.

Scootie ran as fast as he could, but he was not a Cadillac Escalade. Before long, he could hear the engine's terrible voice as the black SUV screamed towards him.

Carter and the Escalade were really getting closer and closer. Scootie wasn't even sure where he was going, but he took a route he knew well. As he ran he tried to think of what to do, but it started to feel like it was inevitable that he would be crushed under the tires of the truck.

Then he noticed he was running on grass, which quickly gave way to another lake of concrete, but this time the lake of concrete comprised three basketball courts.

With his energy failing, Scootie ran, but he knew he was slowing down, and the Escalade behind him was accelerating rapidly.

That's when Scootie saw the shooter, who was driving to the hoop against an imaginary defender.

"HELP!" Scootie shouted, hoping to be heard over the waves of music in the shooter's ears.

"HELP! HELP!" Scootie shouted again.

The shooter noticed, of course; he would know Scootie's little voice, shouted or quiet, anywhere.

The Escalade drove over the grass on the outskirts of the park and was tearing across the courts as the shooter turned, found the trajectory he was looking for, and, with one hand, he overhand-fired the basketball with genius velocity through the open window of the speeding Escalade, smashing Carter Little across the side of the head, knocking him silly and sending the Escalade speeding into a pole of one of the basketball hoops, which the front of the SUV wrapped itself around with a metallic crunch and then hissed loudly.

Scootie collapsed on the far court, panting desperately, his lungs and body burning in pain, and the shooter walked over to make sure the heaving little Throwist was okay.

Many years later, the paved pond of basketball courts in the downtown park were wiped away with a blast, and the Throw-ist shooter returned to the ghost of the independent human spirit—twisting through the air and arcing a ball through the netless rim. Over time, after the blasts, the skyscrapers that remained standing slowly decayed and one by one fell to the ground and were covered with forests, and the field of forests froze and grew and burned repeatedly until the sun in the sky itself swelled and scorched the ground deep brown, then black, and swallowed the whole planet, threw a bright golden pulse as the Throwist ghost was consumed as well, and eventually itself burned out, and there was nothing left to note about that place in the universe.

Happy Hour

DUANE PLATT ambled home from class and enthusiastically slammed the door closed behind him when he got there. He only had one final exam left, and that one would be a cakewalk, so pretty much school, for the semester at least, was finally-fuckingover.

His off-campus studio apartment was silent. Outside: layered, multispecies' bird-chirps and the rising and falling murmurs of duets and triplets of undergrads awalk. As Duane made his way across the room, he pulled out his cell phone, which had been turned off *qua* propriety for the exam. When it powered to life, he saw that nobody had called, texted, or emailed. In fact, he hadn't received an incoming call in . . . he checked the phone . . . nine days.

He thought to himself, *But that's right, right? Sought silence is golden, yes?*

If so, Duane, then why are you asking?

He blasted his music at floor-thumping volume, and out of those speakers tore the unholy wail of raw punk rock, which raised the ire of his blood good and up and spiky and electric, and he was all wings of excitement in the perfect colliding energies of two wonderful-yet-temporary wonders: perfect weather, and freedom from regimented responsibilities.

Duane's off-campus apartment was one of the closest to the arboreal grounds. Out his window, two stories down, streams of backpacked students continued crisscrossing the large, magnificent lawn that gleamed between his apartment and a new, redbrick, large-glassed, school building. The late-spring grass—glossy green and well-tended by its caretakers—sometimes looked like a surreal moat surrounding the stately J. Samuel Simpson School of Communication, or "The J." Behind The

J, shimmering and glowing and twinkling in the distance, was the considerable and dark blue Lake Turgeon. Above it all was a completely cloudless, metallic-blue sky.

Duane's studio apartment mainly consisted of books and booze, and he kept a bottle of liquor almost everywhere in the fuckin' place. He hoisted the closest heavy bottle to his mouth and sucked its insides out like he was getting his soul back.

HOLY FUCKING—YES! Feels gooooooooood when it hits my insides like that, fuckin' hits home—the dragon finds its lair and lays its smoldering eggs.

The bottle still had a little bit of hope left in it, and that hope was whispered into every cell in his body the moment the thick glass tilted back and again flooded his mouth with culti-vated spirits—years of aged hydrodynamic scientific goodness for a few moments of the right goddam feeling for once in a fucking lifetime.

He stared at the ground for a little bit, while he felt his stomach bleed that warmth and those spirits all through him—the best—and then he walked across the apartment and put his shoes back on and grabbed his skateboard near the door. He turned off the music, and he was almost knocked over by the sudden void of that punk-rock insanity. He quickly surveyed the place to make sure—before that second chug rocketed him into the gonzosphere—that nothing in the place would catch fire while he was gone.

Then he was outside, in the late-spring sun, and the air was a delight on his face. It felt refreshing now. Just earlier, on his walk back from class, it felt like any other air in his life. Now, as he looked around at the breezy May afternoon, it felt invigorating. With a well-practiced quickness he rolled his old therapist ahead and jogged up and leapt aboard and pushed forward on a rolling glide over the smooth concrete here in the better-kept section of the school's grounds. When he was up to a plodding pace he put his left foot down and started pushing with real force as his blood cells turned to steel under a power-ful chemical *influence*.

People don't look at you for too long when you're on a skateboard, unless they're just plainly gawking. They glance up and see you and they turn back to the thoughts that otherwise occupy their minds, and you're fifty feet away by then anyway. Duane liked to look at them as they looked at him because he was *influenced* and felt that dangerous-yet-in-control sensation as the wheels clacked and scrambled over small divots and bumps in the concrete, as he weaved in and out of pedestrian and vehicular traffic. Amidst the clattering and weaving, he could be amongst people, around people, and yet completely and obliviously separated from them in a way that was absolutely necessary.

The feeling of a smooth, gliding-yet-intoxicated movement through space, and the feeling of velocity buttressed by a brief, strong wind at his back, and then the absolutely amazing feeling of being mentally undressed by a pretty little thing wearing mighty-big sunglasses as she walked home from an exam and thought about getting drunk and fucked that night, maybe, or something else probably, what the hell.

Duane thought to himself, *Christ, Duane, you drunk piece of shit, let other people be who and what they are—these people who actually do have lives beyond your presumptions of them—and besides, the sun is two hands from the horizon!*

Which, to Duane, made these the first golden moments of twilight—his own, this poor, heartbroken, drunken loner's own, personal happy hour.

The sidewalk gave way to the local town's jagged streets, and from a particularly heinous side street near the business building—The Edward Bernays School of Marketing and Business (the door handles and windows of which Duane had loogied on many times)—he found a little-known paved pathway that quickly flung him down a tall hill that was dotted here and there with supine students studying their books and notebooks. The path wound 'round this tall hill and down to the lowest part of the university grounds, where it continued by tracing along the grassy and reeded edges of the lazily chopping

Lake Turgeon, which was rarely studentless but was studentless today because it was finals week.

Now the wind, not broken and divided by buildings, nor now buttressing his velocity, flew across the flat lake and jumped into Duane's standing lap, and he pushed and pedaled faster and faster to blast past and through it. He was getting away from the campus now, into the rural, nemophilous town that surrounded the university, into the natural quiet of the backwoods. *Oh, that quiet*—an environmental symphony! It was one of the many lovely features of this beautiful place that he sought when he needed to get away from all those people and their overstuft droning and fragile overconfidence.

The path traced along the widest part of Lake Turgeon, and Duane skated thoughtlessly in a solitary reverie as the warm, spring-loaded breeze crossed the far flora and fauna of the fields and swept across the shimmering lake and pushed against his pedaling and flavored the air as it did. He rolled and listened to the wind in his ears as well as the lazy chop of the lake just feet from his feet, and he pedaled and rolled and tried not to think about anything the fuck at all.

Eventually, after a wonderful while, he saw that a hundred yards ahead, like always, the path left the border of the lake and entered the dark maw of the forest.

The sun was now four fingers from the horizon, and the air, and water, and everything the sunrays reached, it all radiated with a beautiful golden hue, but as he passed into the forest's mouth, he went from the glow of early evening to a dark barely relieved by a few rivers of canopy-piercing sunlight.

Immediately upon entering the comparatively cave-like dark, Duane heard a feminine voice say "LOOK—!" and before his eyes could fully adjust to the world of shade, he saw a human-shaped shape five feet directly in front of him on the path, and with the athletic reflexes of his sporting youth, and because he was not nearly as drunk as when he started back at his apartment, he was able to launch himself out of the way of the terrified shape, but the angle of the way Duane pivoted on the board sent him flying off of it, and he crashed half into/out of a patch of weeds next to the paved path.

Following Duane's brief after-crash moment of abject panic—where he checked to make sure that he could still move all of his limbs—he heard some restrained, melodious laughter, and a brief snort.

He could move, and he laughed at the snort while the snorter laughed at him.

Duane's leg was bleeding. When he stood up and started brushing himself off, he saw blood trickling down his leg and into his sock (a whole side of which was growing wet with blood). *Oh, shit*, he thought to himself and, yes, here it came . . . He started to feel nauseous, like he was going to pass out, and he had to sit down, so he plopped right down on the ground, right there, in the fuckin' weeds.

"Hey, are you okay?" the voice said, but Duane couldn't hear it. The tinnitus of his nausea blocked out all external sounds. He was concentrating, with all the singular importance his conscious mind could muster, on not passing out, which, of course, would have been totally uncool.

"Hey!" she said, but he could barely hear anything over the rising chiming in his ears. This overdramatic internal reaction of his—to basically any physical injury above a bruise—really bothered him. He'd asked a doctor about it, and the doctor'd told him not to worry, had said that it was normal. *It might be normal*, Duane thought to himself, *but it sucks donkey cock.*

He felt a hand on his shoulder. "Hey, are you okay?"

"Yeah," Duane said to the concrete, his head swimming between his knees. "My doctor says this is normal."

He started tilting over—he was really passing out this time—and she sat down next to him, and he dropped against her shoulder. "Well, your doctor is *wrong*," she said and laughed at her own joke.

"I just need a few minutes," he said weakly. "Autonomicreactionorsomethn . . ." he said and trailed off, and his head dipped and then sprang back and then dipped again.

"Uh, you got it," she said—she had one of those voices that kids have sometimes that's kind of cutely and tomboyishly gravelly. "I really didn't mean to scare you like that. Could you not see me? Holy jeez, sir, your leg is bleeding bad!"

"I know, kid. 'S'why I'm passin' out." His voice, to himself, sounded as if he were encased in an avalanche of cotton balls.

He felt freezing-cold water crash on the back of his neck and rush down the back of his shirt, and ZING! he was fully awake, no cotton anywhere.

"Thanks," he said.

Finally, he was clearheaded enough to look at this girl and her water bottle. She was small and thin and young, and she had a mouth full of braces on teeth that looked like they were close to becoming braceless. She wore a baggy pair of basketball shorts and a black sleeveless T-shirt. She couldn't have been older than thirteen, but she didn't look scared of or at all worried about the big bleeding college boy unknowingly leaning against her ribcage and shoulder and part of her arm.

"No problem," she said. "Anyway, I feel real bad. Our house ain't too far from here. You should wash up that ugly cut. That okay by you?"

He tested the strength in his legs as he tried to stand. They held, so he stood, but when he stood, the blood rushed from his head, and again he began to stumble, and again she caught him before he fell. "Jesus, you're really strong," he said to her.

"Preacher says the Lord is quite powerful, indeed," she said and laughed and snorted.

He chuckled.

Duane had a decision to make: he could bleed back to his place and take care of the wound there, like an adult, or he could go with this little girl to her house and risk looking like a gigantic creep, but like a man who, when he actually makes his way out there, goes where out there takes him—like Duane.

The girl could see and sense the man's dilemma and added, "I know you're a good person or you'd'a yelled at me for bein' in your way or somethin' just now, so it's fine with me if it's fine with you."

What a cool little chick, Duane thought, and he felt an unanticipated pang of pain, both in his leg and within himself, as he realized something very painful indeed, and for a moment he regretted going on this skate today, but then his mind made more sense of the sudden reminiscence, and he returned to the moment.

"Whoa, you okay?" she asked after she saw him wince and wonder.

"Yeah, sorry—the leg," he said. "And a weird little déjà vu . . . . You just somehow kind of remind me of someone I know . . . used to know . . . hard to explain."

"Was she cool—whoever it was?" the girl asked hopefully, and because of that wonderfully hopeful tone, Duane couldn't resist.

"Actually she was an Arabian horse named Kloppy," Duane said and started to make a silly face when he saw how mad the girl was getting, and the girl realized it was a joke and punched him in the arm.

"Which way to the house?" Duane asked.

Duane collected himself, and they walked together along the paved path under the forest canopy, and neither said much of anything; they just walked along. Duane carried his skateboard.

The cut on Duane's leg wasn't long like a fault line; it was small and deep, like a bullet hole. His leg had slammed down on top of a pointed rock when he fell, and the point had gone straight into some legmeat above the ankle. He thought back on the fall, and he could swear he now remembered a *schwuck* sound when he lifted his leg off the point of the rock. For a moment, he felt sick again.

The thirteen-year-old looked down at Duane's leg, and

the wound was streaming blood at what the girl considered an alarming rate. "Hey, uh, let me see somethin'," she said, and he felt her fingers probe the collar of his shirt. "Oh, man. So, um, your leg's really bleedin' there, and, well . . ."

"Yeah?"

"I was hopin' you were wearin' two of 'em 'cause I need you to take off your shirt," she said, and her face went red as ketchup as she finished her thought into the ground. "They told us last year that when it's bleedin' like this you should tie somethin' around it."

"Well what about your shirt?" he said with a faux-childish, faux-petulant sarcasm. "Totally kidding," he continued normally and, after a moment's hesitation—because, let's face it, undressing in front of a thirteen-year-old girl is awkward and potentially illegal for a twenty-one-year-old guy—he took off his shirt and handed it to her. She was able to make quick work of their makeshift tourniquet, and they proceeded down the path.

Her house wasn't that far—up the trail a decent hike from the mouth of the forest—and indeed just past a small forest pond they turned left through some shrubbery and emerged in a large lawn.

At the far end of the open field stood a time-weathered farmhouse. It was very old, but it had been maintained well by someone who clearly loved it.

"This is it, huh?" he said as they took it all in from the long lawn. "Cool place."

"Ain't nobody home right now, and Daddy said not to let anyone in, so you gotta get cleaned up and outta here quick, 'kay?"

"My name's Duane, by the way," he said and lowered himself onto the porch swing, "and I'm outta here the moment your generous hospitality no longer sustains my emergent hematic presence."

"Good," she said cutting through Duane's narrative fustian. "M'name's Lynne, but most people call me Bug."

"Which do you prefer?"

"Bug works," she said. "Hold on a minute."

She went inside.

Duane looked over the field before him, which rolled down to the woods. He could see—here and there between the trunks of trees—some birds and insects spearing through the air under the canopy. The only sounds he heard were the buzz and click of the natural wild, as well as some footsteps tromping through the homestead behind him.

Bug returned and kneeled and set her supplies on the ground by his feet. "You get lightheaded when you fall down?"

"Sort of," he said. "Anytime I get a bad cut or break a bone or something. It's pretty embarrassing."

As she unscrewed the cap of a brown plastic bottle, she said, "I . . . I push wind when I get nervous sometimes." Her face blushed red again, but he could see she had the constitution to get through it intact. He enjoyed her youthful forthrightness, and he loved that phrasing—*push wind*.

"That's pretty bad, I'll admit," he said. "But I don't think it's that uncomm—"

"It's worse than that," she said. She started unwrapping the blood-soaked ankle. "Two weeks ago a boy in my class tried to kiss me at a dance, but I got so nervous I . . . fluttered . . . really loud."

"Oh man," Duane said, unable to fight off the smile this brought out of him.

"He ain't talked to me since."

"Ah, fuck him," Duane said and then realized he was talking to a youngster and added, "—Whoops."

"Oh, don't worry about it; Daddy swears all the damn time 'round here."

"Cool. I guess what I meant is that that boy's just immature. Everyone farts."

"Yeah, but girls ain't sup*posed*ta, not like that. . . . One boy started calling me *Stink Beetle*."

Duane gave that another half-smile. *It's so easy to be honest with people we barely know.* He bet she needed to get this off her chest to someone, and he was surprised to find that he felt good that he could provide the service.

"Well, Bug, it looks like we both got some pretty embarrassing personality traits."

"Yeah," she said. "This is gonna burn."

She poured the rubbing alcohol into the cut, and, well, to Duane it felt like a hundred-thousand molten needles had been simultaneously jammed into the bullet hole. He suppressed a yelp of pain by clenching his jaws pitbull-tight and breathing erratically through his teeth, but the suppression of the expression was so holistically straining to his body that the erratic breathing quickly gave way to a high-pitched, prolonged squeaking that came from Duane's tensed throat—a truly pathetic, unmanly sound.

They both broke into laughter.

Duane's leg was still bleeding, so he tore off a handful of paper towels and pressed them against the bullet hole and cleared his throat.

"Here," she said and took them from his hand and carefully pressed two crisscrossing bandages over the wound.

"Why are you nervous about kissing a boy?" Duane asked. "Shouldn't you be excited? You're growing up!"

"I'm real excited, it's just . . . I don't know. I never kissed anyone before and meant it. How could I be any good at it? I just start thinkin' so much I get all nervous and my guts feel like a bag of shook soda."

"Well, really, it's no rush, Bug," Duane said. "I didn't kiss my first girl until I was seventeen."

"Really?"

"I swear it."

"Why not?"

"I was very shy," he said. "And fat."

"Oh," she said, paused for a moment, and continued with earnest curiosity, "how'd it go, though?"

Duane thought back to his first kiss, and his face filled

with an emotional strain while his mind watched, once again, from beginning to end, his own deeply personal, brief, ugly love story.

"It was great, Bug," he said with a break in his voice.

Even Bug could tell that the kiss might have been a success but that things didn't end very well at all.

She wrapped a few layers of gauze around his leg and taped them in place and looked at her handiwork, satisfied and happy to have something to say to get past the awkward moment, but unfortunately it was just more awkwardness.

"Here, uh," she said. "Here's your shirt." She handed him the blood-soaked shirt, and he rose off the swing and wrung some of the wet blood out into a patch of dirt next to the porch. He hopped down and mixed the blood into the dirt, so no one was the wiser. Then he put the shirt on, and it looked like he'd been stabbed in the chest. Bug laughed.

"You look a*wful!*" she said, but he could see that she didn't really mean it in the mean way.

"That's pretty accurate," he said. "But I do want to thank you, little Bug."

"So you're leavin'?"

"I probably should. If I had a daughter your age, and I saw her home alone with a blood-soaked college boy with a skateboard, I'd put a bullet through each of his knees and let him crawl his way towards explaining things."

Bug looked up the long driveway to where she'd seen her father returning home so many times before. "Yeah, I could see that. But you ain't no threat—you almost passed out from a little spill."

Duane picked up his board. "Yeah, whatever—just try not to poison the air anymore, Paul McFartney."

Bug was hit, and she loved it, and she fired back.

"Whatever you say, Squeaky!" she said, and they both laughed.

He again tested the strength in his leg. It was throbbing, but it would hold. He turned back to Bug, who was picking up her supplies. "You're a cool little chick, Bug. I'm glad to've run into you." After a moment, he added, "Almost literally!"

Lynne looked up from her stooped vantage and stood, facing him more squarely. "Thanks, Duane. Daddy says you college boys are all rapists and faggots, but I had fun."

The sun was down, but there was still a small orange-purple blushing of afterlight along the western horizon. The rest of the sky was dark but not yet star-filled. The full dark and stars were only ten to fifteen minutes away.

"You gonna be okay goin' back in the dark?" she asked.

"Bug, I ain't ever been okay," he said. "Not once." He looked at the orange-purple blush, took a deep breath, let it out, turned back to the girl, and continued, "So, yes."

She didn't know what to say to that, so she just watched him.

"Take care, little one," he said and started walking away, but then he turned and acted on an impulse that he simply couldn't resist. He jogged quickly up the steps and boldly kissed little Bug on her nervous lips. She pursed her mouth and accepted the kiss, and for a moment replied, and it became a mutual kiss, and Duane pulled away and winked.

"Maybe now you won't be so nervous next time your little boyfriends want to kiss you," he said and turned and started walking towards the university.

"Ain't nothin' to it at all," he called over his shoulder while she stood there red-faced and almost vibrating from her page-turning thrill in the late evening. She watched Duane hobble across the long lawn. "But it means so much!"

He skated back to his house in the dark, his leg throbbing with each push and pedal. He could feel the eerily empty void of the lake to his left as he rolled along the barely visible concrete. He listened to the mellow chop of the water on the lake's reedy shores, and he gazed into the stars, and he thought about her—not Bug, but—

Do the completely fucked in life finally get a break when they die, Duane asked himself and his therapist and whatever

God can be found in every living thing. *If she's gone, where is she now? It was only five years ago—our kiss, what we loved in each other's nearness—but you know, Duane: she's gone as gone goes.*

She was gone from birth. Avuncular, violently penetrative childhood molestation begets years of silent tears and internal confusion, which begets sexual self-abuse with virtually any willing male until she leaps into an awkward teenage noose, which begets a persistent vegetative state, which begets a parents-pulled plug and a stupid gray piece of goddam concrete with her stupid fucking name on it and nothing fucking else. And somewhere, in some small and unremarkable song, or even mere note, in that pathetic, tragic, and short opera, I kissed her. She had been reduced to loving everyone and therefore no one, and I've only ever loved her.

Why didn't she ask for help? Had she? She had, Duane, but never directly, and you missed it, and you couldn't have helped her anyway, could you? You missed it, and it was the most important thing you never did, and you know it wasn't really your fault, but you didn't really help, did you? You didn't do enough. You'll never do enough.

The breeze of the skate cooled and pulled away the tears from the corners of his tired eyes. *Where is she now, then? You're going to keep finding her forever, but you know. There's a little bit of her in little Bug back there, and there will be bits more in others your own age and older, but she's* gone *now, is where she is. She's everywhere within, and she's nowhere without, and that's fucking it.*

Look at this: crying, and she didn't even mention you in her note. She just wrote to you what she wrote to everyone else in the world—that five-word, fucked memoir of the damned.

'Bad luck blue eyes goodbye.'

The wheels hummed on the concrete, the stars above twinkled, the phone remained silent in his pocket, and happy hour was over.

Four Microfictions For My Old English Teacher, Who Could Appreciate Them But Who Proabably Would Not Like Them Because He Always Thought I Was "Capable Of More," The Prick

1.

THERE WAS no time left on the game clock.

A play earlier, the season had ended. The desperately scrambling quarterback, improvising his way out of a badly busted play, had chucked the football into the air, far down the field, but the ball had inexplicably sailed through the equally improvising Division I Scholarship Winning receiver's all-state hands, and the cold pigskin had fallen nose-first into the dewy turf and bounced obtusely a couple times before rocking to rest with grim finality, and the other team and their fans had gone into a wild celebration. The whole stadium, in fact, had started going crazy.

But the game wasn't over.

A weighted yellow flag sat on the turf, in the defensive backfield.

Pass interference.

A game can't end on a defensive penalty, and the fifteen yards given to the offense put them within distance to score. The offense's kicker was good from there. In practice, he could hit field goals from twenty yards deeper, but that was against no rush, with the ball held up by one of those always-faultless placeholder contraptions. This kick would be his record distance for the season, or it would be a turd atop their season's sundae.

Down the line, the defense's chests rose and fell rapidly—still winded and dazed from their efforts before and during the unintentionally premature celebration.

The offensive line walked out to the line of scrimmage and assumed pre-snap positions.

The kicker stepped back in rhythm and found his starting point while the holder kneeled to his own.

The players could barely hear the crowd over the thrum of their own concentration. In the moments before the snap, the fans were noisy, but the players were silent.

The placeholder gestured to the longsnapper, who zipped the ball back, and the placeholder caught the ball and swiftly pivoted it into place while the kicker stepped forward, forward, and struck!

The ball flew, end over end, high into the air.

And whether the ball went through the uprights or not, we've been given this wonderful moment.

2.

JOSEPHINE TOOK a long time deliberating while the clerk eyed her with confusion. The first one was surprisingly heavy, and its weight made her feel good, in a way. Confident. The second one was much lighter, much easier to hold, and in fact, it made her feel just as good as the first one, but she just didn't know. In a way, she felt like she was comparing a million dollars in twenties to a million dollars in hundreds—same thing, pretty much. But this wasn't that, now, was it? Both sat on the counter, in a heavy, ominous, powerful silence. Thunderous silence, as they say. The clerk asked her if she needed any more help. She didn't. She didn't need his help, is what she meant. She alternately picked up one, set it down, and picked up the other, set it down.

"Same price?" she asked.

"Yeawhp," the clerk said.

A young man walked in and looked at her standing by the counter. She felt like she needed to hurry now, but still, which to choose? She was never good at making decisions. Her father had always told her that.

"I guess I'll take both," she said.

"You want both?" the clerk asked, eying her possible worth, which didn't look like much.

"I don't want either of them, really," she said, "but I'll take both."

She paid for and brought both home, but she still couldn't decide which one.

3.

"Dad, what's meatloaf made of?"

"Leave me alone."

4.

Gabriel Garry was getting sick of all the jokes about his sister Cherry. The kids in school, and especially on the bus, made fun of Cherry for all sorts of reasons, but obviously the biggest reason was her glasses, which were very ugly. Ugly but interesting. You see, Cherry Garry had a magical pair of glasses that allowed her to see a little timer floating above everyone's head, and it was the countdown to the moment that that person would die.

(How's THAT for a one-paragraph plot twist?)

Gabriel wanted to tell people about his sister's magical glasses, but the last time he did that the government agents came, and they were even worse than the kids who made fun of his sister. So he just bit his lip in frustration and did what he could to shield her from torment on the rides to and from school.

But he couldn't help her with Johnny Gelfhound, who was gigantic and who, because it always got a laugh, could never resist saying to Cherry as she walked down the aisle in the morning, "Cherry Garry, everyone—whose glasses are as stupid as her face!"

As usual, everyone laughed.

Gabriel, beating be damned, couldn't take it anymore, but just before he turned and socked Johnny in the mouth, he heard the always-reticent Cherry finally defend herself.

"Do you know why I let you make fun of me, Johnny?"

Cherry, who'd always been scared of him, had never spoken a single word to her tormentor, who was so shocked by her response that he just looked at her, mouth agape.

"You don't know?" she asked him earnestly.

He shook his head. "I just figured it's 'cause I could beat up your brother."

"Nope," she said. "It's because I've always known this: today, this morning, seven minutes from now, one of your parents is going to die, and there's nothing you can do about it, and basically I feel really bad for you."

As you can imagine, the interior of the bus suddenly became deeply silent.

George's Black Dog

THREE FAIRLY handsome men—longtime friends Creighton, George, and Jason—met up at a bar in Santa Monica on a Saturday night in late November. Outside the bar, on the black streets, the air was cold, and a chilly, driving rain, born that morning, was still out there. The amazingly-named meteorologists on television ("Windy Steppe," "Cloudy Bolt") had all predicted that this rainfall wouldn't let up until Tuesday—a rare, protracted Southern California rainstorm—and mudslide warnings were already hitting all the news stations. Inside the bar, it was intentionally dark—any man-made light was coming exclusively from the simple centerpieces on all the tables, as well as on shelves on the walls, which produced soothing, candle-like flickers of light. All the windowpanes had been affixed with a transparent, red-tinted layer of plastic, which turned the small amount of light coming from outside streetlights into a burlesque, dim radiance inside, and the whole effect gave the interior of the bar a swanky, opium-den look that the three friends found satisfactory for their purposes, particularly, and pragmatically, because the youngest of them, George, was recovering from an eye injury.

Creighton wore his usual weird-shirt-and-tight-pants combination. Today's shirt featured a scuba diver sitting on a rock, underwater, looking at a rainbow of shades of blue. George wore black pants and a black, button-up shirt, with his hair hanging in wet, careless, essentially unwashed but not smelly twists. Jason, by far the classiest of the friends, wore his usual spectacles-and-suit routine. ("This is Los Angeles, man; the only way to stand out is to look like a normal guy from another city.")

It was still early, around eight o'clock, and the large room was only a quarter-full. The three friends found a booth in the back corner, near the bar. The waitress on call who took their order was a hot-bodied Asian with an unfortunately mangled set of choppers.

"They look like Oriental lamps hanging from her gums," George said. "Just a whisper of yellow—perfect for this place."

Jason said it looked like her teeth were "drunk."

All three men agreed, however, that not a single gentleman at the table was above giving her some sweet lovin' if that's what she wanted. But it was just bar talk because it was pretty obvious that she wasn't exactly all that *into* any of them anyway.

"Probably one of those Asians who's only into other Asians," Creighton said dismissively as he watched her walk away to fill their order.

The plan being carried out was to meet at this bar, get a few drinks, and head over to the concert at the college later. George's brother Harold was playing in a jazz quartet there as part of a national tour of some of the most prominent young contemporary jazz musicians in America. Creighton had come all the way from Van Nuys, George had come from Venice, and Jason had come from Manhattan Beach. For those unacquainted with the wide breadth of the Los Angeles sprawl, each was about an hour's drive from the other, so meeting up was tough, but they always liked it at this bar. It's hard to meet up with your friends in Los Angeles; you need a pretty friggin' good excuse.

Creighton turned to George, who had a troubled look on his face, and began to ask him what was on his mind.

The two ladies who entered the bar, just then, were best friends from college. They'd both moved to Marina Del Rey two years ago, after graduating, and had come up to the bar early tonight in order to sneak in a few drinks together before the rest of the alumni showed up for the annual LA meetup of fellow whatever-that-college-was graduates. The three friends—Creighton, George, and Jason—noticed the women enter because Creighton had been stopped midsentence by the sight of the two of them walking in through the front doors.

"So, Georgie, you look like you—I call the one on the left!"

Jason and George followed Creighton's gaze to the front door, where they saw two beautiful young women sharing a laugh as they entered the bar. The one on the left was short, stacked (big-titted), and had ear-length, raven-black hair. The one on the right was taller (though not tall), less stacked, but more slim, and had glinting ringlets of red hair. Both women were uncharacteristically pale for the sunny California clime. They were young, though, so they were probably as skin-obsessive as anyone today—given all the warnings about the dangers of sunlight adults have been launching at young people for years now.

The girls walked together to the bar. A few minutes earlier, Jacob, the aspiring actor with long brown hair and light-blue eyes, who looked like every other bartender and waiter in the city, had gone to the stock room to restock some depleted bottles before the nightly rush arrived. Consequently, the girls began to feel stupid standing there waiting to be helped.

"I think Duder just went to stock up the bar," Jason informed the girls. "I'm sure he'll be back in a couple minutes."

Creighton and George thanked their respective G/gods for Jason. He was the kind of guy who could do something like that. He was their X factor, and without him and his ability to capture the attentions of women, George probably never would have lost his virginity.

The girls turned—wary looks on their faces from being addressed so casually by men they didn't know—and saw generally handsome, friendly faces checking them out as they checked out the friendly faces. The looks of non-rapey-ness were unmistakable, and the girls were put a little at ease, although of course they still had their womanly guards up. The ice had simply gone from cloudy to clear.

"Please join us, until he gets back," Jason said. "We've got plenty of room, and it should just be a couple minutes—I promise."

The girls looked at each other and then back at Jason. "Sure," said the redhead. "This could be fun," she said to the men, but also to her friend, who looked much more apprehensive.

"Wonderful," Jason said as the girls slid into the seat next to George, who slid himself and his beer down farther into the booth and then turned and tried to smile but then turned back to looking into the bubbles climbing the sides of his now jostle-headed glass of beer.

"Introductions!" Jason announced. "Ladies, I am Jason—*Sagitarius*, haha!—and this is Creighton, *Leo*, and George, our poor little Virgo."

"I'm a Virgo, too," said the one with the black hair, clutching at this commonality in order to keep herself acquainted with the group and conversation.

"It's the worst, isn't it?" Jason said. "Are you as miserable as George here, black-haired Virgo?"

"Michelle," the black-haired Virgo said. "And no, I'm not miserable at all. He's miserable? He doesn't look that miserable."

"Oh he's not *miserable*-miserable, but he's got his problems. Creighton here was just asking ol' Georgie what was on his mind when you two walked in. You mind if we continue with that?"

"Not at all," the redhead said, who herself was a bit of an armchair psychologist and was happy to give picking-over the newly met George a try.

"Excellent! So, Creighton, you were saying—"

"I was just about to ask George what's on his mind. George, do you mind if we get into it with our new friends?"

"I'd prefer it," George said to Creighton and the girls. "You can only hear these guys say *'Just get over it, man'* so many times before it begins to lose its prescriptive utility."

"Well then, smartass," Creighton said sarcastically, "please enlighten us. I mean it. What's wrong, buddy?"

George took a sip of his beer and set it back on the table and again gazed into the jouncing fluid's effects on the bubbles—it was a method he used for collecting his thoughts. Then he cleared his voice.

"Well . . . I'm trying to make peace with being . . . what I am," he said. "I'm sure you girls have noticed the extraordinary level of optimism and positivity expected out of people today. It's especially ubiquitous in this Southern California no-worries culture. Everyone here is as optimistic and positive as anything, but I'm just . . . not. I really never have been. I get down. I get problems, and the problems get me down, and I stay down. In fact, it's gotten to the point that I almost *like* being down. I feel *comfortable* when I'm down here. I get *un*comfortable when I feel the way I imagine most people feel most of the time."

Michelle was already pretty disturbed by what George had to say. "Why would you say that?"

"Why would I say what?" George asked, turning to her briefly before turning back to the bubbles.

"All of that. You really feel that way?"

"No, actually; this is an elaborate seduction," George said in his genius way, with his tone saying yes to her question and his words producing some levity.

"Well I think that's pretty disturbing. What's wrong with being positive?"

"I guess I'd answer that question with another question: what's wrong with being negative?"

"Are you joking?" Michelle asked. She actually looked insulted by the question. She had the same look George was used to: that of someone who wanted to leave his curious presence and get back to the normal world. "You obviously haven't given this very much thought. Wait, were you being *serious* when you asked that?"

The way she hammered on her mounting incredulity hit George like similar lines of thinking always hit him. It drove him deeper into his depression. He said, "Please humor me." He turned to the redhead. "Michelle's-friend, let's play a quick game, so I can make my point to the horrified Michelle."

"Stephanie," Stephanie said, meaning her name

"A beautiful name, Stephanie," George said.

"Okay," she said, curious to see where he was going with this, but also looking over her shoulder for the bartender.

"Okay," he said. "This might seem weird to you, but just play along. You seem like you sort of agree with Michelle here, that I'm being inhuman when I'm depressed. So try to think of a reason why it's actually beneficial to be depressed, and I'll give you a reason why it's harmful to be optimistic."

"This doesn't sound like a fun game," Michelle announced with her growingly uninterested voice. There followed a moment of awkward silence.

"She's right," George said. "We can talk about anything else. I don't think this is going well, anyw—"

"Can I help anyone?" the Asian waitress with the party teeth asked as she arrived at the table with three more beers for the boys.

"What do you girls want?" Creighton asked. "It's on me."

"Oh, you don't have to buy our—" Michelle said.

"Michelle, don't worry about it," Creighton said. "I'm rich as fuck. Get whatever you want."

The girls placed their orders and thanked Creighton when the waitress returned with the drinks. In the meantime, Creighton and Jason had learned that the girls knew each other from college, and that the college was having an alumni event at this bar tonight.

"I'm kind of interested in hearing more from George," Stephanie said. She wasn't lying; she had no reason to lie. She was as curious as Michelle was disturbed. "So, George, I think it's okay to be depressed because . . . it helps to really feel something, if you really feel it. You've got to get it out."

"Excellent," George said. "Couldn't have said it better myself. Would you like to discuss that for a moment or wait for my first blast across the bow of positivism?"

"Blast the bow!" Jason called out.

"Right. We'll circle around to your point, Stephanie. But I arm my cannon thus. Consider not one but *three* clichés: 'Ignorance is bliss,' 'If you're not outraged, you're not paying attention,' and 'Pride cometh before the fall.' Clichés exist because the things they describe are true, more or less. People who are relentlessly positive, then, if you believe those three clichés, are . . . well . . . they're dumb. They're stupid, and ignorant, and arguably destined to fail. But they're *happy*. Anyway, even if you don't believe those clichés are accurate or true, for millions of years of our evolutionary history, there was very little reason for us to ever be what people today consider as having a 'healthy' optimism—meaning an endless goddam parade of smiles. Sorry for cursing. That kind of optimism is an outgrowth of very recent civilization, but that doesn't necessarily make it more virtuous than pessimism. After all, it's pessimism and negativity that may have gotten us here. And please don't get me wrong; don't think that I consider my depressive self to be superior to optimistic people—"

"What? That's *exactly* what you sound like," Michelle said. "I know people like you—*men* like you," she said and took a drink.

"Consider the caveman," George plowed ahead. "One of his kids just died of the flu, only he doesn't know it was the flu. He just saw his kid die, is all he knows. His wife or woman or whatever is coughing, too. She's probably going to die soon. The caveman's not exactly going to be brimming with optimism, right? But we descended from cavemen, so we're descended from very serious, very troubled people. The caveman is depressed. He's pessimistic. But he's not totally depressed or totally pessimistic or else he'd probably kill himself, right? He's predominantly pessimistic—I mean only a complete *maniac* would be predominantly optimistic while living the caveman life, if you can call it a life—but obviously there's at least a pilot light of optimism within him. He's got that need, that drive to go on and get better and survive, to figure things out. But he's certainly down. Anyway, what I'm getting at is that there are psychologists who are now saying that there are actually benefits to being depressed. Stephanie, let me give you another quick test. This one will be fun—I promise. Well, at least more fun than the first game."

"Sure," said Stephanie, tipping her martini to her puffy red lips while Michelle continued a small flirtatious game she had begun with Jason ("who looked so cute in that suit," she would later tell Stephanie, in the can).

"Okay, Stephanie," George said. "Please close your eyes."

Stephanie played right along, and she dramatically closed her eyes tight.

"What's your favorite color?"

"Blue," she said.

"Excellent, now, keep your eyes closed, and tell us what your earliest, first memory is, unless it's too personal."

"No, it's not too personal. I think it was of me playing with a deck of cards on the floor while my mom was on the phone. I think."

"Wonderful, now those were just questions to clear your mind. Now is the real question for our little game: what kind of clothes are the three of us—the three men at the table—wearing?"

"What's this supposed to prove?" Michelle asked. "What's this got to do with being positive?"

"Let's hear this out," Jason said with an authority that Michelle liked. Jason genuinely sounded interested, and manly.

"George, you're wearing a black shirt, button-up . . . Jason is wearing a nice, dark blue suit . . . and Creighton is wearing a T-shirt with a crazy picture on it . . . a scuba diver?"

"Right you are!" Jason said. "So what was the point, George?"

Stephanie giggled at her success and opened her eyes.

"Great job, Stephanie. So these people did a study. They went to a store and placed random knickknacks on the checkout counter. When people were leaving the store, they were asked to recall all the knickknacks they could remember seeing on the counter. The study-holders found that people did significantly better on days when it was raining or when they were playing somber music over the store's speakers. If you'll notice, it's raining tonight, and this place has somewhat of a somber aesthetic, if I may"—as usual Creighton added, "*Of course you may not!*" but George kept going—"and you just remembered all our names and exactly what we were wearing without even knowing that you'd be asked about it."

"Wow!" Stephanie said.

"Our minds evolved over time, but they mostly evolved under the fog of depression and worry. So why have we stigmatized those moods? Why are we running from them? Because they are unpleasant? Sure, they're unpleasant, but they *lead* to pleasantness. They *lead* to innovations in our thinking. Yes, they represent a lesser-evolved mode of being, but they produce a greater evolution. I am reminded of how we must till the soil and plant the seeds before anything grows. Modern optimists seem to suggest that the only thing you need to do in order to make your crops grow is have full faith in the idea that if you want the plants to grow, they will grow as an extension of that desire."

"That's kind of like *The Secret*," Stephanie said. "Michelle loves *The Secret*. I like it, too."

"I can totally understand that," George said. "It would be wonderful if it were true, but I unintentionally disproved *The Secret* years ago. Here's how. When I was eighteen, I was still a virgin. All my friends were having all kinds of sex with all kinds of girls, and I had *nothin'*. It was killing me. It was like a heavy weight tied around my neck, right? So in this moment of total desperation, I did exactly what *The Secret* purports to be the secret of the universe, and this was obviously way before I even know what *The Secret* was. I asked the universe, I put out *vibes* to the universe, and I asked the universe to make it so that I would lose my virginity with this really pretty girl I used to 'go out with' named Maggie. I put all of my most hopeful and optimistic intentions into this request to the universe, and I desperately wanted it to happen, and I channeled my vibes and continued doing good things for people and everything. Do you know what happened? I didn't get laid until I was twenty-four years old, and it was definitely NOT with Maggie. It was with my friend's older sister, who let's be honest was a very . . . well, let's call her libertine . . . she was a very *libertine* girl. It wasn't special or anything like everyone hopes. It was just a drunk fuck orchestrated by a maniac."

"You're welcome," Jason said.

"Well then obviously you weren't doing it right," Michelle said. "I don't think you're capable of the kind of optimism and hopefulness that you need for *The Secret* to work."

"So you're telling me, then, that because the chemicals in my brain are a certain way, that the universe will never give me anything I hope for?"

"I guess so—yes," Michelle said, but she didn't sound very convinced.

"I love this shit!" Creighton said, totally enraptured by the ping-ponging of ideas at the table.

"So, yes, being depressed is unpleasant, but I think it has been unfairly stigmatized. Just because we don't like something doesn't mean it's not good for us. So I get depressed and pessimistic. I have my reasons, and perhaps the depressions are necessary for my brain to enter into an elevated mode of thinking. I mean, after all, name me some happy, optimistic, *great* people from history. Charles Darwin was incredibly depressed. Winston Churchill called his depression his 'black dog.' Supposedly J.D. Salinger collected piss in jars. Can anyone at this table think of one happy-go-lucky genius?"

"So, you're calling yourself a genius?"

"Michelle, calm down, geez," Stephanie said. "He's obviously a smart guy. I think this stuff is interesting. You don't find this interesting?"

"Not really—it's *morbid*," Michelle said. "There's nothing okay about being depressed, no matter what Genius Boy here says."

"I can understand why you think that, Michelle, but an important distinction should be made here, with the slight risk of repeating myself. I'm not saying being depressed is always better than being happy—"

"That's *exactly* what you've been saying this whole time, George," Michelle said.

George let her finish and continued, "A different group of psychologists did a massive study, and one of the things they discovered in the study was that a certain group of people consistently tested with the highest levels of self-esteem in our society; do you know who they were?"

Everyone's silence was an unspoken answer no.

"Violent criminals," George said. "But on the other hand, I've read enough and I know from shameful personal experience that too much negativity can be just as bad: can lead to cowardice and deadly panic. So I guess this isn't a perfect application of it, but I like the line, so it's kind of like a great writer once said, 'You've got to touch both walls before you can find the middle.'"

This time the table's silence was the thoughtful kind.

"But I can understand if you want to talk about something else," George continued. "It's just what was on my mind when Creighton asked. I agree with Stephanie, however, that this stuff is interesting. I had just read an article about 'Depression's Upside' before I came out here tonight, and I'd been feeling kind of down, kind of jealous of my brother—"

"His brother's playing in a jazz show tonight at Santa Monica College," Jason said, continuing his emcee responsibilities. "He's a big-time, hot-shot jazz pianist. Cool dude, too. We're all going to the show in a little bit."

"*Jazz*," Michelle said dismissively. She was done with this whole conversation. Fortunately, Jason picked up on it, and even though she was pretty, he'd had prettier, and this chick wasn't doing George any favors, so he said to her, "Okay, ladies, well, bartending duder Jacob is back, and we've probably got to get going soon. Certainly we hope you enjoy your little event tonight."

Both Stephanie and Michelle looked disappointed. Michelle looked at Jason with her disappointment, and Stephanie looked at George with a hint of flirtation George missed. Creighton just kind of sat there and slammed down the rest of his drink. *These chicks suck anyway*, he told himself, and he felt better sitting there not being looked at. *Fuck it*, he thought, and he spoke up.

"Yeah, I think you need to go," he said to Michelle. "Stephanie, you seem as lovely and pretty as anything, and we thank you for playing along with our depressed friend's speechiness. I think we'd all marry you and have your babies. Michelle, you're the one who should go. You're kind of a huge bitch. It's probably some sort of defense mechanism you've assembled for yourself, and we all have them, but I suggest giving yours the same amount of consideration as George has given his depression, because nobody here likes what you are. I know you and Jason have been flirting while George plays the role of theoretical evolutionary psychologist or some usual George shit, but it's just because you're sexy as hell physically. If he's actually into your personality, he and I aren't friends anymore."

Everyone looked at Jason, who took a long drink and shrugged.

"You guys are losers," Michelle said as she stood up. "Let's go, Steph."

Stephanie looked at George with sad eyes and then at Michelle with sadder eyes, but the look on Michelle's face then triggered her into a feeling of defiance, defensiveness. "Thanks for the drinks," she said, and the two walked away.

"Nice job, George," Creighton said, and all three men laughed.

They went to the concert. George's brother and the whole show were great. Everyone had a good time. George was able to lose himself in the complexities of the music. He listened to the storms of notes fall like raindrops on the fields of his arid soul, and he lost himself in the spiritual give and take.

After the show, the three friends walked through the auditorium's front room. Creighton said to George, "I think that Stephanie chick from earlier was into you."

"Really?"

"Yeah, man. She was eating up everything you were saying. Kept eying you down like she needed your rod in her bod."

They laughed.

"But seriously, I think she dug ya."

"Maybe," George said. "Maybe not. Good times, though. I liked your speech at the end."

"People who suck need to be told they suck, or they'll never learn," Creighton said.

"Well I had a fine time tonight, gentlemen," Jason said magnanimously, putting his arms around his two friends' shoulders. "And I thank you. What's Harold up to now, George?"

"He and his wife are going back to the hotel," George said. "We're going to meet up and go to the Getty tomorrow."

"Ah, the young bride—what a beauty!" Jason said of George's brother's wife.

"Totally," said Creighton.

"She's a peach," George said.

They reached the doors, re-met the falling rain, and prepared themselves for the dash to their respective cars.

"Nice fuckin' weather," Jason said. "I feel smarter already, George!"

They laughed.

"Later, guys," Creighton said. They all said it and they left.

As he walked across the parking lot, being battered by rain, George thought about Stephanie and her puffy red lips and wonderful modest breasts and the way she looked at him—flirtation? Could she actually have been into him? Immediately he began to regret not noticing it.

"Goddammit," he said, pulling the door closed, listening to the rain tap-dance on the body of the car.

"I'm so broken," he said. "I should just fucking kill myself."

He said it, but he didn't really mean it, kind of. It was just something he said when he felt like this—something he wanted to do without doing it.

He turned over the engine achingly and faintly hoped this new depression, which he could feel flooding into himself—another hollowing, black deluge—would be the one that would actually bring him into a better mode of being.

Some Open-Ended Thoughts On The Importance Of Our Circuses

MY FRIEND Anthony Di Franco is the smartest person I know—his C.V. alone must be stored behind several inches of lead to prevent radiation burns to passersby, and Anthony himself is, one might say, rather intense. I remember once during one of what he would call our "headbutts" (our borderline-autistic method of being social together: repeatedly hitting each other in the temples with the most intellectually weighty ideas on our minds), during a brief respite from the open-water swim of trying to keep up with Anthony's newest concerns (ideas from the brink separating genius and insanity), I attempted to change the subject from something like the probable effects of large-scale drone warfare on civil liberties and domestic policing to something closer to my ken, and asked Anthony, who like me is from Cleveland, what he thought about the recent personnel maneuverings of my beloved Cleveland Browns. With a pert but disgusted, rattlingly glottal clear of his throat, and straining to look down his nose at me across the several decimeters that separated us, his face slightly but visibly perturbed by the struggle to tactfully acknowledge the petty concerns I had raised, he cynically mumbled a line paraphrased from the ancient Roman satirist and poet Decimus Iunius Iuvenalis, known in English as Juvenal, (which Anthony silently left me to look up on Wikipedia when I asked,) who was referring to the frivolous attitudes of the lower-class Roman people during the decline of their civilization when he wrote bitterly, "Already long ago, from when we sold our vote to no man, the People have abdicated our duties; for the People who once upon a time handed out military command, high civil office, legions—everything, now restrains itself and anxiously hopes for just two things: bread and circuses."

My understanding is that as long as a cowed and passive

people aren't starving, and as long as they're distracted with manufactured hopes, fears, and spectacles, the leaders of Rome, as well as those of our present world, could and can perpetrate outrageous crimes against the rest of humanity, without suffering the actual outrage.

Soon thereafter, we quickly returned to the task of plowing through the murky intellectual battlefield of whatever subject had been momentarily tabled by my question, and I spent the next five years thinking about the fact that the smartest— and not only smartest, but most interesting—person I knew believed my beloved (and more often beloathed) Cleveland Browns to be nothing more than a silly, and frankly even evil, distraction for sheeple.

Today, after all these years, I think of myself as a man of coarser intellectual sinew and higher brain-horsepower than the chump I was back then, and though I'm still not the swift and sleek nuclear intellectual submarine Anthony is, I'm now a man who's better-prepared to reconsider the idea and think around in its terms, and I'm ready to leap face-first back into this old headbutt.

The NFL currently carries the torch in America's great spectacle.

It would be hard to argue against anyone who claims that football has become America's new national pastime, and I will not attempt it. (Football has a commanding lead over baseball in measures of viewership and percentage of the national conversation.) (citation needed) Meanwhile, in the rest of the developed world, another football, known to us as soccer, has served the same role throughout the history of both sports. "American" football, and soccer ("football")—the two circuses of the modern world.

Assuming this, the questions I'm interested in are, first: why football in America, and soccer in the rest of the world? And second: hasn't anything changed to make the world a more democratic, or at least vaguely better, place since the times of the decadence and decay of the late Roman empire?

In other words, why do so many people care *this much* (in terms of time and money) about sports?

I humbly offer my brief sketch of an analysis.

Let me start by saying, with all the eloquence I can muster, that human events are complicated as fuck, so it's not like I or anyone can really answer these questions definitively—this I point out in the spirit of Mr. Nassim Nicholas Taleb as presented in his books *Fooled by Randomness* and *The Black Swan*—but the following is my theory for why Americans like their football, why the rest of the world likes their other football, and why so many of us care more about sports than about the effects of large-scale drone warfare on civil liberties and domestic policing, or any number of other pressing questions.

While watching my four-thousandth consecutive hour of World Cup soccer/football in 2009, I realized that soccer (forgive my Americanism) is very much like an interpretive dance about people trying to get laid. Everyone is hurrying all over the place, running themselves ragged trying to set up the perfect shot on goal, and a lot of the time it's seemingly endless repetitions of the same back and forth, only occasionally the matching of wits and dexterity in an awkward tackling maneuver meticulously calculated to be as viciously aggressive as possible without outwardly appearing so, and very rarely someone overtly getting shoved to the ground when the culprit thinks no one important is looking. No satisfaction at all, or even palpable progress towards it, for forty-four minutes out of forty-five, but when the magic finally happens and the ball goes in the net, sweet Jesus' hammer, it is something worth celebrating!

I've never been to another country, (since Canada doesn't count,) so I can't say this for sure, but from what I can tell from being a human and interacting with other human beings on a regular basis, people, American or not, spend a lot of their time thinking about sex. And in the rest of the world, the national spectacle consists essentially of an exaggerated form of the drama of the pursuit of sex, (I don't dare say love,) ironically a drama much more convoluted than all but that which few in the world but Puritanical Americans have to routinely experience in that pursuit—Anthony informs me that the Italian slang *fare un 'zicco*, derived from the term *inziccare*, can refer just as well to the ball penetrating the bounds of the goal in soccer as well as the analogous carnal phenomenon.

Here in America, though, thanks to our Puritan heritage and our ongoing moral/religious underdevelopment, we're not allowed to talk about sex or see it or anything, never mind actually experiencing it. Consider the peculiarly American conundrum that it's okay for children watching prime-time television or playing a video game to see someone get shot in the head and the subsequent explosion of said head into a cloud of bloody mist and chunky gore and slimy brain, but it's a national scandal when a woman's nipple slips out of her dress and is visible for a fraction of a second on television. To put another face to the phenomenon, consider the fact that one of the biggest shows in America today—*Dexter*—is about a man in Miami who commits ritualistic homicides.

The result of all of this is that America's game of choice reflects the dynamics not of sex, which is the rest of the world's obsession, but of war, which is ours.

If you think of the American football as a flag, then the object of the game is to stop your opponent from planting his flag in your territory with the touchdown spike.

There is a playbook of squad tactics by which the assaults are coordinated, there are "bombs," yards gained, ground lost, "trenches."

Far from the case in soccer—where after a firm tackle the man left standing backs away and raises his hands in mock disbelief, signaling his passivity, innocence, and gentlemanly spirit of good sportsmanship to the referee—in the American national pastime we use our hands to dig in for the ball and charge armored-shoulder-first into the other guy's breadbasket, trying to lay him out cold and generally beating the living shit out of each other.

It's war, and we Americans love it.

Ultimately, obviously, they're both, football and soccer, silly games, but I think one of the reasons we like them, beyond the fact that some incredible physical poetry, as moving as it is raw, can result from these contests—let me take a quick em-dash second to emphasize: the athleticism driving sports can produce art as moving as any—one of the reasons we adore them is because we live in a dauntingly complicated era of history, and nearly all of the world's systems are so convoluted and complex, so vast and global and specialized and optimized and leveraged, are in every way of a scale that heaps scorn on the individual and leaves the individual lying passively at their mercy, that one is left feeling like neither a Lover nor a Warrior when one confronts them: one is merely left feeling impotent. But by following our favorite teams, or the sport in general, we can relate to something that is complex and nuanced, but also comprehensible and observable, that is presented to us rather than hidden from us, that we are invited to have an opinion on, rather than being told to mind our own business for our own good.

I don't know shit about currencies or banking, and I'm revolted by the idea of holding power over other people or of speaking for anyone other than myself. I have an apathy/antipathy towards the goings-on on Capitol Hill and thus have no useful or informed opinions on political matters (if I can't know it all, it's rather pointless for me to know any of it), but I did play quarterback in the eighth grade, I've logged hundreds of thousands of Madden hours, and I've been watching football since before I can remember, so I have enough time and experience with the sport to generally understand what I'm seeing and be able to have my own opinions about what's going on.

With how complicated things are in every other area these days, it's been years since—outside of sports—I've heard anyone who actually had his own opinion about anything.

All my thoughts and opinions on political matters come from writer Isabel Paterson and show host Dan Carlin; all my opinions and thoughts on fiscal matters come from my aforementioned friend Anthony and another friend, Jack. And I'll bet Isabel, Dan, Anthony, and Jack all got most of their thoughts/opinions from someone else—someone working with better perspicacity from a better vantage.

It's a whole lot of eyes and brains, but it's just flashlights in a lightless airplane hangar—something so big it doesn't even come close to all fitting inside your head at once. I don't have any original thoughts on most things that matter.

All my thoughts on the Cleveland Browns, though? Where do those come from?

I stand here proudly and point, simultaneously, at the head that computes and the heart that burns with love (and hatred).

I see (pretty much) the whole thing, and I see (pretty much) all the relevant details, and I'm happy or sad with this or that, but I'm happiest just to be able to feel happy or sad of my own accord, these days.

Perhaps I'm writing this out because I'm still trying to figure out if I'm stupid. Are sports a circus? A distracting waste of time? Or do they resonate with us because they give us, in socially acceptable form, things we deeply crave as humans but are usually denied: physicality, striving aggressively after tangible goals, the pursuit of victory over others and self-improvement, and an understanding of the world through one's own faculties? Could sports, then, be both somehow useless and useful? In giving us what we lack, do they enrich us or distract us?

Anthony has the kind of brain that can see further and with acuity in the pitch-black airplane hangar of important human concerns, but all I and most of us have is a little keychain light that only lets us see our own feet.

Meanwhile, the lights are blazing at the football stadia,

and every pore on the center's face is beamed to us regularly in full HD.

Sure, it's just a circus, but better a circus than nothing. In the current paradigm, most people will be ignorant of most important things by necessity.

And all politics is money, so there go the lights.

Good luck, Anthony, and I mean that honestly.

And Go Browns.

I submitted that to Anthony for his consideration—I was curious to see what he thought about my latest forehead to his temple. His reply—his counterheadbutt—follows in italics.

In Orwell's Nineteen Eighty-Four, *the lower class was kept constantly distracted by a frivolous and superficial media apparatus and the spectacles they engineered to keep them (the lower class) from learning enough about the world to know that they should revolt. It is implicit in the considerable effort put into manufacturing spectacle that without a massive, sustained effort to distract the people, they can and will quickly learn that what's best for them is not what's going on, and all the complexity that makes people feel helpless to appreciate the truth will quickly be rejected for serving no purpose but that. 20th century mass media played and play exactly this role of manufacturing distracting spectacles, but the alternatives to mass media are beginning to significantly undermine this agenda. The Internet in particular has made it possible to circumvent the homogenizing, neutering bottleneck of mass media and has made learning about the ways of the world practical again, and people no longer have any reason to feel helplessly ignorant next to people supposed to be experts, and an ongoing, globally networked protest has followed. Peer-to-peer communication on the Internet has made this all possible. Examples that can take anyone in the world to the forefront of thinking on war: a few of the best blogs in my feed reader, written by military and government insiders, free for all to read:*

John Robb:
http://globalguerrillas.typepad.com/globalguerrillas/
Don Vandergriff:
http://donvandergriff.wordpress.com/
The Foreigner, written in part by co-Clevelander Rahul Ravi:
http://alajnabee.wordpress.com/
Zenpundit:
http://zenpundit.com/

One can do as well for any given subject.

It's not quite as prepackaged for your consumption as football is, and I know you've been raised since birth to fear any kind of disintermediated, spontaneous, non-prepackaged, potentially interesting experience, but maybe have a peek, dip a toe in, because really all things considered it's much better out here in the vast world of real concerns of real significance.

Speaking of war, I've picked up a bit of the theory of the history of war, much from reading the blogs I mentioned, and as a result, football to me reflects not war in general but a certain terribly destructive, ineffective, and obsolete kind of war known in warrior circles as second-generation or industrial war—the kind that overgrown bureaucratic nation-states wage against each other, and the kind that gets its ass unceremoniously handed to it for pennies on the billion whenever it encounters agile, decentralized, so-called fourth-generation opponents, as it did famously in Vietnam, Iraq, Afghanistan, and really most of the colonies in the 20th century.

It's no surprise that industrial warfare loses so breathtakingly to anything unlike itself, because what at first glance is a problem is in the context of a capitalist system suffering from excess productive capacity a very useful feature: war, better than most anything else, can burn off and blow up economic surpluses so that the wheels of capitalism can keep spinning without too much wealth becoming too widespread—that is, war, by wasting so much, is an excellent means of preserving the status quo despite the growth that threatens it. Whenever people are serious about winning a war in an ex-

pedient fashion, they don't wage it in any way that remotely resembles industrial warfare. Likewise, American football is a maze of arcane, bureaucratic rules enforced by an entire third team of officials to make sure the ball is only in motion 5 seconds of every 2 minutes of the game. So it's a great way to train people to accept similar routine bullshit in daily life. But it's nothing I'd like to spend an afternoon paying attention to. Waiting in line at the DMV once a year or so is bad enough as it is.

As for the sexiness of soccer's tension, you have found something wryly poetic there, and as for the poetry of athletes doing athletic things athletically, I am all for it. I am not all for it having a place at the center of human consciousness to the exclusion of things that, once widely appreciated, would unleash sweeping change for the better. And, now that the practical means exist for people to educate themselves and engage with each other to come directly to grips with the challenges of living in the world, I am glad to look forward to a near future where those things are appreciated and such changes are realized.

The Third Pastel Parade: Another Clutch Of Balloons Rises To The Sky

-The slow-witted child who, when his name was called in class, never seemed to know the answer, yet who, when he joined the Marines, went on to commit many heroic life- and battle-saving actions for his unit and country—a country that the genius next to him in class, who went to Harvard for his undergrad and got an MBA from the Wharton School, further corrupted and made insolvent.

-The skinny Atlantic City prostitute who didn't charge the nervous young man her usual rate because she thought he was cute and she was pretty sure she just gave him herpes, or whatever that sore is in her mouth—hurts like hell.

-The anxious mother who scolded the man for waiting to pick up his brother from work outside the building where the mother was waiting to pick up her daughter from daycare. "Ex*cuse* me, could you *move?*"—HONK, HONK,—"I'm *here* to pick up my *daughter!*" And the angry-eyebrow look the man gave her for being so petty and disagreeable, for he was in no way in her way. He rolls down the window and says, "I'm sorry, lady, but shitting out a kid doesn't give you license to be a bitch."

-The inconsiderate young woman who asked for a favor, changed her plans, and had to ask for several more favors because of it—turning a young man's nice deed into a marathon of blowjobless annoyances.

-The writer who set out to cross a continent with words and who found himself circling the same corner of the same sad desert for decades until he shot himself in the same place he'd been sitting the whole time.

-The mechanic who fixed what was wrong and broke what was working, and the things he did with both payments before, we can only hope, he burned in Hell forever.

-The father of one who went out for a drink with his friends, met a woman in a short blue dress, and in the course of a few hours, a few of the right glances, a few more drinks, and a short walk across the parking lot, became the father of one more.

-The criminal who remained a criminal until he died a violent death, and the amount of money his family sued for.

-The visiting cousin who did an absurd imitation of a dog playing basketball, and his little cute-as-a-button cousin laughing so hard she's not even making any sound, just a red face of ongoing five-alarm laughter, who is so overcome with the silliness of the idea of the dog repeatedly dribbling the basketball with the side of its face that she soon finds herself urgently and unabashedly announcing, "I'm *peeeeeing!* I'm *peeeeeeeeeeing!*"

-(They say that if you love something, set it free, and if it comes back, then it loves you too, was meant to be.) The little girl who loved her balloons so much that she set them free, wanted to see where they were so eager to go. So she unclenched her clutch, and silently their big colorful heads climbed into the sky and were carried away by breezes and never returned to her again, to tell her where they wanted to go but up and away from her. "I guess balloons just don't love us back," she said to herself one afternoon twenty-five years later, watching a crying little girl's colorful clutch of balloons make a rapid rise into the blue-gray November sky.

A Modern Relationship

Amber and Tony had just finished eating—in fact, Tony had just placed his knife next to his fork, across the plate, indicating to the wait staff that the plate was safe for taking away, according to a custom he'd learned in an eighth-grade Home-Ec class—when Amber placed a cigarette between her lips, fished around in her purse, pulled out a lighter, deftly struck the lighter's head—producing a flame—and lit the cigarette. She breathed it in deeply with a look that bordered on a smile of almost dopey contentment.

"What is this, a joke?" Tony said, pulling the burning cigarette from her fingers and putting it out in his mashed potatoes. "Do you know how unhealthy that is for the baby?"

"It's *my* baby," she said. "I'll do what I want with it, and right now, Mama needs a smoke, okay, *Dad?*"

"*No!*" he said, with unintended volume. He looked around—no one had noticed or cared—and, as a way of compensating for his previous loudness, continued in a voice lower than normal, "It's not okay, Amber. As the father, I won't have you giving our child any more birth-defects because Mama doesn't have any willpower."

"Oh, yeah, and you're just Mr. Discipline, aren't you? If I'm the only weak one here, how'd you get me pregnant? I don't see any ring on my finger," she said and pointed to a naked finger on her left hand. "Hello, pot, the kettle thinks you—"

"That's what I'm saying!" Tony said, again uncharacteristically loud, and again he continued quieter than before. "I'm a fucking mess. And so are you. We don't need to make that kid's life any worse than it's already going to be."

It wasn't the words, it was the way he said them—it must have been—that turned her on, because all of a sudden in the middle of his sentence, she was really turned on, so much so that she started to blush. She turned away. Tony misread this as her reaction to his being overly mean—hurting her—so he backpedaled.

"I'm sorry, Amber," he said. "It's just that this whole thing's got me so worried—"

She stopped listening right then because all of her horniness vanished the moment he apologized. She was angry again, and she wanted a cigarette. Needed one. *This fucking kid*, she thought, with disgust, as her mind's eye lingered on the bump below her blouse.

"—would happen to us," he said, finishing his backpedal with the soft dying-away of his voice. *He sure is one charming son of a bitch*, she thought angrily.

"It's not your baby," she said.

"It's—What?"

"It's mine."

Tony wasn't sure how to respond to that, so he didn't. He took a drink and looked with a mild contempt at this *child* in front of him. He loved her? He couldn't say. Sometimes he did, really. Sometimes, like now, it was hard for him to do anything but eye her, like he did, with loathing. He loved her despite who she was, and the whole confusing shitheap of their coupling left him unbalanced. He took another drink. It warmed his body, but his thoughts were a bucket of washwater. What could he tell her? She pressed on.

"It's *in* my body, so it's *my* baby," she said defiantly. "It might be *ours* when it's born, but it's *mine* while it's not, *okay?*"

At this point, the waiter came over and cleared Tony's plate while Amber was still playing with her salad greens. As the waiter turned and walked away with the plate, Tony called after him, "Check, when you get a chance." The waiter nodded his understanding.

"Just please, for me, or for yourself, or for our baby, please don't smoke right now. You've got the rest of your life to smoke—"

"Your mom smoked," she said, interrupting.

"Yes, bu—"

"So did mine, what of it? We're fine."

"Amber—We're not fine."

"You might not be fine, but I'm fine. I'm better than fine."

She meant this. Suddenly, she found herself gleaming with glee, feeling better than she ever had at any point that day. Defiant, even. "Maybe smoking helps the baby, you ever think of that, doctor? Maybe it builds up immunities. You don't know."

"You're breathing burnt carbon into your lungs—carbon loaded with *shit*—so you tell me how that's any good for the baby, doctor."

She didn't listen to him. Her fingers were numb, but she was kind of excited about it. *Numby numby*, she kept thinking to herself and giggling. She giggled aloud but then covered her mouth immediately with her hands—sarcastic fear.

Across the restaurant, Tony saw a man sitting alone, in a dark blue suit, reading a newspaper in a booth. The man was probably about twenty years older than Tony. The man had no date, no friend, no ring on his finger. He had a fine head of hair, but almost everything else about him was shabby. His suit needed to be cleaned and pressed, but he was distinctly not homeless. His skin was more gray than peach. What Tony noticed most, though, were the man's eyes. They were so dark brown as to be almost black, and the way they stalked across the paper reminded Tony of the look he'd seen in a tiger's eyes when he and Amber went to the zoo a few years ago. He remembered how impressed he'd been by the intensity he'd seen. He saw that same intensity within the eyes of this average-looking man who sat alone in a sit-down restaurant reading a newspaper. But why?

"Look at that guy over there," Tony said.

Distracted from her *numby*ness, and therefore immediately forgetting it, Amber turned quickly in the direction of Tony's gaze. "Which one, the old man with the big ears?"

"No," Tony said. "To that guy's left. Guy alone, reading the paper."

"Oh, *him*," Amber said. "He's boring. I'm bored just looking at him."

"Look at his eyes."

"Yeah, what about 'em?"

"Aren't they intense?"

There was a moment when she really squinted and tried to give it all her concentration.

"He's just some boring guy," Amber said, turning back, "with boring eyes. What do you care?"

"He reminds me of something."

"Of something? What *thing* does he remind you of?"

The waiter came by and dropped off their check, thanking them.

"Hey, wait!" Amber called to the waiter. "That man over there—I think my boyfriend wants his phone number."

The waiter looked at Tony, who gave the waiter a please-forgive-my-crazy-pregnant-and-obviously-hormone-addled girlfriend shrug.

The waiter, smirking, walked away.

"Well?!" Amber asked dramatically.

"He kind of reminds me of that tiger we saw at the zoo a few years ago—same look in his eyes. It's weird."

"We never went to the zoo."

"Sure, we did—a few years ago."

"No, we didn't, asshole."

To prove his point, Tony dug into the banks of his memory and pulled up his trip to the zoo. They had seen the tiger, and he had made a joke about—

He had taken his last girlfriend, Katie, to the zoo. He'd never gone with Amber.

Tony swilled the last remnants of his drink and ran his fingers through his hair.

Just Be Happy We're Not The McGuffins Across The Street

THE YOUNGEST member of the family—fourteen-year-old Michael—took a bite of his dinner, chewed, grimaced, and grunted a sound like *blechk*. "Christ, Mom, what is this crap—boiled skunk penis?"

"It's a hamburger, Michael," his mom, Dorothy, said.

"You wish it was a penis, fag," Michael's eighteen-year-old brother, Donald, added. "Just eat it. The stoned teenagers at Valu-Burger slaved over a microwave for several moments to bring you this fine meal."

"You wish I wish it was a penis, shitneck," Michael said. "Then maybe your ugly girlfriend wouldn't keep putting her hand down my pants and asking me what a *real man* is like."

"You guys are so gross," sixteen-year-old Kristen said.

"Honestly, boys," Dorothy said, "can't we have one meal where someone's hand doesn't go down someone's pants?"

"You said 'go down,'" Michael said and started laughing. "You slut."

"Don't call your mom a slut, Mike," Donald said, "or I'll tell Dad and he'll turn your face to paste when he gets back."

"You wish I had paste—"

"Mom, where is Dad, anyway?" Kristen asked.

"Probably eating a gorilla's baby," Michael said.

"What?" Donald asked his brother, truly confused.

"Your father is LARPing this weekend with Cousin Dale," Dorothy said. "Somewhere in that forest outside Bovary."

"LARPing?" Kristen asked, more confused than Donald. "Is that what they—"

"Live-Action Role Playing, genius," Michael said. "That crap's gayer than a vampire."

"For the last time, vampires are *not* gay!" Kristen insisted.

"Oh, no? All those vampires have all these women hot

to trot, but instead of fucking them, those fags kill the horny women by sucking blood from their necks. They want to kill all the females in the world, and why? Because they're gay."

"Why are Dad and Cousin Dale LARPing?" Donald asked. "I thought Dad gave that up."

"Your father is a Kellpannian Warlock," Dorothy said. "The most powerful in the county, in fact."

"But didn't his character, Krankel the Wolfchucker, die last year in the battle between the Army of Nevin and the Praxis Warrior Division?" Donald asked.

Kristen and Michael both turned red with embarrassment from this revelation.

"Very good memory, Donald," Dorothy said, ignoring Donald's heavy sarcasm. "He did die, yes, but as you may know it is only in death that a warlock truly achieves the full spectrum of his magical abilities."

"But—" Donald said but was interrupted by Michael.

"I think Nicole threw Dale out of the house again, is probably why."

"Where did you hear that?" Dorothy asked.

"Kristen told me," Michael said, and Dorothy turned her attention to Kristen with an upturned eyebrow.

Kristen shot Michael a dirty look and then turned to her mom and said, "Cousin Albert said he heard from Uncle Richie that Aunt Judy heard Nicole caught Cousin Dale training to be a Yantrek Sea-Knight."

"A Yantrek Sea-Knight? But he's been a Treylian Fire Goblin since he was a kid!" Dorothy said, shocked.

"I know!" Kristen said. "Pissed Nicole off something fierce, too."

"This is all so dumb I want to kill myself," Donald said.

"Go ahead!" Michael said and turned to his mom. "Seriously, I call Don's room if he kills himself."

"You'd like that, wouldn't you?" Donald asked.

"Hell yeah! Room over the garage out back? That's the best! And bring that rat-faced girlfriend of yours with you, too," Michael said. "I don't want her sneaking into my room again and giving me nightmares."

"You shouldn't make suicide jokes like that, Donald," Dorothy said.

"I don't think he's joking, Mom," Michael said. "Have you met his girlfriend yet? She looks like a hairy oven. Don's a huge loser, and he should kill himself. We learned about that in science class last year; it's called Evolution."

"You know we don't believe in evolution in this household, Michael," Dorothy said.

"Well what *do* we believe in?" Michael asked.

"We don't believe in killing ourselves, that's for sure, so pop that nasty thought right out of your head, Donald," Dorothy said to Donald and turned to Michael. "And Michael, you know this family believes in the elongation of suffering as a pain payment to the gods of battle. Is there something wrong with that?"

"Actually—"

"Mom," Kristen interrupted. "Why can't we just be a normal family?"

"There's no such thing as a normal family," Donald said. "Just be happy we're not the McGuffins across the street."

"Why?"

"They're Catholic."

Everyone at the table shuddered.

Cavemare

DARK GRAY clouds swirled above, no blue anywhere. The nauseous sky churned, cold, sweated—drizzled, rained, and sometimes shivered with a thunderous, frozen downpour. Giant atmospheres of biting air lay still and then howled and roared and swept across the plain and nearly froze the thin layer of accumulated water that coated the trees, the grass, the gray exposed rocks, the shrubs, and his arms, legs, face.

The coats of rain mixed with the film of dirt on his skin and ran over a frozen brown mask of mud on his face, and he continued moving forward. The tracks of water trickled into the sundry animal fur he wore around his chest and waist and lap. He crouched low in the tall grass, so as not to be seen by anything that might want to see him. His family-group was gone; he didn't know when or where he had lost them, but he wandered in any favorable direction, in search of them while the icy thunderstorm abated and merely drizzled, while the surging winds whipped around and skirled over the sides of the mountains that ringed the canyon.

As he inhaled, the heavy mucus in his lungs forced out a painful, wet, hacking cough, which triggered a continuous fit of coughing. He hunched low in the tall grass and tried to muffle the sound. A pool of green and yellow phlegm and the white bubbles of spittle collected under his face—a face brown with mud and red from breathless exertion. When the coughing stopped, he remained low and tucked to the ground. He heard movement in the grass around him. He listened to the sound of four paws quietly padding through the field, not far away at all, and he briefly shuddered with fear when he heard the heavy, gravelly grunt from what was unmistakably an adult male saber-tooth. He heard it sniffing around. It must have had his trail. He could sense that it was there for him, that it had followed him here.

He had to find shelter, and in this search he found a beaten down path in the grass, which he followed in the direction of the far side of the canyon, where the sky was just a bit lighter, where maybe the storms were finally dissolving. A strong gust of wind sent spears of grass slapping into his face and arms. Some of the spears stuck to his skin, and they pulled at him as he moved forward. He couldn't hear the tiger anymore, and that only made him more anxious to find shelter—we are at our quietest in the moments before we attack.

He scurried forward, attempting a matched soundlessness. He could feel the rattle in his chest, and in his desperate surge forward along the narrow path he began to wheeze. Again he heard the gravelly sound of the saber-tooth, and he redoubled his already breathless pace.

Until he came upon a wall.

A wall?

How had he not seen this wall before? He'd kept his head down, yes, and his eyes, too. Still, he would have seen the wall on his way down into the canyon. Standing a foot taller than himself—made of stacked boulders an armful each—it continued in both directions in a wide angle, a big circle curving away. He was outside of the circle, and behind him he could hear the massive tiger's body pushing through the tall grass. For a moment, though still scared, he was relieved. If it grunted, maybe it was moving along . . . but then he could hear the sounds picking up pace, coming in his direction. Another horrible, gravelly rumble, and then a piercing roar. Intended, with such frightening volume, to paralyze the prey with fear, it had the opposite effect on him. He leapt and scrambled over the wall and fell to the ground and winced when the beast smashed against the wall of rocks, dislodging a few of stones from the ancient structure—the stones thudded heavily on the ground, and presumably on the tiger. He heard a wild howl of animalistic pain and rage from the other side, and then he heard nothing.

Panting, again he fell into a rasping coughing fit, and he spent several minutes in its grasp, with his eyes squeezed shut from exertion and anguish. Another pool of mucus and spittle, this time unseen. Suddenly, he found himself exhausted. Tired. He was already lying on his side, facing the wall, with his eyes still closed, wheezing and coughing. Though the flecks of rain still tapped loudly on all around, he seemed inured to them, probably because the wind blasted against the other side of the wall, and this side was heavenly calm in comparison.

He awoke facing the wall—a puddle of mucus at his cheek—and he rolled onto his pained back. Immediately his throat closed and he coughed in painful waves for several minutes. He ended up on his hands and knees, coughing straight down so the phlegm could drain out, and afterwards he fell back to sitting on his feet, and he started to look around dizzily.

Huts.

He had seen huts before. He and his family-group, they had avoided them. They had circled around.

They did stay in a hut once, many bright moons ago. They were caught in a snowstorm, and there was no shelter anywhere, and their snow cave kept collapsing on them, so they decided they had to investigate it—that they would die if they did not. They would rush in and kill whatever was inside.

They approached silently and then stormed in, howling and belligerent, but the hut was empty.

They left early the next morning, having never seen the beings who'd erected it.

Now he saw many huts. The grass was all gone. Brown ground. Not even any rocks. Fine brown. Dark brown. It was more than agreeable to his feet. He liked it.

It had stopped raining. The sky was still gray, but it was that post-sunset gray, not storm-gray.

He needed to look around.

At this time of year, night came very quickly, so with

what energy he had left, he shuffled over to the nearest hut. Still, he heard nothing but distant wind.

The hut, like the wall, was about a foot taller than he. It was made of a very dark brown wood, darker even than the fine rich dirt on the ground. It too was circular, and besides the door facing him, there were no other entrances or exits or portals. He circled it once, trying to find some hidden danger, looking for someone or anything else that might be in the hut or in this place.

It was already getting much darker out, so he went inside.

A few trickles of muted light flowed in through the imperfect edges of the planks that made the wall. The hut was twice his height across, and he could recline pretty much wherever he wanted because there was nothing else in the hut besides a few hand-sized stones strewn about. Other than that, it was just more fine dirt and darkness.

He sought out the darkest corner and fell into it. Nearly choking on mucus and coughing with excruciating exertion, he was soon again on his side, again oddly unafraid about his situation—just tired and relieved to be out of that days-long ice storm. As he fell asleep, he could swear he heard rats or mice, and he was strangely comforted by their squeaks. He slept to the sound of them.

He heard them as he felt himself coming out of sleep.

As he got further from sleep and closer to wakefulness, the squeaks kept getting louder. Considerably louder. They began to take on a slightly different pitch and effect. Louder and ghastlier, it became more apparent: it was not a squeak; it was a woman screaming. He opened his eyes, and there was a small fire in the center of the room, not made of wood but rather it was a few of the hand-sized stones, and they were burning with a furious heat and throwing an orange glow on the face of a kneeling young woman with skin much more colorless than his own. She was crying and screaming. He leapt to his feet and looked around for danger, but then he saw the blood running out of the fur by her lap, and then he saw the dead child, the size of a normal baby, cradled to her chest. The girl looked at the child and cried and screamed and began vomiting a horrible black chunky liquid. His heart beat on the walls of his chest. He tried to run out, but there was no door anymore. He was fully encircled by the dark walls of the hut. As he turned in circles, the female finally noticed his presence, and she let out another terrible wail.

She ran at him and with her open hand she pounded on his chest and face. She kicked his leg from under him and he fell to the ground and she leapt on top of him, and senselessly she started screaming at him so ecstatically that she started vomiting on him, and he positioned himself with his back pressed against the wall and he put his foot square into her chest while she was on top of him, and the force of his kick sent her back tumbling through the air, and she landed face-down in the volcanic rock-fire, where she briefly flailed in agony but then fell silent and disgustingly dead.

He felt a draft of cool air, and while the hut filled with the smoke from the woman's charring head, he turned around and saw the doorway behind him, where his back had been pressed moments before. The smoke and smell were unbearable, and he rushed out.

On emerging into the night, there was a massive pop of light, and everything he saw went backwards: all darkness was light; all light was darkness—the negative. He swatted at his face and rubbed his eyes, but when he opened them he still saw the unnatural colors. His hands, he noticed, were themselves white and fiery orange. He closed his eyes, but it was nothing but whiteness, and it made his head hurt terribly.

A full sprint away, another disturbing cry tore into the air, and it was followed by others all around him. Confused and frightened by the wretched orchestra, he allowed the swiftness of his feet to carry him in the direction of the quietest place nearby. As he headed so, he briefly looked into some of the huts he passed. He could see, in the reverse colors of the night, men cutting off other men's legs by hammering down on them with sharpened rocks; women and children being raped by gangs of bloody attackers; a man being whipped to death, his skin and muscles hanging off his bones like torn cloth; an already-dead-man's body being bludgeoned further by a drunken soldier . . . .

But he had made it past the huts, breathing heavily—his cough gone. He was now in an empty field. The people in the huts were still screaming and wailing, but here the open felt safe.

Almost immediately after that feeling of safety formed, the open started closing around him, and all comfort disappeared. In a far distance, he could see a huge group of warriors moving towards him. He turned in the other direction—another group. Every direction brought a similar group, all rapidly advancing towards him, themselves screaming and carrying spears and clubs, and some carrying nothing but muscle and bone and violence. There were no openings. There was no escape. The orange and white and red and yellow warriors surged at him and closed on him, and then they were all around him, gouging their spears into him and screaming and attacking.

The first spear to enter his body came in through the rib cage just under his right arm. He could feel the sharpened wood tip break the bones and push into and hemorrhage the organs beneath. He let out his own awful cry, and another spear entered his leg, and he fell to the ground. And he was at the bottom of it—a human chamber of dolorous attack. Spears stabbed horribly into his stomach. His legs and arms were bludgeoned with heavy clubs. He could feel each injury individually, but he would not die. Each attack was as painful as the first, but he was no closer to unconsciousness than he was back when he felt safe, only minutes ago.

He closed his eyes tight, and the horrible white static of his closed eyes tore into his brain, and he felt relief in the pain that blotted everything else, and he moved, in his head, into that light, and the pain was so much worse. The pressure in his head was palpable. It squeezed him down, down, into the depths of who he was, and in those depths, he saw his group, huddled against a mountainside, hugging close together, slowly dying of exposure in the freezing storm outside. They shivered and clung together, and one by one he saw them stop shivering and dislodge from each other and fall lifeless.

There was another pop of light, and the colors switched again. And another pop and another switch. With each blink of his eyes, the world underwent phantasmagorical changes. The groups were on him now, chewing into his body, their teeth clacking on and crunching into his bones, but he would not die.

He heard, above the orgiastic din of the cannibalistic feast of the spirits, the piercing cry of a bird of prey, and immediately the warriors attacking him fled away with surreal quickness—whole fields of land crossed in single strides.

The bird was above him and circling. He did not see if it could see him, but he knew it knew he was there. Paralyzed with fear, supine, he felt the air move from the flap of the bird's tree-sized wings. He could not scream. His throat was pinched shut in the helpless choke of absolute terror.

The bird dove, and its claws dug into his stomach and wrapped around his body, and he was jerked into the air. High into the air. The beast was almost soundless as it flapped and coasted up higher and higher. He could see the full circle below him, the wall and all within it, lit up a glowing orange by the furious heat of hand-sized-stone fires. He could see fields of huts filled with anguish and open fields covered with blood-soaked warriors, and he turned his head to the sky, just past the pointed tip of the beak, and he could see a field of stars from long ago when he was still with his parents, when he stared at those stars all night and guessed at what they were.

The bird arched over and swooped down, and they glided down to the ground just by the wall, between a circle of empty, glowing huts, and the bird reared back and buried its beak into his chest, and he cried out in anguish as it pulled his insides out. A talon—pierced through his upper thigh—burned in pain each time the bird leaned forward to tear out more flesh and organs, which sang in agony as they were ripped from him, an agony which was continual, because his insides would regenerate, and the bird would feast on his body again and again.

It lasted what felt like lifetimes. Eventually, as always, however, the eastern horizon yielded to the gray and blue of dawn, and then the pink, and the first glint of raw light from our provider, and the bird flew straight into the air higher and higher until it was so small it disappeared.

Then there was nothing but the sound of distant wind.

He awoke in the circle of huts, and the first thing he saw when he opened his eyes was a wall about a foot taller than himself, made of armful-big boulders. He fled to it and climbed and sat on top. In the field within the circle, to his left, he saw brown huts and brown ground that stretched on and on. In the field outside the circle, to his right, the storm was far away, and the golden sunlight blanketed a snowy-white mountainside. Halfway between himself and the mountain, in the wild, floral field, he saw long spears of grass being flattened by the leisurely stroll of something massively passing through.

Five True-ish Stories—
For Better Or Worse

1.

NAUSEOUS, MARK Horn sat in his turned-off car on the side of a New Mexico freeway and gazed into the flashing blue-and-red lights in his rearview mirror. It was just like a year ago, when he got his first DUI—a completely fucked occurrence that ended up costing him a little over ten-thousand dollars in court fees and fifteen goddam Saturdays of community service, ladling bowls of watery soup and dogshit chili into tiny bowls for the scuzzy New Mexico homeless.

Mark knew he wasn't exactly sober when he found himself giggling as he got pulled over. Definitely not good. Nevertheless, he wasn't drunk. He knew because he could feel it when he tugged on one of the hairs on his arm. It was an old Horn trick—you know you're drunk when you can yank on your arm hairs and not feel it. It always worked for all Horn men. But he didn't think the officer would accept that as an acceptable proof of sobriety, so his mind reeled. Between his every desperate thought *(How do I get out of this?)* was another desperate thought-reaction *(I'm going to jail!)*. Somewhere in this tornado of powerful pressure systems, he heard a loud knock at his window.

"Good evening, young man," the cop said. "Do you know why I pulled you over?"

"I was all over the road, wasn't I?" Mark asked. This caught the cop off guard, but he collected himself.

"Yes, indeed. Now I'm gonna need you to step out of the car—"

"I'm really sorry, officer," Mark said, "but it's just that I really—" (he looked around, even though nobody could possibly be near, and he lowered his voice to just above an urgent whisper) " . . . I really have to take a shit. I mean, like, bad. It's gonna be bad."

The officer, this time, was unfazed. "Please step out of the car, son."

And that's when Mark, without alerting the cop to the effort, flexed his stomach muscles and drove a log of shit into his underpants.

"It was totally worth it," he told his friends the next day, at the bar. "Ten-thousand-dollar shit, man."

2.

CORNELIUS LIKED Penelope, but Penelope wasn't sure if she liked Cornelius. She was drunk, and she wasn't really into him even though he was hitting on her again, so that wasn't good. She and her friends were leaving the party, and Cornelius asked Penelope where they were going. She drunkenly shouted back, *"Not to make out with you!"*

People all around, mostly strangers, laughed at Cornelius for being so shamelessly and drunkenly and somewhat wittily rejected. This kind of broke Cornelius's heart a little bit—we've already mentioned how he liked Penelope. He didn't have much confidence to begin with, so he walked home to his dorm. All glorious wind gone from his sails, he let the tide bring him back to where he started. On the way back, he kept hearing her shout about her not making out with him, and he could see the mockery in people's faces as they laughed at the unconfident guy who got shot down by the pretty girl from one of his classes, and he would alternate between shame and rage when he thought about how he didn't even have a comeback for such a lame line.

There were a few people left in the dorm, but it was the height of party night, so he made it to his room without having to explain himself or his tears. When he opened the door, he could see that directly across from him, by the window, in the small aquarium he shared with his roommate, that his fish— Suckface—was dead. Belly up, floating, and lifeless—its dead eye looking into Cornelius's bloodshot eyes.

The parallel was not lost on Cornelius, and he spent the rest of the night crying and thinking about finally just killing himself.

When he awoke the next morning, he led a one-man pity parade to the dining hall, where he ate his breakfast alone and did the crossword puzzle in the paper.

3.

TYRUS TRAPP dug his right cleat into the batter's box and leaned over on his left leg as he looked at his third-base coach for the sign. The sign was nonsense, which basically meant that the coach wanted Tyrus to swing away.

"That's a pretty fucked-up pair of cleats you got there," the catcher said to Tyrus as he pulled his left leg into the batter's box, tapped the top two corners of the plate with his bat, and settled into a balanced stance. "You, like, *weird* or something?"

The catcher was right on both counts; Tyrus's cleats were pretty fucked up, and he was weird. It had been a long spring and summer on those cheap shoes. Tyrus was the team's ace pitcher, and he played first base when he wasn't pitching. The beast-like effort he put into pitching, and the way he threw his feet around like they were pack animals when he pitched, played their part in fraying and splaying the shoes into their current, almost-ripped-apart condition. So too did the metal cleats from runners who angled their cleats' teeth into Tyrus's pathetically ripped fabric when he was playing first base. So too from the way Tyrus energetically dug his feet into the batter's box in all his at-bats.

But in that time, over the course of that cleat-destruction, he'd gone 12-1 as a pitcher (his lone loss coming during a game he forgot those cleats and had to wear a pair of oversized rubber cleats his parents bought at a local swap meet), batted .415 as a hitter, and played error-free ball at first base. Tyrus loved those cleats and wasn't embarrassed at all by them. Embarrassment never occurred to him like it did immediately to the catcher and the chuckling umpire.

So when Tyrus stepped up to the plate on that fiery-hot Saturday afternoon of the Great Lakes Legends Baseball Tournament, the catcher and laughing umpire had good reason to give Tyrus shit about his cleats. Plainly, everyone even in the farthest ends of the bleachers could see the red socks showing through the large holes in the toes of the black shoes.

The pitcher began his long windup.

Calmly, in Tyrus's Zen-like at-bat mindset, he replied to the shit-talking catcher, "Yeah, I know." The pitcher gathered himself at the top of his windup and began his delivery to the plate, and Tyrus added, "But they're lucky."

Tyrus swung the bat, connected, and drove the ball at least sixty feet over the left-field fence, and he jogged to first base with a grin he still wears sometimes to this day.

4.

APPROXIMATELY EIGHTY people dressed in a whimsically confounding array of costumes had drunkenly gathered at the Wendy's restaurant on Main Street, around midnight of the annual Halloween megaparty, and they were having a hell of a good time, but there was a warning on its way.

At the far table, beneath the corner-mounted television, Chewbacca-wearing-a-wedding-dress was appropriately/incoherently shouting at Willy Wonka while God's Gift To Women thoughtfully chewed a double cheeseburger and drooled on his wrapping paper. Across from them, a slutty nurse, a slutty demon, and a slutty bumblebee spooned Frosties into their inebriated gobs and babbled and cackled to each other in that slurred, incomprehensible language of theirs. A pirate was throwing ketchup packets at a passed-out Hunter S. Thompson while Thompson's girlfriend, dressed as a slutty homeless person, tried to wake him up. In the bathroom, Jesus was puking Jägermeister into a sink while Bob Dole took a dump.

Needless to say, Wendy's was hopping.

And then Ronald McDonald walked in. He looked around tremendously disappointed and shouted, "Don't eat this shit—it'll kill you!"

Everyone—*everyone*—cheered!

5.

PATRICIA PHYLLIS glanced down from her windshield to adjust the car's heater—she was still too cold. She thumbed the nodule all the way down to the reddest bar and brought her eyes back up to the road. She saw a rabbit standing on the curb about fifty yards down the street. Rabbits always made her nervous. Her first image of death from her childhood had been that of seeing the flattened, bloody remains of a rabbit that had been crushed by a car's tire. Ever since then, she could barely stomach the thought of them. "You just stay there," she said to herself, to the rabbit.

The rabbit didn't listen. It shot across the street, and in a panic, Patricia wrestled her steering wheel savagely to the right. The car's velocity and the force of her turn threw the car out of control. Patricia lost sight of the rabbit and oriented herself just in time to watch her car's hood slam into a tree. The airbag popped into her face, smearing her makeup, and a jet of steam hissed from the engine. "Shit!" she said (and this is a woman who never swore).

She clambered out of the car angrily and slammed the door shut. She looked for the rabbit, so she could shout at it, and then she found it—in the middle of the road, flattened and bloody, its back leg still twitching.

Buyer's Remorse: A Half-Assed Story About Stoners

"He's never early, he's always late:
First thing you learn is that you always gotta wait."
—Lou Reed, "I'm Waiting for the Man"

ONCE-A-FUCKING-GAIN, CALVIN was waiting for his weed dealer. If there's anything or anyone on Earth more unreliable than a drug dealer—any more convincing argument for the unsettling unpredictability of physical reality at the very smallest levels, which you'd swear could result in a perfectly benevolent dealer being in his living room one minute and then popping out of existence and appearing somewhere else in the universe the moment Calvin's knuckles rapped upon the dealer's door— Calvin had never seen it, and he probably couldn't.

Calvin's phone rang.

"Sorry, brah," Mr. Green Genes said. "Totally forgot you were coming. Had my yoga class tonight, man."

"It's cool, man," Calvin lied (the dealer's always right).

Calvin waited on Mr. Green Genes' front steps for the next twenty minutes. Then, fucking *finally*, Mr. Green Genes arrived.

"Come on in, brah. Sorry it's such a mess in here."

Inside: basic furniture, splayed clothes, various media, and general filth blended together and settled at the bottom of the room.

Calvin honestly didn't give a fuck; he barely knew this guy—a friend of a friend. (More accurately, a "friend" of a "friend.")

"So how's it been, man?" Mr. Green Genes inquired.

"Not too bad, man," Calvin said while he tried to think of

the quickest and best answer for killing the chitchat without provoking a deeper discussion. "Just been doing a lot of *math* at work."

A moment of thought. "Right, bro." Another moment. "That sucks, man."

Calvin laughed. "So yeah I just need some weed, you know what I'm saying? Too much math fucks my shit up. Gotta relax."

"Oh, dude, you don't gotta tell me about relaxation."

I'll bet not, Calvin thought to himself.

"So what do you need? The standard eight-track?"

"I was thinking about going top shelf this time," Calvin said. "You got anything good?"

"Brah, I got all sorts of crazy shit."

He rummaged through his supplies.

"You ever heard of Sour Jungle?" Mr. Green Genes asked.

Calvin laughed. "No, man."

"Smell this," Mr. Green Genes said holding an open jarette to Calvin's face. It smelled like fresh, really good weed—like all of the other weed Calvin had smelled since he moved to Venice two years ago.

"Wow, that's great, man," Calvin said.

"This stuff's a total body buzz. Shit'll leave you feeling like a stegosaurus, you know? Swinging your tail everywhere you look. It's bad rad! Eighty bucks. But I also got this stuff—"

He put the Sour Jungle down and picked up another jarette.

"This is some shit I just got from one of my buddies in Detroit. They call it Ted Nugget."

Calvin forced another fake laugh again. (*God, this shit is stupid*, he thought.) "Like the Motor City Madman, eh?"

Mr. Green Genes looked amazingly impressed by this. "Right on, man!"

"But I heard Ted Nugent doesn't even smoke weed."

"Yeah man, this is the weed he *doesn't smoke!*" Mr. Green Genes said and really went into a massive extended laugh.

When he collected himself, he continued: "Classic, brah. Anyway, this stuff's more of a head buzz, but a little later it turns into a body buzz, and then at the end it goes right back to the head."

In Calvin's experience, he got high, and then he got less high, and then he got hungry. It was always a holistic thing—head and body flying like carpets; it was never something that he could break down like a football game or election results.

"Sounds good, man," Calvin said. "What's that stuff in the red jar over there?"

Mr. Green Genes' face lit up like a fake Christmas tree on the day after Thanksgiving. "That's the hotness. You ever seen the movie *Pineapple Express*?"

"Yeah," Calvin said. "Of course, man. You have some Pineapple Express? I thought they made that shit up."

"They did, brah," Mr. Green Genes said. "But this is the shit it was *based on!*"

He unscrewed the lid, and the sweetest and greenest of smells—a giggle-inducing, *verdant* smell—floated out of the jar like fresh green roses blossoming in their noses. "This shit is like a combination of that P.O.W./M.I.A. shit I sold you last time and this stuff my buddy Martine used to sell called The Holy Moly Qu'ran."

Calvin held the jar in his hands and looked into its lovely open maw. Inside he saw a winter wonderland of frosted nuggets gleaming an alluring red from the lamplight hitting the tinted jar.

Mr. Green Genes smiled and commented, "It's The Poops."

"It's called The Poops?"

Mr. Green Genes laughed a big, one-breath laugh. "No, man. 'The Poops' is The Shit!"

Calvin smirked. "Indeed," he said. "So what do you call this one? Besides The Poops."

"That shit's The Manhattan Projects."

Calvin actually laughed for real.

"Good name," he said.

"Ninety," Mr. Green Genes said. "I also got some Rebel Yellow and some Arachnid Whirleybird for fifty each if you're also lookin' for something on a lower shelf. And I still have a little bit of Eskimo Daymare."

"Okay, well, I think I'll just have an eighter of The Manhattan Projects."

"Good choice, brah," Mr. Green Genes said. "Damn good choice."

Mr. Green Genes dropped single nugs into a mechanical scale and weighed out the three-point-five grams while Calvin pulled the money from his pocket.

Ah, shit, Calvin thought to himself. He only had twenties, and Mr. Green Genes, being the usual shitty dealer, rarely had change. But Calvin went ahead and asked anyway. "Hey, Mr. Green Genes, I only got twenties. You got a ten for change?"

Mr. Green Genes clicked the cap shut on the jarette, and Calvin could see him scanning his brain for the answer. "Oh, no, sorry, brah. No change today."

Calvin thought to himself, *You're a fucking drug dealer! You have like three responsibilities! One, have drugs for purchase. Two, be a-fucking-round. Three, have some fucking change for your customers, who all pay in cash!*

Mr. Green Genes failed on the last two counts, and he failed on those counts just about every time. It's just harder to find a good dealer than you'd think.

But see, I'm going to stop this story here. I've had my fun, but ultimately this is a story for the narrator, not the reader. The reader doesn't care about the griping nature of the narrator's problems with weed dealers. If Lou Reed had to wait for his man, then so— unfortunately—must I. Plus, and I meant to touch on this as the story progressed, but even as an avid weed smoker, I've never been too into movies and TV shows and writings about marijuana. It never translates.

I guess, and this is as recklessly-thrown-together a comparison as I've put into these pages so far, I think writing stories about weed is like an artist laboring over a painting of a canvas. But no, that's wrong. So reckless it ventured right into nonsense. At least with the story above I was able to paint a hasty-and-silly picture of the state of the weed-buying world here in our A.D. 2010 modernity, but even that story doesn't sate me much, which is probably why I've collapsed again into this meta-commentary.

To round the story out and be even more accurate with my slight satire, this fucker would end with some sort of delay—like Mr. Green Genes fielding a long phone call, with MGG uttering inscrutable, jejune, weed-dealer phrasings while Calvin inwardly peels off his own skin from the painful hope of trying to get out of there soon—followed by another delay as Mr. Green Genes decides to smoke with Calvin, thus delaying Calvin's leaving by at least another half-hour to forty-five minutes. Because, after all, you can't turn down a smoke-offering from your dealer, and you also can't smoke and run. You just have to deal with it. And wait.

Mr. President, tear down these laws!

Until then, here's a hasty-silly ending for the literary fuck of it.

"Well then can you pop a ten-buck nugget in there so we're even?" Calvin asked.

"Good call, brah," Mr. Green Genes said. "Here you go."

He popped another nugget into the packed jarette and handed it to Calvin, who handed the hundred bucks over.

"Okay, so I better—"

But before Calvin could make his escape, there was a knock at the door.

"Who the fuck is that?" Mr. Green Genes asked. "Calvin, check the door."

Calvin looked through the peephole, and it was someone who looked like Mr. Green Genes, but to the millionth degree.

His hair had never been combed, and his shirt was on backwards. His beard had actual twigs coming out of it.

"It's a guy who looks like a cross between a homeless person and a tree," Calvin said.

"My dealer! Let him in!"

Calvin opened the door, and Johnny Applebong walked through the door.

"Sup, Mr. Green Genes," Johnny said.

"Sup, Johnny," Mr. Green Genes said. "Meet my brah Calvin."

"You cool, Calvin?" Johnny asked.

"He's cooler than Walt Disney's head," Mr. Green Genes said.

"Sure, I'm kinda cool," Calvin said.

Mr. Green Genes motioned for Johnny and Calvin to sit down. Johnny shrugged over to the couch and slumped down. Calvin hesitated for a moment and did the same.

"So what do you got for me? By the way, I called you like *four weeks* ago," Mr. Green Genes said.

"Sorry, brah, forgot I had a yoga class," Johnny said. "Anyway, I got all sorts of stuff for you this time.

"Ukulele Jazz Strike.

"Afghani Rainsplosion.

"Glory Holy Shit Kebabs.

"Elephant Foot Kush Boogie.

"Hooked On Phonics, Nigga.

"And Two Women Rubbing Their Clits Together."

"Fuck yeah," Mr. Green Genes said. "I'll take an ounce of Jazz Strike, Kush Boogie, Phonics, and Clit Rub."

"Okay," Johnny Applebong said and unslung his ratty backpack.

He opened four Ziploc bags and labeled them.

Then he pulled out a huge bag of weed and, from the same big bag, fed an ounce into each of the labeled Ziplocs.

"People are really picky about the names of their shit," Mr. Green Genes said.

"Totally," Calvin said and fished his phone out of his pocket, faking like he was receiving a call, standing, to leave, to get the hell away from there.

"Hello?"

The White Dog Of Light

"God is not a second-rate novelist."
—Richard Price

I WAS MAKING $33,000/year doing copy-and-functionality quality control for a multimedia firm in Santa Monica CA, but I had moved to Los Angeles on the wings of an aspiration to get paid to write jokes and stories, and consequently I was steadily proofreading and quality-controlling downwards into a life-threatening depression.

The world's economy hit a wall in A.D. 2008, and one by one, over the course of that year and the following, my peers at work were let go, and I, The Mouse (my childhood nickname amongst my brothers and their cruel friends), could see that it was time to find a new ship to gnaw on.

I was what in the hobo vernacular is referred to as a "barnacle"—fully clinging, not going anywhere on my own.

Although I had abandoned all organized religions, I started praying for direction and hope—that's how despairing I'd become. One rosary per day for fifty-four straight days. They call it a novena. I come from Catholic stock, and although I have very little respect for the bear's share of that organization's pathetic philosophy, I have yet to unyoke whatever faith I still have in the when-you-have-no-fucking-idea-what-else-to-do aspects of earnest, honest, truly desperate prayer.

And wouldn't you know it, near the end of the novena, I got a new job! . . . doing quality control for the websites ("Web sites," at the time) of a health-and-fitness firm in Santa Monica that paid me the healthy sum of $51,500/year.

In addition to the possible benefit of a divine reply to my E-H-T-D prayers, I got the job, or at least the interview, by including on my résumé, under a section called "Awards and

Accomplishments," the fact that I was "*TIME* magazine's 2006 Person of the Year."

They looked it up, laughed, and called me to come in for the interview.

There is also the possibility that during the subsequent interview I pointed out a few mistakes in their Proofreading Test that they didn't even intend to be there. I never followed up on whether that was actually the case, however, because some theories are just too precious to investigate. The only arguments I concretely have on my side are that I got the job and they subsequently changed the test for new applicants.

Here's a snapshot of my life after I settled into my new, higher-paying job: a hard breeze (not quite a wind) is leaning against me as I'm pedaling my mountain bike down the ever-sunny streets of Santa Monica (it's a little too far to walk or longboard), and I'm heading to an office building where I am making a ridiculous amount of money to be a glorified proofreader . . . and I'm so depressed that I'm literally *bawling* as I'm pedaling, praying aloud for God to send a careening bus to just fucking kill me. Now. No grudges, just relief—so I wouldn't have to be responsible for the death I wanted so desperately.

I'm prone to depressions, but this was Something Else.

So I tried another novena, for more direction and hope. *("Dear God, WTF?")*

On the exact final night of the second novena, I swear on my life this is all true, my SoCal roommate of six years—my longtime friend Jordan, from my hometown—told me he had just suddenly quit his job and was moving back to Columbus OH, where he'd gone to college.

By that point, I had been through a traumatic (and unintentionally, darkly hilarious) "you're-fired/I-quit" moment at the job where I was *TIME* magazine's Person of the Year—an epic story in itself which I plan on writing separately, but long story short: it turned out I had been hired by a very successful, very poorly run cult—and I ended up collecting unemployment insurance while testing the job market and working on my novels and a screenplay like a real SoCal dickhole.

After the meltdown, the unemployment-insurance people said they would send the checks anywhere I lived, as long
as I was able to accept work there, so I decided to move back
to Cleveland—back into my parents' basement—so I could
stockpile the unemployment checks rent-free (I called it the
"double dip") while I tested the Cleveland job market.

I spent six months there, and I didn't find shit.

I thought maybe my wife was back in Cleveland. I hadn't
had any luck with the women of SoCal—who were always
looking over my shoulder for Someone Better—so I thought
maybe the point of the response to my novenas was to get me
back to Ohio so I could meet the woman I would marry. But in
those six months the only female I met who had what I considered any real substance was a fifteen-year-old high-school freshman named Shannon, so, clearly I was exactly wrong about
finding my wife back in Ohio.

So I drove back to California two weeks ago.

But on the drive in, on a real humdinger of a highway
they call "The Ten," (I-10 West) I began to feel myself fill with
an unanticipated dread.

*Do I really want to be here? Don't I fucking hate most of
these idiots? The fake-it-till-you-make-it crowd? Why the fuck did
I come back?*

I changed my plans. My original plan was to try to find
an apartment as soon as I got there, take the best of what was
available, and give SoCal one last eighteen-month shot at getting hired to write professionally.

If, at the end of those eighteen months—in December of
2012—if I didn't have anything going by then, then I would
know it was time to go back to college, get a PhD, and become
a broke, broken professor. Or maybe, if there weren't a cool
apocalypse to try to survive—if January 2013 rolled around,
and the Mayans were full of shit, and everything was just a
continuation of the same ongoing national and personal dé-
gringolade—I'd just call it a life, go somewhere where I could

wait for my parents to die, and then once they were dead I could take the silver train to somewhere better than this shit.

But I jammed on the brakes (metaphorically, as I was still on the freeway), and instead of doing that, I decided to try to surf couches in California for a month. If nothing of clear awesomeness developed in that time, I'd go to my friend Sean's wedding in Malibu in early July and then head back to Ohio or move to Denver—a city I visited on both legs of my double-dip trip, a place I had enjoyed particularly. (I once opined, "What Denver lacks in oxygen it makes up for in women I want to bang," and my friend joked back, "In Denver, you don't need the belt.")

It used to matter to me that I get a job writing jokes for TV or the movies; now, when I give it the full brunt of my consideration, I honestly don't care as much as I used to. Today's sitcoms and movies are all so terrible, and like so many things in this day and age the mechanism for greatness appears to be broken. A great idea no longer has a prayer. Unless, as was my greatest ambition in LA, you work at *South Park*, which I realized was the only show I wanted to work for, which was pretty astoundingly unlikely considering how hard I tried to get a job there to absolutely no avail or even response.

The sad part is that my possibly permanent departure from Southern California would, in a way, mean I completely failed—failed pathetically—at reaching my intended goal.

But if it were meant to happen, it would have happened, or I would have at least received an encouraging sign. I got a sign once, but I couldn't read it.

Either way, my change of plans resulted in my needing to find somewhere to stay while I surfed out the month before the wedding. Every day became a struggle to find a place to rest my head under a friendly roof in an unfriendly economic climate. I was part of the Homeless 2.0. A new mass movement resulting from whatever the hell the first decade of the 21st century ends up being called. (In Japan they once had what they called a "lost decade," and I think it's kind of funny that during what was arguably America's "lost decade" the biggest hit show on television was called *Lost*.)

I was freed from rent, a neo-hobo, and my clothes-loaded Jeep Cherokee became my hobo bindle.

Fortunately, my friend Ben had an open couch at his place, so I spent a few nights there in a ramshackle spot near my first apartment in LA, in a rough part of what Jordan and I still call "The Void"—an area of Los Angeles that includes the Marina Del Rey/Palms/Mar Vista/Culver City/Venice/Playa Del Rey area that nobody wants to claim, so they call it "Los Angeles" in official atlases.

Ben advised me where to park so as to lower the chances of someone stealing my automo-bindle overnight, and he also pointed out "where a dude got shot to death a few weeks ago."

Then I learned that another friendly roof had some room underneath—more distant from the bullet chorus—so I moved my life over to the Culver City apartment rented by my engaged friends Billy and Marie.

On a side-but-soon-to-be-related-note, I've often had curious qualms about some of the classic literature I've read from the present and the past, which seemed to so conveniently place a capably perceptive and able writer in the middle of intriguing events involving curious people—largely because it always felt unearned, like too peachy a coincidence.

With that in mind, it was at the tail end of a five-day stay with Billy, a friend from my hometown, and Marie, his fiancé, with whom I'd become well acquainted in my previous six years in California, and their new dog Peppermint, which's name was almost immediately changed to "Pippa" . . . it was then and with them that I found myself in the center of a comedy of errors which, as a writer who prefers to craft fiction, must have comprised a truly remarkable and memorable story if I, The Mouse, am here remembering it and telling it and gnawing on it.

And indeed I am.

May this true story stand as a testament to the fact that sometimes an interested writer just happens to end up in the middle of intriguing events involving unusual points in vibrant people's daily lives.

Billy and I have a nickname for where we grew up: Fight Town. In fact, I was talking with Billy one time at a bar in Venice, and he was fuming mad because he'd almost just gotten into a fight before I arrived, and as he calmed down, we were talking about fights. I'll never forget the gem of wisdom he revealed to me, which we both later agreed should be the motto on the Fight Town city crest.

"And Dan, I'm sure you remember what we all learned in our years of living in Fight Town." He looked at me abstractly, and then his face changed to a sort of axiomatic certainty, and he punctuated his point by shouting: 'STRIKE . . . FIRST!'"

I once asked someone I knew from a nearby high school, ten years after we both graduated, at a bar in my hometown, whether the people in his town got in as many fights every weekend as the people from Fight Town. I should clarify that this person went to our rival high school. The Rules Of Man would normally state that Wherever I'm From Is Sweet, And Wherever You're From Is Full Of Faggot Pussies. But:

"Dude, *no. Nobody* got in as many fights as you guys. You guys were *insane*."

(Literally ten minutes later, there was a fight at the bar.)

I once looked up my hometown on Wikipedia, and it said, amongst so many other boring things, that Fight Town has 0.0% water.

It has 0.0% of anything else, either, besides houses and lawns and angst.

There *is* water, though—in the sky. It rains and snows all the time. (Shitty Fact: Seattle gets more rain, but Cleveland gets more rainy days, which obviously is way more existressful.)

I once asked my friend and fellow Fight Town native

Chris—who is also Billy's friend—what he thought about all the fights in our neighborhood.

"Let me ask you to think about something," he replied. "Picture all the fights you saw in our hometown. How many *girls* were there at the party or in the bar when the fight happened?"

Chris is right; there is always at least a five-to-one ratio of guys to girls at house parties and in the bars. It becomes inevitable that someone will shoot a furtive glance at someone else's girlfriend, and then everyone's jaws get broken.

Despite growing up in Fight Town, I've never been in a fight. I learned how to sense impending violence, and I was always able to avoid it—particularly because I never really gave enough of a shit about anything to fight someone over it.

But that's not to say that I'm above the fighters; in fact, I bear some pretty horrid scars, but they're internal—my rage turns inward.

What I am saying is that Fight Town fucked with everyone I know who was from there.

We're a unique breed—survivors of some kind of unintentional social punishment: an unintentional punishment that has actually resulted in the violent suicides of several people I've known well, including one I loved as much as my demented soul can love.

Anyway, I'm not sure if my friend Billy was ever in a real clusterfuck of a fight in Mayfield. I do know for a fact, however, that someone once cracked him in the face with a crowbar out in California.

Billy was a Fight Town survivor. He survived the crowbar, too.

Out here, in Los Angeles, where I'm writing this story, he is a free spirit among free spirits. He's from Ohio, but he's more of what California seemingly represents than any Californian I've ever met. I love hanging out with him in a place where he truly belongs. Which is why I was so happy to spend some time with him and his awesome girlfriend-turned-fiancé Marie.

* * * * *

Billy and Marie, as I arrive again in their lives—on their perfectly comfortable couch—are just coming off the buzz of an intriguing trifecta of Life, Death, and Emotions.

In short, within a few weeks of one another, Marie's beloved and final grandparent passed away, Billy and Marie got engaged, and Billy and Marie adopted a rescue dog.

I've described Pippa as "The White Dog Of Light" because just as you can refract a beam of sunlight and see all the colors of the rainbow, so too could you refract this two-year-old mutt and find every shade of dog. She barks like a beagle, does the front-leg point, has spots like a Dalmatian and the heterochromia of a husky—she is every dog in one.

And evidently she is also the embodiment of the extent to which this life can sometimes grind even the cutest mutts to the literal marrow.

During my stay with my friends, I would often go on sunny walks with Pippa and Billy, and on the first of those walks Billy told me Pippa's backstory.

"The woman at the rescue shelter said that Pippa's from the streets of South Central, probably the product of two strays doin' it—"

"Doggystyle," I say and Billy laughs and Pippa looks at me.

"Anyway, when she's one year old, she gets pregnant."

"Ah, shit," I say.

"Yeah, but I mean it's not bad when you consider that in human years she was . . . seven."

"That's *fucked*," I say, feeling bad for The White Dog Of Light. Sarcastically I look back at Pippa and add, "You little slut!"

"Huge slut, dude," Billy says. "Disgusting."

Then he laughs ("HA!") and continues seriously. "But there's more. Eventually, she gets clipped by a car—fuckin' destroys her hip, needs surgery. They had to *fuse* the bones together because there was so much damage."

I watch Pippa walk as Billy takes us on his extremely brisk pace. Every few steps, it's clear that Pippa has learned to take a compensatory double-step, favoring the once-shattered leg. Again I feel bad for the dog. She, too, has scars like she's from Fight Town.

As we walk in the heat of the day, I feel that Pippa is lucky to have Billy and Marie as owners. I tell Billy as much, too. This dog won the rescue lottery.

I feel certain of that. (It's funny to think about it now, knowing what happens later.)

"But dude there's even more!" Billy continues emphatically. "While Pippa was getting the surgery on her hip, the woman who'd just adopted her *died mysteriously!* We still don't know what happened!"

"*What?*" I ask, literally incredulous.

"That's what the woman at the place told us, man," Billy says.

Pippa survived the streets of South Central, childhood pregnancy, getting hit by a car, and a mysterious owner-death before finally landing in the arms of Billy and Marie, who, like many serious couples Looking To Take The Next Step, ended up adopting a dog to indeed learn about and refine their abilities for caring and being responsible for another living being. In the middle of this, they also adopted an Uncle Dan.

This is kind of how things went when I settled into my temporary spot with them: for most of the week, I would wake up when Marie left for work (she works with autistic children at a specialty school), and I would begin my daily shit-ton of reading while waiting for zero replies to my transcontinental job inquiries. About an hour later, Billy would wake up, and we'd both do our work, occasionally remarking to each other when a conversational interlude felt appropriate. (Billy divides his day between two work-at-home part-time jobs in this crony- and banker-fucked economic shitshow.)

Meanwhile, Pippa would lie on her dog-mattress while we both worked, until it was time to go for a walk, around noon, at which point she would be bouncing up and down, tail awag, into and out of Billy's standing lap.

As we get ready for the walk, Billy tells me that he has a "whole, sick routine" he does every time he leaves the apartment—making sure everything is off and locked.

I used to do the same thing when I had an apartment, and I tell him that my old therapist told me that that's a form of obsessive-compulsive disorder. I thought that was interesting.

I'm not sure if Billy hears me because he doesn't say anything when he emerges from the apartment with the leash around his wrist, ushering the tail-wagging Pippa out the door. It doesn't matter to me, so I move on to the next subject, which isn't hard because we both just got really baked.

I'm one of the most empathetic people I know, and on our stoned walks—through streets laden with a word I call Culversity—I begin thinking about what the other pedestrians and motorists are thinking when they see me and Billy out walking Billy's dog in the middle of a workday:

"Oh, look at those two unemployed gay men with their cute dog."

I tell that to Billy, and we both laugh.

Pippa takes a skyscraper dump when we stop. It's a medium-sized mutt putting out St. Bernard shits.

The White Dog Of Light.

When we get back to the apartment, I say to Billy, "I was just thinking about Pippa's massive shits, and I wonder . . . Do you think maybe Marie feeds her when we're not looking?"

Billy doesn't respond for a few seconds, but when he does he just bursts out laughing.

"I just had to think about what you said, and that is unbelievable! We've already turned into those shitty people from reality TV shows! *Maybe Marie feeds her when we're not looking!*"

I am fucking dying with laughter. What an insane thing to say.

Don't do drugs, kids.

The hobo lifestyle has many advantages, but I quickly ran into one of the setbacks. I'm the type of person who just wants a solitary place to be miserable when I'm sick, and I could tell I had started to feel sick the night before. I was about to go through two days of misery and two weeks of clearing unsightly mucus from my lungs, and I had no place of my own to hole up in and get through it alone. I tend to get upper-respiratory infections frequently here in California. Probably because of the poor air quality and shit-tons of weed I smoke.

Anyway, I even mention it at all because there is a certain shift in our consciousness when we get sick. Everyday things seem a little . . . different. There is a shift in the way our bodies feel, and our minds and bodies are heavily intertwined, so there must also be a shift in our minds.

That might help you understand that not only were the bizarre things to come happening, but they were hitting me as I was not only superbaked but also while my mind was itching against influenza's crumbs under the covers.

Billy is a tremendously positive person.

He is a freethinker, and he's done a shit-ton of different kinds of drugs. He was Neal Cassady before he even read *On the Road*. And then afterwards he was Neal Cassady with rocket skates.

Always getting after it.

One time Billy tried to get my roommate and me to join him at a drum circle on Venice Beach by saying, "Dude, you guys should come up—there is going to be an *explosion*."

Jordan and I started cracking up because we knew that, to Billy, what that meant was that somehow everyone at the drum circle was going to experience something so phenomenally numinous and paradigm-shifting that people's consciousnesses were going to shoot out of the top of their heads like lasers, and all the lasers of everyone's consciousnesses were going to join in the sky and create an immense explosion of transcendent truth that would fill everyone's life with permanent meaning.

It's that kind of positivity.

There is both Romanticism and delusion within it, and what could be more human than Romanticism and delusion?

So when I say that Billy was being extremely positive on the night in question, understand that that kind of positivity is truly remarkable, and I felt lucky to be along for the ride.

A brief note about Pippa:

The White Dog Of Light certainly knows who rescued her. The love and devotion she shows to Billy and Marie are almost off-putting.

For instance, there have been a few times when Marie was at work and Billy has needed to leave the apartment for a little bit, and during those times, when it's just the two of us, Pippa presses her nose against the very last point that Billy left the apartment, and keeps her nose there, with her body draped across the doorway, for twenty minutes at a time, at which point she pads over, checks the other door, then the bedroom, and returns to the very last spot Billy was inside the house.

Occasionally, she'll eye me warily like, "Get the fuck out of here, you."

"Isn't she just a fantastic dog?" Billy asks exuberantly as I return from a walk in the sun—hoping some sunlight might boost my immune system. Billy is petting the dog vigorously.

"She's terrific," I say as I step into the apartment.

Billy is still going nuts on Pippa, who is loving every second of it.

"Awesome dog, good friend visiting—I feel great!" Billy says and bongo-drum/rib-slaps Pippa to finish the turbo-petting session.

As I get myself situated and ready for the shower, Billy goes into the bedroom, and Pippa follows him.

A few moments later, Billy emerges from the bedroom to

tell me, "Dude, Pippa just puked all over the floor."

"Huge puke, dude," Billy says. "Ridiculous."

I take a look, and indeed it's an unbelievably large pile of dog-vomit.

"I must have gotten her so riled up just now that she puked," Billy finally deduces.

The only thing I can do is laugh in my mystified mind's malaise.

After my shower, it's time to go to the bar. Billy has already downed a beer from the fridge and is frothing over with his transcendent vibrations, and he reminds me that we need to close everything up because the last time they left the dog alone, Marie had thought dogs liked smaller spaces, so they'd decided to lock Pippa in the bathroom, and after they were gone, Pippa went completely nuts on the frame of the closed bathroom door—trying, presumably, to be reunited with her beloved rescuers.

They decided that the next time they had to leave her alone in the apartment, they would close the bathroom and bedroom doors and give her the bigger space of the apartment to wander around while they were away, hoping she wouldn't just go nuts again.

So I leave Billy to his "sick routine" and guzzle the rest of some flu medicine and head outside, where Billy joins me after a few moments.

When we get to the bar, it turns out that they're not selling empanadas tonight, so my influenza-charged hunger must wait.

Billy has a few brews, and we talk about the terribly cunty bartender who barely gave me the time of nothing when I asked her for the empanada menu.

Fortunately, the shitty broad is shift-replaced by a boobie-jiggling piece of sex art with blonde pigtails. I openly lick her entire body with my eyes while we sit there.

Also while we're at the bar, Billy is telling me about more great things he's feeling and thinking. It's funny in a way because I'm not feeling well, but it's also funny because Billy is like a living cartoon character. It's usually inspiring for me to watch him go into one of his life-eruptions, but tonight there's something different about it. There's a weird, raw edge to the things he's saying.

Unfortunately, there are whole hours of conversations in my life that I'm simply too much of a stoner to ever recount with any accuracy or truthful grace.

Anyway, I'm actually starting to feel a little weird about it there at the bar, but again I attribute it to the general weird feeling of the soon-to-be flu.

After a few hours, we decide to walk back to the place to check on the dog and so I can order some Chinese delivery.

When we get back, the screen for the window of Billy and Marie's bedroom is lying in the bushes, and the window that is always partly open is completely shut.

"What the fuck?" both Billy and I ask simultaneously as we see the screen.

Billy's eyes dart back and forth frantically in thought as he hurries across the driveway and unlocks the bolt and watches Pippa sprint from the bedroom to the front door, looking up at him happily.

"What happened?" Billy asks the dog that's jumping into and out of his standing lap.

He goes into the bedroom and I hear him moan, "Oh, I left the door open."

From the evidence, we deduce that Billy must have left the bedroom door open, and Pippa had gone into the bedroom and tried to jump from the bed through the window, presumably to be reunited with her beloved rescuers. In my head, without telling Billy, I also deduce that Pippa must have succeeded in knocking the screen out, but the force of her jump must have dislodged the open, now-guillotine-like window, and sent it slamming down.

In a way, we're incredibly lucky the window didn't catch her neck and kill her.

Of course, this too I keep from saying out loud to Billy.

Once the mystery is solved, I get the number of a Chinese-food place that delivers. I call them and order sweet-and-sour chicken and an egg roll and give them Billy's address. The plan was that he and I were going to get super baked and I was going to absolutely crush the Chinese food. But then the Asian guy on the line says, "That be eighteen se'enty-fi'e."

I say, "Okay," and hang up. And then two seconds later it hits me: *eighteen seventy-five? What?!*

I confer with Billy, and he too agrees that that is an unacceptable price.

"You should cancel that order, dude," Billy says. And he's right.

I call them back and ask them to walk me through the math that makes an entree and an egg roll cost that much. He does, and I tell him, "Please cancel my order."

He says, "Okay," and we both hang up.

When I return to the living room, Billy is putting on his coat.

"Headed out again, man. Gonna go pick up some goodness."

"Sweet," I say because he was telling me about this earlier. We were going to go to his weed-connection's apartment—a dude with a serious amount of goodness.

As I pull on a sweatshirt, Billy says, "I gotta make sure all these doors are closed," and I hear him closing all the doors.

Then Billy gives Pippa a good, calming pet session, and I head out the door. But when he gets to the threshold, Billy tells me to hold on a second. I wait outside for a few minutes while he goes back inside, and then he emerges and leads the way, and we walk to the goodness-dude's nearby apartment.

It's strange to me how normal the dealer's apartment is, considering how much goodness is in the place. Billy and the guy know each other pretty well, but the guy's never met me before.

While Billy and the dude do their illicit thing, I talk to

the dude's girlfriend about how I'm part of the Homeless 2.0, and it really worked out for the both of us because she said she couldn't finish her food and gave it to me when I said that I hadn't eaten.

Suddenly Both Billy and I were getting what we needed.

So I'm munching away happily, and all is well, and then my phone rings.

To answer it, I step into the kitchen area, away from everyone. It's a California number I don't otherwise recognize, but I decide to answer it because I had reason to hope/believe a sexy Asian woman I used to work with might be calling while I was in town.

"Herro?" a female Asian voice says.

"Hello?" I say, kind of in shock. "Madoka?"

"You orda Chinee foo?" the female voice says.

Then it all clicks, and I realize that the dude on the phone never canceled the order.

"Ma'am, I *canceled* that order," I say testily because I did not want to take a ridiculously expensive Chinese-food charge on my hobo credit card.

"You no wan' foo'?" the woman asks.

"No, ma'am," I say. "I swear I canceled that ord—"

Suddenly, there is a man's deep voice on the phone.

"DUDE, YOUR DOG IS OUTSIDE!"

I literally pull the phone away from my ear and look at it in disbelief.

"What?"

"YOUR DOG IS OUTSIDE."

I recognize the voice as Billy's neighbor, whom I'd met earlier in the week.

"Okay," I say, so completely confused. "Can you . . . corral it?"

"GET OVER HERE."

He hangs up the delivery-woman's phone.

I put my phone in my pocket and say to Billy, who is hitting a huge bong on the couch, "Dude, your dog is outside. I think we have to go."

"*What?*" Billy asks just as incredulously as I did.

"That's what your neighbor just told me on the phone."

Billy looks at the dude with apologies all over his face. He stands up, hands me the bong, and says, "Take a big rip because we gotta go."

I do just that, and we both fill the room with hasty apologies and smoke.

(The next morning I was thinking about how much of a drug bust–looking thing that was for me to do: step away from the room, field a call, and return announcing, "Billy, your dog is outside.")

Anyway, we get out of there safely.

I've never seen Billy look the way he looked on the walk back to his apartment, with a hefty amount of pot in a nondescript bag in his hand. I tried several different conversation starters, but he just kept walking without saying anything, with that crazed look in his darting eyes.

When we get back, the window is closed, the neighbor is putting the screen back on the window again, and the front door is open. Marie is standing there with her friend Casey—both of them with their arms crossed as they look at us with disgust.

Pippa is running around their legs happily, tail wagging high and fast.

"What happened?!" Billy asks.

"You tell *us!*" Marie counters appropriately.

"We've been gone for like *ten minutes!*" Billy argues.

"Well in that time *our* dog got out of the apartment. And the *screen* is broken—"

"That was broken earlier, Marie," Billy says, which doesn't help, and I start laughing.

My laughter makes them realize they're arguing in front of people, so they go into the bedroom to discuss the night's events while I sit down at the kitchen table with Marie's friend Casey, whom I know from my previous six years here.

"Thank fucking FUCK you are here right now, Casey," I say as I sit down.

"Why?" she asks.

"Because I'm crashing here tonight, and if you weren't here I'd be the only one bearing the awkwardness of being here right now."

Casey seems inured to relationship dramatics.

"Yeah, well, Marie promised me a night of fun, so I'm not leaving," she says.

We smoke a bowl and talk about her job. She's in marketing, and after she endures a small rant about how I hate marketing, she tells me how I might try to market my novels. In fact, it sounds like she knows what she's talking about enough that I make it a point to get the name of her company just in case I ever decide to sign over to the marketing dark side.

As we reach this point in our conversation, Billy and Marie emerge from their bedroom with questions about the events of the night, which, to the extent I know them, have already been written here.

The war ends with a cease-fire wherein Marie and Casey are going up to the bar for a head-clearing drink while Billy and I watch the dog.

After a few minutes, Billy leaves me with the dog because he can't stand the thought of Marie being upset with him. As he's considering whether to leave, I ask him if he's clearheaded enough to argue his case because I'd seen enough disasters happen as a result of drunken logic. To reassure me as he leaves, Billy says, "Dude, by the time we're done talking, we're going to be so happy I'll be carrying her across the threshold of the apartment like we just got married."

So I laugh and he chases her down and they talk while I write down an outline of the night's events—I know enough to recognize that I am living the peachy part of the writer who happens to be in the middle of a bizarre swirl of events, and with my completely destroyed stoner-memory I know I have to write down some details or I'll forget them for sure.

While her owners are gone, Pippa presses her nose against the last point where Billy was in the room, and—probably sensing the drama in the air—makes soft crying sounds every few minutes while, scribbling, I try to reassure her from the couch that she's okay and that everything will be fine.

Ten minutes later, Billy returns as manic as ever, assuring me that everything is now strawberries and sunshine between himself and Marie. Pippa is doing backflips of happiness that one of her rescuers has returned, and my cough continues to get worse.

Billy makes a ridiculous amount of drunk-food while I read Billy's copy of Darwin's *Origin of Species*, until eventually, just as the food is ready, Marie and Casey return.

Casey and I have a seat and smoke a bowl and continue our conversation from earlier while Billy and Marie continue their whispered argument about the events of the night. Eventually, however, Casey's cab arrives. When her phone rings, to indicate that the cab is here, she says, "Ah, my cab's here— Thank God."

What, I'm such a terrible person to talk to?

Anyway, after Casey leaves, Billy offers to take Pippa out for her last walk of the night, before bed.

There is a writer named Richard Price who was once asked why he sometimes uses stories from real life in his works, and he explained, "Because God is not a second-rate novelist."

To that end, I offer this final image of the night:

Billy, who's already made two fundamental mistakes with the dog tonight, holds Pippa's leash as he throws open the screen door and walks out, but the screen door has a pretty quick kick-back, and consequently Marie and I hear the sound of a quick-kick-back screen door slapping against the hip of The White Dog Of Light, which consequently yelps softly.

"She got . . . under the door . . . I swear."

As Billy says this, Marie is looking at me with utter horror while I cannot laugh hard enough.

It is such a fitting end to the night that the first thought that pops into my head is that quotation by Richard Price.

Eventually, the night winds down. I ask Marie if she wants me to GTFO so they can have privacy for their argument, but she tells me I'm perfectly welcome to stay.

I cough a few times before I slam into sleep.

The next morning, when everyone's awake, Billy walks out of the bedroom, positions his arms like he's holding a dog by the sides of its body, and says to me, "Dude, I just held Pippa up by the window and said, *'No!'*"

My Ideal Man/Woman: A Case Study

MEN ALSO have a biological clock, kind of—when they're in certain circumstances, such as weather-choked suburbia.

My friend is a suburbanite from the outskirts of Cleveland, like myself, and, like myself, he is unmarried as of this writing. Also like myself, he's discovered a mild despair in the idea that all of his friends are now happily in their first marriages, while he has found no one to share his life with besides himself, who is a very old and intimate friend, indeed.

I've written about it elsewhere, but the fact remains that there are nearly always more men than women at the bars in our 'hood. Significantly more. To the point where there are usually huge fistfights at said bars—violent brawls involving at least a dozen men who have zero chance of taking a woman home that night through no fault of their own other than the fact that they live in a city where women, and specifically attractive women, don't go out much—are already married to douchebags or are dating hipster fuckfaces. Sure, there is usually a pack of pumas (aged cougars, past their first and second marriages and primes) to pick from, but they're the sort of women who are, frankly and literally, beer goggle–proof.

My friend and I have been emailing back and forth about this problem. In the process of our conversation, we've discussed the fact that we barely ever go out anymore because of how pointless it is. It brings up one of the major dilemmas of my life: I detest nearly everything about the suburbs of Cleveland, and yet this is where the majority of my friends and loved ones live. There are no better people in the country, probably because there is no worse place in America, in a way—it snows seven months of the year, and it's utterly flat, which means we don't get to snowboard or ski, but we do get to have our frozen cars careen off the road into an icy ditch. The long and short of it is that I wish I could leave, but my experiences with living in California taught me that it's important for me to have people around me whom I enjoy and love. I come from a city where fistfights are happening on an hourly basis, so how could I ever get along in a city containing upwards of ten million of the biggest passive-aggressive pussies in North America? And we (my Cleveland friend and I) realize we've run into a real shituation: we can't leave because we love the people here, but we can't stay because this place is an ongoing castration.

I decided to take one last tack: I would ask my friend to describe his ideal woman, because perhaps in that process we could discover where we might find such a person.

The following is the both-serious-and-joking reply my friend sent, which cracked me up, and which launched this current essay.

… Until then I will keep waiting for my doorbell to ring and have the perfect brunette standing there waiting for me to invite her in. She is about 5'4" or 5'5", 100 to 110 lbs. She has perfect fake tits, jeans that just barely cover her clit, and a thong that is just barely starting to creep up her perfectly shaven asshole. She has light eyes, either blue or green, her skin is smooth but not too dark, she has both German and Irish blood in her. Her name is Stacy, no, Megan. She has no guy friends, two girlfriends who don't live in Ohio, and her parents are dead. She has no brothers, one sister who is 2 years younger than she is. She is educated but not smarter than me, she has an odd obsession with cleanliness and giving me blow jobs randomly throughout the day. She loves sex to the point it sometimes scares me when I am alone. She laughs at everything I say and has good advice when I ask a question. She is Catholic so my mom will get off my back. She has no tattoos but thinks mine is the best one ever.

So, like I said, until then.....I wait.

I don't know why, but that description struck me as hilarious and profound. If you knew my friend, you could picture him hammering out this description, aware of and inured to his own insanity and late-stage immaturity, probably typing with his thumbs on a BlackBerry with a noose around his neck. He's a pretty classic dude in my small world.

I sent out an email, with this essay in mind, to a few of my friends whose minds I liked, who I thought could send back a reply as interesting as the first one I received.

The following are the responses that arrived (for which I guaranteed the senders' anonymity), in the order I received them.

The first reply, quite quickly and quite briefly, came from a married male in his early thirties:

This is perfect because I have to send you a Cronin [surname of a friend of ours] quote from this week:

"I don't care if my wife works . . . but her grandfather better have worked really hard."

I got a good laugh out of that, and I've repeated the line many times since.

So far, so good.

The second response, also quick and brief, came from a bachelor in his mid-thirties:

My ideal woman is a tube sock that has the ability to hug back!

Clearly, he didn't take the exercise seriously, which he readily admitted to in the more personal parts of the email, saying that it was a good idea and that he should do it, but as of this publication he has never submitted anything else. It's funny how little any of us has as an immediate response to this question, which means either we're stupid or the question is (more on this second possibility later).

The third reply—and probably my favorite—arrived a few hours later, from a married male in his mid-thirties:

Dan,

This seems like an article for GQ magazine. Thanks for helping me endure a boring-ass meeting. I feigned interest while surreptitiously jotting down some notes for this email for the last two hours.

The real woman/perfect mate: someone with whom you enjoy spending time possessing mutual physical attraction.

This woman should also demonstrate a realistic/normal degree of the following values/traits (in no particular order):

Humility
Loyalty
Respect (for self & others; possesses self-esteem)
Patience
Understanding
Loving
Honor
Responsibility
Compassion
Integrity/Honesty
Courage
Diligence

I am sure there are plenty more values/traits that we can add to the dirty dozen, but these were the ones that kept jumping into my mind during the aforementioned struggle-to-keep-my-eyes open meeting.

For me personally, the "someone with whom you enjoy spending time" part of my real woman definition equates to three components: intelligence, sense of humor, and civility. Without those three items, I typically don't enjoy being around someone. To each his own though. Additionally, I have seen quite a few marriages fall apart recently because of the "mutual physical attraction" component to my definition, or lack thereof over time.

Further, my preference for a real woman involves someone who does not define or characterize themselves by any one trait or accomplishment in life—basically, one-sided people who can only talk about/do one thing: raise children, train for and discuss marathons/workouts, constantly remind me they graduated from an Ivy League School, fail to refrain from mentioning they are a lawyer within the first two minutes of any conversation, etc.

The ideal woman is a figment of man's imagination. Yes, it's fun to dream and fantasize about the ideal woman, but like the Loch Ness Monster and Bigfoot, she simply does not exist. There are many women out there who will fit some of your wish-list requirements, but I doubt any one woman out there could possibly possess all of man's wish-list items:

Smoking hot, yet humble about it (possible)
Harvard Law School Graduate, yet humble about it (probably not possible)
Between 5'10" and 6'
Intelligent
Athletic
Can run at a 7-minute mile pace for at least 6x miles
Enjoys mountain biking, tennis, or some other outdoor physical activity (in addition to the occasional outdoor intimate activity)
Body morphs back to 22-year-old hotness after having babies
Cooks better and healthier than Martha Stewart
Can't say no to sex (unless someone other than her husband/mate asks)
Understands the concept of saving money; does not burn through your paycheck on frivolous junk
Is a great mom; raises fantastic children
Has a satisfying, fantastic career that brings in enough revenue to make it worthwhile
Reads books with reckless abandon and enjoys discussing them

Can drive a stick shift car
Can drink wine, beer, or do shots; can also have fun/be comfortable not drinking depending on the occasion
Has at least a moderate interest in sports
Has a fantastic sense of humor
Enjoys a clean, organized house
Enjoys traveling
Enjoys outdoor activities
Gets along well with your family
Enjoys hanging out with your friends
Remembers everything you forget but doesn't nag you about it
Buys you clothes so that you don't dress like a total douchebag
Forgives you for being less than ideal
Smiles and laughs a lot; enjoys life; positive person
Can handle life's hardships
Is there for you during life's hardships
Is somehow still there every time you come home

The problem with this list is that it is never ending. Feel free to add to the list, use, cut, delete, or modify as you see fit. I apologize for the overarching semi-serious tone of this reply. Although I greatly appreciate humor, I am not as gifted as a La Famiglia Donatelli.

Take care, Dan. Thanks again for making a 2+ hour meeting endurable. I had to exercise an extremely stable bearing to prevent from laughing out loud during the meeting though.

As the Editor-in-Chief of a publishing company, I will admit to you right now that I've already asked the man who submitted that reply to write a book for me to publish—not necessarily about that answer but rather about the stories he's accumulated in his life's work, which is quite interesting but which I can't get into without violating his anonymity. Needless to say, I was blown away by his response. It was as thorough as anything I could've expected, and it was funny, and it would be hard for anyone to argue with a single thing he wrote.

In fact, I'm pissed at him right now because of how smart he is.

Anyway, the next reply came from a bachelorette in her mid-thirties:

My ideal man is nice, intelligent, kind, considerate, attractive (or appealing enough that I want to sleep with him), doesn't fear commitment, is financially responsible, likes dogs, has a good sense of humor, doesn't check his iPhone or BlackBerry during a movie in a dark theater, likes to have fun but won't judge me when I just want to lay around and watch bad TV, doesn't snore and keep me up all night, isn't a morning person and/or will not force me to get up at 7am to hike on a Saturday or some nonsense, remembers birthdays and anniversaries, is up for dating someone his own age and is not automatically looking for a 25 year old, knows when to rein me in when I'm boring people or being obnoxious, and realizes housework & cooking is to be shared by all and is not solely a woman's domain.

What I think is realistic at 37: someone nice, who has a checking account, and knows how to boil water. (For the record, I can work with this.)

It breaks my heart that a woman as wonderful as the one who submitted this reply has had to take such a hedged approach to her ideal. But if here in the weather-worn suburbs my friend and I are already starting to hear a distant biological clock, I can only imagine how thunderous each tick and tock resounds for a thirty-seven-year-old woman, and perhaps that kind of noise sharpens the clarity and knocks off the superfluous.

Or are we starting to notice a pattern: those who are married, so far, have lots to say, and those who aren't, don't.

Immediately, however, that pattern is broken by a bachelor in his forties, whose reply comes in the form of a checklist:

* Sane! That is, not only by DSM (Diagnostic and Statistical Manual) standards, but my community standards;

* *Reasonably attractive - That is, all her original teeth (and, preferably, all her original limbs), original hair, but tits, if not too, too big, can be fake;*

* *Smart - She needn't be an MD or PhD, but at least a high school graduate and preferably a college graduate, but not one of those schools that have commercials on television during the afternoon where you can "Get a degree in JUST 2 weeks!";*

* *High sex drive - That is, I don't have to beg for sex, and, frankly, she is not apprehensive about initiating it. And, I don't have to negotiate for sex, meaning I don't have to take her on a $1,000 shopping spree at Lord & Taylors just to get laid;*

* *Employed - She has a job making, hopefully, at least over $50,000 per year, legally! Her work hours are manageable, meaning she doesn't drive an ice cream truck from 11a.m. to 10p.m. or work overnight as a security guard;*

* *Never been incarcerated, or, at least, has no felonies, particularly felonious assaults, burglaries, stalking, etc. You know, the usual stuff;*

* *Business-savvy - She understands it's NOT a fucking good idea to go shopping at the mall instead of helping to pay for the mortgage;*

* *Well-read - she appreciates reading newspapers, novels, and even academic literature and understands that "good reading" is not bullshit Harlequin Romance novels;*

* *Appreciates art - Art is NOT watching* The Hills *or* Jersey Shore, *it's going to the fucking museum!*

I think that's about it, but those are the primary things I look for in a woman. So, if there are any women who can't even read what you're compiling for your project, tell them to stay the hell away from me. lol

That was another great reply from another interesting dude. He seemed to know what he wanted, which, from the voice of his reply, suggests he's no stranger to doing some bangin'. What I really liked about this one is that I thought the previous long, list-heavy reply was seamless, but the next one had even more filling. Now how the hell can I write something that isn't a total ripoff of what's been said already?

I'll have to figure that out later, because shortly thereafter another reply comes, which further breaks up the aforementioned pattern, from a married male in his mid-thirties:

My ideal woman challenges me to be her ideal man. She holds me up to a high standard of excellence and refuses to let me doubt myself or degrade myself in any way. She lets me have my alone time when I need it. She takes care of my needs, and fully expects me to take care of hers. She doesn't let me off the hook easily. She makes me answer difficult questions about myself and our relationship. She has patience, lots of patience. She is forgiving and loving. She laughs hard. She is silly and fun. My ideal woman needs me and relies on me. She leans on me, which makes me stronger. I know I can rely on her, which makes me feel safe and secure.

Jesus Christ, I don't know what to say about that reply. I'm not sure that I agree with almost any of that, but that's not really the point here, so in that regard the reply is quite interesting, because evidently not all men are alike. This is good stuff.

Speaking of good stuff, a few days later (the responses really start to slow down here, unfortunately) I got this amazing photographic reply from a bachelor in his late twenties living in Saudi Arabia:

My friend wrote: *"Because I can see her ankles."*

That's one of the best pictures I've ever seen, and the reply made me laugh out loud. But it's just a joke (I mean, I could get into the whole idea of how interesting this question would be in cultures outside of the United States, but the bulk of whatever I wrote here would be even more rampant speculation, and the reader can speculate as well as I can), so I prefer to go on.

Next came a reply from a bachelor in his early thirties, which coincides with my pet theory:

She has to laugh at my jokes and shut the fuck up the rest of the time. Joking.

She has to be confident and comfortable with herself, and have a sense of humor. Not be a nag. Witty and caring. She can't have a jealous heart. No drama.

I could go on, but in a nutshell, the ideal woman should act as un-womanly as possible. I'm a no-nonsense kind of guy. The minute jealousy, worry, and "overthinking" enters the equation, I will see myself out. She should be able to accept me for who I am, and not try to change me.

Evidently, that dude has had some shitty relationships, eh? Look at what he did there: instead of drawing a portrait, he created a silhouette.

I got another reply, terse, from another bachelor, mid-thirties:

My ideal woman does not exist. But if she did, she would be beautiful and kind, love movies, have a great sense of humor, love baseball and video games, understand the importance of family, follow politics but not get nuts about it. She needs to be religious like me, and she has to love me as much as I love her. Needs to be a dog person. And smart. I'm sick of chicks who are idiots or who pretend to be. That's fine for one night stands but I'm not bringing that to Sunday dinner. Honestly, I would settle for someone with a beautiful soul.

Look at that! Perhaps it's because I know who sent it, but to me there is a deep sadness in that description. That line about the soul really stands out, though. I've wondered if it was a sort of poetic add-on, to try to bend his description to my poetic bullshit, or is there something there? Has he been looking for all the right things and still not finding them? Don't we usually presume that our way was lost because we didn't know what to look for? What if we did and yet we see nothing but an endlessly wintry field?

Anyway, by this time I've been pressured a little bit by some of the respondents and some of the still-considering-how-to-respondents to supply them with the one I wrote.

The fact was that I had not written mine yet, but I felt it only fair to supply my own if I were being given this look into my friends' personal considerations of one of life's most important endeavors.

Consequently, I wrote this one and sent it to those who asked for it.

My Ideal Woman

I freely admit to being a theorist, and one of my theories involves the idea that on a physical level a large part of our attraction to potential mates results from a subconscious genetic appetite for certain traits lacking within our own code. (This might not even be my theory as much as a possibly unspoken corollary of Darwin's Big One.) To that end, my ideal woman is extremely tall and thin, and she has a waterfall of hair so thick and luxuriant she makes Rapunzel look like Mr. Clean. She has eyes that are any color other than brown (my eyes are so brown and boring they're like a Tyler Perry movie), and her skin is godlike—with a genetic predisposition towards hairlessness—and almost divinely soaks up and glistens with light. It's okay if she doesn't have a Joan of Arc–like physical coordination (although my genes are rather rancid, I've always been a well-above-average athlete) as long as she can dance convincingly when she's happy and isn't a total klutz otherwise. (Nevertheless, I have to admit that sometimes when I see a woman who has sports talents, like, say, a fluid and effective volleyball spike, my balls became a pair of heated animals, howling, "It's her! It's her!") They say that beauty can be found in symmetry and recognition (symmetry is rather self-explanatory, but by recognition I mean the ability to look like other people—I read of a study where men and women assigned higher levels of attraction to people whose faces were general-looking, rather than unique), and in a way those (symmetry and recognition) are kind of the same thing, but I keep them broken into two distinct parts because of my own preference for symmetry in art, as well as the possibly understandable hope that a general recognition in my ideal woman's face would allow me to imagine, in certain different copulative settings and lights, that she was a number of different women from my life, whom she would kind of necessarily look like, whom I never got to have sex with.

In a poem I once wrote, I discussed the idea of the "self-contained gleam"—THAT! And by that (!) I mean she has developed an impregnable sense of self—cannot be led around by the nose by anyone but herself.

Additionally, I have certain aesthetic preferences with regard to the composition and countenance of her vagina (I'm not exactly sure how to account for that, considering I have no vagina of my own to wish were bettered somehow through our children), but I'll withhold those details nonetheless because nobody else went there.

It's been my experience that women as attractive as I just described maintain categorically deplorable personalities and senses of humor, so there is a developmental twist I would require in my ideal: she is a woman who was homely as a mule's hoof until she turned eighteen, at which point her features all streamed together, became harmonious, and a newly beautiful woman who had been forced to forge her own amazing and independent personality in her formative years would be born, to be able to laugh confidently and resoundingly at the punch-lines of my jokes while despite being super-hot still not considering herself worthy of my mediocre, hirsute flab, and consequently becoming greatly turned on when I made even the slightest move on her, which, when combined with her unusually small vagina (making my standard package all the more satisfying), meant she would instantly have a cascade of breathlessly satisfying orgasms at the mere moment of penile intromission, making my shameful tendency towards premature ejaculation appear somehow merciful and heroic.

I agree with one of the more esteemed of my colleagues when I say that I would like her to be intelligent in a variety of ways— rather than only ever having one possible mode of conversation. To quote the great Walt Whitman, "I contain multitudes," and so too should she.

To that end, despite a difficult and self-confidence-deteriorating childhood, her development and maturation and forged sense of self have left her with the ability to be as comfortable at a crowded cocktail party as she would be while going to a movie theater alone (while her husband is out of town at a conference of fantastically successful author-publishers on Mistress Island).

But alas I have fooled you, and myself, because I could keep going, or I could edit what I had, and it still would never be right, because humans are so complicated and layered, and so too with life, where everything together is further convoluted, compounding the complication exponentially, to the point where it's like oh fuck it I can't really explain anything I do or think, and somehow at the same time I mean everything I just said.

I tried to have it both ways with that ending, which might have been the problem, because not a single person I sent it to replied in any way, as of this publishing.

I go for long walks, and the day after nobody replied to my description, you cannot imagine how much I hated myself and kept pleading with the sky to just please give me a break from this silence . . . Am I really that obnoxious, or that much of a fucking maniac that nobody had anything to say to me at all?

A few days later, I got another reply from one of the people who hadn't been sent the Ideal I wrote—a married male, mid-thirties:

My ideal woman has legs as long as a Tolstoy novel, breasts that conjure the words "Higgs boson," a rear end like a Ferrari, and a face that makes sculptors throw their tools in the river out of sheer hopelessness. She has the intelligence of an engineer combined with the indomitable spirit of a 1960s-era female TV writer and the sexual daring of a first-year acting student. When she vacuums and dusts it is with the force and efficiency of 1,000 maids. Her cooking makes Paula Dean punch cigarette machines and Gordon Ramsay quiet. Her favorite drink is whatever you're having, but make it a double. She has all of the presidents memorized up until Lincoln, because after that, she says, they don't matter. She has been on two aircraft carriers, but is not allowed to talk about why. We will meet in jail. In Amsterdam.

Entertaining and funny, but not truly revealing. What are you hiding, sir? You have your bride—nothing of the realities with her? Only hyperbole!? You wish for a female Ron Swanson?!? But I know sometimes it is more fun to jest—earnest and sober answers are usually the parents of boring essays. Again, that was something else I tried to have both ways with my description (look, for instance, at the enormous tongue in the gigantic cheek in the one I wrote), and I elicited not a chuckle nor daps from my asking audience. You try to do it all and you don't end up doing anything well.

And then I received the last answer I would receive from my inquiry. It was an email from a bachelor, late twenties:

She should be attractive but not everyone needs to think so.

She should be a laugher.

She should be able to carry a car conversation for hours at a time, but she mustn't dislike silence.

She should be tall and hot or short and cute.

She should like sports but not as much as me.

She should work out and watch what she eats, but she doesn't have to be thin in the modern sense.

She should want kids but not for a few years.

She should have lots of friends and at least one enemy.

She should like to shop and hike.

She should be willing to return the favor. Nothing more.

She should like to travel but miss home.

She should be comfortable in her own skin but not too comfortable.

She should look good dressed up and dressed down.

She should like one reality TV show. Only one.

She should be smarter than me.

She should be a better dancer than me.

She shouldn't be Type A but she should make enough money.

She shouldn't be offended if I bought her an apron as a gift.

She is not allowed to listen to music on syndicated radio.

I have to be comfortable with her meeting both my family and my cool friends. And I can leave her alone with either.

A left handed woman is preferred.

Musical inclination is a plus.

From that reply, I learned that my friend likes to write his descriptions like Craigslist ads. And actually in my opinion if he wrote that back when Craigslist was a slut factory he could have done some damage as an importer/exporter (*ifyouknowwhatI'msaying*). But for now he's doing just fine, anyway, so my question and I are just a moment of his time, and he's already balls deep in any, all, or none of the above.

So what have we learned here?

Nothing we didn't already know, and for that, among so many other things, I apologize.

See how I apologize, ladies? I'm very sensitive, and I was just joking about the vagina and premature-ejaculation things—after all, a beggar can't be a chooser.

Postscript

I'M HAPPY to say that I don't have to end this essay on that joke, because in the period during which this fucker was being edited into the sloppy shape it's in today, one of the respondents ("Higgs boson") told me why he'd sent the jesting description rather than something closer to the truth. He and I are both fans of Robert M. Pirsig's book *Zen and the Art of Motorcycle Maintenance*, and I believe he was properly channeling Mr. Pirsig when his notes contained the following line, which, I argue, when read properly, delightfully avoids the tautology: *"The reason I didn't give you a straight answer is because I believe you won't know her until you meet her."*

I love that idea—it means there's hope for us all.

Going Green With Envy

ENVY POWERS was gonna save the goddam Planet Earth whether you liked it or not, because that's the kind of woman—No . . . Humanitarian! NO! *GLOBALITARIAN!*—she fucking was.

It was morning; she knew because a bird shit on her forehead and woke her up.

"Good morning, Mr. Cardinal!" she called out, flinging the bird shit off her fingers and into her composting/manure pile a couple feet away. "Isn't it a lovely day?"

And indeed it was: between the golden-green leaves of the forest canopy she could see that the sky was blue, the clouds were puffy white, and on the ground, her dog, Algore, was eating the skin off of a dead forest rat for breakfast.

She picked up and folded her bed—a large, rotten, Army blanket. When done, she tossed the folded-up bed into the basement—a big hole she'd dug. Then, she shook all the insects and dirt off her body and got dressed in her dirty-as-hell, flair-coated jumpsuit, with large pictures of diseased, dying animals and the word *"REALLY?"* pinned on the back, and walked a few hundred yards out of the forest and towards the road, where she caught the bus.

Once again, no one sat next to her, but that was fine—she didn't want anyone sitting next to her, those Earth-murdering retardo-Fascists. She was fine with being alone because it gave her a chance to make up some new chants. She pricked her finger with the pin of a "Horses Are People, Too!" button and pulled out one of the crumpled up sheets of newspaper from within her jumpsuit, which she used as insulation during the chill of the day, and she wrote down some of the choicest lines that flooded into her mind as she looked at all of those negligent assholes. It didn't take her very long before she ended up in the two places she always ended up: one, finishing a piece of writing with a scathing rant about the environmental impact of Dylan going electric, and, two, looking around self-satisfied—smirking and smug—at the other fuckbastards on the bus.

Then she saw the driver—Hector—and remembered something unpleasant.

"Excuse me!" Envy called over the heads of the other passengers—who, on hearing the quavering pitch of Envy's voice again, all groaned—all the way to the front of the bus. "Excuse me, Hector!"

The driver tried to ignore her.

"Hector, sir! *¡Señor!*"

"Ye', ma'm?" Hector said, glancing into the mirror he used to see the passengers while he drove.

"Did you ever speak to your manager about my ideas for converting these buses to run on compost and corn oil?"

"Yea' ma'm. He sa' he ge' ba' to me, bu' he nev' di'."

"OKAY, THANK YOU, HECTOR. YOU STICK TO IT, OKAY!"

His manager's another one of those fuckbastard neocons, she thought to herself.

"Pigs," she spluttered aloud, without meaning to, but not feeling bad about it either. But then she felt bad about it because pigs are majestic, beautiful animals. *(All the heavens in a pig's hoof!) Neo*cons, however . . . she spat at the back of the seat, and some of the spit hit the peach-hued pate of a bald Caucasian man in the seat in front of her. He slowly wiped off his head, stood up, and turned around.

"Watch where you're spitting, you crazy bitch."

He had a—oh my goodness, she started to see red, and she had to start her thought over again—he had a STYROFOAM CUP in the hand that wasn't wiping the collected spit into her oily hair.

The bald man pulled his now-oily hand away with a disgusted look on his face, but all Envy could see were the cup and the little whisper of steam rising from the unseen contents' surface. Coffee. Had to be. Another careless piece of shitgarbage who raped the ground of Coffea plants and then ejaculated immortal waste on Mother Earth's pretty clothes.

"Oh. My. *Gawd!* Do you have any idea how long it takes for Styrofoam to decompose?"

She couldn't pull her eyes from the white offense of the cup in his hand. It was like looking at a dead baby being repeatedly smashed with a spiky sledgehammer. But worse. Way worse.

He looked at the cup and then back at Envy and said, "About as long as it's been since you had a cock in that crow's nest of a pussy, I bet. Leave us alone, okay? We're all *normal*, and you're *fucking crazy*. See the difference?"

Fortunately for everyone, the bus came to a stop. The bald man sat back down, and Envy shuffled down the aisle and stepped onto the downtown city street.

"Fucking shit," one exasperated man said as Envy walked by, "she smells!"

There were further groans of agreement, but Envy didn't hear them because she was preparing herself for what she was about to enter.

It was like stepping into the bowels of Hell. Cars! Wasteful buildings! Concrete! High fructose corn syrup! She could hear the Earth, below this wretched mess of a city, and it was moaning in pain and crying out to her for help.

Oh, Envy! You have your work cut out for you!

The first thing she did when she was able to remind herself of her mission and stabilize herself in the putrid swirls of everything around her—after she had hidden behind a bench and closed her eyes and repeatedly whispered a mantra she had made up years ago: *num, boing, num num boing*—was start foraging for breakfast. This was always the hardest part of the day when she came downtown.

She went to the nearest garbage can and looked inside. She almost cried. In fact, she did cry, and weep, and look pleadingly skyward, and someone threw an empty paint can at her head.

Barely able to breathe, sick with contempt, she found there were perfectly recyclable plastic bags and containers in the garbage can, which she diligently and desperately separated into some extra bags she had brought, to be recycled later. After that, all the paper products: newspaper, paper bags, pamphlets, her friend Bent Spoon's manifesto about "the choking ubiquity of Foreign-Oil Capito-Narco-Subliminalists swirling down the crony pipes of our pseudo-suffixed American culture-gurgitation."

It was ugly work, but she was a surgeon, in a way. Like a doctor! A war surgeon! Her task was to prolong the life of her patient by helping to make the body healthy again, and, like a surgeon, she had to get her hands dirty. She wasn't sure she had the stomach for it, and after crying and dry-heaving for quite a while, she returned to her task.

Soon, in the garbage can, there was only organic matter remaining: apple cores, banana peels, half-eaten candy bars, a dead pigeon, hobo puke, sundry insects, and some other unidentifiable bits. Envy lifted this bag out of the garbage can and carried it behind a building, where she made herself a stew. She dumped the contents of the bag into a big pot she had hidden back there, and she scooped some rainwater from a puddle into the pot, and she set the whole thing to boil after she siphoned some gasoline out of an SUV (assholes) and used it to dowse a rotted old wooden palette, which she set ablaze with the rock and flint that was given to her by her great grandmonkey. She let the stew boil for a bit while she cleaned up the alley, and then when she could smell that it was done—she knew it was done when the alley started to smell like hot dogs—she pulled the pot from the smoldering golden bones of the burnt palette, let the stew cool a bit, and drank it all down.

And she was able to keep it down this time!

Nourished and energized and only mildly nauseous, Envy set out for her main goal today. She started heading towards the tallest building downtown: the Clarence E. Snarpletooth Building, headquarters of Earth Cure International.

Earth Cure's mission statement—which a quarter-million workers worldwide were endeavoring to live up to—promised sensible, technological answers to the problems presented by our otherwise hateful planet: diseases, floods, earthquakes, storms, animal attacks, etc. They made everything from vaccines to houses to heaters to penguin spray. In every way that the Earth tried to make things miserable for humans, Earth Cure sought a remedy.

Envy had already been arrested, on three different occasions, for spitting her own blood into the open window of the CEO's fancy car. It was worth it.

Today, however, she had an even better plan.

People knew she was coming, that's for sure, because when she hid the stew pot, she pulled out her old deerskin drum (she'd harvested the skin from roadkill, the motherfuckers). Having memorized the new chants she had written earlier, she walked the downtown street wailing on that drum and howling her shrieking slogans into the ears of the morons who passed her.

"Earth's our friend, Earth's our friend, if Earth can't do it, no one can!"

"Hey hey, ho ho, the human race has got to go! Hey hey, ho ho!"

Eventually, however, she, like most protesters, found herself just hammering on that drum and shouting stuff.

"Mother Earth!" "Recyclables!" "Animo-harmony!" and later, when she was really warmed up, a repeated barrage of "Slings and sparrows! Slings and sparrows! Slings and sparrows!"

It didn't even really make sense to her, but making sense wasn't important. Formal logic was so *capitalist*. What she had was even better: sentiment! She could feel the Earth crying out to her. She could feel that she was doing the right thing. I mean, how can you argue with the most important fucking mission in the goddam world?

She thought of children of the future, holding hands under a rainbow, dancing and singing her praises. But then in her dream one of the kids took a shit and didn't compost the feces, and the whole thing was ruined. Had she taught them *nothing?*

She was really lost in this thought, it seems, because all of a sudden she was being shoved into a wall. The drumming stopped as she picked herself up.

"I told you to get lost, ya fuckin' hippie!" It was a middle-aged man in a suit. Next to him, his child was looking at her and crying. "You think my kid wants to see those fuckin' pictures on your back? What the hell is wrong with you?"

"Your kid needs to see the truth!"

The man placed the drum over her head and started pounding on it and yelling at her, "No-bod-y cares! Do-you-hear-me?"

She couldn't hear shit. The pounded drum had fuckin' blown out her eardrums.

The man carried his crying child away when he saw that Envy'd started vomiting up a dead pigeon, and as she wiped her mouth with her sleeve, she thought of the trials and tribulations of all the world's great people—the evangelical saints who'd had their heads cut off, the intrepid explorers who'd had their heads cut off, the glorious astronauts whose heads she'd tried to cut off. With this thought, she was re-fortified. She was strengthened.

It was time.

Her letters to her state senators had not worked. Her letters to her district's representatives had yielded no results or even replies. Her letters to the editor of the city paper had gone unpublished. Her appearance on *Larry King Live* had garnered the lowest ratings in that show's pitiful history. Her every argument in her life, so far, had been like the equivalent of trying to level a mountain with a shovel. One shovelful at a time. Fifteen years into the effort, the mountain stood, tall as ever, and her hands were calloused, and she probably had tuberculosis, and her vagina was just *on fire*.

Now or never.

Earlier in her life, she had been taught the Ways of the Animal by an Apache shaman, and he had spoken to her of a fabled incantation of unfathomable power. She discovered the roots of the incantation while in a lethal battle with a mountain lion in her kitchen. The mountain lion ended up teaching her the full incantation, and she ended up teaching the mountain lion the follies of man, to love.

She had to get as close to the Earth itself as she could for the incantation to work, so she took the cap off a sewer and plunged deep into the rank darkness below and kept scuttling her way deeper and deeper. She saw many people she knew in the sewers, but the deeper she went, the fewer people she saw, and the more she could sense that she was climbing right down into Mother Earth's tired heart.

But then, wouldn't you know it, as Envy was working her way down into the deepest depths of the city sewer system, a gigantic, cosmic meteor plummeted massively into the Pacific Ocean, and in the resulting explosions, tidal waves, and volcanic eruptions, everyone and everything died—humans, animals, plants, and all.

The Earth was reduced to the sound of only wind on barren plains and waves on empty shores. All was quiet around the world as the blackened air hung like a death shroud over the unforgiving day.

Envy Powers heard and felt the chaos far above, and eventually she worked her way out of the sewers and discovered she was the only one to survive the meteor strike. Awestruck and stumbling through the eerie quiet of the new world, she made her way up to an empty downtown street, amongst the broken, eggshell leavings of blown-apart buildings, and she looked around, dusted off the old deerskin drum, and started a new chant.

"Hey hey, ho ho, these meteors have got to go! Hey hey, ho ho!"

The Pilot, Part One

Introductory Note

NOBODY ASKED or paid me to write them (we're off to a great start already), but the following are two teleplays I wrote for an animated-comedy TV show I invented called The Pilot. *Essentially the idea for the show was that each week would be a different program—each episode would be either the pilot of a completely new and different show I/we invented, or the completion of the previous week's pilot. I loved the idea of having that kind of creative/comedic freedom.*

And really it's the only way I could ever get away with writing something as unabashedly fucked-up as what I now present to you in two parts, for your reading pleasure. Fuck yeah.

[Publisher's Note: With the author's permission, *The Pilot* has been formatted uniquely for this book.]

The Pilot

INT. SUBURBAN CHILD'S BEDROOM—MORNING

The sun is just rising, and a cute little girl is still asleep in her little bed, peaceful and comfortable.

Then a huge, stuffy, ancient hardback book floats into frame.

VOICE: (PLEASANT, OFFSCREEN)
Wake up and read this book, little girl.

The girl is startled awake. She still looks sleepy, and the book is slowly coming closer to her face. She backs away, kind of scared, and voices a noise of rejection.

VOICE: (WITH EMPHASIS, OFFSCREEN)
Time to read this book, kid.

The wide-eyed girl is backed into a corner and can't escape. She begins whimpering and crying as the book draws closer. There is now a crowd of boys and girls circled around her, pointing at her and calling her fat and ugly.

VOICE: (DEMONIC, OFFSCREEN)
READ IT, YOU BITCH!

A huge, shadowy, ghastly figure is now forcefully holding the back of the little girl's head with the book open in her face. She is sobbing in hysterics. Total insanity.

GHASTLY FIGURE: (MONSTROUSLY DEMONIC)
REEAAD IIIIIITTTT!!!

The image and horror fade to black.

Screen: "PAID FOR BY THE U.S. DEPT. OF EDUCATION"

INT. MODEST SUBURBAN LIVING ROOM—CONTINUOUS

Pull back from the TV that was showing the previous commercial, and a generally average man is standing and walking away from the television. He is our hero, and his name is UNCLE MEAT.

UNCLE MEAT:
God, I hated that book. (PAUSE) Well, off to work.

Uncle Meat spots himself in the mirror across the room. He looks himself in the eyes.

UNCLE MEAT:
Go fuck yourself, loser!

Uncle Meat jingles his keys and walks out of the room.

OPENING CREDIT SEQUENCE: Pleasant music plays while Uncle Meat drives through the city of Hayfield, smiling and waving and letting people in and out of traffic lanes, and intermixed with this sequence are quick cutaways where a maniacal Uncle Meat is violently sawing into something that's alive, with blood spraying into Uncle Meat's chest and face, and then back to the traffic, and so on.

EXT. UNCLE MEAT'S MUSCLE GARDEN AND VAN RENTALS—MORNING

The music trails off, and we open on a parking lot where Uncle Meat's van comes to a stop. He gets out and puts on a hardhat and goggles.

Pull back to reveal the name of the business: "Uncle Meat's Muscle Garden and Van Rentals."

SIGN: a photograph of Uncle Meat's proud smiling face and the guarantee: "You Can't Beat My Meat!"

Uncle Meat is walking towards the front door.

INT. UNCLE MEAT'S OFFICE—MORNING

Uncle Meat steps into his office. On his desk is a picture of a handsome cut of raw meat, and across the front of his desk is a placard that reads: "Hi, I'm the Owner—Nice to MEAT You."

He puts on a pair of heavy-duty gloves and pulls his goggles into place. Pleasant, classical music is playing over the speakers. A section of the wall opens, and a fatted pig cautiously steps out.

Uncle Meat picks up a cleaver and implodes the pig's head with it—blood erupting in every direction. Then he starts with his perfect-form, expert cutting. When he's done: loin cuts, ribs, links, and bacon strips are stacked beautifully on the table.

UNCLE MEAT: (TO HIMSELF)
This little piggy went with hash browns.

He chuckles.

The wall opens again, and there's an adorable baby lamb standing there.

A head-on look at the little lamb's sad face. Then a knife cuts horribly into the face, and there's another absolute bloodbath. When he's done, it's nothing but white bones and gorgeous shanks of veal.

Uncle Meat stabs his cutting utensils into the lamb's still-enbrained skull and attempts to wipe himself off because he's soaked in blood.

UNCLE MEAT: (ANNOYED)
Damn blood.

The wall opens again, and it's an adorable puppy, which Uncle Meat picks up.

UNCLE MEAT: (TO THE PUPPY, IN A CREEPY SOUTHERN DRAWL)
Ah'm go'n' en-joy this'n'.

EXT. UNCLE MEAT'S MUSCLE GARDEN AND VAN RENTALS—EARLY EVENING

Screen: "8 Hours Later"

Uncle Meat walks out, dripping with blood, insane in the eyes. Another employee, equally drenched with blood and brain matter, walks up.

EMPLOYEE:
Hey, Uncle Meat. Long day. Wanna get a drink?

UNCLE MEAT:
Does a duck shit when you crack its beak with a hammer?

They both laugh like bastards, until their laughter dies down.

UNCLE MEAT:
Okay, let's go.

INT. SPOOKY OLD MANSION—EVENING

A group of blank-faced cult followers form a perfect circle around a BEAUTIFUL MAN. In the background is some particularly wild music from the opioid depths of acid-jazz history.

BEAUTIFUL MAN:

Tonight is the Sacred Quintipia Eroximotica, and the Cleansing Hour is unfolding as predicted, brothers and sisters! The time has come to place the Seed of Tranquility into our mouths and enter the perfection of Our Glorious Eternity.

The group responds in eerily similar orchestration as they place a pill in their mouths. (Beautiful Man only fakes like he's taking his pill.)

BEAUTIFUL MAN: (SPIRITUALLY MOVED)
Let it happen.

Everyone waits, heads bowed and serious.

BEAUTIFUL MAN: (SPIRITUALLY ECSTATIC)
Let it *grow*.

Beautiful Man seemingly reaches the height of existential bliss, as does the music.

BEAUTIFUL MAN: (WHISPERING)
We're going.

He bows his head with them. Someone behind him starts to twitch. Then two people. Then suddenly everyone is convulsing violently, their bodies jerking around horribly until at last they come to a final and permanent rest. And just for good measure, blood and excrement then rocket out of their mouths, noses, ears, and anuses.

Beautiful Man turns off the music, pulls out a cell phone, and makes a call.

BEAUTIFUL MAN: (INTO THE PHONE, NORMAL VOICE)
Yeah, it's done. Bring the van around.

He clicks the phone shut and leans over, reaching his hand into the back pocket of one of the dead bodies. He pulls out a wallet.

BEAUTIFUL MAN: (TO THE WALLET)
Hello, my name is—

He pulls out a wad of money.

BEAUTIFUL MAN: (TO THE SKY)
Cash Money, baby!

EXT. SPOOKY OLD MANSION—EVENING

A shitty van pulls around and stops in front of the spooky mansion.

INT. HAR DEE HAR'S BAR—EVENING

Uncle Meat and Employee are having a beer and staring at the beautiful bartender, CHASEY BROOKE. Uncle Meat then slams down a drink.

EMPLOYEE:
Anyway, so then real quick I says to the horse, I says, "If you didn't want me to gut you to chunks, Horse, maybe you should have addressed me by my CHRISTIAN NAME!"

Employee laughs uproariously at his own story. Uncle Meat just nods knowingly.

UNCLE MEAT:
Fuckin' horses.

Uncle Meat spits, and Chasey walks over with a couple more drinks.

CHASEY:
Sounds like you boys had a long day at the Garden.

UNCLE MEAT:
Boy howdy, Chasey.

EMPLOYEE:
You got that right.

CHASEY:
Uh-huh. Thought so.

Silence.

For a while.

CHASEY:
Well hey, I just had an idea—

EMPLOYEE:
Not interested.

CHASEY:
Oh.

INT. SPOOKY OLD MANSION—NIGHT

Beautiful Man has cobbled together a new wardrobe for himself by stripping various dead people of random bits of clothing. The rest of the gear he likes he stuffs into the duffel bag that he carries with him as he walks out.

EXT. SPOOKY OLD MANSION—NIGHT

Beautiful Man tosses his shit into the van, gets in, and looks upon his driver, a smoking-hot babe.

HOT DRIVER:
There you are, baby. I missed you.

BEAUTIFUL MAN: (FAUX-EUROTRASH ACCENT)
I missed you oodles, poodle. Now get me avay *from zese* loosssers.

The both cackle with laughter as the van rattles away from the spooky mansion full of dead bodies.

INT. HAR DEE HAR'S BAR—NIGHT

Uncle Meat and employee are still silent, staring at what Uncle Meat describes as Chasey's "amaze-bags." Then a heavily drunk child sits down next to them at the bar.

DRUNK CHILD:
You do coke, bub?

The child hiccups and vomits.

DRUNK CHILD:
This happen ever' fu'n' time . . . Shi', bub! (PAUSE) 'Ey! You know m'parents, bub?

Chasey wipes the vomit off the bar.

CHASEY:
JACK, you've gotta learn to control your drinking.

DRUNK CHILD (JACK):
What's 'at mean, bub?

EMPLOYEE:
IT MEANS MODERATING YOUR ALCOHOLIC IN-DULGENCE, YA SOILED IMP! Now get outta here, orphan scum! Away!

UNCLE MEAT:
Your parents are dead, boy.

JACK:
You seen 'em?

UNCLE MEAT:
You mean when they died?

JACK:
'Eah!

Uncle Meat and Employee lean back and think.

EXT. HAYFIELD CITY PARK—DAY (PAST)

A handsome mother, father, and little boy walk together through a modest park. They are the picture of contentment.

JACK:
Daddy, cuh I get some owce cweam?

JACK'S DAD:
Not right now, son. We have to hurry if we're going to make it to grandma's big birthday party!

Jack looks at his father resentfully and begins to cry. The parents exchange looks like, "Here we go again."

A homeless man, drunk like crazy, puts a bullet in both parents' brains.

HOMELESS MAN:
That'll teach you not to indulge yer child's ever' whim!

He swings the gun on the ice cream man.

HOMELESS MAN:
Gi' the boy all the ice cream 'e wants!

The terrified ice cream man does just that. Heaps of it.

JACK:
Wow! Thanks, mista! Hey, Mom and Dad, look at all this owce cweam!

Jack's parents remain shot dead.

HOMELESS MAN:
Well, my work here is done. Take care of yourself, kid.

Pull back to see that Uncle Meat was there in the park that day. And he was horrified.

INT. HAR DEE HAR'S BAR—CONTINUOUS WITH BE-FORE

Jack is vomiting again. Uncle Meat has the same look of horror as he did that day.

UNCLE MEAT:
Yes, I saw it all. (SHAKES THE MEMORY AWAY, NOW

OVERLY NORMAL) Why?

JACK:
They ever say an'thin' t'you 'bout co-*hic!*-caine?

CHASEY:
What are you talking about, Jack?

EMPLOYEE:
The little bastard's just hammered as balls.

UNCLE MEAT:
You're fired. Go on, Jack.

JACK:
Woke up this mornin'—shitload of cocaine on my front porch. How 'm s'posedta get a drink when I gotta climb over 'at shit. *Sheeeeit!*

UNCLE MEAT:
Jack, let me take you home and we'll figure this all out. Chasey, how much do we owe you?

CHASEY:
Fifteen dollars, gentlemen.

UNCLE MEAT:
Jack, pay the lady. I'll bring my van around.

JACK:
Aw fuck you, Meat.

Jack slugs down the rest of Uncle Meat's beer, fishes in his pocket, and pulls out a twenty.

JACK:

Keep the change, baby.

EXT. JACK'S HOUSE—LATE EVENING

Jack's house is a real shithole. Sure enough, there's a huge pile of cocaine bricks on the porch. Uncle Meat's van pulls into the driveway, and he and Jack exit. Uncle Meat's eyes light up.

UNCLE MEAT:
Well, right you are, Jack. That there is one *assload* of cocaine!

JACK:
Tol' ya—*hic!*

Uncle Meat pulls a butcher's knife from his belt and cuts into one of the packages. He licks the blade.

UNCLE MEAT:
Not Columbian . . .

He licks the blade again.

UNCLE MEAT:
Not Haitian . . .

He picks up the cut brick, puts his nose into the slit, and sucks half the contents into his brain.

UNCLE MEAT:
WOWWWW! FUCK! . . . YEAH!

JACK:
Whatchu think?

UNCLE MEAT:

This is angel-dandruff, Jack! This is what God puts on Her tits when She's pregnant! Jesus, Jack who the fuck gave you this shit? My gums feel like my face's moon lasers.

JACK:
Fuck if I know, Meat. 'S'what I's asking you for—*hic!*

UNCLE MEAT:
You're right. Right right right. Well, either way, let's get this stuff into the house before that cocksucker CHIEF DICK sees it.

Uncle Meat and Jack grab armfuls of cocaine and carry them inside.

INT. JACK'S HOUSE—CONTINUOUS

The inside of Jack's house is about as shitty as the outside. In the living room, on the couch and recliner, are Jack's parents' rotting corpses.

JACK:
Sorry 'bout the mess. Been meaning to clean up. Hey, Mom and Dad.

UNCLE MEAT:
No worries, Jacky. No worries no worries no worries no worries nwownownwownwownwnw—Christ I gotta get a handle on myself this cocaine is really kicking into high gear hello Mr. and Mrs. Jackson I was just drinking with your fine son Jack at the bar and he told me about this cocaine and do you know anything about this of course you don't you're dead I need to sell this stuff or do something jeez do you think anyone's looking for it I sure hope not my feet feel like cosmic vapor ghosts!

JACK:
Hey, Meat.

UNCLE MEAT:
Yeah, Jacky? Jacky Jacky Jacky!

Jack vomits on himself.

INT. SPOOKY OLD MANSION—NIGHT

Police Chief Chuck Dick and DEPUTY BUCKY are poring over the crime scene: the same collection of dead bodies the Beautiful Man left.

CHIEF DICK:
This fella here ain't got no shirt.

DEPUTY BUCKY:
The big pile, Chief Dick?

CHIEF DICK:
Best be safe.

Deputy Bucky drags the body over to two piles of bodies, one labeled "PROBABLY RAPED" (big pile) and the other labeled "MAYBE RAPED" (small pile) and deposits the shirtless body in the big pile. Chief Dick pulls out a voice recorder.

CHIEF DICK: (INTO VOICE RECORDER)
Kevin, I'm at the crime scene. There are dead bodies everywhere, some of them shirtless or in various states of undress. I would imagine those and most else were raped savagely. I know that much. No signs of a struggle, though there was one lamp knocked over, probably during a rape. I'll keep looking, but for now this is what I call a goddam mystery science theater

three-thousand.

Dick pockets the voice recorder.

INT. VAN—NIGHT

Hot Driver is now Hot Passenger. Beautiful Man is driving down a long, lonely, dark road. Hot Passenger is blowing Beautiful Man, who is driving with his eyes closed. He turns off the headlights and floors it. Hot Passenger is lustily grinding on her seatbelt and moaning with pleasure.

BEAUTIFUL MAN:
Fuck yeah.

INT. JACK'S HOUSE—NIGHT

Uncle Meat and Jack are stashing cocaine under the floorboards in Jack's parents' old room, which is now where Jack goes to break things when he gets emotional.

JACK:
A'ight so wha' we gon' do wi' all 'is coke?

UNCLE MEAT:
I don't know yet, Jacky. Let me think a sec.

INT. UNCLE MEAT'S FANTASY

In First-Uncle-Meat's Idea of what to do with all of the coke, Uncle Meat and about fifty strippers nakedly pie each other in the face with pie tins full of cocaine, and then they run around laughing and fucking.

In Second-Uncle-Meat's Idea, Uncle Meat successfully completes a drug deal, the buyer walks out, and Uncle Meat tells Jack that he (Jack) can afford a college education. Jack is hammered, and he (Jack) vomits. Uncle Meat looks less sure of his decision.

Then in Third-Uncle-Meat's Idea, Uncle Meat looks back at himself and shrugs, as if to say, "I have no idea."

INT. JACK'S HOUSE—CONTINUOUS WITH BEFORE

Uncle Meat returns to the here and now, though his ideas still hang in the air.

UNCLE MEAT: (TO HIS IDEAS)
Don't worry, fellas. I got it.

INT. SPOOKY OLD MANSION—NIGHT

Chief Dick head on. He's grunting and grimacing with effort.

CHIEF DICK: (INTO VOICE RECORDER)
Victim A0221…

Reveal Chuck Dick's other hand is down the back of a corpse's pants.

He pulls the hand out and examines his index finger.

CHIEF DICK:
Not raped.

Deputy Bucky bursts in.

CHIEF DICK:
This guy wasn't raped, Bucky.

DEPUTY BUCKY:
Excellent news, sir.

CHIEF DICK:
I'll say! You know what else I found out?

DEPUTY BUCKY:
What's that, sir?

CHIEF DICK:
None of these people has any money. Bunch of homeless people—in a home!

DEPUTY BUCKY:
I have more news, sir. I found tire tracks outside.

CHIEF DICK:
Fuck if I care, Buckface.

DEPUTY BUCKY:
They could belong to the perpetrator, sir.

CHIEF DICK:
You know what, you're right. I know that. I knew that. You asked me a trick question.

DEPUTY BUCKY:
Anyway, there's something peculiar about these tracks. They don't appear to have any tread.

CHIEF DICK:
Bucky, are you really suggesting that this perp has some sort of *smooth* car?!

Chief Dick makes a "What's with this guy?" face.

DEPUTY BUCKY:
Actually, I was thinking, sir, that we should be on the lookout for any cars with bald tires.

CHIEF DICK: (GETTING IT NOW)
Oh, fuck yeah. (THINKING) *Hmmmmmm* . . . .

DEPUTY BUCKY:
You know what? The vans that shitbuckle Uncle Meat rents out are real pieces of suck, and I bet half of 'em have bald tires. I'll go find Uncle Meat and see what he knows.

CHIEF DICK:
Excellent. I'll stay here and check the rest of these for rape.

Chief Dick's eyes move over to a hot dead woman in one of the piles.

CHIEF DICK:
Hey Bucky, we don't have any, uh, forensic, uh, forensic *lubricant* . . . do we?

Deputy Bucky shudders and walks out.

CHIEF DICK:
Maybe there's some Pam in the kitchen. (INTO VOICE RE-CORDER) Kevin, I'm checking the kitchen for some Pam.

EXT. HIDEOUT—NIGHT

The van drives along the wooded road until it pulls into a worn section of grass in the field and follows it down to a shack by a lake. The shack is in an oft-used hideout for various Hayfield scumbags.

It's a porch, a small room, and a garage. Beautiful Man pulls the van into the garage.

INT. HIDEOUT—NIGHT

The small room consists of a mini-fridge, a poker table with chairs, and a couch.

BEAUTIFUL MAN:
Sweet—poker table.

HOT CHICK:
Baby, what are we doing here?

BEAUTIFUL MAN:
Mini-fridge! Hello!

Hot Chick is still nervous and confused.

BEAUTIFUL MAN:
Relax, *Brenda*. I'm meeting the guy here, he's gonna give me the shit, I'm gonna drop it off, and then you and I are gonna party like hardcore speed monkeys in a shithouse prison grotto, baby, so don't get yo' bananas in a bunch, bitch, *ouw*! (BEAU-TIFUL MAN AS ANDREW DICE CLAY)

HOT CHICK:
My name *isn't Brenda*.

BEAUTIFUL MAN:
Gah, you really shouldn't be so negative, babe. I get really nega-tive vibes from you sometimes. Like right now, for instance.

HOT CHICK:
Hey, you know what? Fuck you, you condescending mystical weirdo! Call me when you wanna fuck again.

Hot Chick leaves in a huff.

BEAUTIFUL MAN:
It's not me, baby: it's your vibes!

Beautiful Man sits down at the poker table and begins air-shuffling cards.

BEAUTIFUL MAN:
Okay, sorry 'bout that. Hope y'all brought your wallets, 'cause I'm feeling lucky tonight! General Patton, put out that shitty cigar and tell your girlfriend you'll text her later. And Mohammad, keep the preachy shit to yourself tonight—we just wanna play some cards here. Okay, your deal, Ayn Rand.

EXT. JACK'S HOUSE—NIGHT

Uncle Meat and Jack are now loading the cocaine into a meat van.

JACK:
So whatchu gon' do wi' all 'is shi'?

Uncle Meat stops and turns his full attention to Jack.

UNCLE MEAT:
Jack, I asked myself that same question. And you know what I realized? The answer lies within the question! What am I going to do with all this shit? Why, I'm going to DO all this shit!

Uncle Meat holds his hand to his heart in a gesture of honesty and stares off onto a truthful plane.

UNCLE MEAT:
All my life I've wanted to be a life-blistering, coked-out mess. But let's face it: I'm a meat-man. Meat is a high-risk commodity . . . hard to turn a profit . . . terrible moral cost . . . . And don't get me started on the van-rental business. (RHETORICALLY) You ever been raped by that knife-cock from the movie *Se7en*? (BACK TO SERIOUS) Jack, cocaine just never made fiscal sense for a meat-and-van-man like me. But now . . . now I'm going to spend the rest of my life with this big beautiful bitchin' batch of brain-blowing snort joy, and I have you and the Fates to thank, my friend.

JACK:
'S nice, Meat.

Jack pukes.

JACK:
Whatchu go'n' gimme for it?

At first Uncle Meat just shrugs his shoulders and makes one of those "I don't know" sounds. But then he throws a deal out there.

UNCLE MEAT:
How's a shit-load of meat sound?

JACK:
S'nds good. What else, mothe'fu'?

UNCLE MEAT:
Want a van, too?

JACK:

Fuck yeah. Deal.

They shake hands.

UNCLE MEAT:
Well, Jack, I gotta hit the road. Remember to pass out on your stomach, man. I once watched a dude choke to death on his own puke. Shit was fucked up. Tell your folks I said goodnight.

JACK:
'Night, Meat.

Uncle Meat gets in the van, and as he's turning the van around, he accidentally clips Jack and sends the drunk boy headfirst (landing prone) onto the lawn, where Jack remains presumably until he wakes up the next morning.

INT. UNCLE MEAT'S VAN—NIGHT—CONTINUOUS

Uncle Meat is looking with concern into his rearview mirror as he speeds away.

UNCLE MEAT:
Whoopsie.

He keeps driving.

INT. HIDEOUT—NIGHT

Beautiful Man is in an argument with what he believes is the prophet Mohammad.

BEAUTIFUL MAN:
But you don't even know if Allah exists, Mohammad! There is

an inherent uncertainty of God's existence built into the very core of your admitted faith! So why don't you take your—

There's a knocking at the door.

BEAUTIFUL MAN:
Finally.

Beautiful Man pulls the door open and reveals SENATOR JOHN YUDA—one of those characters whose calm face cloaks a malicious insanity. He is wearing the obligatory "Senator" sash, and he is followed by a posse of toughs/bodyguards, one of whom is named HAM-WHIP.

JOHN YUDA:
Sorry I'm late. The boys 'n' I came across a lovely young thing walking up the road about a mile from here. (PAUSE) Helped ourselves.

Beautiful Man is not one to scare, but he is obviously intimidated.

BEAUTIFUL MAN:
No problem at all.

JOHN YUDA:
Oh?

BEAUTIFUL MAN:
Yeah?

JOHN YUDA: (NODDING)
Fuck yeah. So, listen, I don't have the, uh, "package." The "package" is gone.

BEAUTIFUL MAN:

Okay. Shit. Okay. Do you know where it is?

JOHN YUDA:
No.

BEAUTIFUL MAN:
Okay, so—?

JOHN YUDA:
So no deal.

BEAUTIFUL MAN:
No deal. It makes sense this way.

Two gunshots ring out in the garage. In response, Beautiful Man winces twice, and all of Yuda's bodyguards unsheathe their weapons (each is a specialist: knife, bazooka, fists of fire), and John Yuda doesn't even fucking blink. A few moments later, the final bodyguard—assault rifle—steps through the door.

BODYGUARD:
Was a van in the garage, boss. Scared me, so I shot it like you says I should shoot things. I shot the tires. They go boom.

BEAUTIFUL MAN:
Shit again.

JOHN YUDA:
You sayin' you don't appreciate my team's handiwork, son?

BEAUTIFUL MAN:
No, sir. I appreciate everything you do for us, Senator Yuda.

JOHN YUDA:
Thank ye kindly. But now, uh, Ham-Whip . . . .

Ham-Whip steps forward.

JOHN YUDA:
Give one of our fine upstanding citizens here something else to remember me by.

HAM-WHIP:
Huh huh. He sure is pretty.

Ham-Whip approaches slowly, unbuckles his belt, pulls down his pants, and unsheathes a knife hidden down near his ankle, which he uses to cut Beautiful Man's cheek. He then puts the knife back and pulls his pants up.

BEAUTIFUL MAN:
You'll regret this, Senator Yuda.

JOHN YUDA:
Men like me don't regret, son. We just fuck ya and forget ya name.

John Yuda and his crew start walking out.

JOHN YUDA: (TO BODYGUARD)
Take the mini-fridge. (TO BEAUTIFUL MAN) Little campaign contribution.

They take the mini-fridge, and everyone else leaves except Yuda, who stops at the door.

JOHN YUDA: (OVER HIS SHOULDER)
Don't forget to vote.

Yuda chuckles as he walks away.

EXT. DARK COUNTRY ROAD—NIGHT

Deputy Bucky and Uncle Meat drive past each other going in opposite directions. Recognizing Uncle Meat's van, Bucky swings around and turns on his lights.

INT. UNCLE MEAT'S VAN—NIGHT

A knockoff version of AC/DC's "TNT" is absolutely blaring while Uncle Meat dangerously and greedily snorts down handfuls of cocaine and rocks out.

UNCLE MEAT:
'CAUSE I'M *DY-NA-MITE*! OY! OY! OY!

His gaze goes up to his rearview mirror, and he sees he's being pulled over.

UNCLE MEAT:
Son of a bitch!

Uncle Meat checks his face/nose in the mirror as he pulls over, and there's a ton of coke below his nose. He tries to wipe it off with his hand, and his hand becomes chalky white. He uses the other hand, and it's just spreading it even more around his face, and it's even beginning to cloud up the air around him.

EXT. DARK COUNTRY ROAD—CONTINUOUS

Uncle Meat's van slows at the side of the road. While in motion, the two front windows open, and a cloud of white coke dust whips out, and the van stops.

Deputy Bucky arrives at Uncle Meat's window.

DEPUTY BUCKY:
Evenin', Meat.

UNCLE MEAT:
Bucky.

DEPUTY BUCKY:
Chief Dick 'n' I found some fucked-up shit tonight at the spooky old mansion on Murder Hill. Also found some bald tire tracks leading away from the scene . . . *of the crime!* First thing I see when I hear the words "bald tires" is an image of your ugly mug trying to rent me one of your broken-ass jalopies, so tell me what you know, Meat Man, or I will bring the hammer down on your crown, King Nothing!

UNCLE MEAT:
So it's come to this, has it? The third amendment versus the eleventh, those war-weary, longstanding gladiators. The age-old question of personal rights vee pesky bureaucratic legal intrusions for the sake of the general goo—

DEPUTY BUCKY:
Listen, I can see that you're high as balls right now. Just tell me who you got vans rented out to tonight. I'm not here to annoy you (HE DOES SOMETHING EXTREMELY AN-NOYING). It's just that we got a forty-gallon bucket of dead bodies on our hands and bald tire tracks as our only clue, so stop wasting my time with your incredibly long-winded rambling incoherent ironic loquaciousness, you douchebagguette.

UNCLE MEAT:
Fine, Bucky. I care about Hayfield as much as the next asshole. I lent one out to my grandma and one to that hot guy.

DEPUTY BUCKY:
What "hot guy"?

UNCLE MEAT:
Some guy. He's real hot. Before I knew what I was doing, I gave him the van for half price. That's below my profit margin. And I'm straight! He was just so . . . beautiful. It's weird.

DEPUTY BUCKY:
Okay, fruitcake, this hot guy got a name?

UNCLE MEAT:
Now look who's interested!

DEPUTY BUCKY:
Buckets of blood up there, Meat!

UNCLE MEAT:
Right. No, I didn't get a name. He paid in cash. If it helps, he was about six-three, real hot, and he had two eyes that were a shade of blue I thought only existed in my fantasies.

DEPUTY BUCKY: (WRITING IN A NOTEBOOK)
—existed in his fantasies. Right. Anything else?

UNCLE MEAT:
Oh, and he was traveling with some sexy slut. I overheard something about them going to that creepy cabin by the lake. I remember because she was so hot I thought about how great it would be to bend her over the mini-fridge in there. Now are we done?

DEPUTY BUCKY: (SUDDENLY WEARING AVIATORS)
Move along, sir. Nothing to see here.

Uncle Meat rolls up his window, cranks up the music, and floors it out of there, running over Deputy Bucky's toes.

DEPUTY BUCKY:
FUCK! Fuck! Fuck! Fuck! Fuck! Fuck! That was my fault.
(PAUSE) That was my fault.

INT. SPOOKY OLD MANSION—NIGHT

Chief Dick is on a cell phone.

CHIEF DICK:
What? The creepy cabin by the lake? I'll go now and meet you there.

Chief Dick hangs up.

CHIEF DICK:
Got you now, you one-armed son of a bitch!

Behind Chief Dick is a blackboard with a bunch of information on it. The dominant idea is the words "one arm/two arms" with both heavily circled, but one, "one arm," has a bold arrow pointing at it.

INT. HIDEOUT—NIGHT

The light is on. Chief Dick bursts through the door with his gun drawn while his other hand holds the voice recorder.

CHIEF DICK:
Kevin, I'm in the cabin.

Chief Dick looks around.

CHIEF DICK:
What the hell happened here? (PAUSE) And why does it feel

like it's going to be a *week* until I find out?

END OF PART ONE

The Pilot, Part Two

INT. HIDEOUT—NIGHT

Chief Dick, voice recorder in hand, scans the hideout.

CHIEF DICK:
Kevin, it feels like a *week* since I've walked into this room. Now let's see what we've got.

Chief Dick looks around and describes.

CHIEF DICK:
Not much to go by. Your standard hideout. Kind of a letdown, really. Looks like there used to be some sort of mini-fridge in the corner—thing was probably sweet. Gone, though. *Why?* Also looks like somebody was playing some poker here. Not bad. I myself don't gamble, as you know, Kevin—not after what those lottery winners did to my mother. Anyway, there's an unusual smell in the air. In the Academy they trained us to look for this smell. (SNIFF) Somebody took a cut here. (SNIFF) Cut in the face, with a knife. All the telltale olfactory signs are present . . . . What could all of this have to do with a spooky mansion full of dead, raped, homeless immigrants? I'll be honest with you, Kevin: right now, this here remains what I call one sssssssssssssssssssssssssexy riddle. I can't wait to see how it plays out.

A car pulls up.

CHIEF DICK:
Sounds like Bucky is here.

INT. JOHN YUDA'S LIMO—NIGHT

Senator Yuda swirls his drink in the back of the limo. His four henchmen are crammed in right next to him.

JOHN YUDA:
What the *fuck*, gentlemen?

HAM-WHIP:
Sir?

JOHN YUDA:
Where . . . are . . . the . . . drugs. (PAUSE) (NOW PETU-LANT) You made me look like an asshole in front of that hot guy, Ham-Whip!

HAM-WHIP:
We delivered 'em, sir, like you says.

JOHN YUDA:
I TOLD you to bring them BACK.

HAM-WHIP:
Well, you should have specified, boss.

John Yuda quietly suppresses his rage.

JOHN YUDA:
GLENN.

Glenn, the biggest and burliest of the bodyguards, nods his head into the conversation.

GLENN:
Yeah, boss?

JOHN YUDA:
I'm afraid it's time for you to administer some Southern Justice

on Mr. Ham-Whip T. Kirkpatrick.

Glenn smirks and eyes Ham-Whip.

GLENN:
Ah kin do 'at, sir. How deep you wan' it?

JOHN YUDA:
All the way, of course!

HAM-WHIP:
But . . . but—

John Yuda pinches the bridge of his nose, restraining his frustration.

JOHN YUDA:
Do you love your country, Ham-Whip?

HAM-WHIP:
Yes, sir, one hundred per-cent. America is the best. But . . . we ain't in the South right now.

JOHN YUDA:
I am an *American* Senator! I AM the people . . . including the dimwitted South! Therefore, to deny me anything . . . anything at all, boy . . . is high treason. You know what we do with men who commit acts of treasitude in the South?

GLENN:
We fuck 'em.

JOHN YUDA:
We fuck 'em forever, Ham-Whip. We fuck 'em 'til our hips shrivel.

HAM-WHIP:
So if I love my country, I get Southern Justice, and if I don't love my country—

JOHN YUDA:
All the way in, Ham. Forever and always.

John Yuda begins unzipping his fly.

JOHN YUDA:
Well, let's get this started then, I guess. Right?

Yuda's phone rings.

JOHN YUDA:
Ah, fuck it, I gotta get this. (INTO PHONE) You got'n Yuda, ya'n'.

INT. UNCLE MEAT'S OFFICE—MORNING

Uncle Meat's office is now a total party, with loud rock music, weird lighting, candles, etc.

Uncle Meat dips his bloody butcher's knife in the pile of cocaine on the floor in the corner, puts his face to it, and ingests it in every way possible at once, and then he rocks over to the waiting pig. He picks up a chainsaw and swings it above his head, but then he leans over and BITES the pig's neck open and cackles like a ripped maniac.

UNCLE MEAT: (TO THE SKY)
IMMORTAL!

EXT. JACK'S HOUSE—MORNING

The sun is just coming out. The birds are chirping. It is actually a very pleasant morning. Jack blinks awake in the same position he was in when he was hit by the van and drunkenly knocked unconscious by Uncle Meat the previous evening.

JACK:
Fuck.

Long pause. He's miserable.

JACK:
Still here.

Another pause. A real moment. Not just still here on the lawn, but still here alive. This kid has almost no hope, and he seems resigned to accept that, and to drink the pain away. He gets up and walks towards his house in the dewy pleasant morning, with the birds still chirping.

As he crunches down the street and out of sight, the sound of a speeding engine grows louder and louder, tearing down the long road. As it gets closer there are numerous voices coming from a pickup truck maniacally ululating "yi-yi-yi!" and dancing like crazed Indians.

SFX: the whooshing sound of someone throwing something

SFX: a bottle breaking on Jack's skull

JACK: (OFFSCREEN)
Ow! What the *fuck?!*

INT. CULT HEIGHTS HOSPITAL—MORNING

Beautiful Man is being tended to by a doctor for his (B.M.'s) facial cut while at the same time consoling a young mother whose child is very ill.

BEAUTIFUL MAN:
I'm sorry; I was unable to get the drugs the child requires. My connection fell through, and then he cut me. I'm so sorry.

DOCTOR:
Without those drugs, the child cannot fight the infection.

The mother begins crying. Behind them is a window to the outside. During the following conversation, a number of people fly past the window, falling to their deaths (one of whom shoots himself in the head on the way down).

BEAUTIFUL MAN:
What were the drugs anyway, doctor? Maybe I can pull off a miracle and get them myself.

DOCTOR:
It is a highly potent fungal powder called Hexokike. It is almost identical to cocaine in appearance, and it is the only known substance in the world that can kill the infection in the child's brain.

BEAUTIFUL MAN:
Hexokike, huh? Let me see what I can do.

DOCTOR:
I should warn you: it's a rare and dangerous substance that can have ramifications on the human body on a nearly metaphysical level. Be extremely careful with it. Only an expert pharmacist can safely assemble it into a useful drug without triggering its profound side-effects, and—

BEAUTIFUL MAN:

Yeah, yeah, got it. Real careful.

DOCTOR:
I'm deadly serious—

BEAUTIFUL MAN:
So am I! Just get your best pill-pusher on the horn, doc, 'cause he or she's about to save this black baby's life.

Beautiful Man is gone.

<u>INT. JACK'S KITCHEN—MORNING</u>

Jack is eating cereal (Meaty-O's) and reading the comics. In the background, the TV is on, and Jack's dead parents are arranged to look like they're watching.

JACK: (LOOKING AT COMICS)
"Who drew on the wall?" "Not Me!" Huh-huh-huh!

Jack pours himself a shot and slings it back.

Outside, there can be heard a shitty-sounding van blaring a ripoff of Guns N' Roses' "Welcome to the Jungle" backing into Jack's driveway.

UNCLE MEAT: (OFFSCREEN)
JACK!

Jack gets super pumped.

JACK:
Meat van!

EXT. JACK'S DRIVEWAY—CONTINUOUS

Uncle Meat is doing push-ups on top of the van until he swings down to the ground when Jack arrives outside.

UNCLE MEAT:
Meat van!

JACK:
Meat van!

UNCLE MEAT:
As promised, Jacky m'boy! Your own van—

Uncle Meat swings the two back doors open, revealing grotesque, huge, still-bloody shanks of meat.

UNCLE MEAT:
And a shitload of meat!

Jack goes from excited to extremely let down, looking at that horrible meat.

JACK:
What the fuck is this, Meat Man?

UNCLE MEAT:
Whadda ya mean?

JACK:
Look at that shit! All bloody and raw! Christ, Meat, what did you use a chainsaw? This meat sucks.

UNCLE MEAT:
Point of order, Jacky, the bow and arrow is to the Scythian horse-archer what a chainsaw is to any high-quality meat man.

The chainsaw *tenderizes* the meat while it *terrorizes* the soul—and any good meat man knows that when you combine those two elements, it really gives the meat flavor some *kick*!

Uncle Meat does a big KICK when he says kick.

JACK:
And there's blood all over the van!

UNCLE MEAT:
All my vans got blood. Look, kid, this is what you wanted, and this is what you're getting. Now I gotta split, so you . . . do whatever the hell it is you do, and I'll see you later, all right?

JACK:
Whatever. Fuck you, Meat.

UNCLE MEAT:
Well fuck you very much, too, ya drunk loser orphan piece of shit.

As Uncle Meat walks away a pang of regret crosses his face, and above his shoulder an angel appears.

GOOD ANGEL:
Uncle Meat, you know it's wrong to say such hurtful things to such an unfortunate child.

Uncle Meat looks over to the other shoulder, and an angel snorting a huge line appears.

BAD ANGEL:
(BAD ANGEL JUST GETS A HUGE RUSH OF ENERGY AND YELLS "YEAH! YEAH! WOOOOOO!!")

Uncle Meat just keeps walking as the Good Angel frustratedly shakes his fist at the Bad Angel. But then Uncle Meat stops.

UNCLE MEAT: (TO JACK)
Say, kid.

There is a shift in the mood and music of the scene. Maybe goodness will prevail.

JACK:
What?

UNCLE MEAT:
You wanna hang out with me today on my meat deliveries, maybe?

JACK:
Gee, Uncle Meat . . . you really must think I'm retarded. You're so coked out right now getting in the van with you behind the wheel would be like killing myself.

UNCLE MEAT:
So what? You got something better to do, shitfucker? (ANOTHER PANG) I mean, kid?

Jack considers.

JACK:
I'll get my things.

INT. HIDEOUT GARAGE—MORNING

Chief Dick and Deputy Bucky are analyzing the van that was left there by Beautiful Man.

CHIEF DICK:

The garage, of course! 'Nother good call, Bucky.

DEPUTY BUCKY:
God, Uncle Meat's vans are such pieces of shit. Look at this thing!

It really is pathetic.

CHIEF DICK: (INTO VOICE RECORDER)
Kevin, there is an early '80s Dorge van in the garage by the lake. It's got two shot-out tires, and closer investigation indicated there's been quite a number of sexual encounters in the van, which is a nice way of saying we found fifteen soiled condoms, three of which were banana-flavored. (TO BUCKY) The agency needs all this information. (INTO VOICE RECORDER) Lastly, there are tire tracks leading away from the cabin, and by their lie Bucky seems to think we're looking for a limousine—I myself finding limousines uncomfortably ostentatious for personal use, of course.

DEPUTY BUCKY:
Sir, I think I found something. It looks like a woman's pair of panties.

Chief Dick hurries over.

CHIEF DICK:
Let me see!

Chief Dick snatches the panties from Deputy Bucky and then presses them to his nose/face and breathes in heavily, like he was about to suffocate.

CHIEF DICK: (SATISFIED)
Fuck yeah. (PAUSE) Let's bring these with us.

Chief Dick pockets the panties and depockets his voice recorder.

CHIEF DICK: (INTO VOICE RECORDER)
Kevin, Bucky found some woman's panties, and I conducted some brief forensics on them. We're bringing them with us in our pursuit of the alleged limousine. I'll give you a full analysis on the road.

EXT. HAYFIELD PUBLIC SQUARE—AFTERNOON

Senator John Yuda is addressing a sizable crowd of cheering citizens. A stage and the requisite banners and flair have been erected.

JOHN YUDA:
One time, a reporter asked me if I loved my country. I said, "Son, I love my country like the fox loves the henhouse!" *Yee-haw!*

The crowd goes nuts over this, particularly the men, who grunt and holler and make salacious air-gyrations.

JOHN YUDA:
And when they said, "John, you can't say that: it gives the wrong message." I said, "Message? Folks don't a want message. Folks want folks. And folk's what I am. Fags are queer!"

The crowd continues to go apeshit.

JOHN YUDA:
And now, to wrap things up, let us bow our heads and pray. As we step forward into our proudiful future, let's never forget who we came from, and what we were when things were what they were then. May the Lord Our God individually bless

the hopes and healthitude of all past, present, and future pious American taxpayers. I'll see you all at the cookout!

The crowd hits a fever pitch for the speech's ending. In this crowd, the camera settles on the unimpressed Beautiful Man, who catches Yuda's eye, and Yuda nods towards the waiting limousine, and they both head in that direction.

INT. UNCLE MEAT'S VAN—DAY

Uncle Meat and Jack are flying down the street. Uncle Meat is frantically checking his mirrors, and Jack's upper body is out the window, looking back.

UNCLE MEAT:
Can you see 'em?!

Jack leans back into the truck.

JACK:
I think we lost 'em.

They both relax.

UNCLE MEAT:
Goddam bees.

Uncle Meat pulls the van over.

UNCLE MEAT:
Okay, I think we need to take a break and relax.

Jack picks up his bottle of rum, and Uncle Meat opens a briefcase full of cocaine. Then they both greedily ingest their respective intoxicants.

Uncle Meat punches it into tenth gear and tears down the street again.

EXT. PLEASANT HAYFIELD HOME—DAY

A well-framed shot of the façade of a standard Hayfield home in midafternoon. A sound grows in the distance, from left to right. It sounds like one of Uncle Meat's shitty vans, hauling ass.

UNCLE MEAT:
MEAT!

Uncle Meat's van goes whipping past, tunes blaring, with drunk Jack driving and Uncle Meat on top of the van hurling a sack of shanks hammerthrow-style through the home's metal garage door. He does a dance and flexes like a bodybuilder as the van speeds away.

INT. HAYFIELD POLICE CAR—AFTERNOON

Chief Dick and Deputy Bucky are in the car. The lights/siren is on, the engine is at full throttle, and the wind is whipping around like crazy.

Pulling back it turns out they are riding in a fake police car that was never going anywhere. They get out of the Police Simulator and get into the real police cruiser.

CHIEF DICK:
Bucky, once again, you're right: that was awesome.

DEPUTY BUCKY:
Thanks, Chief. Let's roll. We gotta find that limousine and that

hot guy!

They haul ass out of there.

INT. JOHN YUDA'S LIMO—DAY

John Yuda and Beautiful Man sit in the limo while Yuda's henchmen wait just outside.

JOHN YUDA:
You got balls the size of my balls comin' here, son.

BEAUTIFUL MAN:
I'm a desperate man, Senator. There is a black baby in my city who will die soon without Hexokike. Believe me when I say that it is NOT her time to die.

JOHN YUDA:
I understand, y'an', but my shitknuckle henchmen don't remember where they forgot it, y'see.

BEAUTIFUL MAN:
Well do you know where you got that original shipment? Perhaps I could go there and try to get some myself. Senator Yuda, as I said, it's not her time to die, and besides, you should see the set of bongos on her mother.

John Yuda laughs his quiet, sinister laugh.

JOHN YUDA:
Yip. I c'n 'magine. I want to help; Hell, I live to serve the people!

They both have a good laugh at that.

JOHN YUDA:

I like you, son. I want to help you save that black baby, but I'm real busy today. Havin' a big party at Hayfield City Park in two hours 'n' I got to get another speech ready.

BEAUTIFUL MAN:

Let me do it.

JOHN YUDA:

Give the speech? Young man, I respect your ambition, but—

BEAUTIFUL MAN:

No, not the speech. Tell me where you got the drugs, and I'll go there myself. Senator Yuda, if this baby doesn't die right, it will face an eternity of suffering.

JOHN YUDA:

Well to quote our forefathers: "How the fuck do you know, shitbuckle?"

BEAUTIFUL MAN:

It's not well known around here because of the controversy surrounding the title, but if you must know, I am a Deathicist, Senator. I'm sure you've heard of my kind.

JOHN YUDA:

You mean them con-jobs what tell people they know how they supposed to die?

BEAUTIFUL MAN:

I guide people to their proper deaths, Senator. And I can assure you: there is no con here. It is one of my many fantastic abilities, and my greatest curse.

JOHN YUDA:

Oh, yeah? How'm I s'posed to die?

Beautiful Man channels beautiful energy and returns to normal.

BEAUTIFUL MAN:
Plane crash in about fifteen years.

JOHN YUDA:
Shit. Really? Well that blows.

BEAUTIFUL MAN:
On the contrary, sir. If you die like that, your eternal results will be wonderful.

JOHN YUDA:
Oh? The fuck's that mean, boy?

BEAUTIFUL MAN:
I don't exactly know, but it was once described to me, by a very wise shaman from Otherton. He said, "Picture a long and powerful liquid pleasure eruption, and then hold that feeling forever while hot monkey sluts spank you with smooth ice-cream paddles."

JOHN YUDA:
Gol damn, son! Sounds mighty fine!

There is a knocking on the window, and Ham-Whip opens the door and leans his head in.

HAM-WHIP:
Sir, Glenn was wondering if we could get some sandwiches.

JOHN YUDA:
We're going to a barbecue soon. He'll have to wait.

The door closes.

GLENN: (OFFSCREEN)
Oh, man!

JOHN YUDA:
Idiots. Anyway . . . hey, you got a name, fella?

BEAUTIFUL MAN:
No.

JOHN YUDA:
Oh, okay.

BEAUTIFUL MAN:
The drugs. Where do I find the drugs, Senator Yuda?

JOHN YUDA:
How's Glenn supposed to die?

BEAUTIFUL MAN:
If I tell you, will you tell me what I need to know?

JOHN YUDA:
Uh, sure.

Beautiful Man channels beautiful energy.

BEAUTIFUL MAN:
He will be crushed and burned alive.

Senator Yuda whistles.

JOHN YUDA:
Nice.

BEAUTIFUL MAN:
So, yeah, now I get the Hexokike from—?

John Yuda looks around and then leans in and whispers to Beautiful Man.

BEAUTIFUL MAN:
Ah, shit.

<u>INT. UNCLE MEAT'S VAN—DAY</u>

Uncle Meat and Jack are eating lunch.

They have fast-food bags, which they each unwrap. Jack "eats" (drinks) his "hamburger" (large glass of whiskey), and Uncle Meat "has" (greedily snorts) a "quesadilla meal" (pile of white powder). Once again, hardcore rock 'n' roll music rattles the windows. Best day ever, man.

Impulsively Jack sort of yells and sings along, but the "words" are completely nonsensical. Uncle Meat does the same thing right after him.

Uncle Meat realizes something.

UNCLE MEAT:
JACK!

JACK:
WHAT?!

UNCLE MEAT:
FUCK YEAH!

JACK:
FUCK YEAH!

They continue rocking out. As they rock out, Uncle Meat's

world begins to swirl and change. Sounds and colors get all screwy. In the midst of this strange turn, which is the result of his snorting a shitload of Hexokike, Uncle Meat's altered perception moves over to the numbers on his watch.

UNCLE MEAT: (SHOUTING STILL, VOICE WARBLY) HOLY SHIT! THIS FUCKING DELIVERY IS LATE AS BALLS! STRAP IN, JACK!

Uncle Meat hauls ass out of there.

EXT. HAYFIELD CITY PARK—LATE AFTERNOON

The park is packed with picnic tables and people, banners, and a big tent celebrating the "Hayfield Annual Event!" Senator Yuda's limo is parked just outside, and the Senator is currently under the tent, standing onstage, addressing the crowd. Just outside the tent is the big feature of the park: "Hayfield's Strongest Pole!" (It is a rather strong-looking pole, indeed.)

JOHN YUDA:
I understand the barbecue's a little late, so I thought I'd say a few words.

There is a highly welcoming reception from the crowd.

INT. CHIEF DICK'S SQUAD CAR—CONTINUOUS

Chief Dick and Bucky pull up to the Hayfield Annual Event. They see the limo and the Senator, and it all clicks.

CHIEF DICK: (UNDERSTANDING)
Ohhhhh.

DEPUTY BUCKY:
Sir, Senator Yuda?

CHIEF DICK:
Bucky, we got a nightmare homicidal rape orgy back there and a description of a charismatic hot guy. Sounds to me exactly like a United States Senator! (INTO VOICE RECORDER) Kevin, I've solved the case. It was Senator John Yuda, who has full legal immunity. I can only assume that one of his arms is fake. Case closed!

INT. UNCLE MEAT'S VAN—CONTINUOUS

Inside of Uncle Meat's consciousness, the world is an insane blur of sounds and colors. It's just a continuous swirl of utter insanity.

Seen from the outside, he just looks ripped, and he's shredding up the street in his dangerously speeding van.

Zooming into his brain, and then into the cells that make up his brain, and then into the parts that make up that, the things on that level are awash with drugs and begin to pop into a radically different shape, and it begins to change the shape of things on each level on the way out.

Back in the van, Jack is drunkenly taunting or pleading with the Fates.

JACK:
Come on! I'm right here! Hit me! KILL WHAT I AM!

Uncle Meat starts screaming. Jack starts screaming, too.

<u>EXT. HAYFIELD CITY PARK—CONTINUOUS</u>

Yuda is still speechifying.

JOHN YUDA:
You see, when I was a boy—

Something catches Yuda's eye. Way in the background there's a van speeding erratically. It plows through the outside fence and shoots towards the crowd.

JOHN YUDA:
—What the fuck?

People hear the shitty van coming at them and get excited.

ENTHUSIASTIC TOWNSPERSON:
Hey, it's Uncle Meat, with some of his Muscle Garden victuals!

The crowd cheers for their favorite Meat Man. Unfortunately, their favorite Meat Man is now swerving straight into the path of "Hayfield's Strongest Pole!"

ENTHUSIASTIC TOWNSPERSON:
Look out, Uncle Meat!

Someone else in the background yells.

BG PERSON:
The pole!

Glenn, eating a sandwich finally, is also unknowingly walking right into the path of the runaway van.

JOHN YUDA:
Look out, Glenn!

Too late. Uncle Meat plows his Meat Van into Glenn, and then Hayfield's Strongest Pole, which absorbs the impact. Both front tires pop, and the van's engine instantaneously bursts into flames.

Next to Uncle Meat, Jack is dead. His skull is cracked open, and bits of his brain are strewn about the cabin.

Uncle Meat stumbles out of the Meat Van, carrying the last bag of what he thought was cocaine. He drops the bag and speaks.

UNCLE MEAT:
(A SOUND THAT IS UTTERLY UNINTELLIGIBLE, KIND OF SOUNDS LIKE "G'MMMAFFANAH*OOOUU*")

As he says this gibberish, his drug-induced metamorphosis speeds up rapidly until Uncle Meat's entire body goes from its normal humanesque structure to being radically puffed out, with a fungal texture. He flowers into a large and Uncle Meat–looking dead mushroom. It is certainly one of the most unusual deaths anyone has ever witnessed. Because of this, there is an unbroken quiet as the Hayfield townspeople take in what just happened. Then, finally:

ENTHUSIASTIC TOWNSPERSON:
Fuck Yeah!

ENTIRE TOWN:
Fuck Yeah!

The place goes nuts. Eventually they settle down.

CONCERNED TOWNSWOMAN:
Uh, shouldn't we put out that fire?

This is met with a mild general agreement.

ENTHUSIASTIC TOWNSPERSON:
Hey, that's a Meat Van! I say we just let the fire cook the meat!

The crowd loves this idea, including Senator Yuda.

SENATOR YUDA:
Let it burn!

The crowd goes nuts again.

A fire crew hurriedly drives up, unrolls the fire hose, and then attaches it to the fire engine—the slot labeled "Barbecue Sauce." They then open up the back doors of the van, revealing a king's ransom in drugged-out massacre meat, and they spray it all down and party.

A man sprays Dead Glenn's flame-engulfed head with a fire extinguisher and walks away.

Pull back from a pleasant cookout, with a burning van cooking the barbecue to perfection.

ENTHUSIASTIC TOWNSPERSON:
I got dibs on the veal riding shotgun!

INT. CULT HEIGHTS CITY HALL—LATE AFTER-
NOON

Beautiful Man stands before the seven members of the city council. He is first addressed by town Mayor ERNEST LAW-JUSTICE.

MAYOR LAW-JUSTICE:
Well, well, well! If it isn't Cult's very own shotgun outlaw—the hero every man wants to be and every woman wants to bed!

Our very own Uncle Jesse James Dean Moriarty! The human dynamo who—

BEAUTIFUL MAN:
Sir! There is a matter of vital importance before the Council. Can we please—?

FEMALE COUNCIL MEMBER:
What's so important? Your hot buns? 'Cause I'm ready to vote on that!

GAY COUNCIL MEMBER:
Mmm-hmm!

MAYOR LAW-JUSTICE: (LOOKING AROUND)
Okay, we'll put it to a vote, then.

BEAUTIFUL MAN:
Ladies and gentlemen, a child is going to die!

GAY COUNCIL MEMBER:
If that whole dying kid thing is a metaphor for those shoes, you're right, honey.

FEMALE COUNCIL MEMBER:
I think they're cute.

GAY COUNCIL MEMBER:
Oh, please. You would.

BEAUTIFUL MAN:
My shoes? I am talking about a real baby, here!

Beautiful Man motions behind himself to where the worried mother and pathetically ill baby are seated.

MAYOR LAW-JUSTICE:
His shoes are not the issue here!

BEAUTIFUL MAN:
Thank you, Mayor. Now if I could humbly request—

MAYOR LAW-JUSTICE:
The issue here is that we hate this guy, right?

The councillors are kind of wishy-washy with their replies.

MAYOR LAW-JUSTICE:
What's this? C'mon, guys, just last night you were talking about how much you hated him! This is our big chance to screw him over! *C'mooonnnnn!*

MALE COUNCIL MEMBER:
Well, yeah, that's true. But he's here now, and he's got a dying black baby with him. I can respect that.

BEAUTIFUL MAN:
Ladies and gentlemen of the council, no matter your opinions of me, is it not your job as governors to listen and react to the needs of your citizens?

There is a long silence in the room, and then the council starts laughing uproariously.

MALE COUNCIL MEMBER:
Oh, oh, that's rich. C'mon, Ernest, this guy's not that bad!

FEMALE COUNCIL MEMBER:
I'll say!

MAYOR LAW-JUSTICE:
Oh, fuck you, you *whores*. (TO BEAUTIFUL MAN) What

the fuck do you want, fucknut?

Beautiful Man motions to the doctor from before.

DOCTOR: (TO THE MAYOR)
The child needs some . . . Hexokike.

The room goes silent. That which shall not be named hath been named! A slow, tense heartbeat sounds as the stern faces of the city council members and the gathered citizens react to this unspeakable revelation. There is some deep history between this city council and that drug. After a long, tense moment:

MAYOR LAW-JUSTICE:
Yeah, sure. Rocco, gi' da doc' summa da 'Kike!

A big burly bailiff goes behind chambers and into the Riff-Raff Room, which is stocked with everything that is fun/relaxing and unapproved of by the pious if eclectic leadership of the Hayfield-neighboring town of Cult.

The bailiff returns with a package of white powder matching Uncle Meat's stash and tosses it to the Mayor, who tosses it to the Beautiful Man, who tosses it to the doctor, who tosses it to the pharmacist, who is just finishing her lunch. She half-hurriedly finishes her sandwich, wipes off her mouth a bit, and then hastens over to a table where she mixes it into a liquid loaded into a helluva needle, and then she hands it to the doctor from before, who jams the needle into the baby's face and deep into its brain.

Everyone gathers around and waits for a reaction from the baby. It takes a beat, but the baby begins to look better. Better and better. Too better.

The baby flowers into a dead baby mushroom.

DOCTOR:
Oop. Too much. Sorry about that. But don't worry, everybody, because—

He throws his hands and the dead baby into the air in celebration and is joined by everyone from the entire show in shouting out something that also appears in giant words on the screen.

EVERYONE:
"None Of This Is Real, Anyway!"

FADE TO BLACK.
SFX: POLICE SIREN

END OF SHOW

Twenty-eight

What The Hell

I HAVE my suspicions, and I've written about them frequently enough that I'm not even going to get into them here, but the thing is I doubt I'll ever completely understand how in the months leading up to my twenty-eighth birthday I began to feel a wretched dread that I was somehow literally falling into the sort of existential void that I knew could claim me forever unless I did something.

I wonder: does everyone else know exactly what they want to do from the age of twelve onward? And what could I say to others about being someone who worked towards a virtuous goal from twelve to twenty-eight—swam the Styx for sixteen years—and seemingly didn't see a single sign of hope that things would ever work out for the better?

It seems to me the only thing to do is tell the story of what I myself did, which was: double down!

I forced myself to write more than ever—at least one-thousand words per day for every day that I was twenty-eight years old, which, considering how long it takes for me to write Something New, is like deciding to spend a year traveling at a speed where the force of acceleration flattens you entirely and crushes your bones to dust. But I had decided that I had to grind my aspirations against the powerful force of reality—do something!—and in the process I lifted my eyes from my otherwise horrible labors and began building the holy metropolis I'd been seeking myself all along.

This book, this sundry collection—Oh, Title!—is largely the result of that harrowing desperation and those efforts. Any light within these pages was produced within a very dark, lonely place.

And if there is any value in this book, should I and we all be thankful for that darkness and that loneliness?

There are times when I am out socially, and I am staring into my thoughts, and people ask me what I'm thinking about.

The following offering, eruption, stack . . . *is a carefully refined, entire countryside of the poetry that intermittently burst from me over the course of my twenty-eighth year—the year I was a freaked-out pulsar with a pulse.*

I attach it, the following poem, a gigantic caboose, to the back of the Oh, Title! Express, *because for one thing I love poetry and would wish to introduce it to anyone unacquainted, and for another thing I think careful readers will find on the walls of this caboose a few paintings and mirrors of ideas and images they might remember from the more engineward cars of this passenger train—how the mind finds ways to rhyme!*

Before I go, for now, I would also like you to know that I was at an art gallery this past April—performing in, you guessed it, a "Grammar Smackdown"—and before the finals (where my team eventually lost, goddammit), on one of the floating walls of art displayed there, I first observed the framed piece that ended up being used as the cover image of this book. I mention it because as I stared at the piece I realized it was an unintentionally perfect visual representation of the last line of my beloved, colossal poem, "Twenty-eight"—the final line being a piece of advice I wisely stole from a man far wiser than I.

By starting with Mr. Kuzmic's image and ending with Mr. Aurelius's words of wisdom, I've tried to abstractly link the back of the caboose right to the front of the engine, completing a sort of circle—when people go somewhere, they like to be brought back, too.

On that note, as before and always, to the greatest you are capable, please enjoy what's next, and . . .

Be well.

—Daniel Donatelli
25 May 2012
Fight Town OH

Twenty-eight

Aaaaahhhhhhaaaaahhhsssssssshhhhhh
Aaaahhhhhaaaaaahhhhsssssssssshhhhhhhhh
CreakcreakWhOOOOOoosssshhCreakBOOM
(((((WITH LOTS OF WINDY, BROKEN ECHOES)))))

Amidst chilling bursts of chirping squeaks, the
misty, salty, skyblue breeze rushes towards a golden horizon
that leaps and leans just atop a steady chop that
gurgles and froths forth like a drunk and
falls away in a heavy hurry on
deft little saline tiptoes—
(a heavy hurry that is always,
as we all know,
coming back with more
strength and roar than before)—
and I have dipped my hands well deep into the shore here.
And I imagine at the base of these columns I've created,
around my slim wrists,
the silt is hopefully too scuttled over
by all those old silent claws.
For when my fingertips find and settle at the base plates,
when my spine begins to feel the
tremble of two colliding continents,
I can find the means to meditate about this life and myself,
while these tremendous masses slowly rub together
and sometimes kill us all.

Everything is so heavy, even the
light things come at us in overwhelming quantity,
and the heavy things only get heavier,
until they and everything else here are
lighted and lightened and burnt,

and then unfortunately you've got nothin'.

Mother! Father! My Brothers and Sisters!
Aunts, Uncles, Cousins, and you too the Estranged from Me!
You have to see our blood!
You have to have seen our crossed forearms
and their fat muscles' bulging!
(The Exclamations Of Poetry!)
Oh, what a thing to consider all the
billions of ways
it could have gone differently
and yet didn't, because ours is the kingdom,
the power,
and the glory,
they say.

Ours,
Ours,
Ours!

The hours are ours—they insist!

Ha-*haaa*!

(My mother always warned: first the laughter, then the tears.)

So,
shall I set the stage or the table? Or
shall I set the house afire
and tell the authorities
it wasn't me
or the dog?
(Well?)

"I'll await your word to tell me it's okay to advance, sir,
and meanwhile I'll cast about for direction

in the radiant dusty air of this empty living room."
"The light through these windows is exquisite,
is how it was sold (and is indifferent to
anything it touches and glows, but
nobody mentioned that
when we signed the goddam contract!)."
"Sometimes there are voices in these staid rooms,
is what I'm saying, sir, and
they bound about the air like bombs
and rattle the floorboards like this war."
"I listen for them, and I listen all the time,
and I can't see how I'll ever stop listening
always."

Outside, now and then, away, and
it's so nice out here on this side of the wall,
and it feels good, and there aren't any problems at all.
(Except for those problems
which never left at all,
and which come with me,
and with you,
and with us all.)

Now the trees are bending to shade us.
(They never do that when it's just me.)

The Heartbeat Of My Youth:

Smile—
the dangerous hiss of a well-thrown ball,
and the satisfying snap on the other side;
following the ball through wind-ript space as it hisses
and snaps into your glove with an echoing pop.
Over and over and again and again and over
and *ooooohhhhhhmmmmmmmmmmmmmmmm*
(until I feel foolish, which is its own sort of enlightenment).

Recognizing a sweeping bend and striking
before the moment is past,
and running savagely to save yourself,
or else it is another oblivion.
Until, that is, you run out, and then
you go home to your family,
and you notice how things
haven't changed at all and never have,
and it's another oblivion also.
(Except sometimes you stop
  or they die
  and then you cry yourself blind.)

A Secular Confessional:

Oftentimes at night, the sky is clear over the desert,
and the universe bends over to show us
her every twinkling freckle, and it's shamelessly wonderful
to observe, if you're capable of it.

I am at least having strange thoughts at all times,
and certainly I am damned, for that or anything else.
So there is not the Why but to bear shoulder and carry it, it
and everything else that it consequently chokes,
yoked between me and whatever else is real.
This is what surfaces:

To leave! To return! To see others leave or return,
and to know that when your heart hurts
it is good sometimes.
The stunning natural wonder
met with the things we do to improve it,
and how only the natural wonder never seems
to be any less glorious.
(And people wonder how
I can possibly be so big-minded and yet humble,

except they never wonder about that at all, either part of it.)
Questions to be asked and answered and re-answered,
and how we keep getting better all the time
while we get there and ask
for more of course.

A coy smile from a real woman, unobserved, but it was *there*.
A job well done, heralded or tossed aside; it was *there*.

Is it possible to be known? Is it like a movie written,
and we are the writers? The actors?
Or are we musical instruments?
I've never considered a fart, belch, or groan to be a song,
and I change: all farts, belches, and groans make music.
Like the way the roundly moving sun makes the day,
and still everything is moving,
even the dead and the long dead.

What we need here is a bridge—
something to get me from here
down to there, just below me,
where the movie and the soundtrack meet.

A hammer smashes a nail into place,
a board is laid,
and a hammer smashes the next nail into place,
and the next board is laid.
I walk from plank to plank,
and between the planks I can see the canyon below,
and it's a dry riverbed,
for better or worse;
there's a dry riverbed down there.
From plank to plank I walk,
and I can see the canyon below,
between the planks,
and there's a dry riverbed down there,

for better or worse;
it's a dry riverbed.

What happened to these continents?

Suddenly I am slammed into motion, racing forward,
raised on the very wind and I am weightless and
speeding along at my favorite pace, and
thinking fantastic thoughts I simply cut my path between you
like an unexpected gust and around all things
make my way every day.
Marking the progress of time
with the clack of hard rubber wheels
and swiftly swooping into shadows to see but not seen,
I go, I go, I go, trousers rolled, Michaelangelo,
with peaches, beaches, and mermaids singing their asses off.

Fragrant as rainwater on tulip bulb and just as colorful
and giving fragrance as I am given fragrance. Ho,
what name could I give the things I know here
(and what name do those things give themselves)?
What is really that numinous afterlight that
bends around the Earth
and paints the bottoms of clouds those astonishing colors?
What are really the gulping piles of air that press against me
and swim into me and fill me with sustaining life? And why?
Yearning to be free, I am the same as it all, yet here I am,
complete as a vacuum,
and the things I do are different always and never complete.
Never complete and never to be completed,
and not only that, but always for good and never godly.
No longer seeking godliness, frowning at the thought
and offering the alternative: the self-contained gleam.
A diamond born within the greatest
grinding pressures there are,
and remember: they remember the diamond;

they seldom remember the pressures.

The diamond is self-contained; the tulip is self-contained,
and the coin, the silver ore, the marble, the gold bricks blown
to the ocean's bottom are self-contained.
We have to be self-contained
or we will be smashed to ungodly goo by these pressures.

Oh, philosophers! I churn and have borders and
would rather freeze my core than be blasted
and blasted and blasted until
there is no trace of me whatsoever.
Just water rolling up and down a dry coast,
churning everything to indistinguishable grains.

Popping In And Out Of My Life And Time Now,
Like I Do Because My Existence Is Unkempt:

Wholly enveloped in the cool,
calm chill of my former friend's blue pool,
and draping myself on the ropes of a hammock
in southern Ohio as the insects click and buzz about.
Fully saturated with sweat, my head in my arms,
between innings, and sitting with friends near a lake as a boy
in white shorts, then sitting with strangers on an airplane
as this troubled man, then letting the anger out in one
explosion of immature petulance.
Rip-roarin' to take it easy.
Repeatedly looking in the mirror at some flaw,
and obsessing over it like a little bitch.
Getting stoned on the marijuana
and stoned on the mushrooms
and stoned for my rude behavior
and laughing and laughing.

Sub-Category: Portraits Of General Times

Where the wind thrashes dry twigs,
the sky gray but not threatening rain,
where the air is fine but the
air within the wind is cold,
and those wisps kick orange red and brown leaves
into a clumsy little journey atop cool green
blades done growing for now,
where the football arcs through the sharp evening air—
GODDAM! it feels great out here!—
and dives into my friend or brother's hands,
where it was going without knowing.
Where I am layered in clothes, happily,
where the trees have turned into splayed bird skeletons,
where the air moves but the space is quiet,
where the savory smell of a distant hearth spikes the feeling,
I am there,
I am there right now,
but I am here, of course.

Where the sun's heat bakes the tar gooey and
my bike's tires press little divots in. Like a stern,
ever-watchful parent's eye,
looking down to see what's happening,
that star, ninety-three-million miles away,
isn't like a parent's eye at all;
it just burns. It's big and burns and burns and burns;
the light is incidental.
But it is the air it warms I wish to embrace
and fill myself with: the lush fragrance of LIFE.
Oh, Life!
The plants are alive and stretching,
The plants and all the plants are green and growing,
And the insects scuttle in their excess,
between soft green blades drooping contentedly,
the air stirring lazily, and sometimes not at all,
but always the air is that life-breathing summer air.

And it is all there,
but the sunlight is incidental.

Isn't that just horrible?

The ground is repaved with a dense layer of translucent ice,
and the sun is presumably vacationing in Florida.
Gray days precede gray days, which proceed in like fashion.
The air is a million little icepicks spinning through space
And hacking at my chubby little exposed face.
Squinting from the unbroken fields of brightness,
I see the white of snow and the gray of sky, but what of black?
Black is the early night—the five pee em sunset.
Black is the ice-covered street where my car and I
are spinning into a snow-capped fire hydrant.
Socks and another set of socks,
then undershirt, pants, long-sleeved shirt,
and sweatshirt, heavy jacket, thick boots, hat, gloves,
all bundled up, everyone. Ready to get the paper.
It lasts forever, and it doesn't ever stop until it finally does.

The acute arrows of the air of winter widen, eventually,
and become rounded on "The Day."
Oh, The Day! That most blessed and perfect
and welcome and empyrean day!
When the surprisingly strong grasp of
Old Man Winter finally unclenches and melts away,
And the sun and pretty girls come out to display
what they are again.
That smell returns—it is life!
Those colors return—they are life!
The rain returns and drives us all inside.
And *BLAST!* the comfort and terror of a well-timed
crack of thunder and lightning!
Spring! Undress the cold world and return
its scorched face to color and life.

In the one before, I eagerly await the next,
and I love them all so much it kills me.

Closing Ruminations, or Pay Attention, Donkey:

And what is that shadow, then? I thought I was made
out of space and electromagnetism.
(Note to self: *look that up.*)
So what is that shadow at my feet if I am so empty?
Surely, it signifies something.
It could mean exactly what I think it means,
and it could be something else entirely,
and both could be right, and neither.
Something is right,
but this poet's mother and father—heart and brain—
know not,
and as ever there are several brotherly conjectures:
-It is the dark stain of my sinful soul made visible
through God's holy searchlight.
-It is what a ghost is when a ghost is still alive.
-It is a shadow, you idiot.

I sound my call and hear its return,
and it is but only one small corner of all sounds,
and in sum the sounds they all make makes this perfect
white buzz that is probably also like enlightenment.
Oh, foolish man. Oh, pregnant woman. Oh, you child.
Oh, oh, you march on! The beat carries you!

Drained of passion, drained of love,
drained of all mood or sentiment, emptied of optimistics,
and jar-dumped of all courage and romance,
there it sits in its angst, and emptily it tries to do something,
to move forward for unknown reasons,
for what's forward to fall off for unknown reasons.
That thronging beat!

The peeling clang of the first bell—
the minds it must have rung! and
to have heard it, that unnatural sound,
that aural human signature,
and to have rung!
The Earth turns away
from the sun and
winter falls and
that is also part of that chilling beat!

Sometimes when I am walking between warm trees,
a small breeze will rise up to greet me,
and my knees will be momentarily weakened
by all the sweet beauty of this planet we inhabit.
We are on the acid jazz of planets, man;
we are layin' down
wit'out a doubt
da grooviest beat.

To sit and laze and lean and loafe at your ease, Uncle Walt.
To frame thy fearful symmetry, Mr. Blake.

Would you be my friends?

I pour water in the mortar and
with my pestle I try to break it down even *furthur* because
I want to see what's in there, what's below the
already-chopped-and-grinded—
silvery or maybe goldeny or maybe refractional
like light off of diamonds : . : . :
That is all the treasure in the world to me,
all the mounds and mounds of treasure
there could be, right there in that littlest bit there is—is it.
But I give up on the task when I see
that it won't happen today either.

"Excuse us, Tubby Writer Of This 'Twenty-eight,'"
the letters from the orchestra pit addressed me
before our performance,
"we were just wondering why it is that You always seem to
have such a loquacious 'n' *cute* way of getting to whatever
so-called poetical point ever Ye prance
daintily and inexactly towards.
Do Ye hope to charm an audience with
indirection and fluff all the while?
Do Ye puff out Yr chest and
surround us in nonlinear fog for the feel of it?
Or is the fog another convoluting byproduct
of Yr misguided huffery and puffery?"

(The letters in the orchestra pit
are biting when they speak up, no? *Insolence!*)

It took me a while before I could
come up with a satisfactory response for them,
as it usually does:
"It is," I said, "what concern of yours, exactly? Please
do your job."

(Things have gone well enough between us since then—
possibly because I overheard one of them murmur that I,
the tubby author of this "Twenty-eight,"
am probably no more or better than a letter
in someone else's poem myself.)

Where there are victories there I went and
where there are defeats there I went and
where there are open spaces or crowds or others traveling.
Yet I remained here, seated here, in this numbskull's skull,
the whole time.

Are virtue and victory assured?

Experience says no, but they endure.
Is there a way—one way?
Experience says there are any and many,
but there is really only one.
Can a man's heart be contained?
Experience says that it cannot,
but sometimes it often can.

Do you see that torch there in the distance?
Its flame slashes violently in the cold mountain
wind tonight, there.
It is hot, and it will provide us with heat.

Can you feel it yet?

Guess my name and win a prize, if you guess it correctly.
Oh no no no, none of you is correct today.
My name is Jamo, George, Danimal, and
now my name is A Victim Of The Lord, and
now my name isn't anything but letters and sound, and
now my name is everything, like a solipsism.
We are all my name.

Oh, humanity, and your vacuuming dance in the jungle!

Wheeling around and down
these long gray stretches of road,
chugging along at wind speed,
the tires howling down the street,
I feel your warmth and the heat
of your blood beneath your pale skin
across the way from me.

Grant and Lee and Patton,
and today we don't seem
to have anything or anyone like that.

(Well, we have plenty of people like that,
but not in any of the good ways.)

Oh yes me and my bloated brain but where are the balls
upon which such a brain must rest?
My brain rests on the ground,
like boots,
and no longer wonders why it gets kicked around so much.

I've read the great poems and felt them
being etched onto the windows of my soul;
I've read the great novels and
felt them filling me with images moving and unreal;
I've read the great correspondences and felt
those crushing feelings of similarity and dissimilarity;
and I will continue to read them all,
to be etched and filled and crushed, inevitably.

Think about the wolf starving to death in the forest.
Think about the baby thrown in the dumpster by her mother.
And now think about red ribbons
tied tight in bouncy golden pigtails.
A jet carrying benevolent strangers to fancy new places.
That exhilarating feeling
when their hand first reaches down there.

Fucking life, man! Fucking life, you hear me!

Who is it passing on that windswept, rainswept,
overgrown plain, across which the sun and
animals and plants plod at their grave, timely pace, and
how long will it be before they raise their heads
and acknowledge that we are here with them?

Have you ever seen a baby twinkle in the evening?
No, but have you seen one vomit?

Have you ever seen a rainbow smile back?
I stood on my head once and almost broke my shit.

When giving advice, consider the deeper implications
of what you're saying.

For example:

When retching into a potted plant, be sure to say
you're welcome
afterwards.

Is it because I am unkind, or insufficiently kind,
or is it because I find so much unkindness, or
is it like a vacuum cleaner,
which to the carpet is like a reverse hurricane nightmare,
or is it just an acid rain
that falls on any many and maybe all of us, or
is the root of it different,
like a carrot that above ground
doesn't appear a carrot at all,
or like an old neighbor,
an old friend who snickers at your foibles, or
is the stench of it a dead giveaway—
a giveaway that died and rotted—
or do words fail at the walls of its kingdom,
like describing the taste of milk, or
is a technician needed here, here, and
over there and there, and there,
or is the lazy bastard in a creepy van
already on his way over, or
is waiting it out even worth it,
when it's like it is now,
because storms on Jupiter can last for ten years,
and that's nothing compared to this.

'Round me the founders founder—they found her.
Great mistakes were made,
and panicking we caught our cots on fire and
carried them like shields into the screaming crowds,
and we found her, too, despite their rage and our errs.

When I carry the rain in my arms,
I cannot help it that some of it drops to the ground.
And anyway, who wouldn't
be delighted by that wonderful sound?

I owe tribute and am owed tribute.

I carry whatever I please.

Is there anything so beautiful as a young person's smile?
Before they've been lifed in the heart,
before their character has been shaped to
such a certain mold that
there is no smile without also
an easily perceptible cloud of miseries
overhanging the parade,
there is the young person's smile—
that better glimpse into the fountainhead of joy.

Of course there are other things so beautiful,
but I stand by my point and smile my aged smile.

Sub-Category: Two Haiku Out Of Nowhere

A tree in the spring,
and a tree in the winter,
the water always.

&

The ground is wet there;
try not to step into it,
for it's the ocean.

When will they shoot? Must I gnaw on their rifle-butts?
Ice Cube? Rimbaud? I'm shouting and shouting!
I sound my barbaric yawp into the vacuum of this oblivion::::::

What's the sound of one hand clapping
if there's no one there to hear it?

::::::and jump around in my cage and fling shit in the mirror.

Mother, I blame you.
And father, I blame you, too.
And I love you, too.
The blame is all mine.

Sub-Category: Songs Of The Nemophilous Author

How high you reach your hands to the sky! and
how much I love the shade-room you offer
to me and my family, Tree.
I picture the palms of your fingers
as they are warmed and fed by the sun,
I have held the fingers of your hands
to my face and loved them and
have felt their coarsened backs and wondered about them.
There are some who call you nothing but a Big Shrub.
I cast those people out.
They are dead to me.
I loathe them.
How could I not love you?
       In the heat of the summer,
        when the wind blows,
        you applaud.

I am at peace in your cathedral.
Some would argue that man's buildings are prettier than you.
I would argue that a few of man's buildings are
prettier than you, but you are prettier than
all of man's other buildings besides those few.
You see, there are many things I wish there weren't,
so I thought it right to say that
I am glad that you exist,
despite the fact that I aim to make books
out of the marrow of your bones.
But 'pon consideration, that's not such a bad fate.
I am destined to be dined 'pon by a rather
sordid and sundry gathering of unmentionables
(critics and insects).
My ink and your bones, Tree.
We end up making something more than what we are.
As if there weren't enough shit already.

&

A tiny bird once chanced upon a branch
above my head while I awoke from a nap,
and the bird greeted me with a tweetly-twee,
and I greeted him with a groan.
Then I lighted my pipe,
and he preened his between-feathers,
singing between feathers,
and the two of us got along
as well as anything got along—
as along as anything got along with anything.
But I had my day, and he had his worm,
and alas the moment could not last,
and though our paths had passed
our ways were two ways—
one each—and each one went one
and could not the other.

But in that moment
we were brothers.

The hum of traffic is constant, and on top of that plops
any number of toppers like
dog bark
bird chirp
vacuum yowl
lawnmower groan
horn honk
crowd applause
and crowd cheer
child eek
cat growl
ball boing or
door slam
and atop all that is the clickety clack
as the silent author types—
it is the nearest and most soothing sound of all.

Yet at the same time, amidst the mid-clack,
I ask, *Whom am I fooling?*
What is all this mess?
This is progress? What is all this mess?

Charging through the field, my bow slung o'er my shoulder,
my dog far ahead, on the scent, and I on her trail,
the swirling gray clouds blacken and
spring rain and vicious winds.
The first lightning strike touches a tree
that burns and is soaked out.
The scent ahead leads my dog to a cave,
out of the storm, but unknown and dark.
Just like every time before.
The way a seed is carried by the wind,
I am carried by my wisdom and wits.

My watchfire is a lamp; my horse is an old SUV.

Grief is a tectonic pressure;
the first event is colossal,
and you quake, and
there are aftershocks forever after that.
There is always movement below.

I will write each individual letter
with a determined twist of my wrist.
I will promise each person better,
of my mind, meaning, and dopey hopes.
I will return the things I've taken and
take back the things that were
mine if they are no longer wanted.
I will own them, and they will own me,
and we will give each other meaning.
I will cast them away, and
I will shine as my own meaning.

Grace and grit, is how she was described, she who is gone.
A newspaperman
once described me as gritty.
A gritty pitcher.
Which sounds like a gay-sex euphemism now.
Back then it meant,
when it came to my body and throwing a baseball,
that I used the whole buffalo.
Treya was full of grace and grit.
She died.
And this is life—
it's a blind sniper playing Russian roulette
with everyone we love (including especially ourselves).

With this I add unto you
all the glories set before us:

the weathered vines aclimb,
the battle tanks in the hedgerows,
the bees busily buzzing about,
an unkindness of ravens seen upon a walk,
and we, aclimb, in the hedgerows, buzzing, unkind, walking
and squawking—
we who are to be great—
make great mistakes.
But I set out to add unto, and here shall I too:
though there will be many more mistakes than successes,
consider how far we've come thanks to those successes,
and all those goddam mistakes.
After all, I just masturbated to a
musically scored composition of
hardcore pornography seen in the
quiet and safety of my own warm bedroom.
Lotsa mistakes and a few successes got me
(and by me I mean
so-called civilized humanity)
here.
So let this be a note to myself
and to anyone who needs to be reminded:
cowboy up and get over it.

The stacked packs of dead rats make
a ballast for the silver ship
that glides through the hopping chop
of glassy, green water—
a drunken boat, a season in Hell,
the wicked Arthurian anguish
of sensitive, delicate talent
emboldened by sloshing spirits
and sent to labor in oblivion thereafter.

Toss it over the side and watch it struggle,
go down, drown,

and float back to the surface pale already,
weaving 'tween the waves.
The whisperers whisper and splash
cool fingers of water
into the eyes and ears and
mouth and face, signifying nothing,
remembered by no one—
the threads of water a tiny host to something already gone.

The way the light hits the pale corpse,
the stained sides of the ship, the gurgling froth,
it is the same way I think of you
now that you have left, are gone,
are moving away soundlessly.
For it to be my island, your vacation, the glints of light,
the shining suntan oil on your shy T-zone,
they would call me resplendent, transcendent even, and
in my eloquent thanks I would sing of you.
But there's always a but
and the unbroken dunes of this beach are a but
and my feet leave a single set of footprints.
In my wandering wonderings and memories
of you I am led out to where a heavy ocean suffocates me—
my lips two inches from the surface,
I drown and cry out, and these bubbles, this proof, pops,
and then they and I are gone.

Around the wounded,
sound rebounded and clattered
against the coming coffins.

Planes cut scars across the sky,
and still sounds rebound in the thin air up there.
And in the smallest moments and on ungodly scales,
there is sound that bounds and rebounds.
As a beggar and not a chooser,

I choose to beg to hear the universe
(that's how pleasantly unsteady
my head and heels feel here).

Big night in the life of my soul mate,
for tonight she will meet the love of her life,
while I read a novel alone in my apartment.

Can you see how I could keep going?
Can you see how there's no goddam point?

I hope not.

Z.

Without the guarantee of victory,
there is every possibility of defeat.
Hello, Anxiety,
so glad you could show up again, you coward.
("This whole scroll is just the jejune and offensively smelly
phlegm horked out of a set of mind-lungs
with shitbrain tuberculosis,"
Depression's best friend,
My Catholic Self-Esteem, parenthetically added
before it left again immediately.)
Oh, and you, Depression, so nice of you to make it,
ya pale creepo fuckface.
Hey, they both say,
and we chill out for a bit.
Or at least we try in what ways we can—
the coming dark made Anxiety nervous
and Depression sad, you see.
I turned our attention to that smoldering light on the river.
Depression thought about
how I won't have any moments like this when I'm dead.
Anxiety blurred the vision and returned my attention

to the chilly fingers of the suffocating coming night.
I shut them out and shivered and thought
about this brief crack of life and
returned my attention,
with Mr. Whitman, to the stars of the night sky,
but unlike Mr. Whitman my silence was quite imperfect.

The neighbor's dog is bark a day,
the aunt's cat is pad and mewl.
The father is barrel cough often,
the friend replaces verbs with sounds.

The fastest fish in all the sea
the fleetest of the fleet,
the unusually courageous, bold, and strong,
the sharpest with their teeth:
Oh to be to be to be and how truly wonderful it would be.

The oak tree leaves bright with nighttime starlight,
the predator and its corollary death-fright,
the prey that pray exposed, alone, and afraid,
the things that are wrong, the things that are right,
the newborn star that burns with white heat,
the half-illumined planets and their moons,
the universe itself:

will die like you, will die like we, for all of us,
evenly and eventually.

It looks like the only sure way to make it matter
is to make it matter ourselves.

Which is horseshit, if you ask me.

Oh, Voice, why do you seem to leave me so often?
Without you I am most unguarded.

When unguarded, I am anxious.
I am anxious often, and therefore too unguarded.
So where do you go, Voice?
You who is best of me.

It is a miracle I am here.
(At first I accidentally wrote "miseracle" there,
and I cried out, *"Le mot juste!"*)
It is a miseracle I am here and there are
millions of miracles more; I know.
Shouldn't you be with me at all times,
my Voice, to join me in these miracles too?
I need you to survive, and
not only that, but to brightly thrive.
Neither of us is capable of doing it alone,
and it's no guarantee we'll even do it
when we work together.
So come on!

Would it be too hippie of me to say that
I really do hope that things turn out okay for everyone,
and that I consider that possible?

Yes.

How many words will it take? Is it millions? Is it beyond that?
Mayhap there is no number great enough—
a hoofer can only go so fast.
A hoofer can't run enough to become an attacking cat;
he dumbly becomes a somewhat faster fool,
and his accomplishment is dubious.
Is that what I am? A dubious perhaps quick udderer
delusionally pounding these
hooves into plastic electronic clatterboxes?
Standing next to a tiger as it drinks from the river and
drinking from the river like the tiger?

The tiger is sated; I stupidly mimic it insatiable
but self-righteous in my clumsy aims.

What an unintelligent, bovine design:
a slow hoofer that pines to race with
the dynamic animal grace
that the great ones have.
But a hoofer is to be yoked—
yoked and worked until its dumb death.
Its only value is purely physical—
spare us the silent philosophy; we never asked!
Work!
Pay attention!
Quit staring at the ocean, you ruminant,
you who ruminates . . . .
After all,
there are no tigers or donkeys or oceans anyway!

None is truly separate, nor could it ever be,
for everything is connected—
tender cradle to bloated grave—
on every level there is.

So dislodging my thin wrists from the silt of the sea floor,
I once again return to my ordinary life, and at twenty-eight,
faced with the same interconnected cosmic stakes as
everyone else who ever lived,
I think of the old diaries that show that even the
powerful Roman Emperor Marcus Aurelius
sometimes, oftentimes, had to remind himself:

"It's Up To You!"

About The Author

Daniel Donatelli is the author of the novels *Jibba And Jibba* and *Music Made By Bears*, as well as the sundry collection of stories and essays *Oh, Title!* He currently lives in Fight Town, Ohio.

For more information, visit www.hhbpublishing.com.